Julia Jones is the pseudonym of Mary Hargreaves, an author of funny fiction set in the north of England. Her debut novel was shortlisted for the Romantic Novelists' Association's Debut Romantic Novel Award.

She has worked in hospitality, healthcare, project management, scientific publishing and – for one brief and regrettable summer – the over-50s club scene.

Splitting her time between Tuscany and Manchester (and the rest of the world when she can), she's never sure where she's going to end up next, but knows that writing, her husband and a general sense of adventure will be her constant companions.

WE NEVER HAVE SEX ANY MORE

JULIA JONES

avon.

Published by AVON
A division of HarperCollins*Publishers* Ltd
1 London Bridge Street
London SE1 9GF

www.harpercollins.co.uk

HarperCollins*Publishers*
Macken House, 39/40 Mayor Street Upper
Dublin 1, D01 C9W8, Ireland

A Paperback Original 2026
1

First published in Great Britain by HarperCollins*Publishers* 2026
Copyright © HarperCollins*Publishers* 2026

A catalogue record for this book is available from the British Library.

ISBN: 9780008793838

This novel is entirely a work of fiction. The names, characters and incidents portrayed in it are the work of the author's imagination. Any resemblance to actual persons, living or dead, events or localities is entirely coincidental.

Set in Sabon by HarperCollins*Publishers* India

Printed and bound in the UK using 100% Renewable Electricity at CPI Group (UK) Ltd

All rights reserved. No part of this publication may be reproduced, stored in a retrieval system, or transmitted, in any form or by any means, electronic, mechanical, photocopying, recording or otherwise, without the prior written permission of the publishers.

Without limiting the exclusive rights of any author, contributor or the publisher of this publication, any unauthorised use of this publication to train generative artificial intelligence (AI) technologies is expressly prohibited. HarperCollins also exercise their rights under Article 4(3) of the Digital Single Market Directive 2019/790 and expressly reserve this publication from the text and data mining exception.

For more information visit: www.harpercollins.co.uk/green

For Salsiccia, who cannot read, but who has still managed to achieve a PhD in chaos and destruction

Chapter One

I think I might be dying.

I squint my eyes open with difficulty and glimpse a sliver of the living room ceiling, cut through with a bright strip of morning sunlight. I quickly close them again. I'm not sure I can move.

I take a minute to dig into my memory troughs and figure out exactly how I got here. I was at Jade's hen party, I remember. I was at Jade's hen party, and we were drinking Screaming Orgasms, and someone started crying because their boyfriend had asked for an open relationship, but then they stopped because a stripper called The Anaconda arrived, and . . . then what? Vague images of a gyrating pelvis in sparkling Speedos flit through my mind, and then there is nothing. I try to picture myself in an Uber, or unlocking the front door, or shovelling down the McDonald's I can smell somewhere nearby, but I draw a blank.

From somewhere else in the room, there's a whimper, and then something wet brushes against my ankle. I force myself up onto my elbows, my head screaming, and peel my eyes open again. Betty is standing over in the open-plan kitchen, by her food bowl, staring at me with round, wet eyes. At my feet, which are hanging off the edge of the sofa, Boodle sits happily, his tongue lapping at my bare leg. Even through my hungover fog, my heart clenches. They are the cutest sausage dogs in the entire world. Everybody says that about their dogs, but it's true. They're short and stumpy and shiny and *perfect*.

'Hi,' I say. Or at least that's what I *attempt* to say, but my tongue is stuck to the roof of my mouth, so a choked grunt comes out instead. I unglue it and swallow uncomfortably before trying again. '*Hi*, you two.'

Betty thuds her tail against the kitchen cupboard door impatiently. *Water.* I need water. You've got to put on your own oxygen mask before helping others. I turn my gaze hopefully to the coffee table beside me, praying that somewhere in my lost memories there's a scene of me pouring myself a pint of water.

But there's something even better: a glistening bottle of Evian, beaded with condensation, and beside it, two paracetamol.

At first I think I'm dreaming. But then I spot the note tucked under the bottle, the paper slowly dampening.

I pick it up gingerly, recoiling at the state of my nails. Another memory flits in: the nail salon after bottomless brunch. My thumb is painted a shining cherry red, and decorated with an alarmingly true-to-life penis, veins and all. I remember it being funny at the time. I pray it's not gel.

I lift the note to my eyes.

L,

Drink me! Swallow me! Gone for a run, see you in an hour.

T x

I raise my eyes to the sky and almost weep. It's official: my husband is the sweetest, kindest human being on the planet. And despite the hangover, there's a stirring in my loins. Before I can get carried away, I have to remind myself that Theo doesn't *mean* to make things sound as sexual as he does sometimes. I know him well enough to know that he quite literally wants me to drink the water and swallow the paracetamol. I sigh and unscrew the cap with a satisfying click, and then chug half the bottle before pausing for breath.

'Right, doggos,' I croak, hauling myself to a standing position and then steadying myself on the arm of the sofa while my head spins. 'Time for breakfast.'

When they were designing torture devices in the Middle Ages, they missed a trick. Forking wet dog food out of a can on a hangover has to be worse than having your thumbs twisted. It doesn't matter that the contents are organic, the beef British and the peas fresh from the field – the smell almost has me bolting for the toilet.

I leave Betty and Boodle to clear up the source of my discomfort and swing open the fridge. The first shelf contains two of the expensive bottles of coconut water I buy for Theo whenever I'm passing his favourite running shop, and in contrast, stacked on the second shelf are twelve iced lattes in my favourite caramel flavour. I yank one out like I've discovered the elixir of life.

Back on the sofa, I swill down the paracetamol with what's left of my water and take a first gratifying sip of my coffee. It's cold and creamy and sweet, and cuts through the fog of the hangover just enough for me to start to believe that I might actually survive.

We had started at Hodge, an upmarket brunch restaurant whose claim to fame is avocado on toast, which is served exactly the same as anywhere else except they sprinkle truffle dust on top and charge double the price. Jade, the bride, is a sixth-form friend; one I've kept in sporadic contact with over the years, and someone whose wedding I expected to be invited to, but not as a bridesmaid. I'd never met any of the twenty other women before, and from the looks of it, very few of them were familiar with each other, either. We had begun awkwardly, introducing ourselves and politely offering each other Bellini top-ups, but by the time we'd consumed enough avocados and Prosecco to offset Greta Thunberg's carbon neutralizing, we'd shared our deepest secrets and I'd been invited to someone's nephew's First Holy Communion.

Well, I say *we* shared our deepest secrets – I did not share mine. When someone – Holly? Harriet? – leaned across the high-top table, her necklace dangling in the feta butter, and divulged in a voice so loud that the people in the next restaurant could hear that she'd started selling feet pics on OnlyFans, I listened and nodded supportively. I offered advice, plucked the necklace out of the butter, and handed her a napkin. I laughed and had fun and linked arms and screeched the lyrics to 'Texas Hold 'Em' when it played over the restaurant speakers, but I kept my woes to myself. The important thing was that Jade had fun, that we all had fun. My private business didn't need to come into it.

After that, there'd been the nail salon, the silent disco walking tour, and the private room at Le Jardin, where The Anaconda had swivelled his hips and someone – Jenny? Jess? – had cried in the bathroom, and tray after tray after tray of Screaming Orgasms had conveyer-belted through from the bar. Then, things start to get murky, images coming in flits and flashes.

An image of Jade, clutching my shoulders, shouting something emotional into my ear.

An image of Holly or Harriet, taking her shoes off and showing the bartender her feet.

An image of The Anaconda's glistening chest, him nodding seriously as I tell him something.

I put my iced coffee down. What was I telling him? I rack my brains, searching fruitlessly for memories that weren't encoded. I recall him earnestly giving me some advice, and that drunkenly optimistic feeling of motivation that comes when a ridiculous idea rears its head. But what would I need advice about?

Not *that*, surely. I'd never have told anyone *that*.

I pick up my phone to distract myself. I was probably complaining about my job, I concede. Slagging off Petra and her new big, soulless ideas. I'm not a complainer, but if I were to complain, it'd be about Petra. The woman could suck the fun out of a five-year-old's birthday party.

I have a new message from Caro, and I tap it open with relief. My best friend has the unique ability to make even the worst hangovers a little less doom-y. I can see from our chat that I messaged her at about two o'clock this morning: *Love u wish you were herr.* She's following up.

> Caro: *How was the hen do, you dirty little stop-out?*

I tap out a reply, and she comes back immediately. I smile; I love it when we ping-pong like this, each of us nursing sore heads on our respective sofas just half a mile away from each other.

> Caro: *I had that awards show, drank enough free Prosecco to take down a horse. Whose hen was it again?*

> Me: *Jade's. From sixth form? Think you've met her a couple of times. She's asked me to be a bridesmaid...*

> Caro: *Oh yeah – weird laugh? Walks all over you? Tenner says she's a bridezilla.*

> Me: *She does not walk all over me!*

I hesitate, remembering the way Jade had run through the itinerary for the wedding rehearsal with us last night, timed to the minute. The 19.47 cake entrance sticks in my mind.

> Me: *She's clear about what she wants, I'll say that.*

> Caro: *Don't let her put you in an ugly dress. Anyway, meeting Peter for brunch. Wish me luck.*

I laugh and settle back into the cushions and lull myself into a comfortable trance as I scroll through TikTok, then Instagram. I can entertain myself for hours like this, and most days, I know it's a problem. But I'm quite adept at ignoring those feelings, and today of all days, I need the comfort of the familiar scrolling routine to block out the searing thud in my skull.

On Instagram, the first post at the top of my feed is a long, long carousel of photos from Jade, documenting the deteriorating events of last night. I swipe through – when did they remove the ten-photo limit? – and watch as perfect makeup and upright postures at brunch descend into wonky grins and mascara stains at Le Jardin. I feature in a few photos: a full-table shot of us all at Hodge; one taken on the walking silent disco, my hands in the air; and one in Le Jardin, where I'm one of three people throwing back a shot of sambuca. The coffee in my stomach curdles.

I let my eyes rest on Jade in the final picture; she's leaning forward, pushing her cleavage together, and The Anaconda is wiggling his bulge alarmingly close to her face. How many times did she talk about sex last night? A hundred? She's notorious for regaling anyone within earshot about her and Matt's adventurous escapades: their frequent romps in the park, secret blow-jobs under his work desk, sneaking into broom cupboards at art galleries. Yesterday, I remember, she told us she'd bought a 'second-generation womanizer mini' for her honeymoon. She'd shown us a picture, and I still hadn't the first clue what it was, but I didn't ask. It's not that I'm jealous, obviously. Or at least, not really. Besides, it's Jade, my third-closest friend from sixth form. She deserves all the good sex.

I keep scrolling, flicking past the same adverts for dachshund carriers and Merit makeup and HelloFresh boxes that I've seen a thousand times, and lose myself in my favourite influencers' holiday pictures and household hauls as I drain the last of my iced coffee. I'll get up in a minute. Get showered, put some fresh clothes on – I'm still wearing last night's spangly bodysuit – and make myself presentable before Theo comes home.

I'm about to force myself to put my phone down when I scroll onto a new post from one of my favourite content creators. Tilly Carter is one of those people you've never heard of until suddenly she's everywhere, making you wonder how there was ever a time when you didn't know her name. She has an extensive background in sex therapy and couple's counselling, but despite her impressive résumé, her popularity seems to rest mainly on her personality – she's funny, doesn't take herself too seriously, and is so relatable that she seems to know what I'm thinking before I've even thought it myself. She hosts one of the most popular women's podcasts in the UK, *The Cliterati*, and it's become so big she now drops three episodes a week. I never miss a single one.

Her 'New Episode!!!' post buoys my mood so much, I almost forget how hungover I am. It's one of her 'Questions and Confessions' episodes, which are my favourite. Listeners send in voice notes or messages detailing their worst dates, biggest secrets, and most burning sex-related questions, and I drink it in like it's nectar. There's something about listening to other people's scandals and frustrations that soothes me, makes me feel more comfortable with where I am.

I hit play on the episode and tuck my phone into my bra

before heaving myself up off the sofa again, Tilly's upbeat voice accompanying me across the room.

'Good morning, Cliterati Club! I'm coming to you today from the second bedroom of my mother-in-law's house, where the window has been painted shut, which is unfortunate because I'd quite like to throw myself out of it.'

I snort to myself and head to the fridge for another iced coffee. I'll need it before embarking on the task of locating the source of the McDonald's smell, which has somehow seeped into every corner of the room. After a quick scan of the kitchen–living area, I locate the familiar brown paper bag wedged under the coffee table, a half-finished double cheeseburger inside.

'Last week, we talked a lot about in-laws, and Samira's question about whether she could legally divorce her husband's mother has had an insane response. It looks like I'm not the only one who'd quite like to have my husband emancipate himself from his parents. It's OK, my mother-in-law doesn't listen – to the episodes, or to me when I ask her to stop commenting on my weight. Anyway! Today, we're moving on to a new topic, and I anticipate that this one will be quite divisive. I've certainly got my thoughts, but before I get ahead of myself, let me read out the message that was sent in to the podcast in the early hours of this morning. Our team have had to edit it for typos, but we've stayed as true to the main text as we can. OK, here goes . . .'

I half listen as I take a sip of my second coffee, my eyes trained on the staircase. I'm weighing up the energy it'll take me to climb the stairs, take off the spangly bodysuit, and get in the shower, as *The Cliterati*'s confessional background music starts playing and Tilly begins reading out the latest of her listeners' confessions.

'Hi, Tilly! Help! I'm sex-starved! I feel like I am a mad, horny, insane nymphomaniac, and the worst part? I'm married!'

I pause in the doorway of the kitchen. Something begins niggling at me, a creeping sort of unease right at the periphery of my thoughts.

'We've been together for seven years, married for three, and I'm only thirty-five years old. I don't think I'm bad-looking, and I haven't really changed much since we met, so . . .'

A sickening lead weight has settled in my stomach. My eyes stare unfocused at the staircase. It can't be. It *can't* be.

'Anyway, I don't get it. All of our friends are at it *all* the time, like five times a day. Although sometimes I think they might be inflating things a bit. But still! Why doesn't he want to jump me? I mean, I guess I don't really make much of an effort. I get into bed most nights and it's just easier to go on my phone and hang out until I'm tired and then turn the light off and go to sleep.'

There's a thud from behind me and I start, spinning around, my heart in my throat. Betty has dropped her ball and it's rolling slowly under the sofa. I blindly cross the room towards her and sink to my knees, my heart hammering in my chest. Betty stares at me expectantly, but I don't move.

'Sometimes I just don't feel like it. But sometimes I do. What's wrong with us? Can you help?'

I can't breathe. Tilly begins dissecting the message, but her voice fades into white noise. Betty nudges my hand with her nose, but I kneel, frozen, my iced coffee clutched in my hand while my phone blares from my bra.

I don't know how long I sit there, but at some point, Boodle plods over and paws at me and I come to. The podcast has gone to an ad break, and a man's enthusiastic voice is waxing lyrical about BetterHelp into the silence of the living room. I half stand up, turn round, and let myself sink back against the sofa before pulling my phone out of my bra with a trembling hand. I swipe through to the comments on Tilly's 'New Episode!!!' Instagram post.

> *Hard relate! I can't tell you how many times me and my friends have this conversation, and it's mad that it feels embarrassing to admit.*
>
> *No advice, but sending solidarity. It's been three years since me and my husband had sex. No end in sight.*
>
> *I'll tell anon one thing: in our sixty-five years of marriage, there wasn't a day when my Bernard didn't jump my bones. And damn good he was at it, too. RIP Bernard.*
>
> *This is what freaks me out about marriage – kills the fire! Long live hookup culture lol.*
>
> *Send her my way, I'd give her a good seeing to ;)*

I feel suddenly explosively hot. The ads finish and Tilly's voice trills from my phone. Beside me, Betty noses at her ball under the sofa, and I reach blindly to fish it out. My heart feels like it's going to beat out of my chest.

'So we just heard from one of our lovely listeners, who sent her confession in at three o'clock this morning, after what I can only assume from the typos was a fucking fantastic night out. And I have a *lot* to say about this, anonymous listener, so pop some headache pills and settle in. First, you need to get that sexy beast of a husband of yours and—'

The key is turning in the front door. I stab at my phone, frantically searching for the pause button, and manage to silence Tilly's voice just as Theo appears in the living room doorway, a grin on his sweaty, bearded face and a bunch of tulips in his hand.

'Happy Valentine's Day!' he cheers.

I stare at him from my seat on the floor, my head spinning and my cheeks hot. Oh my god. What have I done? For a moment, I can't speak.

Because as much as I wish it wasn't true, there's no denying it.

The sex-starved confessor on *The Cliterati* podcast was *me*.

Chapter Two

'A bit bumpy along the canal path, but it's been a few weeks since we've had rain, hasn't it? It'll go to sludge as soon as the weather turns. I'll probably start doing the paved route again, down by the church. What do you reckon? . . . Lottie? Hello?'

I snap to, my heart stuttering. I realize that I'm standing in the middle of the kitchen, the bunch of tulips hanging limply from my hand, and Theo is peering at me with a crease between his eyebrows.

'Yikes, are you that hungover?'

I shake my head, then nod. 'No. I mean, yes. I feel a bit . . .'

'Sit down,' he instructs as he guides me gently towards the nearest dining chair. I slump into it, and then stand back up again.

'I'll put these in some water. They're gorgeous, thank you.'

'I'll do it,' he says, laughing as he eases me back into my seat. 'You sit down. Did you take the paracetamol?'

'Yes, thank you,' I say, nodding more enthusiastically this time. The movement sends a jolt of pain through my skull. Good god, what have I done? I watch Theo's back as he leans over the sink, filling a vase. There's a dark triangle of sweat running between his broad shoulder blades, down to the base of his spine. His dark, curly hair is shiny and damp against his neck. My gorgeous husband, whom I no longer have sex with. And now the whole world knows.

'So!' Theo says, turning around, and I jump. 'How are we going to fix this?'

I blink. My mouth feels very, very dry. He knows. He's heard the episode, put two and two together and figured out it was me. He *knows*. 'Fix . . .'

'This Valentine's Day! We always do something fun.'

I almost collapse from my chair with relief. He doesn't know. Yet. Oh, god.

He peers at me. 'What do you need? Liquid I.V.? I've got a sachet somewhere . . .'

Theo disappears from the room, and I listen to his footsteps on the stairs as I gaze unseeingly at the empty kitchen. Boodle pads over to me and sits by my feet, letting out a sigh. From her spot in the corner, Betty stares at me, and I swear her lips are pursed. 'I know,' I find myself whispering at her. 'What do I do?!'

'I've had a thought!' Theo declares as he bursts back into the kitchen, waving a sachet of rehydration salts between his fingers. He pours them into a glass of water and hands it to me, along with yet another iced caramel latte, before leaning against the kitchen counter and raising his eyebrow suggestively. 'I think you're going to like it.'

Despite my despair, I feel my heart flutter. That's the face he used to pull when we first met, when I'd wear my tiny denim skirt and he'd whisper in my ear that he couldn't wait to get me home and rip it off. That's the exact eyebrow he'd quirk at me across the room at parties before tilting his head towards the stairs and disappearing, and I'd find him waiting for me in a vacant bedroom. Have I willed a solution to our dry spell into existence, just like that? Are we about to hurl ourselves over this sexless hurdle, finally?

'Vegetable curry,' he says.

I haven't been concentrating. He's so good-looking, he takes my breath away even now. Chocolate-brown eyes, a broad chest, his short beard damp with sweat from his run. 'I'm sorry?' I say, coming to as I put my drinks on the table.

He gives me a wink. 'Oh, you heard me. Vegetable curry. That new recipe you've been telling me to try. Ottolenghi. With the chickpeas.'

Oh, god. Forget spicing up our sex life; he wants to spice up the legumes. And he looks so happy. The natural joy of the post-run high and a clean conscience. I feel like I've been hit with a sledgehammer. 'That sounds great,' I manage.

He beams and steps towards me, bending down to plant a kiss on my head. 'Love you, Lottie-lots,' he says.

I want to cry.

*

Six hours, a cool shower, and two more iced coffees later, and I'm physically feeling much better. Mentally, though, I am well and truly spiralling.

I'm lying on my stomach on our bed, scrolling with increasing panic through the comments under Tilly's Instagram post. There are more than three thousand of them now, and they're only growing. I swing between rationalizing and catastrophizing (everything's going to be fine, but there is no way Theo isn't going to find out about this, but it was anonymous, and there weren't too many identifying details, but someone will hear it and suspect it's me and tell him, and—) as the smell of cumin and broccoli wafts up the stairs.

As I'm scrolling, a notification alerts me that Tilly has uploaded a new story. I tap on it hopefully, impatient as the loading wheel spins. Someone else must have confessed something much worse. Or she's announcing tour dates, a new product – anything to draw the hoard away from my drunken ramblings.

It loads, and my stomach flips. It's a picture of Tilly, her beaming face angled towards her laptop screen, which has a barely legible graph on it. The caption reads, 'This morning's confession has gone completely viral! It's officially our most listened-to episode EVER! Who knew sex causes the biggest stir when it ISN'T happening! Thank you so much to all our fab listeners! Something tells me this won't be the last we hear about this . . .'

Oh no. Oh no, oh no, oh no.

Immediately, I navigate to Tilly's profile and tap 'Unfollow'. Then I go to Spotify, delete *The Cliterati* from my favourite shows and launch my phone across the bed. It slips between the pillows and skitters down the back of the bed with a thump. I stare after it, wide-eyed, and then leap from the bed and begin bundling Theo's running clothes frantically into the washing basket.

My phone buzzes from down the back of the bed, and I reluctantly fish it back out. It's a message from the 'Jade's Hennies' group chat. Before last night, I'd only met a couple of the girls before in passing, but the newly created group chat is violently active today.

> Jade: *Amazing night, girlies! Love you all!!*

> Holly: *SO much fun! Can anyone tell me why I've got a vulva on my thumbnail?*

> Jess: *Anyone heard the latest* Cliterati *ep? Good job you and Matt won't have that problem, Jade!*

My pulse quickens for the hundredth time today. My phone buzzes several more times as I stare at the screen.

> Holly: *OMG I thought the exact same thing lol.*

> Jade: *Hahaha think the problem will be stopping us.*

> Melissa: *Has anyone else been sick? That feta stuff tasted a bit off. I think I need to go to A&E.*

> Holly: *The feta was instantly dissolved by the eight gallons of sambuca, Mel, I think you're good.*

Every woman I know listens to *The Cliterati*. I've even seen my boss, Petra, the most inhuman of humans, loading up an episode on her lunch break. Tilly has taken the world by storm, and I've been part of more than a few nights out where the main topic of discussion has been something aired on her show. Myths about the female orgasm. The history of anal sex. Are bigger dicks necessarily better dicks? Whatever Tilly covers, everyone wants to hear about it, and then everyone wants to talk about it. Not only are tens of thousands of women going to know that I'm not getting any, but Theo is *absolutely* going to find out that I've aired his dirty laundry. He's going to divorce me, take the dogs, leave me penniless and unloved. And then I'll *definitely* never have sex again.

'Lottie!' Theo's voice booms from downstairs, and I jerk my head so violently towards the door that I summon my hangover again. 'Dinner!'

It's beer fear, I tell myself as I toss my phone on the bed and descend the stairs so slowly I could be in a funeral procession. Perhaps I am – the funeral of my marriage. Certainly the funeral of my sex life; if Theo wasn't giving me any before, he certainly won't be once he finds out what I've done.

Downstairs, I ease myself into my usual seat at the table and try to make myself look normal. On the placemat in front of me is a bowl of creamy curry and steamed rice, coriander sprinkled artfully on top. In the middle of the table, Theo has put a plate of his homemade naan breads, fresh from the pan.

'This looks fab!' I chirp, picking up my spoon.

I can feel him looking at me as I scoop up a chunk of pepper, and my eyes begin blinking rapidly against my will.

'You seem a bit perkier.'

'I'm feeling much better!' I smile in a way that even to me feels to be bordering on manic. My voice sounds shrill. 'Like a new woman!'

Stop talking, Lottie.

Theo smiles at me strangely. 'You OK?'

'Well, I am still a bit peaky,' I say, smiling weakly. 'But this is just what I need!' I shovel some food into my mouth and chew, making appreciative noises. My stomach is in knots. I swallow and nod. 'Delicious!'

Theo puts his spoon down. 'So. Last night.'

I'm going to be sick. I've plastered a grin to my face, and it's now frozen in place, making my cheeks hurt. Here it is, my reckoning. I try to remember the words I used in my confessional message. *Why doesn't he want to jump me?* I am actually going to perish, right here in Yotam Ottolenghi's vegetable curry.

'The hen party?' he asks, his frown deepening now. 'Seriously, Lotts, are you OK?'

'The hen party!' I cry, dropping my spoon into my bowl with a clatter. 'Of course! It was brilliant. So much fun.'

'Any strippers?' He wiggles his eyebrows.

'Just the one,' I reply, taking another spoonful of rice. 'The Anaconda.'

Theo splutters, and I force out a laugh. We're not the kind of couple to get jealous or analyse each other's every move. We trust each other.

'Remember our first Valentine's Day?' he says once he's swallowed a piece of naan bread, grinning mischievously.

Seven years ago, on our very first Valentine's Day, we'd gone to a museum. We were twenty-eight, had only been together three months, and would happily have spent time together in an asbestos-infested coal bunker if it was on offer. We staggered around the place, arms linked, drunk on each other, laughing at shrunken heads and questionable pieces of artwork. Then Theo spotted an open fire-exit door and pulled me through into the stairwell. We went up as far as we could, our feet clanging on the metal steps and our laughter bouncing off the walls, until we reached the top floor. It was an empty storage room, with the same floor-to-ceiling windows as the rest of the building, and nobody was about. Theo had shut the door behind us, and he'd taken me from behind while I pressed my hands against the glass, the view of the city spread out below us. He's always said it's his story, the one he's going to tell to impress the other senile blokes in his future nursing home. It's an in-joke we've had for our entire relationship, one he whispered in my ear at our wedding: 'This is an all right day and everything, but I'd do anything to be back at the museum.'

Now, we respectfully set our phones to silent while we watch TikToks in bed. We haven't stopped loving each other, but when the hell did we stop wanting each other?

I have to tell him. The realization comes quick and certain, making nerves jump in my belly. If I can get ahead of this, explain what I've done now, before he finds out from someone else, it'll be better. We can laugh about it, maybe try and fix whatever it is that's gone awry between us. It's the right thing to do; he deserves to know.

'And now for dessert,' Theo says before I can speak, getting out of his chair and coming over to stand in front of me. 'I think I've got just the thing to sort you out,' he says, his voice low and suggestive. He runs his finger along my jawline and tilts my chin up, so that his smouldering gaze meets mine. We've been together for so long, but still I feel a stirring in my loins. He is *so* sexy. My breath catches in my throat.

Is now the time? What if this is the moment the dry spell ends, and I ruin it by telling him what I've done? Isn't actually reigniting our sex life more important than some stupid drunk message I sent to a podcast he'll never even listen to?

I'll tell him tomorrow, I decide. When I've had a good sleep, and we've given this evening the chance to redeem things. It's Valentine's Day, after all. Surely if we're going to reignite the fire, Valentine's Day will be when it happens?

Theo lets his finger drop, but continues to hold my gaze as he steps backwards towards the kitchen counter. He turns away, and for a moment, I put my guilt and anxiety to one side and allow my imagination to run wild. He's got me a gift. New lingerie? A sex toy? Maybe he's going to sweep his arm across the counter, sending the utensils flying, and take me right here by the sink. He'll drop to his knees, put his head between my thighs. I can get my fingers tangled in that soft, curly hair.

'Flapjack!' Theo announces, spinning back around, holding a Pyrex dish aloft in his hand.

Or maybe not.

Chapter Three

By Monday morning, I am feeling slightly calmer. I managed to keep Theo away from his phone for almost the entire weekend, and as my hangover abated, so did my catastrophic thinking. Really, there's very little chance anyone's going to realize it was me, and if they do, I can just deny it. I'll tell him soon, I'm certain of it. But he's busy in the run-up to half term, and while I know he loves his job, I can see the pressure it's putting on him. Besides, these things blow over quickly. There should be a new episode of *The Cliterati* out today, and the conversation will shift, thrusting my confession into the annals of history. Once it's old news, and we've started having sex again, I can tell Theo in a fun, off-hand way. Like, 'Remember that dry spell we had? I completely forgot, but I wrote into a bloody *podcast* about it. Can you believe it? What a numpty.'

Not that any of this fixes my actual problem, of course. But I'll think about that later.

I'm sitting at my desk at the arts centre, sipping on a coffee and flicking through the emails that came in over the weekend. As Community Engagement Officer, my incoming correspondence mainly consists of amateur artists reaching out and asking if they can hold an exhibition. The answer, unfortunately, is almost always no. As Petra says, there's no money in unattended art shows. She's right, but it makes me grit my teeth regardless.

In an attempt to avoid replying to an email that came in on Friday evening (a sweet seventeen-year-old girl who paints woodland creatures and whose dreams are about to be crushed), I click through to the company intranet and update my bio. I bought a basil plant at the weekend, so I add 'gardening' to my short list of interests.

'Lottie.'

I start, spinning round on my chair. Petra is standing behind me, and my overreaction obviously makes her suspicious, because she peers at my screen with narrowed eyes. 'Dog walking, socializing, gardening,' she says.

'Yep.' I force a smile. Petra is very keen on staff having their own 'fingerprint' at the arts centre, something she says she learned when working for a law firm. Her own bio lists bouldering and international charity work. Her wardrobe consists of identical pant suits – black for work, navy for social events. She's one of those.

'Got a minute?' she asks, and then before I can reply, continues, 'We're chopping Chatty Tuesdays.'

I sit back in my seat. 'What?'

'The budget's tight, and we've got to cull the herd.' She smooths an invisible flyaway from her short dark hair. 'Sorry,' she adds, like it's an afterthought.

Chatty Tuesdays is my baby. It's an initiative I came up with two years ago, before Petra even worked here: a casual social every Tuesday evening for artists at any stage in their career to have a chat, share their work and give each other tips. It's a networking event, and the only thing we have to pay for is tea, coffee, some own-brand biscuits, and keeping the heating on an extra hour. I don't get paid overtime for hosting it. 'It doesn't cost much,' I say.

'That's as may be.' She folds her arms in her habitual *I won't be persuaded* stance. 'Energy costs are rising, we've had to give Donald a pay rise' – Donald is our long-suffering security guard – 'and frankly, Lottie, nobody ever turns up.'

I have to admit that she's right there. Last week, only one woman showed, and she brought with her a terrible papier-mâché rendition of Jesus Christ. I had to sit with her for an hour and talk about glue. I've tried everything: flyers, posters, Facebook adverts Petra doesn't know I use the arts centre credit card for. Nothing seems to work, but I still don't want to give up on it. I'm sure it's going to grow and get better; it just needs time.

'Good chat, Lottie,' Petra says before I can respond, and then swoops away.

I count to three and then get to my feet and stomp into the staff kitchen. Harry is standing by the kettle, spooning Nescafé into a mug.

'I'm going to scream,' I declare.

'No, you're not,' he replies without turning around.

Mid-forties, with chubby cheeks and a hairline that is running away from him at speed, Harry is a caricature of a jolly uncle, but my mood will not be lifted.

I hoist myself up onto the counter and look up at the ceiling. 'She's cancelling Chatty Tuesdays.'

Harry grimaces at me. 'Well . . .'

'Don't say it.'

'Does anyone ever show up?'

'Yes!' I cry. 'There's always at least one person.'

'A one-person networking event.' He splashes some milk into his mug and then leans against the counter. 'That's novel.'

'You're making it worse.'

'I know,' he says, and then smiles, his face becoming animated. 'But chin up. We'll come up with something new together. I've got loads of ideas. Last night, actually, I was thinking . . .'

I let my attention drift as Harry regales me with yet another of his wild initiatives. He has ten a minute, and if I spend more than half an hour in his company, I need a lie down. Harry is a creative well that can't be drained; his issue is that he can't seem to direct those ideas towards actually getting much done. He sent an email to the whole community engagement team at two o'clock this morning asking if anyone had heard of bacteria-grown portraits and whether we could get the health and safety sign-off to host a class. As of yet, no one has replied.

'I don't want something new.' I interrupt now as he's two minutes into explaining yet another nude drawing session he wants to host. 'I want Chatty Tuesdays. I *believe* in it.'

'Say something, then.'

I purse my lips.

'Lottie.' He comes and stands in front of me, forcing me to meet his eyes. 'You could say all of these things to Petra, you know.'

'Like she'd listen.'

'Probably not, but that's not the point. You can take the reins every once in a while, stand up for yourself.'

'I do!' I retort. 'I fight my corner.'

He raises an eyebrow.

'Whatever,' I say, picking at my jagged fingernail. I spent half an hour last night filing the acrylic penis down to an undecipherable blob – it was gel, after all. 'It won't make a difference.'

He sighs, his smile drooping. 'I know. It's shit. I feel like the whole ethos of my job is being pulverized by the second, hoovered up and scattered over the high seas.'

Harry often words things in ways that take a moment to digest, but his sentiments always hit home regardless. I always think he'd make a brilliant eccentric writer. 'God, me too.'

'Like, I *loved* this job. I got to be creative, engage with the community, have a vision. And then she took over, and it's suddenly a complete one-eighty, style over soul. She's completely—'

I'm nodding enthusiastically when the kitchen door swings open. We both turn around, our faces flaming like naughty school children. Petra stands in the doorway, her arms folded. 'Were you two planning on joining us?'

'Of course!' I say, bouncing off the counter. 'I was just putting my mug in the sink, I . . .' I trail off. Petra has already left the room.

Harry walks past me, nudging me as he goes. 'Way to go standing up for yourself there, buddy.'

*

It's a big meeting, and as late arrivals, we're squished in at the back. Gary from Accounting, who is about seven feet tall and has a thick bush of hair, is sat in front of me and is completely blocking my view. I slouch down in my seat next to Harry and sigh.

'We've had funding cuts,' Petra announces once we're settled, as if they were made by someone other than herself, 'and I know some of you might be disappointed.' Her tone is flat, like she's ordering a sandwich. 'But I do have some good news. We've managed to secure a partnership with a very exclusive gallery in London, which . . .'

Harry nudges me, and I roll my eyes. This is classic Petra – sod the local community, let's get champagne and canapés and mingle with the big city folk. I tune out, sinking down further into my seat, and let my mind travel to something more pressing.

Theo and I need to have sex. At first, the thought was just a niggle. A fleeting *Hm, it's been a while*. Then, I found myself sitting at the kitchen table, trying to remember the last time we did it. A month? More? And then it started to weigh on me a bit. I'd go through my day, determined that that night, we'd break out of the rut we'd found ourselves in. And then we'd get into bed and I'd pick up my phone and get lost in some scrolling activity or other, and by the time I put it down, he was asleep. Once three months had passed, I'd got myself so worked up about it that I questioned whether I should even make a move. Now it's been six, the thought of trying is terrifying. He evidently isn't interested, and the rejection would be far too painful.

So instead, I've taken to mulling it over incessantly. And

anonymously talking about it to thousands of people on chart-topping podcasts.

I glance up to check that Petra's attention isn't on me, and then slide my phone out of my pocket. I google 'How to get mojo back seven year itch' and angle my screen away from Harry. This isn't something I've done before; my general approach to problems in life is to worry ferociously while simultaneously hoping they'll resolve themselves without my input. Obviously, that strategy isn't serving me very well. If I have to tell Theo what I've done, I should at least try to *fix* our problem beforehand.

The results load quickly, and I click into an article from *Elle* that promises 'Ten tips for guaranteed mind-blowing sex after a dry spell'.

I scroll, my eyes scanning the numbered titles. Sex toys, yoni steamers, tantric retreats.

'What's a yoni steamer?' Harry whispers beside me.

I clutch my phone to my chest. 'None of your business!' I hiss. I don't admit that I have no idea myself.

Harry goes back to looking at the front, and I peer at my screen again. I'm about to read the yoni steamer paragraph when an Instagram notification pops up: a DM from an account I don't recognize. The first sentence is partially revealed: *Hey Lottie. My name is Isa; I'm Tilly Carter's agent...*

My heart immediately begins hammering.

'If we can get big artists from London to come to our gallery, we'll get much greater footfall,' Petra is saying. I tap open the DM with a trembling finger, leaning back as far as possible lest Harry catch another glimpse of my screen.

Hey Lottie. My name is Isa; I'm Tilly Carter's agent. Thank you so much for sending your anonymous confession in to The Cliterati's *Instagram page. I hope you don't mind me getting in touch via my own account – less chance of your response drowning in confession submissions! I don't know if you're aware that your message was aired on Saturday morning's episode, but I'm thrilled to tell you about the reaction we've received. It has BLOWN UP. This morning, the BBC wrote an article about a decline in sexual activity in younger generations, and they cited your confession as 'the beginning of a much-needed conversation.' You're famous! We've cancelled our plans for today's episode and are instead doing a deeper dive into your confession this afternoon, with experts chiming in and Tilly giving her view. Needless to say, Lottie, we would love to talk to you. Would you be free for a call with Tilly, just to get some context for your confession? Still anonymous, of course! And this might be a bit premature, but if needed, would you be free to meet Tilly and I at some point this week? We might have an idea we'd like to run by you, but will be able to confirm after today's episode. We can work around you, but would ideally like to set that call ASAP this morning – we're insanely excited about where we could take this, and are keen to jump on the opportunity while the story is fresh. It goes without saying that you'd be well reimbursed for your time. Let me know! Isa x*

A sharp jab in my side makes me snap my head up. The room is quiet, and a few people have turned around to look at me. 'She's said your name three times,' Harry whispers urgently.

'Were you asleep, Lottie?' Petra asks from the front, and I notice that she's moved to the side, where her view of me is unobstructed.

'No!' I reply, my voice shrill. 'Not at all. Sorry, I was just . . .'

'I was asking whether you'd finished the mock-ups for those flyers. Accounts need to know how much the print run is going to cost.'

Shit. I was supposed to do that before this meeting, but I got distracted by the death of Chatty Tuesdays and the near-constant barrage of thoughts about my sex life. I never forget things. What is going on today? I pull myself up straight, swallow the whirling panic momentarily. 'I'll have them in your inbox within five minutes,' I say, my voice squeaky.

'Good. Back to work, everyone.' She claps, keeping her eyes on me. 'Let's make a good day of it.'

'What is going on with you?' Harry asks as people stand up and begin filing out of the room.

I shake my head, anxiety coursing through me. My eyes find the clock on the wall at the front of the meeting room, and my heart begins pounding even faster. Ten o'clock. *The Cliterati*'s latest episode will be airing in just a few hours, and I'm going to be the main feature.

What the hell have I started?

Chapter Four

Obviously I haven't replied to Isa's DM. I've deleted it, removed it from my inbox, purged it from my life. And I'm not thinking about it. I'm putting the whole episode behind me, quite literally, and refusing to give my own stupid mistake any more airtime in my brain.

'Lotts, look at him.'

I've momentarily forgotten where I am. My feet have been carrying me along the ground, my arms swinging by my side, but I have to blink a few times to remember that I'm in the middle of a field, halfway through a dog walk, and that Theo is beside me.

I am *not* thinking about it.

Ahead of us, Boodle has found something, and he's prancing clumsily on his stumpy little legs, circling whatever it is, his ears flapping madly. A couple of metres away, Betty sits and watches with disdain. Betty is often weary of Boodle's reckless-abandon approach to life.

'He's so cute,' I say, linking my arm through Theo's. These are my favourite moments, when it's just us four, our hodge-podge of a chosen nuclear family. Every Sunday, without exception, we do a four-mile loop across the expanse of hills behind our house, through summer storms and crisp winter days, the ground changing beneath us with the seasons.

I take a deep lungful of air, bringing myself back. This is what's important. I have to remember that, and I hope Theo remembers, too. Because I'm about to tell him what I've done.

And *then* I'll stop thinking about it.

'So,' I start, my stomach in knots. 'Funny thing.'

Theo unlinks from my arm and takes a step away from me. I stop, confused.

'Oh, Christ,' he says. 'Boodle, *no*.'

I follow his gaze to the ground, where the object Boodle – the world's cutest sausage dog, with eyes like little brown pools and paws I could stare at for days – has been so transfixed by sits. It's a sheep's skull, half embedded in the grass.

'Ew,' I say. 'Boodle, you're so gross.'

Betty appears by my feet and plonks herself down, surveying the scene with Theo and me as if she, too, is repulsed by Boodle's discovery.

'No, come on, come away,' Theo says, stepping around the skull and chivvying Boodle along. 'Leave it alone, you minger.'

We carry on, eventually getting far enough for Boodle to stop looking over his shoulder, and settle into a steady rhythm again. 'So,' I try again. 'I had—'

'Oh, I wanted to ask you,' Theo says suddenly, turning to me with his eyebrow cocked. 'Is there something you wanted to tell me?'

My legs feel suddenly weak. Does he know? Has he found out from someone else? I feel sick; I was supposed to explain this to him. It was my responsibility to come clean. 'I—'

'I wasn't snooping,' he says. 'Promise. The email popped up when I was doing some marking.'

I stop. Hang on . . . 'What email?'

He grins. 'You're the actual best.'

I shake my head. 'I don't—'

'The model show? I thought it was completely sold out. Seriously, Lotts, I don't know how you do it. I'm . . .'

Relief floods through me as realization dawns, and Theo's voice fades into the distance as we start walking again, the dogs scampering ahead. The model show. Theo loves planes, and it's a bit of a hobby of mine to try and find him tickets to aircraft and model shows to surprise him. Sales almost always start at nine, when he's trying to herd 30 ten-year-olds into their seats to take registration, so he's usually too late to get a ticket by himself. A few weeks ago, he was talking about a particular show that always sells out in seconds, so I sat at my desk at work and refreshed the website until tickets went live and then snagged a pair.

'Any time,' I say, letting out a breath as I link his arm again and give him a squeeze. 'Who are you going to take?'

'Rob and Dasha have just been to AirX, so I'll see if Dev's free. It's going to be so good – you know they're showing the full Michael Webb Concorde collection . . .'

I drift off, my wellies squelching, as Theo talks about the parts of the show he's most excited for. He's got a group chat with three other plane enthusiasts, one of whom is his best friend, Dev, and they have good-natured competitions about who can get the best tickets for what. Most of the popular shows only allow the purchase of two, but it all works out evenly, with each of them inviting another member in tandem if they don't manage to get four between them.

Theo is one of those rare, enviable people who excels at being a multi-faceted adult with a job and hobbies and responsibilities and friends wherever he goes. He teaches a class of mad Year 6 children, and he's made for it. Unlike most people, he returns home from work each day brimming with energy, which I think is due to both his natural cheery temperament and the fact that he works in a nice school, where the kids enjoy learning and the parents see the teachers as allies rather than enemies. I've lived in this small town all my life, aside from a three-year break during uni, and knew I'd come back once I graduated. I worked a few odd jobs for a while until I landed my place at the arts centre, and unbeknownst to me at the time, Theo got a teacher-training post here straight after university. We met a few years later, and I often wonder how my life might have been different if he hadn't taken that job. I like to believe that somehow, wherever we were, we'd have found each other.

I like my life. I like my hometown. I like our house and our friends and our jobs and our routines. I like our marriage. But is it a marriage if you're not having sex with each other? Or is it an intense, legally-binding friendship?

Don't think about it now, Lottie.

Really, is now the time to tell him what I've done? Now, when he's all happy about the model show, with the blue late-winter sky above us and the dogs scampering happily across the soggy ground? Is this a moment I want to ruin with my confession?

Isa's message has gone, removed from my inbox like it never happened. Yesterday's deep-dive episode, as far as I can tell, has not had any ripple effects. No one has contacted me, no one has questioned whether it's me. I haven't listened to it yet, because I have a strange superstition that the moment I do, what I've done will become real. But it's already real; it's done, unchangeable, and maybe – just maybe – it's behind me. But I won't know for sure unless I pluck up the courage to sit down and actually listen to it.

We reach the turning point of the loop, Theo still chattering away, and stop to look out across the view of the rolling hills. Betty and Boodle sit on the grass, their tails swishing, knowing the drill. I reach into my jacket pocket and pull out a Ziploc bag containing two dried anchovy fillets, which I give out simultaneously. The dogs lie down, chewing on their halfway treat, while Theo and I stand, our arms interlinked, staring out across the landscape we've seen every week, no exception, for the last seven years.

I'll tell him soon, I promise myself. First, I have to listen to that episode, establish exactly what it is I'm dealing with. But then I'll tell him. I'll sit him down, hold his hand, and explain the silly little mistake I've made. And then he'll laugh, and everything will be fine. Everything will go back to normal.

I'm sure it will.

*

'Don't do it, Lottie. I can see you're about to. Control yourself.'

Caro is leaning back in her chair, her glass of red wine aloft. Her dark bob is shining under the ambient low lights, her plum lipstick still perfectly in place despite the moussaka she's just wolfed down. We're at our local Greek restaurant, a Sunday-evening tradition we haven't done in too long, and while I love spending time with my friends, there's been a niggle in the back of my mind since the first plate of houmous arrived. I still need to listen to *The Cliterati*'s deep-dive. I need to stop putting it off.

I hold up my hands. 'I wasn't going to say anything,' I protest.

'You were,' Dev, Theo's best friend, chimes in, grinning as he plucks a ring of calamari from the platter in the middle of the table. He looks at Theo. 'She was, wasn't she?'

Theo squeezes my hand under the table. 'Lottie? Never.'

There's a brief pause while everyone watches me. I try to bite my tongue but fail. 'But he was so *nice*, Caro.'

She plonks her glass down and throws her hands up. 'And there it is!'

'But he was! And you really liked him! I thought things were going well!'

She puffs out her cheeks and blows out a stream of air, making her fringe flutter. 'Things were going well and then they weren't. What can I say?'

I swallow down another retort. What's the point? But I can't deny that I'm disappointed. Caro's latest boyfriend was the longest relationship she's ever had – a whole three months – and I'd started to let myself believe that it might actually last. Peter was kind, funny, and the right kind of challenging. Caro met her match, and from the outside, it didn't seem like anything could go wrong.

But this is Caro we're talking about.

She cocks her head at me. 'Come on, Lotts. It's my breakup, not yours.'

She's being flippant, but I can see the apology in her eyes. Caro met Peter shortly after the last guy she was dating – a manchild with mummy issues and a less-than-charming coke habit – disappeared on her a month into their intense situationship. I've never seen her as down as she was when she realized he really wasn't coming back. It took two weeks of her sleeping in our spare room, long walks with Betty and Boodle across the fields, and a home-cooked dinner every evening for her to seem a little more like herself. And then she ran into Peter at a shoot she was doing and the heartbreak was forgotten.

'Why, though?' I ask, unable to leave it alone. There was nothing wrong with Peter; he made her laugh and let her be herself and didn't put any pressure on her to make things more committed than she was comfortable with. I loved having her in our house and looking after her, but it made me even more happy to see her connecting with someone who seemed to really care about her. This is the problem with Caro, though – she seems to like men until they show some genuine interest in her.

'It's easy for you guys,' Dev says before Caro can answer. 'You have no idea what it's like out there.'

I can sense we're veering on to the tried-and-true topic of 'How awful are dating apps?' and I resist the urge to roll my eyes. Caro was *off* the dating apps. She'd done the very thing she's always complaining is impossible in this day and age: she'd met someone nice and normal. Sometimes I think she's in love with the *idea* of love: those first few mad months, where you're so absorbed in each other you don't notice time passing, or each other's flaws.

'Exactly!' Dev nods enthusiastically. 'You and Theo met IRL. Do you know how rare that is?'

'Maybe you two should sign up for some kind of outdated extracurricular activity,' Theo suggests, and I laugh. 'Worked for us.'

I'd been back from uni for a couple of years when I had a minor quarter-life crisis. I realized that the easy friendships and access to community that had carried me through my years of education wasn't replicated in adult life. I was living in a one-bed flat and my days consisted of breakfast alone, walking to work alone, dinner alone, and occasionally seeing Caro. My other friends had all dispersed to far-flung places after graduation and the on-and-off boyfriend I'd had at uni had moved to Australia eighteen months earlier. I realized I needed to put myself out there, seek out a social life now that it was no longer being handed to me on an institutional platter. So in a mad moment – and in my defence, there really wasn't much to choose from – I signed up for a six-week line-dancing course at the town hall.

And it just so happened that Theo had done exactly the same thing.

His school had started a new community wellbeing programme wherein teachers were given money towards pursuing new hobbies that they could share with their pupils during a special 'Reciprocal Learning' hour. The reason Theo chose line dancing is still unclear both to him and me – but really, there probably isn't one. That's just Theo.

We were paired with each other that first day, and I often wonder how things could have been different. He could have done the course another time. He could have been paired with someone else. But he didn't, and he wasn't. By the end of the six-week course, we were no better at line dancing but we were completely in love with each other.

'Right,' Theo says now, slapping his thighs and standing up. 'It's almost eleven and we're too old for later than this on a school night. I'm going to settle up.'

'Let me come and give you a hand,' Dev says, touching Caro's arm as she tries to protest. 'Be my surrogate girlfriend for the evening,' he suggests.

The boys disappear across the restaurant and Caro props her chin against her hand, staring after them. 'Dev is such a sweetheart.'

'You'd destroy the poor man.'

'Hmm. Probably.' She continues gazing wistfully over my shoulder and sighs. 'You're lucky, you know.'

'I know,' I agree, and then decide I can't resist the opportunity to drive my point home once more. 'But Caro, you have to actually stick with someone long enough to—'

'No, not that,' she says, flapping a hand. 'You're just one of those people – or two of those people, the both of you – who don't have *issues*. You've got no baggage, Lotts. It's maddening.'

'I have baggage!' I retort on impulse, though I'm not really sure I do, nor that I particularly want any. Aside, of course, from the sex thing. And the fact I've told thousands of people I don't know about it. The weight of it sits on the tip of my tongue, and I almost confess right here, but it's too risky. The boys will be back any second. Instead, after a moment, I add, 'Our life isn't totally plain sailing.'

She gives me a deadpan look. 'Come on. You don't even argue.'

'Well, no,' I admit. 'But every couple communicates differently, right?'

'I can't imagine what you'd argue *about*.'

I shrug. 'We annoy each other sometimes, I guess. But we find a way around it. We don't need big long chats about things. We just sort of . . . figure it out.'

She rolls her eyes good-naturedly. 'Oh, god. Now you're brilliant *and* telepathic.'

I laugh. 'Neither of those things. My point is, you don't have to have a relationship that's like anybody else's, you know? It doesn't have to be serious chats and bickering over the dishwasher and whatever other stereotypes you've somehow absorbed. You can have whatever kind of dynamic you want.'

For a moment, Caro looks like she might actually be taking on board what I'm saying, and hope bobs up inside me. But then her eyes flick over my shoulder again and she beams. 'My sugar daddy's back,' she says as Dev returns to the table. 'And he's even brought me a complimentary mint. What more could a girl need?'

Chapter Five

It's six o'clock, and the arts centre is almost empty. Through the glass wall of her office, I can see Petra typing intently at her computer, her back ramrod straight. I find myself wondering whether she's listened to *The Cliterati* episode. I stand up from my desk, shrug on my coat, pick up my bag, and walk towards the exit, offering her a wave as I go. She nods, and I push through the door into the stairwell.

I fish my earbuds from my pocket and tentatively tap through to *The Cliterati*'s Spotify page as I tread down the stairs. I've avoided this for too long, and I can't put it off any longer. I spent this morning's commute listening to the BBC's latest report on gut health, which I managed to convince myself was unpostponable. Now, even I've got to admit that I've run out of excuses.

Since I unfollowed the podcast, I didn't receive a notification of the new episode, but here it is. *SEXLESS MARRIAGE DEEP*

DIVE. My stomach flips. It's over an hour long, and for some reason this makes me uneasy. Tilly's episodes are usually around the forty-five-minute mark; is there really so much to say?

My walk home is only around twenty minutes, but Theo is out at the gym this evening. Dev has been on at him to start lifting weights for months, and he finally caved a few weeks ago. Usually, they go for a pint afterwards, so I know I'll have the house to myself. Not that I'm avoiding him, of course. But the thought of listening to a professional deep dive into my marital issues while my husband, who I haven't yet told, is in the other room feels a step too far.

Generally, I've managed to wrangle my thoughts into something less catastrophic over the last few days. Since I deleted Isa's DM, it's become easier to convince myself that all of this is simply going to die away, another social media flash in the pan that will burn itself out. But sometimes, in the middle of the night, I wonder whether Isa might not leave it there. She mentioned a big idea, something she and Tilly are excited about – won't she try and make contact again? And what if they try to reach out through a different medium? What if they find the arts centre and call the front desk? What if they go through my tagged photos and start reaching out to my friends? *Hi, is that Jade? We're trying to get in touch with your friend Lottie about her predicament. What predicament, you ask? You haven't heard? She hasn't had sex with her husband for months, no end in sight. She told you her sex life was good? Well, I think you'll find she was lying. If you'd like to check out Saturday's episode of the podcast, you can hear for yourself.*

No. That's not going to happen. That's middle-of-the-night, paranoid Lottie speaking, and god knows she isn't to be trusted. Once I listen to the deep dive, I'm sure I'll see that the whole thing has taken an entirely new direction. My confession was just a springboard, and they'll be moving on to something new and exciting instead.

Still, I put off starting the episode. Instead of going out of the staff exit at the bottom of the stairwell, I take a right, pushing through the door of the gallery. The bottom floor of the centre is the part that's open to the public. It's four rooms in total: the gallery, where we have our exhibitions; the creation room, where we host classes and workshops; the storage room, where we keep all the art we've sold or need to return to the artist; and the shop. We close at five, so the gallery is empty, with just the low security lights illuminating the polished concrete floor and art-adorned walls. At the moment, we're running an exhibition for a semi-local artist, whose work – splashes of beige paint on a slightly lighter beige background – isn't great, but whose name brings in the crowds.

I wander around, relishing the quiet for a moment, and try not to get too irritated when I spot the space on the wall where my Chatty Tuesdays flyer used to be pinned. It's been replaced by a minimalist, corporate-looking announcement of our new partnership with the London gallery. Say what you want about Petra, but she gets shit done.

Outside, a cold February rain is starting up. Reluctantly, I have to admit that I've put it off long enough – it's time to walk home and listen to what Tilly Carter has to say about my sex life.

*

By the time I make it to our front gate, I am feeling decidedly less confident and decidedly more like I might throw up all over the front path.

Tilly has spent the last twenty minutes doing a review of my confession, analysing it word for word. She's said the words 'Why doesn't he want to jump me' about thirty times. She's explored the ideas I might have about myself, and has deduced that calling myself 'not bad-looking' is a sign that I am struggling with my self-esteem.

Mercifully, Theo's bike isn't outside, which means he's already left. I hurry up the front path with relief and unlock the door before closing it behind me and leaning against the frame. The dogs immediately run to me, their tails thrashing, and I squat down to give them a stroke. In my ear, Tilly says, 'We did reach back out to our anonymous confessor for a follow-up interview, but unfortunately, she hasn't responded. But not to worry! We'll keep trying, and we've got something just as good for you instead. My first expert guest, Dr Fauzia Biswas, is going to give us an insight into exactly what our anonymous confessor meant when she said, "I feel like I am a mad, horny, insane nymphomaniac." Dr Biswas, welcome—'

'Hey.'

I leap a foot into the air. Theo has appeared in the kitchen doorway, dressed in his gym kit.

'Hi!' I manage, scrambling to my feet as I pull out my phone and stab at the pause button. In the seconds it takes my finger to fumble with Spotify's controls, I'm convinced Theo can hear Dr Biswas as she begins to unpack the semantic differences between a nymphomaniac and an *insane* nymphomaniac. I yank out my earbuds. 'Aren't you at the gym?'

'It doesn't look like it.' He laughs. 'I was just about to leave. You OK?'

'Yep!' I nod. 'Yes, great. Great, good day. You? Where's your bike?'

He smiles confusedly. 'I had a great, good day, too. And I've put it round the back, in the shed. The rain's going to be awful, apparently.' He steps towards me, weaving around the dogs. 'Has something happened?'

'No! Like what? Nothing's happened.' Good god, could I *sound* more guilty? I'm rambling, and I know that if I look in the mirror, my face will be bright red. 'I'm fine!'

Theo frowns at me for a moment. 'Lottie—'

A car horn beeps outside, and Theo looks over my shoulder towards the front door. 'That'll be Dev. Are you sure you're OK? I can stay . . .'

'No!' I say too quickly. 'No, I promise, I'm totally fine. Just . . .' I scramble. 'Just annoyed with Petra. She's cancelled my Chatty Tuesdays event.'

Theo's face creases. 'Oh, Lotts, that sucks. I'm so sorry.'

I nod, guilt gnawing at my stomach. 'I know, but hey-ho. Go on, don't keep Dev waiting. Have a lovely evening.'

The horn sounds a second time, and Theo's phone buzzes in his pocket.

'I'll keep it short, OK?' he says, moving past me. 'Then I'll come straight home and we can talk about it. I'll pick you up your favourite curry on my way back?'

'No, no.' I shake my head, thinking on the spot. 'I've got Caro coming over for a drink. You go to the pub, enjoy your evening.'

Reassured that I won't be alone, Theo nods and bends down, planting a big kiss on my lips.

'See you later,' he says, and then disappears through the front door.

Once I've heard the car door slam, I sink down onto the hallway floor and let Betty and Boodle clamber over my legs. I pull out my phone and fire off a text to Caro.

> Me: *Tony's at mine?*

She comes back to me immediately.

> Caro: *Oof, you know how to get a girl going.*

What is it they say? If you're going to lie, keep it as close to the truth as possible. And speaking of lying – maybe this is the perfect way to spend my evening. I need to tell *someone* what I've done, and who better than my best friend?

In less than half an hour, the doorbell is ringing. I race down the stairs with my hair in a towel, wearing leggings and an old T-shirt, and swing the door open.

Caro is standing on the doorstep in a floor-length linen kaftan, holding two bottles of rosé aloft. Her shiny bob appears totally unaffected by the rain, and despite the sun being long gone below the horizon, she has a pair of sunglasses perched on her head. Her lips, as always, are a deep plum colour. I'm not sure I could tell you the colour of her natural lips if I tried.

'I see you've dressed up for the occasion,' she says, stepping past me and kicking off her shoes. She turns back and wraps her arms around me, enveloping me in a patchouli-scented hug, the two bottles clinking together behind my back.

'Sorry,' I say into her soft hair. 'Long day.'

'Well, thank god I'm here. Come on.'

She leads me into my own kitchen–living room, dumps the bottles of wine on the counter and begins fussing with the dogs. Boodle jumps up at her legs while Betty offers a more dignified sniff of her shoes. 'My babies,' she coos.

'So what's new?' I ask, readjusting my hair towel as I pull two wine glasses down from the cupboard. It's less than twenty-four hours since we last saw each other, but knowing Caro, something interesting will have happened.

'Oh, nothing,' Caro breezes, crawling across the floor to Boodle's bed and plonking herself in it. 'Did a photoshoot at an underground kink dungeon this morning. Did you know they did morning sessions for these kinds of things? Anyway, I dropped my camera in some adult baby food, which wasn't ideal. Then some guy offered to clean it but ran off with it instead, so I've spent the day at the police station. And you'll never guess who the desk sergeant was. Phil. Remember Phil? He asked me if we could go for a coffee,' she scoffs. 'I mean, that's an absolute no. Anyway, what about you?'

Caro is one of those people around whom chaos orbits. Her idea of a normal day is my idea of a life event I'd have to take a week off work for. I've known her since we were fifteen, and we have always been the kind of polar opposites that under any logical kind of framework just shouldn't work together. But we do. We've never had an argument, never gone a day without speaking to each other, and never struggled to accept one another for exactly who we are – though we do try to nudge each other in the right direction from time to time, Caro's dating issues being the perfect example. Phil, incidentally, is a guy Caro dated for two months until he forgot he invited her to Ibiza and she turned up to find him in bed with a cocktail waitress. She spent the week's trip staying in the hotel room he'd booked for himself, refusing to leave, smoking cheap cigarettes on the balcony and learning Spanish on Duolingo.

I know better than to be shocked by the last twenty-four hours of Caro's life, so after asking the usual practical questions that come to my mind – has she lost a lot of work, are the police going to pursue the case, does she have insurance – I lead us to the living area and allow her to steer the conversation towards me. 'So?' she asks once she's sat down on the sofa opposite me.

I know she won't be expecting much of a response; nothing much of interest tends to happen to me. 'Work's a bit shit,' I admit. I can't bring up my podcast debut right out of the gate. I'll let it come up naturally. For now, I'll stick to tried-and-true topics.

'Petra the prick?'

I nod, sighing. 'It's fine, there's nothing I can do about it. It's just frustrating. She makes the place feel so corporate and soulless.'

'Well,' Caro says, taking a sip of her wine, 'you know what I think. Give her a piece of your mind and then tell her to shove her job up her arse. You'll find another one.'

I nod, though I have absolutely no intention of doing either of those things, and Caro knows it. This is the way we work – I remind her of the important practical aspects of her life that need attention, and she promptly ignores me; she tells me to do wild, life-altering things on a whim, and I carry on as I am.

'Top-up?' she asks, rising to her feet and striding over to the fridge. 'Shall we order some food?'

We place an order at Tony's, the crappy pizzeria down the road that has been standing as long as both of us have been alive, and which has stubbornly refused to follow the trends of the twenty-first century. The two-inch-thick margherita with luminous tomato sauce and an impenetrable layer of cheese is the same today as it was when we were teenagers. Tony – a man from Newcastle who has never been to Italy in his life – will not be shamed into using phrases like 'fresh ingredients' and 'Neapolitan style'. A pizza is a pizza is a pizza, he says, and while it isn't gourmet and certainly isn't good for us, Caro and I order from him at least once a month.

'So,' Caro says a while later as she pulls a piece of cheesy garlic bread from its greasy box on the coffee table. She leans back on the sofa, watching as the cheese stretches and then snaps. Betty and Boodle stand guard, waiting for something to drop. 'How's Theo? He seemed on good form last night.'

We're on our second bottle of rosé now, and I can feel the edge of my predicament softening. Telling Caro what I've done is exactly what I need to do. We don't keep secrets from each other; there is nothing about me she doesn't know. That said, I haven't exactly been forthcoming about my sex life, or lack thereof. Telling her about the whole ordeal will mean telling her everything, and it feels easier to skirt around it. Omission isn't lying, is it?

Plus, there's a tiny part of me that doesn't want to shatter the illusion of us being the perfect couple. The people who communicate in their own perfect way, who never argue. The people without baggage. I've spent so long inhabiting my role as the lucky, perfect wife, I don't know if I can bear to see in Caro's eyes what it means if I'm not.

But Caro is my rock, one of the two people I trust most in the world. This big thing has been looming over me for days, and if there's anyone in the world I can spill my guts to – aside from Theo for obvious reasons – it's my mad bitch of a best friend.

I swallow a mouthful of stodgy pizza and put my glass down. 'I did something,' I say.

Caro's eyes widen. I know she'll have been expecting the usual 'he's fine' or 'same old'. Of the two of us, I am not the one with scandalous stories. 'What?'

I put my face in my hands. 'Something bad,' I mumble. I can feel my resolve cracking, the pressure of the secret building behind my eyes. 'I've really fucked up, Caro.'

Caro is on her feet in seconds and kneeling in front of me. She prises my hands from my face. 'Listen to me,' she says, holding my gaze intently. 'Was it sex, touching or emotional?'

I blink. 'What?'

'Remember when I was dating Rajesh? And I had that emotional affair with Liam from the printing shop? There are levels to these things, Lottie. And even the best people have weak moments. Who was it? Harry?'

Hang on, what exactly is she saying? I pull my wrists from her hands. 'I haven't *cheated!*' I splutter.

Her face slackens. 'Oh, thank god.'

'And with *Harry*? Who's married to a man?'

'I'm sorry. I was racking my brains. You don't have a tonne of male friends.'

'Jesus Christ.'

'Sorry, sorry,' she says, holding her palms up. She sits back on the rug, her back against the coffee table. 'So what is it, then? Did you steal something?'

'Can we stop the guessing game?'

'Yes, sorry, go ahead.'

I take a breath. Where do I even begin? I decide to rip the plaster off and come right out with it. 'So Theo and I haven't had sex in a while.'

Caro raises one perfect eyebrow. To her credit, I see no smugness in her eyes. 'I see.'

'And it's been weighing on me. Then the other night, I was at Jade's hen do—'

'Jade with the horsey laugh, treats you like a doormat, yes, I remember.' Caro nods.

'Well I wouldn't say . . . OK, never mind. So I had quite a bit to drink, and—'

'I'm really struggling to see how we're not going down the cheating route here.'

'I'm getting to it!'

'Get there faster.'

I take another calming breath. 'So I think I spoke to the stripper about it. About me and Theo not having sex. I remember telling him something, and him giving me some advice, and then my memory goes blank. Anyway, I woke up the next morning and put on the latest episode of *The Cliterati*.'

Caro has been nodding impatiently throughout my story, but now, as I pause, I watch her face change. She frowns. 'What has that . . .' I can see the cogs turning. 'Hang on. Saturday's episode?'

'Yes.'

'About the woman whose husband won't have sex with her.'

'Yes.'

Her mouth drops open. 'And you've been in touch with this woman?'

'No, Caro, Jesus Christ. It was *me*.'

I watch as her brow furrows and then slackens, realization dawning. She sits back heavily against the table with a thump. 'Fuck off.'

I throw my head into my hands again. 'Theo's going to find out. He's going to find out and he's going to leave me.'

'Bloody hell, Lottie, this is very out of character.'

'I know!' I wail. 'Oh, god, what am I going to do? What am I going to—'

She lunges forward and grips my shoulders with her manicured hands. 'Relax,' she says shrilly. 'Relax!'

'You're not making me feel relaxed!' I pull my hands from my face and glare at her.

'Listen to me.' She leans her face towards mine. 'I had *no* idea it was you. And I'm your best friend; I've known you more than half my life. That confession could have been *anyone*. How would anyone know it was you?'

'If you knew Theo and I were having a dry spell—'

'No one knows.'

'Theo does.'

'Theo doesn't listen to the podcast,' she says, 'and I doubt any of his friends do either, if he's confided in them.'

'That's true,' I concede. I press my lips together. 'God, Caro, I feel awful.'

'As would I, if my vagina had gone into hibernation.' She

offers me a smile, and I reluctantly return it. 'You don't need to worry about the podcast,' she says firmly. 'It'll blow over and he'll never know.'

I close my eyes. 'I'm going to tell him.'

'God, don't do that.'

'What?' I open my eyes again. 'Why?'

She releases me and shakes her head. 'Because what's the point? It won't change anything.'

'I can't lie to him.'

'You're not lying. You confessed, anonymously, about something that's been bugging you, and you've received some advice in return. Have you listened to the deep dive?'

'Not all of it.'

She shakes her head. 'God, it's so weird, thinking they were talking about *you*.' She sees my face and grimaces. 'Sorry. But she speaks to this incredible neuroscientist at the end, who's done all this research into . . . yes, OK, no, you listen to it in your own time.' She takes a breath. 'Anyway, my point is, you don't need to worry about it because you haven't done anything wrong.'

'But—'

'What you *do* need to worry about is the state of your marriage,' she continues bluntly. 'You are too young to be sitting in bed with your rollers in and a floor-length nightie on.'

'I don't—'

'So,' she interrupts, reaching behind her for the bottle of rosé. 'You need a plan. A plan of wooing and seduction.'

'Wooing.' I pull a face.

'Don't look at me like that,' she says sternly. 'You're in no position to turn your nose up at advice. Now, get your phone out. You've got some work to do.'

Chapter Six

The next evening, I find myself standing alone in our bedroom, wondering what the fuck I think I'm doing.

Lying on the bed in front of me are two Amazon packages, and I can't bear to open either one of them. The smell of a bubbling lasagne wafts through the doorway from downstairs. I have half an hour until Theo gets home.

Oh, god. Oh, god. Oh, god. *Just do it, Lottie.*

I pluck the first package off the bed and rip it open, tipping its contents out onto the duvet. Instinctively, I wince. It's a black, lacy bra and pants set, horrifyingly thin, and significantly worse quality in person than it seemed in the photos online. I had begged Caro to let me order from somewhere nicer, but her response had been final. 'Better slutty Amazon than M&S, Lottie – don't you dare say you'd have shopped anywhere else – and you don't have time to wait for delivery. The difference between one and three business days could be the difference between a good shag and a hefty marriage counselling bill.'

I pick the bra up by its strap. The cups are about a quarter the size of my actual breast, and the material feels scratchy and cheap. I fling it back down and pick up the other package instead. Inside, there's a silicone rose-shaped thing, along with a USB charger. Just looking at it makes me feel scandalized, and I wonder when I became such a prude.

'The thing is, Lottie,' Caro said last night, 'this is the twenty-first century. Men don't just want to bonk you while you're half asleep any more. They want you to enjoy it. They can *tell* when you're not enjoying it.'

She told me this thing was a female stimulation device, and it doesn't take a tonne of creative leaps and bounds to figure out where it's supposed to go. It's not shaped like a phallus, so I'm pretty sure I'm right in guessing which other part of my anatomy it's designed for. I tentatively press the button and it jumps to life in my hands, buzzing so loudly I'm certain Theo will hear it from the school two miles away. I scramble with the button, my fingers fumbling, and it gets louder. I keep frantically stabbing, somehow taking the device through every available setting, before it falls silent.

Theo and I have never used sex toys in the bedroom, and I have to admit that I'm one of those women who has always claimed that we don't need them. We used to gel so well together; we always seemed to be on the same wavelength at the same time. Neither of us ever needed a hand getting things going, and when we were together, we were more than capable of communicating and experimenting with each other, having fun, getting each other where we needed to be. We were in sync.

And look where that kind of smug thinking has got me.

I check my watch. Twenty minutes until Theo's due home, and I need to check the lasagne. I pluck the lingerie from the bed before I can think too much about it and shimmy into it with difficulty. When everything's in place, I appraise myself in the mirror. I have to admit that I look good; my boobs are bulging in the right places, the razor-thin thong sitting high on my hips and making my bum look bigger.

But Jesus *Christ* is it uncomfortable. The material scratches at the flesh near my armpits and inside my thighs, and the cups of the bra are doing so much work to lift up my boobs that they're cutting off my blood supply.

Ten minutes to go; too late to change my mind now. I fling the wardrobe doors open and pull out my sluttiest dress – one Theo used to go crazy for. It's black and low-cut, the hem reaching just below my knickers. I haven't worn it since we were first dating, and I'm surprised that it still fits, but I'm also surprised to see that I look pretty good. I throw on some makeup and shake my hair out, then head downstairs, my stomach churning.

The lasagne still needs a few minutes, so I busy about setting the table and then resetting it, putting a candle in the middle, and then slightly to the side, and then adding another before deciding it looks too symmetrical and putting it on the coffee table instead.

Aside from the hum of the oven, the kitchen is quiet, so I connect my phone to the speaker and begin searching for some appropriate music as I lean forward on the counter. I can feel a draft on my arse; there's a reason I don't wear this dress any more. Is Adele too emotional? Taylor Swift certainly is;

nothing screams 'shag me' less than a song about typewriters. Chappell Roan? Will having 'Casual' on in the background subconsciously spur Theo to take me for a ride in the car and put his head between my thighs?

In the end, I disconnect my phone and chuck the radio on. I don't want Theo thinking I've made too much of an effort; we're married – a romantic evening and some good sex should be a natural, regular occurrence. Something undertaken with the hum of Capital FM in the background, with a stomach full of pasta and ragu and garlic-bread breath. Too polished and it'll feel forced. I blow out the candle on the coffee table.

The seven o'clock news bulletin is on, and I tune out as I bend to check if the lasagne is ready. It's the recipe I make for Theo every few months, if he's feeling particularly tired or wiped out from a heavy day's marking. Sometimes I make extra and freeze some individual portions for him to take to work to cheer him up during long teacher-training days or to see him through parents' evening. I put little sticky notes on the lids – in-jokes and crappy drawings of Betty or Boodle that he collects and keeps in his bedside drawer.

A hot blast of air flutters my fringe as I pull the oven door open. The lasagne is bubbly and cheesy and smells incredible. Christ, this bra is itchy.

'. . . and a woman's anonymous confession about her sexless marriage on a popular women's podcast has sparked a debate about what experts are calling "a worrying decline in sexual activity in the Western world".'

I stop dead with my hands in the oven gloves.

'One side argue that it's a result of excessive fearmongering during the rise of teenage pregnancies in the nineties and noughties, but the more prevalent view seems to be that social media is, once again, to blame. The conversation began when a listener in her thirties wrote in to complain about the lack of intimacy in her marriage, which—'

The sound of Theo's key in the door sends my heart skyrocketing, and I stab the radio off. Shit. Shit, shit, shit.

When will this *end*?

'Hey!' Theo says as he appears in the kitchen doorway. His eyebrows shoot up as he sees me. 'Oh, *hey*.'

'Hi,' I say, padding over and giving him a kiss. I push thoughts of the podcast down, forcing myself to breathe normally. 'How are you? How was marking night?'

Theo looks beyond me to the candle, the lasagne, the well-set table. 'What's going on?'

'Nothing!' I say, smiling. 'Just thought it'd been a while since we'd had a nice dinner.'

'It's been a while since I've seen you in that dress,' he says, his eyes scanning up and down my body. 'I completely forgot about it.'

I smile, enjoying his attention. He lets his gaze linger for a moment longer and then shrugs off his satchel and removes his coat. 'I should change into something nicer,' he says, gesturing to himself. He's wearing his usual school uniform: a white shirt, the very top button open, and sage green trousers that hug his pert little bum.

'You know I love you in your work outfit,' I say, rubbing his arm and then pulling my hand away. What am I doing, comforting him after the loss of his grandmother? When did I forget what natural touch felt like? 'Come on, wash your hands and sit down. It's ready.'

Oh, good, now I'm his mother.

'How lucky am I, eh?' Theo grins over his shoulder at me as he scrubs his hands at the sink. 'You look incredible.'

'Are you talking to me or the lasagne?'

He flicks the tea towel at me. 'Both of you. How did you have time to do all this?'

'It doesn't take that long,' I say, deciding not to mention that I've been cooking since I got home two and a half hours ago.

He grins and pulls out a chair. 'You're such a liar,' he teases, then sits down and reaches towards the counter for my hand. 'You know, I've started loving marking night because I know you always do something special?'

My heart squeezes with happiness. Theo is such a dynamic, active person; the more sedentary, boring aspects of his job make him fidgety and frustrated, and while it sounds cliché and a bit outdated, there is genuinely nothing that makes me happier than seeing his tired face light up at the sight of his favourite meal at the end of a long day. I love thinking of little ways to cheer him up, and he's so easy to please. He once told me that the day after our wedding, when we were finally at home, blissfully happy but exhausted and a bit shellshocked, was better than the day itself. I made us hot chocolate with great handfuls of teeny little marshmallows and we sat on the sofa curled up with the dogs watching an old warplane documentary, sipping contentedly. Theo had worked right up until the day before the wedding, while I'd taken a week off, and I wanted to start our married life together with a night just for him.

But now, selfishly, I want a night for *us*. Or, more specifically, for our long-neglected genitals. Caro's right; telling Theo at this point just doesn't make any sense. He's never going to find out it was me, and really, what damage has been done? It's not airing the dirty laundry if no one knows whose laundry it *is*, surely. It's just a scabby pair of unclaimed knickers, owner unknown.

Besides, after tonight, there'll be no problem to discuss. Everything will go back to normal, and I can forget all about it.

My phone buzzes on the counter – a text from Caro containing the photos from her latest shoot. She often sends me her pictures once she's edited them; I think it's her way of sharing her work without having to *actually* share it. I reply with a love heart, flick my Do Not Disturb on and set my phone face-down at the back of the counter.

'So how was your day?' Theo asks, and I give him a brief overview as I open a bottle of nice red wine; one I bought on the way home from work. Top shelf, over a tenner. I'm pulling out all the stops.

Once I've poured us both a glass, I pull out my own chair and sit down. The Amazon thong instantly slices into the furthest reaches of my arse crack. I yelp.

Theo makes to stand up. 'What's wrong?'

'Nothing!' I cry, tears in my eyes. I force myself to sit down slowly, wiggling my hips to try and give the fabric some movement. 'Pins and needles.'

His brow crinkles but he lets it go, cutting a slice of lasagne and ladling it onto my plate. 'Garlic bread as well,' he says as he offers me the dish across the table. 'Feels like my birthday.'

'I know how to show a boy a good time,' I say, feeling

clunky, but my cheeks only redden slightly. I've got to get the vibe switched on, get the flirting started. It's just that I've sort of forgotten how to do it.

But Theo sidesteps into another of our routines instead: pretending to be a French food critic.

'And do we know zee provenance of zis delightful baked item? An Italian dish, per'aps?'

'From a small region called Aldi,' I confirm, working to keep my face serious. 'Renowned for its creative use of the freezer.'

'Ah, *bien*. Cheers to zee people of Aldi,' Theo says, clinking his wine glass against mine. He smiles at me warmly and reverts back to his own voice. 'And to my gorgeous wife.'

My tummy flutters. I love him so much. Everything about him is perfect; everything about our lives is perfect. I just need us to get back to that place, refind that one missing piece.

'So we never really talked about Chatty Tuesdays,' Theo says now. 'How are you feeling about it?'

'Oh, fine,' I say, waving my hand. I do not want to allow Petra to infiltrate my romantic evening. 'It's fine.'

'What happened? Why is it being cut? What did Petra say?'

Theo has a way of firing questions so rapidly that you feel like you're under interrogation. I've seen him do it with new friends at the pub, asking everything he can think of about their jobs, their lives, their hopes and dreams and ambitions. At times, it feels like being interviewed, but he gets away with it because he's so warm and kind, and because you can just tell he's genuinely curious. He's interested in people.

'Can we not talk about it this evening?' I find myself saying as I mop up some sauce with a piece of garlic bread. Recently, I've got into the habit of whingeing about work too much, and I want us to talk about happy things – funny things, flirty things. Like we used to.

He frowns, but nods understandingly. It isn't often that I don't want to talk my issues through; my usual MO is to stay quiet in the moment and then vent behind closed doors after the fact. We lapse into silence, broken only by Theo commenting on how cheesy the lasagne is.

Amid the sound of forks on plates, I rack my brains trying to think of a flirty topic of conversation. I've never had to contrive a situation like this before; it used to come so naturally. But what to say? 'I've been thinking about you all day'? No, I'd manage to make it sound like a condolence to someone with an ill relative. 'Fancy taking this upstairs?' But what if he gets the wrong end of the stick, and brings the lasagne tray up to the bedroom? I could just come straight out with it – lean across the table and say, 'Are you horny?' But no; he's got tomato sauce in his beard, it's not the time.

'How was marking, then?' I ask eventually. Seductive, sensual, suggestive. Keeping things strictly away from work. Ticking all the boxes.

'Great,' he replies, laying his knife and fork down. Theo is almost always great, even when he's doing his least favourite thing. 'I got through all of it, which is a relief. They're all doing really well. A few little niggles, but nothing major. Ben is still struggling with his maths, so I think I'll suggest an assessment for additional help at the next parents' evening . . .'

I nod and raise my eyebrows in the right places, offering 'mmm's and 'good idea's where appropriate, but for once, I'm not listening. Half of my mind is on my nipples, one of which I can no longer feel and one of which is itching so intensely I'm wiggling in my chair, and the other half of my mind is on how I can get Theo to initiate sex with me – primarily because we *need* to have sex; secondarily because it will necessitate taking this underwear off.

The problem, I realize, is that I've not often been the one to initiate sex. Usually, Theo will come and nuzzle my neck, or he'll run his hand up my thigh under the table, or we'll be kissing and his hands will roam. I'm overthinking it so much, I'm not actually sure what to *do*.

Kissing. Let's start there.

'Sounds like you've got everything under control as usual.' I smile when Theo pauses for breath, rising from my seat. I circle the table and lean over him, planting a kiss on his lips. I imagine he'll respond, pull my face closer, snake his arm around my waist, but he gives me a peck and then leans back, smiling at me. His eyes travel to my chest, where my boobs are bulging out of my dress.

Leaning over him is now feeling awkward, given that we aren't having the make-out session I envisaged, so I sit on his lap and wrap my arms around his neck. I've done this so many times before, I've lost count, but my heart is hammering. Surely this has to work?

Theo raises an eyebrow and pushes his mouth against mine, letting his lips linger longer this time. 'Mmm,' he murmurs.

And then he pulls back. My heart sinks.

'Shall we head upstairs?' he asks.

I nod, relief and anticipation flooding through me. It's happening! Oh, god, finally. It's happening.

I stand up and take his hand, pulling him to his feet. He leans down and kisses me again, and then picks up the plates from the table. I pause.

'What are you doing?'

'You head up. I'll sort this out and join you.'

I want to tell him that the washing-up can wait, but I'm not about to look a gift-horse in the mouth. I hoick my skirt up just a little bit more and then walk out of the room, swaying my hips. Betty and Boodle follow me, their paws scrabbling adorably against the tiles. I glance over my shoulder when I get to the doorway, looking over at Theo through lowered eyelids.

He's decanting lasagne into a Tupperware box.

Well, that's fine. It's not a problem. I'll go upstairs, make myself as comfortable as this underwear will allow, and wait for him. I'll do the hooker-in-a-hotel-room move, minus the trench coat.

Upstairs, the dogs immediately ask to be let up onto the bed, but I send them to their cushions under the window instead, where they gaze at me with looks of abject betrayal. I pull my dress off and take a quick look in the mirror. The underwear is still making me look like a porn star, but it's giving me red welts around my arms and my crotch. I turn off the main light and flick one of the bedside lamps on instead. Just a moment longer, and Theo can rip it off me and this whole saga will be over.

I sit on the bed in what I imagine is a seductive pose – propped on one hand, my legs tucked beneath me. Downstairs, I can hear the clank of plates being loaded into the dishwasher, the tap running. Any minute now.

I shuffle about on top of the duvet, trying once again to loosen the grip of the thong. Oh, god. I need a wee. I can still hear Theo clanging about, so I make an executive decision, jump off the bed and hurry to the bathroom.

Mid-flow, I hear Theo treading up the stairs. Shit. I don't have time to run back to the bedroom now; he'll see me flitting across the landing in my underwear and think I've gone completely insane. I flush the toilet and wash my hands, listening as he walks into the bedroom. For all my gutsy planning, my ideas of seduction, I suddenly get cold feet. I cannot walk in there dressed like this. It's too embarrassing.

I grab a thin dressing gown off the back of the bathroom door and wrap it around myself. I'll go in there, and he'll be waiting for me, and I'll let him see a little peek of my shoulder. Then he'll stand up and undo the belt of the dressing gown, see the lingerie, and we'll get started.

Good god, am I planning a meeting?

Before I can think too much more, I swing the door open and pad across the landing. Outside the bedroom door, I pause momentarily and take a breath. *Come on, Lottie. It's sex with your husband, not a redundancy one-to-one.*

I step into the bedroom.

Theo is sitting under the duvet, his glasses on the end of his nose. There's a book about the history of Boeing 737s in his hands. He doesn't look up.

For fuck's sake.

'Hi,' I say.

He glances over. 'Hey, you. All cleaned up down there.'

For a horrifying moment, I think he's asking me a question about my trip to the bathroom. But then I realize he's referring to the dishes. I notice that the dogs are now curled up in the middle of the bed, between his side and mine. Boodle wags his tail happily, and Betty looks at me with triumph.

'Thank you,' I manage. Come on, don't give up this easily. Yes, there are obstacles, but they are not insurmountable. 'Can I make it up to—'

'Did you know that since the Sixties, the Boeing 737 has carried nearly seventeen billion passengers?'

Right, no, that's enough for me.

'Fab,' I manage, and then I grab my pyjamas from under the pillow and stride back to the bathroom. I fight back tears as I get changed – tears of relief as the bra comes off, tears of frustration. Why doesn't he want me? What am I doing wrong?

I wash off my makeup with cold water and look at myself in the mirror. It's fine, I tell myself. This was the first attempt; I just have to keep trying.

Back in the bedroom, Theo has put his book down. I don't look at him as I walk around the bed; now that my plan has been thwarted, I'm irritated. I slide under the duvet and open TikTok on my phone.

'What's this?' Theo asks.

I take a breath. If he's going to ask me to identify a plane engine part, I will officially reach my limit. I turn to look at him.

Oh, god.

He's frowning quizzically at a pink, rose-shaped object in his hand. I watch in horror as he turns it this way and that, my words catching in my throat.

'Don't—'

But before I can stop him, Theo has pushed his thumb down on the button, and it jumps to life in his palm.

And this, I realize – this right here – is my actual limit. I have welts on my crotch, I haven't so much as managed to get my husband to even tongue me, and he's now sat beside me holding an active vibrator in the air as his book about passenger planes slips off his lap.

It is quite clear that something has gone terribly wrong in my marriage.

Chapter Seven

I miss him. It sounds so pathetic, doesn't it? Because he's right here. He's next to me while I make coffee in the morning, he's opposite me at the end of the day, asking how it went and listening. Actually listening. He sleeps next to me and he hugs me and he holds my hand when we're out in public. But I miss him. I miss the way we used to be. Why aren't we having sex? I don't even know whose fault it is. I've hardly put the effort in either until recently. Doesn't he want me any more? Isn't he attracted to me? Has he met someone else? God, I hope not. But I love him and I miss him. So, so much.

I take a deep breath and stop typing, then exit the Notes app. It's five in the morning and I'm sitting in the bath, letting chamomile-scented bubbles soothe my lingerie-injured body parts. I haven't slept, which I know is going to ruin my entire day at work, but after three hours lying next to Theo's sleeping back, getting more and more worked up, I gave up. I ran a bath, and I've been sitting in it for the past hour, ruminating.

I told Theo the sex toy was a gag gift from Jade's hen party, and the excuse has raised yet another question in my mind. A normal wife would just come clean, wouldn't she? She'd admit that she'd bought the toy herself, to spice up their sex life, and the husband would probably be quite pleased. He'd insist they try it out, be glad that his wife was invested in having sex with him. What does the fact that I can't be open about these things with Theo say about our marriage?

And what does Theo's reaction say about it, too? When I lied about the sex toy's provenance, Theo laughed it off and tossed it onto the pile of dirty laundry by the door before picking his book back up and resuming his studies of the various fascinating features of Ryanair's favourite aeroplane.

Shouldn't he have seen the opportunity there? Shouldn't he have thrown himself on top of me and insisted we give it a go straight away?

I've never had thoughts like this. In all our years together, I have never questioned the very fundamentals of us. Theo is my best friend, an unquestionable part of me, hooked onto my hip since that first line-dancing class seven years ago. But now it feels like there's a crack running through the foundation of everything, making me question not only our sex life but the emotional bonds that are tied to it by design.

But how do I talk to him about it? *Why* haven't I talked to him about it? It's a stupid question, and one I know the answer to without thinking. This isn't us. We don't have issues. We don't rub up against each other. We don't talk things through, because there's never anything *to* talk through. And how do you change the dynamic of a lifetime?

I lock my phone and reach over to put it on the toilet seat. Beside it, the rose-shaped sex toy stares at me. I plucked it from the washing pile on my way out of the bedroom and brought it in here with me. I'm not sure why – because I didn't want Theo waking up and seeing it again (another decision I'll have to fret over the reason behind), or for some other purpose.

That other purpose is niggling at me.

Aside from wanting more intimacy with my husband for reasons related to the solidity of our relationship, I have to admit that I also have some very selfish motives. I like sex. I'm thirty-five years old, and I'm not ready to hang up my boots on the carnal pleasures of life just yet. I'd prefer to get my kicks from my spouse, but if that's not going to happen, should I just accept that my life is now devoid of physical pleasure?

'It's waterproof,' Caro told me last night. 'See if he'll join you in the shower.'

Theo won't join me in the shower. But maybe this thing can join me in the bath.

It's another hour until I need to start getting ready for work, and the bathwater is already getting cold.

Fuck it.

I lean out of the bath, dripping bubbly water on the floor, and grab the toy. If the mountain won't come to Mohammed . . .

*

I find myself walking to work feeling the strangest mix of emotions I have ever experienced.

The first is pure, unbridled elation, brought on possibly by sleep deprivation but more likely from the earth-shattering orgasm I gave myself in the bath a short while ago. Jesus Christ, I had forgotten how good it felt. Actually, I'm not sure it's *ever* felt that good before. I texted Caro just before I left the house: *Holy shit, the rose toy thing. How doesn't everyone know about this???*

My phone buzzes in my hand as I'm bouncing along the pavement. *They do. Welcome to the beginning of the rest of your life. How was the sex?*

I decline from responding.

The second emotion – and the strongest of the two – is deep, bubbling frustration. Access to this kind of pleasure is our god-given right; why have Theo and I decided to opt out? There's nothing wrong with going solo from time to time, but I want us to be making each other feel this way, to get back to the way we used to be. I've tried to bridge the gap myself, and for whatever reason, it hasn't worked.

Maybe it's time for more drastic measures.

I'm ten minutes early for work, so I step into the café next door and order myself a large iced caramel latte. I'm feeling impulsive, a bit mad – the opposite of my habitual state and a clear sign I haven't slept enough – and suddenly shot through with a weird sort of frustration, a powerful feeling of autonomy that's almost foreign to me. I made myself feel things I've never felt before at five o'clock this morning; I can fix my marriage. I can get my husband to come back to me. I am not hopeless, and we are too good to be given up on this easily. But maybe – just maybe – we need a little outside help.

And maybe it's that feeling, that crazy, impulsive, adrenaline surge of self-certainty, but as I'm standing in line, I find myself doing something I've known I was going to do since I walked into the bedroom last night to find Theo reading in bed.

I pull out my phone and retrieve Isa's DM from my deleted folder.

And then, with the smell of warm coffee filling the steamy air of the café around me on this chilly, ordinary February morning, I reply.

Hi Isa, could we meet this evening?

*

The bar at The Golden Oak Hotel is swarming with people, which is doing precisely nothing for my anxiety. There's some kind of work event wrapping up, and suited workers are filtering through from the function room towards the booze, weary and rumpled after a day of meetings.

I sidestep around people as I scan the seating area around the perimeter, feeling distinctly out of place. The cushioned armchairs are filling up quickly, and I keep my eyes peeled for any redheads with empty seats opposite them.

I spot her in the corner. She's sitting back, her bright red hair twisted into a messy topknot, a luminous drink in a short tumbler in her hand. She's halfheartedly nodding at the person sitting opposite her while scrolling on her phone, her eyes flicking up every so often to scan the bar. I manage to get within a foot of her before she realizes it's me, and I remember suddenly that although I can recognize her a mile away, she has no idea what I look like.

'Lottie?' she says, pocketing her phone and getting to her feet. 'Tilly Carter. *So* great to meet you.'

She's wearing a bright, floral shirt cut low to reveal her milky-white cleavage, and a pair of insane, zigzag-patterned flared trousers with sky-high purple heels. Her wrists are adorned with delicate, shimmering bracelets, which tinkle as she holds her hand out for me to shake. Under her shiny red fringe, her green eyes are rimmed with pink kohl.

I immediately feel horrifyingly boring.

'Hi,' I manage. I smooth my hands over my denim pinafore dress and stand a little taller in my white pumps. 'Lovely to meet you.'

'This is Isa.' She swoops an arm out to the woman sitting in the chair opposite hers. Just like Tilly seems to naturally embody her celebrity status, as if she was born with it, Isa appears to be right at home in her role as 'The Agent', almost like she's been plucked from the streets of 1980s New York City and dropped in a velvet recliner in an unknown British hotel. She's wearing an exquisitely tailored charcoal suit with shoulder pads, a pair of metal-framed glasses and a chunky gold necklace, which she somehow manages to pull off tastefully.

'Hi, Isa,' I say, reaching out my hand. She shakes it and smiles tightly at me.

'Nice to meet you, Lottie. We're very excited.'

A twist of disquiet makes itself known in my belly. What am I doing here? What the *actual* hell am I doing here? In a hotel bar, on a Wednesday afternoon, meeting the UK's biggest podcaster to discuss an anonymous text I sent in about my abysmal sex life, which I still haven't told my husband about? Panic seizes me.

I open my mouth to tell them I've changed my mind, but Tilly gestures to the empty seat beside her. 'Come, sit down. What do you want to drink?'

I hesitate. They've come all the way from London for this, worked around my schedule. The least I can do is hear them out. If I decide it's not for me, I can be a big girl and say I've changed my mind. Over Instagram DM when I'm back home later on.

'Whatever you're having would be lovely, thank you,' I say, taking a seat. On the low table in front of us, Isa's laptop is open next to a shining leather notebook filled with fast scribbles.

'Two more Anna Bananas, please,' Tilly is saying to the waiter who has appeared by our table. He nods and scurries off.

'So!' Isa says, leaning forward in her seat, her pen poised. 'I'll cut straight to it and start off by saying thank you, Lottie. We're extremely glad you're here.'

'Oh,' I say, blushing. 'It's no problem. I only work round the corner, and—'

'Not for meeting us,' Tilly says, reaching out and placing her warm hand on mine. The touch is the kind of casual intimacy Caro does so well, but which I'm terrible at. 'For your confession. It was so raw and brave, and I'm so grateful that you trusted us with it.'

Before I can reply, Isa leans further towards me keenly. 'It's sent the podcast into the stratosphere.'

'Also true,' Tilly says. '*Millennials give no fucks. Not even to their spouses.* Did you see that one?'

'Erm, no . . . I—'

'*Wired,*' Isa says, nodding. 'That organic exposure was exceptional.'

'Anna Banana?' The waiter appears brandishing two full versions of Tilly's cocktail.

'That'll be for us,' Tilly says brightly, gesturing to me. 'And Isa will take another Screaming Orgasm?'

Isa nods once. 'Please.' She swivels towards me once the waiter has disappeared. 'Speaking of . . . it must be a while since your husband's given you one of those.'

I laugh nervously, feeling my face flame. Talking about Theo behind his back feels even worse than I thought it would. 'Well, it's both of our faults, really.'

Tilly nods, her dangling earrings swinging. She throws a quick warning look at Isa. 'Obviously this isn't something we're here to joke about. It's something we're here to fix. It must be incredibly painful for you, Lottie. You love him, but you're not being physically intimate any more.' She sits back in her chair. 'I had a client, back when I was coaching, who was exactly like you. Now she and her husband are at it three times a day.'

Blimey. 'I'm not sure I'd need—'

'And you're absolutely fucking gorgeous,' she continues, squeezing my arm. 'You deserve a bloody good sex life.'

'Oh! Well, I—'

'And your husband knows about all this, I presume?' Isa interrupts.

I feel my mouth open, feel the word 'no' on the tip of my tongue. 'Erm . . .'

Tilly's eyebrows shoot up. 'You haven't told him?'

I should tell the truth, I know that. But this is Tilly Carter, and I'm so star-struck I can barely breathe. I want her to like me. I want her to think I'm a good person. *I* want to believe I'm a good person. So I say the thing I know I should say, the thing I know *should* be true. 'Yes, of course, he knows about it all.'

'Oh, *good*,' Tilly says, beaming. 'I know you wanted general anonymity, but the tasks work so much better when both partners are committed.'

I mentally bury the lie in the rapidly growing pile of things I have to feel guilty about and sit up straight. 'The tasks . . .?'

'Your situation is extremely common,' Isa says before Tilly can answer, flicking through her notebook. 'We've had hundreds of people write in to say they're at their wits' end.'

I brighten. I knew people related to my story, but hearing it out loud is reassuring. 'Do you think it's always been like this? Maybe people just didn't feel comfortable talking about it until now?'

'Probably,' Tilly nods. 'But also, social media. For a million reasons; it's to blame for pretty much everything awful in the world.'

Isa sighs. 'You've got social media to thank for those Missoni trousers, Tilly.'

'Unfortunately true,' Tilly admits, but I can feel a frisson of irritation rolling off her in Isa's direction. She straightens and turns in her seat to face me. 'So! Let's get to it. We have a proposal for you, Lottie.'

I've taken a sip of my drink, and I swallow quickly, nodding. It's sweet and banana-y and delicious.

'We'd like you to co-host a new series on the podcast with us: Long-Term Lust. Anonymous, of course,' she adds, catching the terror that must be written all over my face. 'Each week, we'll give you some tasks to do, aimed at reigniting the spark in your marriage. You report back to us and I'll dissect it on-air for our listeners.'

I'm already shaking my head. I shouldn't have come here. What the hell have I got myself into? 'I can't. I'm so sorry. I've completely wasted your time.' I get to my feet, dumping my almost-full glass clumsily on the table. I'm not sure what I expected when I came here; surely there was a part of me that knew it'd be something like this. But hearing it out loud . . . 'This is . . . it's totally out of my comfort zone. I'm so sorry,' I repeat. 'It was lovely to meet you, but—'

Isa thrusts a piece of paper at me, her neutral manicured nails glimmering under the low lights. 'Read the terms first?'

I shake my head again, moving to take a step around the coffee table, but my eyes land on the document in Isa's hand as I go. And the first thing I see, almost as though fate is drawing me to it, is the figure printed about a third of the way down the page.

I hesitate. And then I take the piece of paper from her outstretched hand.

> *. . . and in return for weekly submissions, the contractor will receive a fee each Friday, no later than 17.00 GMT, of . . .*

The number is eye-watering. It's not quit-your-job money, but it's life-changing. Theo and I could finally take that holiday; we could reconnect. We aren't drowning financially, but the mortgage has slowly creeped up to more than we're quite comfortable with, and there isn't much room for luxuries. Neither of us has any kind of pay bump on the horizon, and we've been earning the same for years now, while our expenses seem to keep growing. This would take some of the pressure off.

Not that I'd ever be able to tell him where the money came from.

There's another little flutter of hope in my stomach, though. It's small, but it's there.

What if this actually works?

It's not beyond the wildest realms of possibility. From extensive googling last night, I now know that Tilly is a certified sex coach with years of experience; there are couples who would kill for her input. And to be *paid* for it . . . I'm clearly not getting very far by myself – why not allow someone to guide me, to advise me? It'll be anonymous, written in, so I won't have to speak. And besides, what Caro said was true: if she couldn't even recognize it was me from my confession, how would anyone else? Nobody I know has approached me, asking whether I'm the sexless girl from *The Cliterati*. If people who listen to it haven't twigged, how would Theo? Maybe I've got away with it.

Maybe this is the opportunity of a lifetime.

I sit back down in my chair, holding the document on my lap as I read. Isa and Tilly are watching me, the hum of the bar fading into white noise. Blindly, I reach forward, pick up my Anna Banana and take a long sip.

After a moment, I look up.

'OK,' I say. 'What do I need to do?'

Chapter Eight

Oh, god. I've agreed to help Tilly write the podcast, which will reference me anonymously as 'the Horny Wife'. I'm not the biggest fan of it – it feels like the title of a porn film – but Tilly assures me it'll get clicks and be prioritized on the algorithms. Isa floated the idea of calling me 'the female incel', which I was even less keen on, and my suggestion to call me 'the anonymous sex-starved wife' was vetoed on the premise that it'd inevitably be shortened to 'ASS wife'.

So I'm officially the Horny Wife. And frankly, right now, I feel the moniker is quite fitting. I'm lying in bed next to Theo, feeling equal parts irritated and insecure, with a big fat dash of guilt-ridden panic slopped on top.

We're both scrolling through our phones, Theo on TikTok watching engineering videos, me on Instagram attempting to numb myself with haul content. But tonight, it's not quite working. I keep looking beyond my phone screen, to Betty and Boodle snoozing at the end of the duvet, and thinking – what the hell am I doing?

Beside me, Theo gives an unselfconscious, throaty cough. It's the kind of sound my dad would make, sat in the armchair watching the football. I glance at Theo. The curly hair at his temples is salt and pepper, the first signs of grey taking hold. Every age suits him; he was gorgeous in his twenties and he's gorgeous now, at thirty-five, with the first fine lines settling near his happy eyes.

But Jesus Christ, the noise he just made. I've never heard him make a noise like that before in my life. I've never heard anybody under the age of seventy make a noise like that.

Is this what we're descending into? Silent bedtime routines with hacking single-beat coughs and probably a few trumpeting farts thrown into the mix? Is romance officially, once and for all, dead?

For the fifth time today, I swing towards the 'Good, I'm taking things into my own hands' end of the what-have-I-done spectrum. I'm happy here, on my Lottie-the-family-woman podium. We might not have the traditional family unit, but we've both always been clear about our shared decision not to have children. It's not something I've ever felt drawn to, preferring dogs over kids, and Theo has always maintained that he fills his quota of child-related activities at work, with lots left over. And really, what am I doing now, if not trying to fix our marriage? Our family? I'm trying to bring us together again, even if Theo seems to be quite happy with how things are. But it can't be that he hasn't noticed; we used to have a very active, very healthy sex life. It's like having a giant, prizewinning fern in the middle of your living room and not realizing it's died. When I'm feeling my most frustrated, my most desperate for change, I find myself thinking, *At least one of us is doing something about it.*

But the other side of the spectrum – and the pendulum swings there quite often – is sheer, throat-gripping panic. I thought I was in deep before, when my confession sent the podcast to the top of the charts; how have I somehow managed to procure myself a spade and dig myself six feet deeper? Something's sent me mad, surely. This is not how I usually behave.

And right at the end of that spectrum, in the crimson zone, a place where I occasionally let the pendulum teeter before yanking it back, is the thought of Theo finding out what I'm doing before I've had a chance to fix us and explain everything. The thought of him leaving me.

'We should book that holiday,' I find myself saying into the silence. A guilty conscience, perhaps?

'Hm?' Theo keeps his eyes glued to his phone, only tearing his gaze towards me when his current video has ended.

'The holiday we were talking about. We should book it.'

He smiles wistfully. 'I wish. It's just not in the budget, Lotts. The dog walker has already put her rates up.'

I nod. He goes back to his phone. I'm unsure why I've even brought this up. What can I say? 'Don't worry, I'm getting a hefty weekly sum to write about our endless vacuum of a sex life. We can hire two dog walkers! Load up Booking.com, get us to the Maldives!'

'You're right,' I say after a beat. 'Never mind.'

'Let's talk about it again at the end of the year,' he adds, glancing at me briefly. 'See where we're at.' He leans over and gives me a kiss on the forehead, like I'm his adorable prized niece rather than his wife – am I reading too much into things? – and returns to his phone.

I swipe off Instagram and go to the Notes app on my phone, where I've started a new list. The title of the new *Cliterati* series is Long-Term Lust, and the premise is that it's an exploration of dwindling intimacy in twenty-first century relationships, particularly within the 25–45 age bracket. Almost everyone I know falls into this demographic, so this week I've been tasked with finding out exactly how many of the people in my life are *really* getting it on. Anonymously, of course. I could tell people what I'm doing, see if they'll share their stories with me in a transparent way, but then I'd have to tell them everything. Then I'd have to admit that my own sex life is dreadful, that the façade of my perfect marriage is a lie, and that I'm going behind my husband's back to tell the world about it.

But surreptitiously recording my friends and passing on their secrets feels horrifyingly disloyal.

So I've decided to find a middle ground. I'm going to ask general questions, do some casual probing, and then I'll report on the themes I've found during my research. Once this part's over, we'll start phase two: The Experiment.

And then I'll tell Theo everything. Once we've reconnected, and the spark is back, I'll tell him about my anonymous confession, that nobody knows about but us, and we'll shag our way happily into the sunset.

I feel a bit sick.

I push thoughts of my future conversation with Theo from my mind as I tap out some ideas on my phone, tilting my screen away from Theo. I'll take it one step at a time, focus on this week for now.

And I already know exactly where I'm going to start.

*

'OK, so it's . . . pink?'

'It's not *pink*, Mum. It's *champagne*.'

'I see.'

'Don't purse your lips like that. You know I hate it when you do that. Are you making it your mission to ruin today? I knew I shouldn't have invited you.'

I am perched on the edge of a velvet clam-shaped sofa in a very upmarket wedding-dress boutique. Jade is standing on a podium in a pink (and it *is* pink) silk dress, an assistant standing close beside her, pinning pieces of fabric at her waist. Beside me are a few of the other girls from the hen party, some of whom I slut-dropped to 'Low' with just a week ago, but who now feel like total strangers again.

Jade and I met when she joined my secondary school's sixth form, and we were somewhat close throughout our A levels. Somehow, we've managed to stay vaguely tethered to each other for the seventeen years since we left school, while most of our other classmates drifted away. We've kept our friendship bobbing along but never quite fizzing during that time, with annual lunch catch-ups and the occasional flurry of WhatsApp messages. We don't have a tonne in common outside of having been on the periphery of each other's lives for almost as long as either of us can remember, and when she asked me to be her bridesmaid, I was surprised. It seems, though, that I am not unique in my position in Jade's life and am instead part of a pattern: the hen do saw me and most of the other bridesmaids meeting for the first time, each of us colliding after years of bobbing around in Jade's orbit. The newly formed WhatsApp group is doing a very good job of highlighting our differences.

Now, we are each clutching half a glass of warm champagne and staring at Jade's mum, who is sitting in the mother-of-the-bride armchair with a sour look on her face.

'You're doing a fine job of ruining the day by yourself, Jade. As per usual.'

'For fuck's *sake*,' Jade whimpers, before pulling up her skirt and stumbling clumsily off the podium. She totters back into the changing room and swishes the curtain angrily closed behind her.

There's a beat of silence.

'Should I . . .' The maid of honour peers at us, her eyes wide. We nod. Far be it from us to usurp the leading lady in her duties.

She hurries off. Jade's mum stands up and turns to the assistant, who is standing with a hand full of safety pins looking like this isn't her first rodeo. They begin a hushed and intense conversation that I can't hear.

'Ugh.' Holly – or was it Harriet? – puts her phone in her lap and closes her eyes for a few seconds. She breathes in through her nose, out through her mouth, and then snaps them open again. 'I'm going to kill him.'

'James again?' asks a girl whose name I can't even take a stab at, but who I know is one of Holly's friends. She leans forward with the air of a fortunate person who knows someone else in the group very well and wants everybody to know it. 'What's he done now?'

'He's kicking off about the feet pics again,' she says, sighing.

I remember Holly's feet pics; she showed me her entire page during the hen party. Each to their own, but I'm not sure Theo would be best pleased if my feet pics also contained my naked breasts, so I suppose I can see where James is coming from.

'Holly,' the other girl says wearily – so it *is* Holly – 'he's a misogynist.'

'Lottie!' Jade's voice barks out from the other side of the room, and I look up to see her tear-stained face peeking out from behind the changing-room curtain. 'What's the colour of the bridesmaids' dresses?'

I blink. I'm unsure why I should know this. 'Erm, lilac?' I suggest.

'No, the *colour*,' Jade says impatiently, her voice thick. 'What's the exact name of the *colour*?'

I flick my eyes to the maid of honour, who is standing just outside the curtain, her eyes wide. Shouldn't she know this? I pull my phone out quickly and scroll through our group chat until I find Jade's message from a few weeks ago. 'Dusty lilac petal,' I call over quickly.

Jade yanks the curtain closed again, and I feel inexplicably like I've done something wrong. It's the stress, I tell myself. Planning a wedding is hard, and just because I went with the flow when I had my own doesn't mean everyone can do the same.

'I wouldn't mind,' Holly continues now, dragging the conversation back to her OnlyFans and the disapproving James, 'but he isn't even interested in my feet.'

I'm unsure how this is relevant, but suddenly, I spot my opportunity and clumsily fumble my way inside.

'Do you have a good relationship otherwise?' I ask.

Holly looks at me as though it's the first time she's ever clapped eyes on me. 'I mean . . . I guess.'

'How's your sex life?' It's out of my mouth before I can stop it, and instantly a hush falls over the group.

Holly laughs without smiling, her eyes flitting from person to person. 'Sorry, remind me of your name?'

'Lottie,' I say, mildly offended. I'm pretty sure I had Holly on my shoulders at one point during Jade's hen. But no time to dwell on that; my face is on fire. 'Sorry, that was so forward of me!' Just a bit. I want to die. I'm channelling my inner Caro, my inner Tilly: bold, brash, to the point. Essentially the polar opposite of my own personality. But I've got to get this conversation going, got to push through. I don't know these women, don't have any intention of seeing any of them again after Jade's wedding. *Come on, Lottie.*

'I'm just saying,' I force myself to continue, 'sex is the root of everything in a relationship, right? The foundation.'

Jessica, a quiet girl who I don't remember ever uttering a word in my presence, says, 'I think it's communication.'

'Well, yes,' I agree, nodding. Ironic, coming from her. 'But without the sex, what are you? Roommates who share a bed?'

'Oh!' Holly says, snapping her fingers. 'Sorry, I've just realized you're talking about the podcast.'

At the word 'podcast', my stomach drops. But then I remember the discussion we had about *The Cliterati* on the group chat, and I mentally slap myself for not using it as a segue sooner. 'Yes!' I cry, leaning forward. 'Gosh, sorry, did you think I was just prying into your sex life willy-nilly? I'm mortified!'

'Me and Ralph have a great sex life,' Holly's friend who wants everyone to know she's Holly's friend says smugly before Holly can respond.

'You've been together three weeks, Melissa,' Holly replies deadpan. Melissa blushes.

'Jade and Matt basically hump non-stop,' the final girl in our group says. Her name, I'm pretty sure, is Jenny, and she looks livid. I won't disagree with her; Jade can regale a group all evening about her and her fiancé's sexual exploits. There's a moment of quiet, and I rack my brains. If my confession sparked the conversation it did, at least one of these women must be lying.

'I basically have to force James to do me,' Holly says quietly, picking at her nails.

My heart lifts. We're getting into it now.

'Holly!' Melissa, of the one-sided best friendship, gasps. 'You never told me that.'

'Has something changed?' I ask. Maybe there's a common denominator we share; something in Holly's life that mirrors mine. We both switched to Nivea deodorant at the same time? Both our husbands caught us watching *Bargain Hunt* at three o'clock on a Tuesday afternoon? The feet pics are a more likely story, but I live in hope.

She shrugs. 'No. Not that I can think of. He just . . . doesn't seem into it.'

'Are you still into it?'

'As much as I ever was, I guess.'

I clutch the stem of my champagne flute as a thought forms. 'I wonder if it's a sort of . . . multi-faceted thing,' I muse. 'Men have always wanted more sex than us – or so we've been told. And now we're allowed to own our sexuality, to say what we want and when we want it, they can't keep up. Or they're intimidated by it. Or maybe it's social media? The perfect lives, perfect bodies. Never mind the time it sucks up, which could be used for having sex. Maybe it's not just one thing, and maybe it's just human nature. Perhaps attraction and lust and libido come in waves, and all of life follows this sort of rise and fall, like seasons. Maybe it's just a dry season.'

I realize when I stop talking that everyone is staring at me. Holly's eyebrows are furrowed together.

'I think he just gets his back up about the feet pics, to be honest,' she says.

And thankfully, Jade chooses that moment to stomp out of the changing room wearing another decidedly pink dress, her mother and maid of honour in tow, mascara streaming down her face.

*

'OK, so . . . how did it go?'

I escaped wedding-dress shopping earlier than expected, thanks to Jade declaring, in the middle of the high street, that the whole day was 'a complete write-off' and that her mother wasn't invited to the wedding. I called Caro after saying goodbye to the girls, most of whom I am convinced now think I am either unhinged, intrusive or both, and told her I needed to give her an update. She had a photoshoot round the corner, so suggested we meet for a drink. We're sitting in our small town's version of a romantic bar, at a window table, a tealight flickering between us.

'Wait,' I say, stalling for time. Now that I'm here, I can't seem to get the words out of my mouth. What, precisely, am I doing? 'Tell me how the police investigation went first.'

She frowns. 'Police investigation?'

'Your camera? The kink dungeon thief?'

'Oh! I forgot about that. Erm . . . I don't know, actually. I should give them a call.'

It doesn't surprise me that she's forgotten; things happen to Caro and she sails over them without issue. She is not a past-dweller. 'How are you working without your camera?'

'Oh, I have like three others. Remember that guy, Guglielmo, from the apps?'

'The Mafia guy?'

'Not Mafia, but looks like it. Anyway, he had like a hundred cameras lying around a few months ago and I took a few off his hands on the cheap. God bless Hinge.'

'Were they stolen?' I ask, aghast.

She shrugs and mimes zipping her lips together. 'Ask no questions, Lottie.'

'And Peter?' I ask hopefully.

Her face closes off, her eyes flicking away from mine. 'I've been on a few dates.'

'With . . . Peter?'

'No, not with Peter,' she says, almost snapping at me. She takes a breath. 'Sorry. Things are done with Peter, I told you. I'm back out there, trawling the streets. Lock up your sons.'

I want to ask how she's feeling about it, but I know the response I'll get. *I'm amazing, Lotts. I'm having a great time. Fuck Peter.*

'Anyway, stop stalling,' she says, her face brightening again. 'How was the sexy night in?'

The temptation to stall some more is strong. But she knows me too well, and she's already frowning.

'Shit, Lotts. What happened?'

'Nothing. That's the problem. I wore the lingerie, cooked the dinner. He went to bed and read about aeroplanes.'

'Oh, god, not the bloody aeroplanes.'

'I like that he likes aeroplanes!'

'You would not last three seconds on the apps. They'd eat you alive.'

'I just want him to like aeroplanes *and* shagging me. You know?'

'Jesus Christ. What is wrong with that boy?' She shakes her head, looking out of the window. When she turns back to me, her face is bright. 'Well, at least the whole podcast thing has blown over. They've announced some new series, I hear. Your soul-baring is officially in the past.'

I was planning on easing us into this. I wanted to present it casually, not make it a huge deal. But my face has crumpled against my will.

'What?' She leans across the table. 'Oh, god, Lottie, what?'

I shake my head and lean back in my chair, avoiding her eye as I take a sip of my wine.

'Lottie.'

I blow air into my cheeks and clunk my glass down. 'I might be involved in that series.'

Caro raises her eyebrows. 'Involved how?'

'I might have met Tilly Carter and her agent. And I might have agreed to help them host it.'

For a moment, Caro doesn't speak. She just looks at me, her face blank. When she eventually opens her mouth, her tone is that of someone who has just been told the moon is made of cheese. 'Fuck. Off.'

I grimace.

'Are you for real? Are you actually for real? What do you *mean*?'

'Can I get you anything, ladies?' A waiter has appeared at our table.

'Two more of these, please,' Caro says, gesturing to our almost-empty glasses. 'We're going to need them.'

Once he's clipped away, I fill her in on the whole thing, the story leaving my chest like a physical weight as I share it. She stares at me, her mouth open. By the time I'm done, we have two fresh drinks in front of us and the bar has filled up, chatter swarming around us. I fall silent, biting my lip as I wait for her judgement.

Caro sits back in her chair and begins slow clapping. 'Fina-fucking-lly,' she says.

'What?'

'I've been waiting twenty-five years for you to do something absolutely mental, and my prayers have finally been answered.'

'Oh my god, Caro! This isn't a soap opera, it's my life!'

'Precisely! And it's about to finally get interesting.'

I reach across the table and slap her on the arm. That kind of comment from anyone else would offend me, but from her, it's the playful reinstating of our roles. I'm the sensible one, who wishes Caro would be a bit more careful; Caro's the mad one, who wishes I'd make more questionable decisions every once in a while. We're both perfectly happy with who we are, so this kind of banter doesn't cut deep.

'I need to tell Theo.'

'You don't.'

'I do! I can't lie.'

'You're not *lying*. You're doing, like, a surprise gift. Right? Ta-da! I got you a remedy for our barren wasteland of a sex life! You're welcome, darling!'

'Caro, I have to tell him,' I say firmly. 'If he finds out from someone else . . .'

'He won't.'

'How do you know?'

'He just won't.' She shrugs. 'Believe.'

I bite down a frustrated retort. Caro goes through life believing everything's going to work out for the best. It doesn't seem to matter that many times it hasn't; her faith is unshakeable. 'OK,' I say slowly. 'But let's imagine he did.'

'He's obsessed with you. He's the nicest, kindest, warmest human being on the planet and he loves you to death. He'd try to understand why you did what you did and he'd forgive you.'

And now I want to kiss her. She is incredible at making everything better. 'You think so?' I ask hopefully.

'I know so. Now, let's get down to it. Do you want to interview me? Ask me about my favourite vibrator?' Her eyes widen. 'Actually, what if *Tilly* interviews me? I could tell her some stories.'

'I mean, we're looking at people who *aren't* having sex, really. I'm not sure you're the best candidate.'

'God, Lottie, you can't be in cahoots with the host of my favourite podcast and *not* introduce me. I can be the opposing view. Can you at least interview me yourself so I can get on the show?' She beams.

I nod, slowly. 'Actually, that's a good idea. Maybe we can figure out what's different between you and people who aren't having as much sex.'

'I shop around, for a start.'

'God, Caro, I can't renounce monogamy.'

'But what if that's the answer? What if we're just not meant to have sex with one person for the rest of our lives?'

I shake my head. The repercussions for me if polygamy is the answer to my problems are too horrifying to imagine.

'Think about it,' she carries on, tucking her shiny black hair behind her ear and leaning forward. 'Of all the people that wrote in to *The Cliterati* after your confession, how many were single?'

'I didn't listen—'

'None,' she says. 'All of them were married, or in long-term relationships.'

'That's because that was what we were *talking* about,' I say forcefully. 'Relationships that have lost their spark, sex-wise. We weren't talking about single people struggling to find hook-ups.'

Caro shrugs – her usual response when she knows I might have a point but doesn't want to admit it. 'I think it's worth considering,' she says, taking a sip of her wine.

We finish up and step out onto the blustery street, saying goodbye as the first splats of rain start hitting the pavement. I walk the ten minutes home slowly; the wine has made me mellow and reflective, and I'm not in a rush to get back and see Theo. I pull the hood of my raincoat tighter around my head and listen to the rhythmic patter of the raindrops on the fabric.

Despite my earlier protestations, I've got a worried feeling in my stomach.

What if Caro's right? What if we're not meant to have sex with the same person for the rest of our lives? What if the flame can't be sustained for that long, no matter how compatible you are?

Because if that's true, the stakes just got higher. If monogamy doesn't always work, this isn't just a question of me getting my sex life back on track. It's a question of making sure my husband doesn't go looking elsewhere.

Chapter Nine

In the office kitchen the next morning, I sit on the counter and watch as Harry wrangles ineffectively with the new coffee machine – a purchase made by Petra, despite her claims that the budget was tight.

'We can't afford some rich teas for Chatty Tuesdays, but we can afford a Nespresso Nimbus two-thousand or whatever that thing is,' I complain.

'I don't think there are any beans in it,' Harry says, angling his head to look around the back. 'Does that look like where the beans are supposed to go?'

I sigh, tapping my heels against the cupboard doors as I sip a can of iced caramel latte. 'Is Petra married?'

Harry pushes a button, and the machine lets out an ominous screech. 'Is she what?'

'Married.'

'Oops,' he says, wagging his finger at me. 'Inappropriate personal question.'

I laugh. Last week, we had a 'Respect in the Workplace' seminar, whose overall message seemed to be 'treat your colleagues like personality-less cyborgs or *else*'. Harry and I have been joking about it ever since. On Friday, he asked if I wanted a plain M&M or a peanut one, and I threatened to report him to HR.

'But is she?' I push.

He gives up with the machine and flicks the kettle on. 'Don't think so. I think her and Robin have just been together forever.'

'Do you reckon they still have sex?'

Harry looks at me, half frowning, half smiling. 'You OK?'

'I can't imagine Petra losing herself in the throes of passion. Do you think she's written a Standard Operating Procedure for date night?'

Now, Harry laughs. 'You're weird recently.'

'I know,' I sigh. 'What about you? How are things with Jas?'

'Don't you start asking about my sex life. I really will report you to HR.'

'I won't!' I say, making myself look shocked. That's exactly what I was going to try and do. In a roundabout way, of course.

'Everything's good,' he says. 'We should have you guys round for dinner soon. I've seen this recipe for a roasted aubergine with a courgette *inside* it. Like a bird in a bird, but vegetables. And then I was thinking: what about putting asparagus inside the *courgette*? Then it's a bird in a bird in a bird . . .'

I've lost him. Once Harry gets going on something he's excited about, there's no bringing him back. I nod and smile as I swing myself off the counter and head towards the kitchen door. When he pauses for breath – having described the way he wants to cook the accompanying rice (in coconut milk and chicken stock, with some sautéed garlic and onions) – I leap in. 'That sounds so good – let's get a date in the diary. I'll check my calendar now when I get back to my computer.'

On my way back to my desk, I glance into Petra's office. She's typing away at her computer as usual, her face unreadable. God help me if Petra is having sex and I'm not. I remember her partner from the Christmas do: a serious-looking, bespectacled Dutch man with an unexpectedly loud and infectious laugh.

'Lottie.' I hear my name being called as I slide into my seat, and I swivel round. Petra is poking her head out of her office door, and I admonish myself for the blood that rushes to my face. It's not like she heard me talking to Harry – what is wrong with me? 'Can I see you for a second?'

Ominous. I get to my feet and walk across the room, the eyes of my colleagues following me. Harry emerges from the kitchen and raises his eyebrows in my direction. I shrug in response, unease curdling in my belly.

I step inside Petra's office and she closes the door behind me – only a partially useful move, as the walls are made entirely of glass, and I know with certainty that if I turn around, everybody will be watching.

'Take a seat,' she says, gesturing to the chair in front of her desk. I sit down.

'I got rid of Chatty Tuesdays,' she says, sliding into her

own seat and immediately starting to pound at her keyboard with her long fingers. 'And I know that was important to you.'

Is she reading this off her screen? The words she's saying are correct, but there's no emotion to them. I feel like I'm at the GP. But . . . is she going to bring Chatty Tuesdays back? A little flicker of hope alights in my chest.

'Yes,' I say, leaning forward. 'I really think if we can give it another push—'

'So I've decided to put you front and centre of our new initiative,' she continues, cutting me off. 'We're trying to attract the more affluent members of the community to the gallery, and at the same time, bring in less affluent people to buy the things they can afford from the shop. Tea towels and knick-knacks and the like.'

I pause. 'So you'd like me to . . .'

'I want you in charge of the second part. Engaging with the customers who are inspired by the art but can't afford it. The people who might buy a tote bag with the latest Emma Raynor print on it, for example. Do you think you can handle that?'

I'm not sure what to say. I swallow. 'Isn't that marketing?'

For the first time since I walked in, she looks up from her computer. 'It's engaging with the community. And you are a community engagement officer.'

'I mean . . . it sounds really great.' It doesn't. 'But also, I really enjoyed what I was doing before. Bringing people into the centre to create art and talk about it. Creating a community within the centre itself.'

'This is a business, Lottie,' Petra says flatly. 'And businesses by definition need money. Giving people free biscuits and letting them show off their pencil drawings *costs* us money.'

Does she think I don't know that? We're partially funded by the council – a big part of us achieving that funding each year is what we offer the community. Not just people who can afford to shop here and buy our artwork and postcards – everybody.

'I just think, in terms of our funding—'

'We offer seven classes a week, all of which have extremely generous concession rates. The council doesn't need more than that.'

I want to scream. I remember what Harry said to me in the kitchen the other day, about standing up for myself. About taking the reins and challenging Petra on the changes she's making around here, the soul she's sucking out of the work that we do. I started working here over ten years ago, and it has been challenging and rewarding, and I had never even thought about leaving until Petra came along and tried to turn the whole place into a big corporate show pony. She's showing no signs of going anywhere, and she's making such big changes that I can't imagine it ever going back to how it was before.

'I'd also like you to get your thinking cap on,' she says. 'One of our goals for Q4 is to host a high-profile event at the gallery, get ourselves on the map. Londa seems to think we can get Katie Price in – apparently she's friends with her niece? If you know any contemporary, abstract artists . . .'

Not for the first time, I'm hit by the stark contrast between how my work used to be and how it is now. Harry and I used to go out on the street and offer people free portrait classes. We used to stay open late on Thursdays so that homeless people could come in for some warmth and enjoy the art with a free cup of tea. We used to have 9 a.m. meetings where we'd discuss the best and cheapest ways to get more people involved in the centre. It was the most creative job, figuring out how to access the least visible areas of our community.

Now that's all gone.

I open my mouth to say something. To tell Petra that I won't be going along with her thinly disguised marketing campaign. To finally, once and for all, let her know what I think – that our community matters more than the size of our profit margins.

But instead, I find myself saying, 'That's fine. Where would you like me to start?'

*

Despite the fact that I walked home in a rage, recording a thirteen-minute ranting voice note for Harry about Petra's new initiative, the new direction at work actually proves to be quite helpful. I tell Theo I've got a new project that requires some overtime and close myself in the study to write up my first bit of work for the podcast.

I open a Word document and tap out everything I've discovered or thought this week, from social media and selling sex online to monogamy and riding the waves of dry spells. I know Tilly will put her qualified slant on it, only reporting the hypotheses that have some research to back them up, so I spew every thought I have onto the page. At the end, I write a personal paragraph at her request – something she can use to weave in the individual element, the 'case study' as she calls it.

I love my husband more than I can put into words; he is kind, funny, and smart, and he's my best friend. But recently, it's felt like we are just that: best friends. Where we once used to spoon in bed, now we read or scroll on our phones. We used to have sex on top of the washing machine; now we discuss which spin cycle is appropriate for his gym wear more than we touch each other. It feels like we've morphed into a caricature of a middle-aged sexless couple overnight, and we're only thirty-five. I'm taking part in The Cliterati's Long-Term Lust *experiment to try and bring some spark back into my marriage, to reconnect with my husband, and to fix what has gone wrong. I also hope that my story will have a happy ending, and that it will give some hope to other women in similar situations.*

I lift my fingers off the keys and sit back in my chair. I read through what I've written, doubting myself. Am I identifiable from this? Should I change my age, the references to Theo's gym clothes? No, I decide. If I'm going to do this, I want to be honest, and besides, these descriptions could fit thousands of couples. I have plausible deniability. While Tilly is still under the impression that Theo is totally on board with my little experiment, she has agreed not to share where I'm from to protect my identity, so there'll be no geographical narrowing-down of who I might be.

Besides, Theo doesn't listen to the podcast, and neither do his friends. And would he even pay any attention if someone was talking about it in his presence?

The sound of the doorbell ringing startles me, and I quickly paste my notes into a blank email and delete the document. I don't hear Theo's footsteps going down the stairs, so I come out onto the landing. The dogs are going ballistic down in the hallway, but the shower is running, so Theo mustn't have heard. I hurry down the stairs and swing the door open.

'All right, Lottie?' Dev is standing on the doorstep. I'd completely forgotten he was coming over.

'Hey!' I say, stepping forward to give him a hug. He's huge, with biceps the size of my head, and as usual, I struggle to get my arms around his barrel of a chest. 'Come in, come in. Theo's just in the shower.'

He slips his shoes off and follows me into the kitchen–living room, where he promptly collapses on the sofa. I've known Dev as long as I've known Theo; they met at football club the first week of uni and have been inseparable ever since. Like Caro and me, they're not the most obvious coupling: where Theo is a bit rumpled and cerebral, Dev is a certified gym bro, and at first glance, you'd never guess he and Theo share an obsessive love of aeroplanes. He's tall, bald, and straight-faced, but also one of the kindest people I've ever met. Since Theo and I got together, we've done frequent 'double dates' with a twist: me and Caro with Theo and Dev – our two single best friends get on like a house on fire, and our evenings together are some of my favourite memories.

'Drink?' I ask, opening the fridge and pulling out a six-pack of beers I got in for Theo to have over the weekend.

'Go on then,' he says. 'Cheers.'

I crack one open and pour it into a glass. 'How are things?'

'Oh, you know, SSDD.'

I smile. This is one of Dev's famous catchphrases: same

shit, different day. He works in financial sales and, while he's brilliant at it, he absolutely hates it. 'That good, eh?'

'What about you?' he asks, taking a swig of his beer.

'Fine, yeah,' I say, nodding. I have to be careful here; Dev is perceptive, and he'll know if something's up. He's also Theo's best friend, and god only knows what Theo's told him. Does Dev know we don't have sex? Another thought hits me: does Dev know *why* we don't have sex? Has Theo confided in him?

The shower falls silent upstairs, the boiler in the kitchen cupboard clunking off. Dev flicks his eyes towards the door and the stairs beyond it, and then back to me. 'You sure?'

My heart picks up pace. 'Of course.' I laugh but it sounds forced. 'Why wouldn't I be?'

He doesn't speak for a moment; he just looks at me, his eyes narrowed, his head slightly cocked. And then he opens his mouth to say something, but the noise of Theo's footsteps thundering down the stairs has him pausing.

'Hey, mate! Sorry, got in a bit later than expected. You've not been here long, have you?' Theo enters the room in a waft of peppery shower gel, his curly hair wet, dampening the collar of his clean white T-shirt. He grabs a beer from the counter, offers me one and, when I decline, joins Dev on the sofa.

'Forty minutes 'til kick-off,' Dev observes. 'Shall we get food ordered?'

'Good shout. Let me get the menus.'

I chat with Dev about the latest date he's been on – a girl from the gym who he calls 'lovely but intense' – while Theo fetches the takeaway menus we keep in the study.

'Lottie,' Theo says when he returns. 'Computer's pinging up there.'

My heart just about falls out of my arse. How could I be so stupid? I left the computer on while I went to answer the door to Dev, and now I've just sat here as Theo's gone into the study. I rack my brains, trying to remember how I left the screen. Did I minimize the email I was about to send to Tilly? I remember deleting the Word document, but did I leave the email up?

I look at Theo, trying to read his expression. He's flicking through the menus, his face unreadable. He wouldn't make a scene in front of Dev; does he know? Has he read the whole thing? He wasn't gone long enough, surely.

'Probably Petra,' I say eventually, trying to make my tone as light as possible and hoping that only I can hear the tremor in my voice. 'Pestering me about this new project. I'll leave you guys to it. If you want to order from the chippy, give me a shout and I can nip out and pick it up for you while the game's on. Enjoy the footie.'

Dev thanks me, but Theo doesn't answer, instead keeping his eyes fixed on a Chinese restaurant menu he has open in his hands. My heart hammering, I slip out of the room and run up the stairs, the dogs scampering behind me.

In the study, the computer screen is obnoxiously bright against the glum March evening outside. I flick on the big light and slip into the seat. I let out a sigh of relief. The screen is clear, the blank desktop greeting me. When I go down to the taskbar, I can see my email minimised, where I'm sure I left it.

Or did I? Did I leave it open, and Theo's read it and minimised it himself?

Oh, god. I don't know. I quickly type Tilly and Isa's email addresses into the 'to' section and hit send, then lean back in my chair. He was only upstairs for a minute, tops, and surely, if he'd read something like that, he'd have asked Dev to leave so that we could talk. I'm sure he would.

Or maybe he's downstairs now, talking to Dev about it, asking him what he thinks he should do.

I shake my head; thoughts like this are getting me nowhere but deeper into paranoia. Theo said the computer was beeping; I'm sure he was just letting me know, not hinting that he might have seen something. He's not the type for mind games.

I click through to my inbox and the source of the beeping makes itself known: a new email from Isa, sent just five minutes ago.

Hi Lottie,

How are you? We can't wait to read your first submission when you're ready to send it through today; please don't forget to have it with us by six o'clock.

I'm sending your first 'experiment' through (attached), as I want to get ahead of the game and give you time to plan. Tilly has picked this place specially; it's rated incredibly highly, and she feels confident referring her own clients over, so has great hopes for its success for you (and for listeners who may subsequently want to visit). She also has a great sponsorship deal with them, and the exposure will be incredible. Visit on the house and all other costs covered by the podcast, of course; your job will just be to enjoy and report back.

Book whenever you want via the website and expense everything through to me. Needs to be this coming week, though.

Speak soon.

Isa

With great trepidation, I open the attached file.

COUPLE'S TANTRIC YOGA

Join us at our centre in the leafy countryside for a yoga experience the likes of which you've never had before. Using Indian teachings dating back to the early medieval period, you and your partner will reconnect on a deep, spiritual level, with the aim of bringing your souls closer together and, as a result, enhancing your physical intimacy.

Loose clothes recommended.

Oh, good god.

How the hell am I going to get Theo to agree to this? He's an open-minded person, but he's not very interested in self-discovery or hippy culture. And how do I even explain why I want to go? I've never suggested anything even remotely woo-woo before in my life; he'll think I've gone insane.

But there is one thing that I do have going for me – Theo, being the amazing guy that he is, will always say yes to trying something out with me. If he thinks it's important to me, he'll give it a go. He's been at every poorly attended launch of mine at the arts centre; he's shown up for boring colleagues' weddings as my plus-one; he drove me round twelve different shelters until we found Betty and Boodle because I wanted to give a home to brother and sister dogs, who I'd read were much less likely to get adopted than a single puppy. And all of it, whatever I ask of him, he does without complaint. He does it with a smile on his face, just happy to be along for the ride.

So actually, yes, I think he'll come with me.

But how do I explain my motivations?

I google the centre and click through to their website. It's almost mockingly New Age; the banner photo at the top shows a lush green field filled with an unlikely mix of people eating apples and burning incense. 'Join the revolution' the text laid over the top says. Is this a cult?

Amid my doubts, there's a flicker of fire in me. This is what we need: to step out of our comfort zones and try something new, to be proactive. I'm the first to admit that I'm not the most get-up-and-go person in the world; Caro often tells me I let life happen to me, and sometimes I think she's right. But beyond the nerves there's something else. Hope? Optimism? Because why am I doing this if not in some hope of fixing us? I wouldn't be going to these measures if I wasn't desperate for change.

I go through to the booking page and have a look at the free dates. There's an hour's slot on both Wednesday and Thursday evening this week, and when I check on Google Maps I can see that it's near enough for us both to make it after work.

I pick up my phone and tap through to our shared calendar. Theo is at the gym with Dev on Wednesday, but neither of us has anything in for Thursday. I book the session before I can think too much, and as I'm going through the payment and requesting a receipt to send to Isa, an idea hits me.

I know how I'm going to explain this to Theo.

Chapter Ten

'So, explain this to me again. It was a voucher? From Petra?'

It's Thursday evening and we're trundling along a narrow country lane in the dark, the car's headlights illuminating the rain-soaked tarmac ahead of us.

'Yes. She didn't buy it for me; she had it going begging. Her and her partner can't make it.'

'And she gave it to *you*?'

I wish he'd stop asking questions. I wish I'd said the voucher was from Harry or someone. Petra was a stupid idea; it's hardly a state secret that we don't get on. 'Yup. She sort of just . . . offered it to everybody. Nobody else could go.'

'And what is it again?'

I look out of the window in case he turns and sees the barefaced deception in my eyes. 'Some yoga thing? Very exclusive, apparently. People pay hundreds for a session.'

This part is true. The session cost me £250 to book, which Isa has already had refunded with the sponsorship deal.

'I've never done yoga,' Theo says, and when I glance at him, he looks quite excited.

Maybe this is going to be fine? Maybe we're actually going to enjoy this, and then tonight, we'll have incredible, life-affirming sex and our souls will ascend and unite above the bed or something. There's got to be a reason Tilly, a sex coach who has helped thousands of people, recommends this place. I push away the thought that maybe the sponsorship has something to do with it. Tilly has professional integrity; she'll have vetted it.

'It'll be great, I'm sure!' I say, reaching over and putting my hand over his on the gear stick. He interlaces his fingers with mine, throwing me a smile, and I feel a flutter of excitement. Already, this feels good.

After a few miles along unlit roads, the satnav tells us to turn left, and a huge pair of wrought-iron gates materializes in front of us, lit by old-fashioned streetlamps either side. There's a buzzer to the left, but Theo's driven too far over for me to reach, so I duck out of the car and stab it, holding my ear to the speaker as the rain patters down onto my head.

'Hello?' a woman's voice answers.

'Hi! We're here for the—' I stop myself just in time. 'The yoga session?'

'The tantric couple's yoga? Sponsorship deal with Tilly Carter?'

Jesus Christ. How could I have been so stupid? Tilly and Isa think Theo is fully aware that I'm taking part in the podcast; there'll have been no instructions for discretion. My heart jolts, and I glance over at Theo, praying that the rain is too loud and the speaker too tinny and the distance a bit too far for him to hear. He's tapping at something on his phone, so I quickly turn back and lean in to the microphone, lowering my voice.

'Yes, but could you not mention that to my husband, please? He thinks it's a voucher a friend gave me.'

'Pardon?'

God, this is awful. I glance over my shoulder again. Theo is looking at me, a questioning expression on his face. 'Just a second!' I say into the microphone, and then quickly dash back to the car. 'Just got to answer some questions apparently,' I say. 'Don't let rain get into the car.'

I slam the door shut and hurry back to the buzzer, then repeat my request.

'Oh,' the woman says. 'OK. A voucher. Sure. Opening the gates now.'

The gates begin swinging open and I jump back in the car. I grab one of the dogs' towels off the back seat and pat myself dry with it.

'What was all that about?' Theo asks as we begin crawling up a sloping driveway.

'Oh, she just had some questions. About the booking.'

'Couldn't she have asked us inside?'

'It's quite exclusive, I think.' I'm thinking on my feet. 'She was a bit weird about it being Petra's voucher but Petra not being here.'

Theo seems to accept this as an answer, and I take a couple of deep breaths. Is this wrong? Should I have confessed to Theo earlier, given him the chance to decide whether he wanted to take the class? But it's all anonymous. At the end of the day, it really is just us, reconnecting. Finding each other again. I need to relax; I'm here for a reason, and it's time to hand over to the professionals, for the sake of our marriage. I'm wound so tight, and this will all have been pointless if I don't calm down. I close my eyes as we continue up the driveway, breathing in slowly through my nose, out through my mouth. *Connection,* I think. *Intimacy. Love.*

'Lottie?'

I snap my eyes open. We're parked up outside a grand stately home, the imposing front door lit by glowing lights that give a murder-mystery vibe when paired with the gloomy weather.

'Sorry,' I say.

'You OK?' He peers at me.

'Yes! Yep, I'm excited! Come on, let's go.' I get out of the car before he can probe any further and hurry to the main door, hoping I can find whoever runs this place before Theo catches up with me and remind them one more time to keep the arrangement behind this class a secret.

I push the heavy wooden door open and Theo appears by my side. God damn his long legs.

The space we walk into is grand, luxurious, and completely empty. The floor is tiled and shiny, the walls covered in butter-yellow wallpaper, and there's a curved reception desk to our left, with nobody behind it. The whole place is lit with wall lights that cast everything in a warm, dim glow.

Theo walks over and slaps the bell. The ting echoes off the bare floors. 'Ages since I've done that.' He grins.

I find myself mirroring his excitement; it's a long time since we've done something random and new like this. We're so entrenched in our routines, it's easy to forget that activities other than work, the odd social event and scrolling exist. But still, there's a niggle at the back of my mind – I need to tell Theo that this is tantric yoga, at least. He deserves to know what he's getting into.

I open my mouth to speak, but a woman appears soundlessly in a doorway to our left, and I jump. She's wearing a long white kaftan, which perfectly matches her long white hair. I remember her from the picture on the website – she was somewhere near the middle of the group. The cult leader, perhaps?

'Hello,' she says warmly, in the softest voice I've ever heard.

'Hiya!' Theo jumps in. 'What a brilliant place this is. The floors are incredible. How long has it been a yoga centre? Do you know what it was before? If I had to guess, an aristocratic home?' He begins walking around, peering at the nooks and crannies embedded in the walls. 'I'd imagine there's stone behind this wallpaper? I couldn't see much from outside, but I bet in the daylight it's absolutely incredible . . .'

He ventures further into the reception area, propelling himself forward with his usual motor-mouth questioning. I take my chance and turn to the lady, who is staring after Theo, her mouth half open as if she might actually have an opportunity to answer one of his questions.

'Was it you I spoke to over the intercom?' I say quietly.

She tears her eyes away. 'No, that'll have been Bethany.'

'Is this statue original?' Theo calls from the other side of the room. The lady opens her mouth to reply but I jump in.

'Please could you not mention—'

'Incredible!' Theo's voice echoes off the ceiling, and his footsteps begin tapping back towards us.

'Pardon?' the lady asks.

'Could you please not—'

'It's beautiful, isn't it, Lotts?' Theo says, reaching us and wrapping his arm around my shoulder.

'Stunning,' I say, my heart hammering. Any second now, this woman could reveal that we're here at the bequest of Tilly Carter, podcast host, for my experiment to try and reignite my sex life. And I can't stop her.

'I'm sorry, you were about to ask me something?' she says. They both look at me.

I shake my head. 'Oh, I can't remember now. Something about the building probably. Beautiful place!'

She smiles. 'Well, I'm Moonbeam, and it's a pleasure to meet you . . .' We introduce ourselves. 'Well, Lottie and Theo, do you want to follow me?' she says gently, before padding across the room – barefoot, I note – towards a door on the far wall. She lets us through, and we find ourselves in a large studio space with wooden floors and mirrors spanning every wall. In the corners, clusters of white candles have been placed on the floor, and they flicker prettily, casting the space in moving light.

'If you'd like to sit side by side, just in the middle there,' Moonbeam says.

'Oh wow, it's just us,' Theo whispers in my ear as we take our seats on the floor. I realize that for him, this feels co-conspiratorial. He thinks I'm clueless about what's about to happen, too; he thinks we're figuring this out together. I feel a hot rush of guilt. I nudge him once we've sat down, and he nudges me back.

'So,' Moonbeam says, coming to sit in front of us, her legs crossed expertly. 'You're here for tantric couple's yoga.'

Theo's elbow knocks against my ribs. 'Tantric?' he whispers.

'Is everything OK?' Moonbeam asks.

I turn to Theo. 'You don't have to do it if you don't want to.'

Moonbeam shuffles on the floor. 'I'm sorry, were you not aware—'

'No, it's fine,' Theo says.

'Are you sure?' I ask.

There's a brief pause. Theo looks at me, and there's a faint crease between his eyebrows that I'm familiar with. It's his thinking face, the one he pulls when he's untangling a problem, trying to read between the lines. I feel my breath hitch in my throat; does he know? How could he know? After a moment, he looks away, his gaze returning to Moonbeam. 'Why not? Let's do it.'

My heart slows a little.

'Great. This session is aimed at bringing you both closer together, physically and emotionally, on a profound level.'

I feel Theo shuffle beside me. He's uncomfortable. But that's normal, isn't it? I'm uncomfortable; this isn't an everyday occurrence. He's not wriggling with discomfort because he might have to touch me, surely. It's the situation, Moonbeam, the weirdness of it all.

'Let's begin.' From somewhere, Moonbeam produces a tiny gong, and she taps it lightly. The room fills with a melancholy hum. 'If you could turn to face each other,' she says.

We do as she asks, and then we are face to face, cross-legged, the humming receding around us in the flickering candlelight. Theo's eyes meet mine, and his lip quirks ever so slightly. He's trying not to laugh. Instantly, instinctively, I feel my stomach clench. *Don't, Lottie.*

'Maintain eye contact,' Moonbeam says softly.

How? How am I supposed to maintain eye contact? Theo's mouth is quivering now, his nostrils flaring. I feel a bubble of laughter rising in my throat. After a few seconds, he flicks his eyes away from mine.

'It might feel uncomfortable, but I encourage you to keep looking one another in the eye,' Moonbeam reminds us. Theo moves his gaze back, clearing his throat, shuffling from one sit bone to the other. He settles in, his face serious, and his deep brown eyes lock with mine.

God, this is intense. We've never looked at each other for this long. It feels like I'm under the microscope, like he can see every part of me. Against my will, my mind travels to my confession, the podcast, meeting Tilly, the reason we're here. I feel like he can see it all; like it's impossible for me to hide any of it.

I can't do it. I move my eyes a millimetre, so I'm looking at the bridge of his nose.

'Now, Lottie, I want you to bend forward, bowing to Theo, clasping your hands together in prayer and placing them in his lap.'

I turn my head to look at her. She smiles and nods.

I give Theo another glance and lean forward, until my forehead is almost on the floor and my outstretched hands are resting on his crossed ankles. His balls are about an inch away from the tips of my fingers.

'The goddess bows down, expressing that she is open and willing to receive his love,' Moonbeam says in a low voice.

'Ah,' Theo says, making me startle. 'I'm not sure about the whole bowing down thing—'

'It's a respect ritual,' Moonbeam says firmly. 'It's your turn now. Lottie, please sit up. Theo, please bow to Lottie.'

I catch his gaze and he raises his eyebrows. I choke back a laugh. What in holy hell are we doing?

Theo copies the movement I made, and Moonbeam narrates. 'The god bows to his goddess, honouring her essence and opening himself to receive.'

Theo's praying hands land on my ankles and I swear I hear him snort.

When he rises again, Moonbeam sighs deeply. 'Beautiful. Now, maintaining eye contact, kiss, and with the kiss, experience the truest nature of one another.'

Theo throws me a subtle 'oh my god' look, but before he does, I catch the way he stiffens, the way his eyes dart away from mine. Like he doesn't want to kiss me at all.

I lean forward, and he does the same, our lips inching closer together. It's mortifyingly uncomfortable, but I force myself to keep my eyes open, locked on his. He does the same, right until the moment our mouths come together, and then he flicks his eyes shut. When we pull apart, he looks away.

Moonbeam doesn't seem to notice. 'Take each other's hands.'

Resting our forearms on our bent knees, we clasp hands. Moonbeam takes us through a series of chants, instructing us to move our hands together in circles, and I can't look at Theo for any of it. I keep my gaze focused on his nose, his eyebrow. Anywhere but his eyes, where I know, if I look, I'll find him trying to bite back a laugh. But I'll find something else, too, I think. Something that goes further than discomfort at being so intimate in front of a stranger. A general discomfort with *me* – an awkward, cringey feeling. The thought of it makes me feel suddenly small and humiliated.

Anxiety is coursing through me. I don't feel relaxed, or connected. I feel exposed and unattractive and like I want to be alone, somewhere quiet, where nobody can look at me. Where I can't see the distance between us written so plainly on my husband's face.

'Now,' Moonbeam says softly after we've gone through another cycle of chanting, when I'm almost ready to explode, 'we're going to enter into the *Shiva Shakti* position.'

Whatever that is, it doesn't sound good.

'Lottie, if you could position yourself on top of Theo's crossed legs, and wrap your legs around his back. Place your foreheads together. Lift your palms, and intertwine your fingers.'

She's not serious. I am not straddling my husband in front of this woman.

'I'm not sure I feel—'

'Come on, Lotts, let's give it a go,' Theo says to my surprise, sitting up straight. Something like hope bobs to the surface in my chest. He wants to try; he wants us to take this seriously. I stand up and then, hesitating, awkwardly squat down, hovering over Theo before I dump all of my weight on his lap and wrap my legs around him. Moonbeam hums her approval. As Theo presses his palms against mine and our foreheads connect, I try my absolute hardest to get into the moment. To feel the heat of him on my thighs, his strong chest inches from my own.

'Now, wrap your arms around one another and press your bodies together,' Moonbeam murmurs.

We do as we're told, and then just like that, we're

spaghettied to one another, our clothes the only thing stopping us from actually having sex in front of this strange woman we met half an hour ago.

'Eyes closed now, and breathe together. In and out, in and out.'

I close my eyes with relief, immensely grateful to be able to stop focusing on where my gaze is at last. I breathe in and out in time with Theo, and will my heart to slow down. From Moonbeam's direction, the noise of a sound bowl begins, reverberating around the room, vibrating in my chest. After a moment, I flutter my eyes open, but Theo's are closed, his face slack, his breathing steady against my face. The feel of him between my legs is solid and warm, and I grip a little tighter. His arms pull me closer.

I feel myself calming, almost like I've been drugged. My shoulders drop, my breathing slows. And then, with the noise of the sound bowl washing over us, I feel it. A sort of melding, like Theo and I are coming together, our chests merging, becoming one. It's followed by a strange wash of horniness, the likes of which I haven't felt before. It's not frantic or overly lustful, but deep – a sort of need to be as close as possible, to have every part of him connected with me. It grips my throat, and I have an animalistic desire to kiss him, deeply – to have him.

But no. Moonbeam is here, with her sound bowl.

'Now,' she says, and her voice is so out of place here, in this sacred space, that I suddenly despise her. 'Lift your heads, adjust your arms, and hug.'

As we transition, I catch Theo's eye. His expression is unreadable, but he's no longer trying not to laugh. I wrap my arms around his neck, his stay around my waist, and I let my head rest on his shoulder. Every part of us is touching now, my chest pressed against his, my calves against his lower back. I want us to stay like this forever, weird as it is. I've never felt this totally and completely connected with him – with anyone.

Moonbeam smacks her gong. I jump.

'Oops,' she says with a soft little laugh. 'Too strong.'

The spell broken, Theo unlaces his arms from me, and I'm forced to unravel my legs and sit back on the floor.

'Well done, both of you,' Moonbeam murmurs. 'That was beautiful. I could feel the energy between you both; the room came alive.'

I look at Theo. He looks back at me, and his mouth quirks into a half smile. Suddenly, I experience a rush of hope and impatience – I cannot wait to get this man home, to the privacy of our bedroom, and to do that again. Without our clothes on.

Moonbeam talks us through some final closing chants, and then we're on our feet, two separate people again, but it feels like something's shifted between us.

It feels like we might have just tipped the pendulum back in the right direction.

*

Or maybe not.

We're in the car on the way home, and my hope is dwindling fast. Theo is driving again, and he's laughing.

'"I could feel the energy between you both",' he says, grinning. 'How funny was that?'

I swallow. 'Maybe she could? I thought it felt quite nice.'

'It felt awkward,' he says, nudging me across the central

console. 'God, wasn't that nuts? Your boss is a maniac. People pay two-hundred-and-fifty pounds to do that?'

'You didn't like it, then.'

He glances at me, his smile fading. 'I mean . . . it was weird, Lotts. Wasn't it?'

I look out of the window, not trusting myself to speak. Yes, it was weird. But there was a moment there where I thought he was feeling what I was feeling. Where I thought, stupidly, that there'd have to be something wrong with him for him to not feel *anything*, with us wrapped around each other like that, every part of our bodies pressed together.

'Hey,' he says, finding my hand in my lap. 'I had a great time.'

'Me too,' I manage.

'Don't be sad. Why are you sad?'

I weigh up my words as I keep my head angled towards the window, wanting not to be seen for a moment. 'I think it felt nice to connect like that,' I say eventually.

He doesn't speak for a minute. 'Lotts,' he says after a while, 'it was weird. Come on, you know it was weird.'

'Why was it weird?' I say, turning to look at him. 'We're married, we love each other. Why is touching and hugging weird?'

'There was an old woman in a kaftan watching us and hitting a gong.'

'But you didn't feel anything?' I can't stop the words tumbling out of my mouth, months of hurt compiling and rushing out of me. 'You didn't get anything from that?'

Theo sounds bewildered. 'I mean . . . no. I thought it was a laugh. I thought we were going to laugh about it.'

I realize I'm being boring. I realize I could be saving this moment, making it a funny story, writing it off as some weird thing we did once. But it's too deep; the rejection feels too raw.

'Did you know it was going to be a tantric thing?' Theo asks after a beat, his voice gentle.

I don't want to lie, but how can I tell the truth? How can I tell him that I purposefully chose this for us, that I knew it'd be intimate and walked in there with serious hope in my chest? How can I do that, when he's sitting there admitting that he found being close to me so weird and uncomfortable? 'No,' I say. It's yet another tiny lie on top of the pile. 'I just went with the flow, and got something from it. I think it's a shame you didn't.'

'Fucking hell, Lotts. It's not that deep.'

'Maybe it is to me.'

'Why?'

'Because *why* is it weird? Why was that weird between us?'

'I've just said, maybe if there wasn't some weird hippy woman watching our every move—'

'That's not the *point!*' I shout. The car falls silent. I can feel my heart thudding, the tears threatening to break free from behind my eyes. The car rumbles to the end of the country lane, the wipers squeaking against the rain, and the main road comes into view.

'Let's just agree to disagree,' Theo says after a while.

Neither of us speaks for the rest of the journey. What is there to say?

Chapter Eleven

The spa lobby is a flat expanse of shiny marble tiles, ending in a babbling fountain on the far wall. Our therapist disappeared a couple of moments ago, and Caro has been talking at me non-stop ever since.

'Honestly, I'm really worried about you, Lottie. This is *so* out of character.'

'Oh, come on.'

'I'm serious! I mean, I'm thrilled to be invited, but I was under the impression that you'd be doing all your task thingies with Theo. Though I suppose Theo doesn't have the requisite bits to get involved in this one, thinking about it. I just can't imagine you *ever* choosing to do something like this. I mean—'

'Shh!' I hiss as our therapist returns carrying a bundle of white clothes.

'The changing rooms are just through here, ladies. Here are your gowns and slippers.'

Caro waits until the spa therapist has walked away before turning to me. 'No, but have you actually had a knock to the head?'

'Stop it!' I say, laughing as I barge past her and push open the door to the changing rooms.

'Seriously,' she continues, hot on my heels. 'I genuinely am not kidding. Have you seen a doctor?'

'Caro,' I say, pulling my jumper over my head and bundling it into an available locker. 'I am physically totally fine.'

'Sure,' she says, crossing her arms and staring at me. 'But *mentally* . . .'

'Mentally I'm fine, too. Get changed, we're late.'

Caro narrows her eyes at me for a moment, and then begrudgingly begins undoing the buttons on her dress. 'I'm just saying, I didn't realize this podcast thing was going to be so . . . intense. The Lottie I know wouldn't even join her work's padel club, never mind *this*.'

'Well, the Lottie you knew also thought she had a pretty healthy relationship. She's resorting to desperate measures.' I pick Caro's dress up off the bench and throw it in the locker with my things, then fish out a pound and slip the key in my gown pocket. 'Come on, our time's being eaten into.'

'Oh dear. God forbid we not get the full session.'

I slap her arm as we flip-flop our way across the tiled changing rooms and through the door to the corridor. Our therapist is waiting outside, her hands clasped below her stomach. 'Ladies,' she says, beaming. 'Are we all ready?'

'I *certainly* am,' Caro says, injecting far too much enthusiasm into her voice. 'I've been feeling like something is missing from my self-care routine, and I really think this might be it.'

I give her a hard jab in the ribs, and the therapist flashes us a wavering smile, as though she's unsure whether we're joking. 'Well . . . good!' she says after a beat. 'Come on through.'

We follow her along the corridor, our slippered feet slapping comically against the tiles. 'It's weird being in a dressing gown in public, isn't it?' I say to Caro.

'I love that *that's* what's weird about this whole thing for you.'

Our therapist stops outside a closed door and pushes down on the handle, gesturing for us to enter first. Caro trots inside and I follow her.

Oh, god.

The room is small and painted a deep, tasteful pink, with glowing salt lamps tucked against the walls. There's some whooshing, ocean-like music playing, and the whole thing gives the impression that we've just walked into a—

'Welcome to the womb room,' the therapist says, sweeping her arm across the space in front of us.

It's then that my eyes land on what's *in* the room: the reason we're both here.

Positioned in the middle of the floor are two steaming buckets, and on top of those buckets are wooden seats with a hole in the middle. I can see that an attempt has been made to *not* have them look like toilets, but that attempt has failed.

'You'll have thirty minutes in here, and a lot of our clients use that time to catch up and enjoy some relaxing time in each other's company while reaping the benefits of the yoni steam. Our unique blend contains mugwort, lavender, oregano – an excellent antiseptic – and rosemary, among a host of other beneficial botanicals. If you'd like to come over here . . .' she gestures to me, and I reluctantly follow her to the furthest steaming toilet, '. . . I assume you've left your underwear in your locker?'

I nod. We were told at reception to remove our clothes entirely. 'Wonderful. Now if you'd like to sit down here, lifting up your dressing gown at the back so there's nothing in the way . . .'

I make the mistake of looking over at Caro as I'm squatting down. She is beaming like it's Christmas Day, and I thank god that our phones are back in the changing rooms.

'I'd encourage you to spread your legs if you can,' the therapist says. 'Really allow the steam to access all areas.'

Sweet baby Jesus. Not only am I sitting on a hot toilet in front of a stranger and my best friend, I've adopted the posture of a man on a train: legs spread, elbows on knees for balance. Ironically, I have never felt less feminine than I do in the womb room.

'Fantastic. Would you like to join your friend?' she asks Caro.

'Oh, I *would*,' Caro says, grinning. She strides across the room and plonks herself unselfconsciously on the toilet – steamer – next to me.

'I'll leave you ladies to it,' the therapist says once we're settled. 'Enjoy, and I'll be back in thirty minutes.'

As soon as the door closes, Caro splutters out a laugh. 'Oh my god,' she says. 'It is *torture* not being able to take a picture. You look like George Clooney.'

'And you look the picture of femininity.'

'Really?'

'No!'

'What is this supposed to do?'

I shrug. 'Cleanse the uterus?'

'Gross. Tilly thinks your dirty uterus is responsible for your shitty sex life?'

The thought hadn't crossed my mind. 'I bloody well hope not.'

'It feels . . . weird.'

It does feel weird. It feels like sitting over a just-boiled kettle. 'Smells nice, though.'

'That it does,' Caro nods.

Around us, the ocean music whooshes, and I have a distinct feeling of being out of my own body – like I'm looking down on myself, wondering how I got here.

'Is it working, then?' Caro asks, tying her dark hair up into a stubby ponytail.

'How would I know? How can you tell when your uterus has been cleansed?'

'Not the steamer, you knob. The experiment.'

I close my eyes momentarily. I haven't seen Caro since the disastrous tantric yoga session, and I'm reluctant to relive it again. It's all I've thought about for the past week, and Theo and I have managed to dance around the topic as usual, keeping our conversations to everyday life admin: the dishwasher, who's cooking, if a package arrived or not. He's upped his gym evenings to three a week, and I've been going in to work earlier, trying to focus on the boring, soulless project Petra has asked me to dedicate all my hours to.

'Not great,' I say when I open my eyes again.

'Oh.' Caro's face falls; for the first time since we met outside the spa twenty minutes ago, she becomes serious. 'What happened?'

I explain our trip to the yoga centre, and when I get to the part about me straddling Theo in front of Moonbeam and her gong, she laughs. I find myself laughing, too; it's easy to see the funny side when I'm here with Caro, looking at it through a non-emotional lens. With Theo, though, I can't. The feeling of rejection is so strong, there's no humour in it whatsoever.

'So let me get this straight,' Caro says, adjusting herself on the toilet seat. 'You dry humped him and he had no reaction whatsoever.'

'Well, I thought he did. I opened my eyes at one point and he looked like he was kind of into it. But then in the car on the way home, he just thought it was funny. We had a bit of an argument about it.'

'You two never argue.'

'No,' I agree. 'It was horrible. It was just . . . I don't understand why it felt so weird.'

'I mean, apart from a woman you've never met being in the room with you . . .' Caro catches the look on my face and presses her lips together. 'No, sure. Did it feel weird for you, too?'

And here's the bit I've been trying not to think about. Because it *did* feel weird. I was uncomfortable almost the whole time, I couldn't make eye contact with my own husband, and my anxiety was sky-high. 'A bit, yes.'

'Do you think maybe you're just taking it a bit too . . . seriously?'

I sigh. 'Maybe. But it's hard, you know? Like, once you've identified something as a problem, how do you *not* take it seriously?'

'He still loves you, you know.'

Caro always knows what I'm thinking. I look down at

my slippered feet. 'I know,' I reply quietly, because I do. The question comes out of my mouth before I can filter it. 'But is he attracted to me any more?'

She doesn't miss a beat. 'Of course he is. You've got yourselves into a rut, that's all. It happens to couples the world over. Most of them don't resort to such drastic measures to fix things, but . . .'

I groan. 'What the fuck am I doing?'

'We. What the fuck are *we* doing?'

I look at my best friend, squatting pant-less over a bucket of steaming herbs, just because I asked her to, and feel such an immense swell of gratitude that I burst out laughing. 'You're the best, you know that?'

She joins in, tipping her head back and whooping. 'Lotts,' she says gleefully, 'this is the most fun I've had in forever.'

'Oh, shut up. You have loads of fun.'

She shrugs, the smile slipping slightly from her face. 'Yeah.'

I sense something here, the way only someone who knows you inside out can. A soreness that needs addressing. 'Have you thought any more about Edinburgh?'

Caro comes from Edinburgh originally, moving here with her family when she was eleven and enrolling in Year 7 with me. She's always harboured a dream of moving back there, and her most notable effort occurred when she was sixteen and ran away to the Fringe, causing a short-lived police search and a series of rapidly deleted 'Have you seen this girl?' posts on Facebook. She claims she came back because the picture they used of her was so awful, but I know it's because the police tracked her down at a dirty puppet show with a twenty-six-year-old small-time weed dealer and convinced her to come home. She'd invited me to go with her, but I didn't have the balls.

Sometimes, I wonder whether Caro keeps Edinburgh as a dream because it means she has a reason not to commit to anything here. I also wonder whether she never makes any serious moves to make it happen because if she acts on it, the fantasy will get tainted with reality, and deep down, she knows she'll carry all her issues with her and there'll be nowhere left to run. Edinburgh is like an escape hatch she keeps in her pocket but never uses, because once she does, it loses its power.

Not that I've ever aired these thoughts to her, of course.

'I'm figuring it out,' she says, fiddling with the cord of her dressing gown.

This is always her response, but my heart sinks, because recently, things had started to shift. She'd begun talking about photography competitions up there that she wanted to submit her work to. Caro is only afraid of one thing in life, and that's vulnerability. She's always wanted to show her work – and it deserves to be seen – but she's never quite managed to pull the trigger on putting herself out there and letting herself be open to feedback. She's been through phases where she submits her collections and is offered places, but she always pulls out at the last minute, and then months go by before she tries again. Recently, I thought she'd turned a corner, especially since she met Peter, but their breakup appears to have made her hit the pause button once again.

Caro is the bravest person I know; her life is chaos, a total absence of routine or structure, and anyone who meets her assumes she's the quintessential free spirit, blowing where the wind takes her. It's only when they really get to know her that they stop to wonder why she hasn't left our little town in over twenty years.

'What's stopping you?' I ask gently.

'I'll miss you,' is her well-practised reply. And god, I'd miss her, too. I'm not actually sure how I'd cope without her. But this time I know it's something else, something more than our friendship. Our friendship would survive; of that I'm certain. But I know not to push. This is where this conversation always ends, no matter what I say. Her dreams still in the planning phase, her connection to me the tether that ostensibly keeps her from pushing the button.

'Maybe once you're in a better place with Theo, I'll go,' she says. Her voice brightens. 'Anyway. Have you written about the yoga thing? For the podcast?'

I let it drop, knowing that pushing her further will just make her close off even more. 'Yeah, I sent it in a couple of days ago.'

'When does it go live?'

'I think they're recording all of it before airing the first episode. There'll be a teaser trailer soon, I'm told.' I feel sick at the thought.

'And what are you going to write about this experience?' she asks, nodding to her compromised position.

'God knows.' I laugh.

'Perhaps something like, "It's the first time I've spread my legs in a long old while".'

'It wouldn't be a lie.'

'To be honest,' she says, looking wistful, 'sitting like this is making me feel quite horny.'

The door to the room swings open as Caro is speaking, and our spa therapist walks in. 'That's time, ladies. How was it?'

'Fantastic,' Caro says, leaping up. 'I could have sat there all day.'

We traipse back up the corridor, and I feel an uncomfortable damp ring where I've been sitting over the yoni steamer. As she deposits us at the changing rooms, the therapist leans in towards us.

'Speaking from experience, you'll have the best sex of your life in the twenty-four hours after a yoni steam. Don't waste the opportunity.'

She raises one eyebrow suggestively and pads off.

Caro turns to face me. 'Well,' she says. 'I'd better find myself a lucky gentleman, hadn't I?'

*

Do you remember the first time you had sex with your partner?

How was it?

Mind-blowing? Earth-shattering? A bit disappointing?

Do you remember the second time, the third? How about the first time it really felt good, when you learned what you wanted and couldn't keep your hands off each other? Maybe that was the first time, or maybe it was the tenth.

Now, let me ask you another question. Do you remember the last time you had sex with your partner?

For some of you, it's yesterday. It's last Wednesday, a week ago, this morning. But for some of you – and it's a big some – it's been so long that you can't quite remember. A month or two. Or six. Or a year.

A few weeks ago, The Cliterati *aired a Questions and Confessions episode that garnered a response so huge, we couldn't ignore it. An anonymous listener sent a message in, explaining that she and her husband of three years didn't have sex any more. She didn't know why, and she didn't know how it had happened, when their sex life until recently had been great. She just knew that she felt sad about it, and increasingly anxious.*

So many of you related to our anonymous confessor's plight that we decided to take action. Shortly, we'll be launching a brand-new six-part series called Long-Term Lust, with me, Tilly Carter, where I'll be dissecting this issue and seeing what we can do to fix it. And the best part: our anonymous confessor will be coming along for the ride. I'm sending her weekly tasks – proven tactics I've been recommending to my clients throughout my ten years of professional practice – to complete and report back on, which we'll unpack together during the episode. Think tantric yoga, yoni-steaming sessions and much, much more . . .

If it works, you'll be the first to know.

So join me as we take a deep dive into stagnant sex and languishing libidos, with the aim of getting you sex-confident for the spring.

I'd quite like to sit down, but I'm in the middle of Boots, and there's not a chair in sight. I pull my earbuds out of my ears and stuff them in my pocket, willing myself to relax.

The teaser trailer gives no indication that I'm the anonymous confessor. The only risk here is that people go back to the original episode to get some context and somehow twig that it was me, but I doubt it. If they haven't figured it out by now, they probably won't.

But what about when the episodes start coming out? What about when Tilly unpacks my detailed description of couple's tantric yoga? If Theo ever heard it, he'd know it was me describing the experience we had together. But he wouldn't listen to *The Cliterati* in a million years – I'm not sure he's ever even heard of it. And surely he hasn't told anyone that we went? If he has, it'll be his male friends, who also don't listen to the podcast, so the risk remains the same.

It's fine.

I push down the unease in my stomach and focus on the positives. My first payment from the podcast came in this morning, and even though I knew the amount beforehand, it still made my heart skip a beat. I'm looking at the expensive nail polishes on the middle shelf, the ones I've never allowed myself to buy before. There's a burnt orange I've always eyed up, and I swipe it into my basket, swallowing the guilt I feel. Have I betrayed Theo's confidence to buy nail polish?

Hurrying along into the next aisle, I search the shelves for the real reason I'm here. I had a phone call with Tilly this morning while I walked to the office, and she talked me through the next experiment. Thankfully, this one is more conventional, and when I raised some concerns she adapted the protocol to fit our lifestyle. So I'm here, now, buying exactly what I've been told to buy.

I scan the shelves until I find it – sore muscles massage oil. Tilly had told me to buy something sexy and fragrant, but I'd pointed out that there was no way I could naturally bring up the idea of a sensual massage to Theo at this point. We're like ships in the night recently, and with the ashes of our sex life hanging over us like a cloud, it'd be too transparent. Too awkward. Tilly suggested I try offering him a sports massage after the gym, using a nice scented oil. Just to get us touching again. She said she's taking us 'back to basics', and admitted that the yoga might have been too much too soon.

I throw the bottle into my basket and head for the till, excitement bubbling in my chest. Because while the experiment so far has yielded no positive results – the yoni steam gave me thrush I've only just got rid of – it has had one unexpected effect.

I am extremely horny.

For the past few months, my libido has felt like a strange, foreign object I can't make sense of. I've thought about sex more than I ever have in my life, but I haven't *wanted* it the way I used to. I haven't felt drawn to Theo in that way; I've been less like a physical being and more like an observant manager, scanning the horizon for signs and opportunities. I've worried and worried about the growing distance between us so much that I've become sex-obsessed, but I've been out of touch with myself, focused on the logistics. Now, with me putting all this focus on my body and how I feel, I can sense that pull again. For the first time in a long while, I feel that familiar flutter. And the idea of an oiled-up massage is sounding incredibly appealing.

Luckily, Theo's at the gym tonight. So I'll have my perfect excuse when he gets home.

Chapter Twelve

I am sitting on the sofa, pretending to relax, but my eyes are focused over the top of my phone screen, to where Theo is greeting the dogs in the kitchen. He's in his gym gear, squatting down and letting Boodle jump all over him while Betty licks his exposed toes.

He looks up and I flick my eyes back to my screen.

'Good day?' he asks.

'Hm?' I glance over as though I've been engrossed in something quite important. 'Oh, yeah, great, thanks! Yours?'

'Brill. Great gym session.'

He stands up and I keep my eagle eyes alert. As he straightens his back, I see it. A wince, his hand to the back of his thigh.

'Sore?' I ask in a wholly unnatural and strange way. It comes out like a strangled bark, and Theo frowns at me before replying.

'Er, yeah, think I've pulled a hamstring.'

I force my eyebrows to shoot up as though I've just remembered something. 'Oh, I got a freebie when I was walking through town earlier.' I stand up and walk over to my bag, which is hanging on the back of one of the dining chairs. My movements feel odd as I go, my legs wooden. I rummage until I find the bottle of oil and then hold it up like it's a long-lost pendant. I am so glaringly obvious, it's painful. 'Some sports massage oil. Do you want me to . . .'

Theo looks at the bottle and smiles. 'That's so sweet, but I'm OK. I'll just have a hot bath. Thank you, though. You're so cute.' He deposits a kiss on my forehead.

For god's sake. 'No worries,' I say, smiling tightly. I need to adapt, to think quickly. 'When you're done, would you mind doing my calf? I think I twinged it or something on my way to work yesterday. It's giving me hell.'

My *calf?* Of all the places – I might as well have asked him to massage my elbow.

'Of course,' he says easily, pulling his top over his head and bundling it into the washing machine under the sink. The evenings at the gym have been paying off; his chest is broad and defined, and there's a light glistening on his toned abdomen, the trail of hair leading into his shorts damp.

'You're looking good,' I say, raising an eyebrow. 'Dev's been working you hard.'

Oh, good idea, Lottie. Bring Dev up – that'll get the mood going.

'God, yeah.' He raises his arms above his head and stretches, and his shorts dip lower on his hips. 'He's a psychopath. It feels good, though. Makes me a stronger runner.'

I bob my head. 'Fab.'

When did things become so generally awkward between us? I've always felt most like myself when I'm with Theo, like I can drop all the pretences and just let words fall out of my mouth. But now, things feel formal and stilted, like there's a wall between us. Is it just the sex, or is something deeper going on?

Before I have the chance to carry on our conversation, to try and shift the tone once more, Theo has disappeared upstairs to run the bath. I hold the bottle of oil in my hand, passing it from palm to palm. Even if I only get a calf massage I don't need, the physical touch will be something. I can't remember the last time Theo touched a bare part of me that wasn't my face or my hands.

The thought brings a sudden rush of sadness. What the hell has happened to us? It feels like our whole life at the moment is stuck in that brief period after an argument, where you're tiptoeing around each other, when all is forgiven but the disturbance still hangs in the air. We're perpetually suspended in the adjustment period, the in-between, the stilted offers of a cup of tea and requests to pass the remote.

Theo is a rare combination of both a chatterbox and an excellent listener, and talking to him has always been like talking to a wide-open book. Over the course of the last years, we must have spent hundreds of hours on the sofa, putting the world to rights over glasses of wine. We must have spent even more time lying in bed, our faces inches apart, whispering about our jobs and our friends and our plans for the future, even though there was nobody to disturb but the dogs. Theo used to tell me about articles he'd read – the future of air transport, automation, and AI, his niche interests – and I'd fall asleep but he wouldn't mind. I'd tell him about the people I met at community events at the arts centre, big ideas I had for bringing art to more diverse groups, which we both knew I probably wouldn't get the budget to act on. He'd listen and offer advice, helping me build plans despite him knowing that they'd almost certainly remain just that.

We haven't done any of those things in a while.

And then I realize that Sunday has been and gone, and we didn't do our dog walk across the fields. We've never missed one before, and the realization is a gut punch. We *always* walk the dogs across the fields on Sundays. How did we forget? It feels, suddenly, like what we have together is made of sand instead of concrete. Like if I look away for a second, it'll slip through my fingers.

The sadness gives way to a renewed sense of purpose. This is the reason I'm doing this; this is what I'm fighting for. Us. What we were, and what we still are, underneath whatever it is that's burrowed itself between us. I take the stairs two at a time until I reach the landing, where I can hear the splash of bathwater coming from the bathroom. I go into the bedroom and strip my work clothes off, putting on a short, comfy dress and no underwear. Then I lie face-down on the bed and scroll through TikTok, waiting for him to emerge.

Ten minutes later, he pads into the bedroom, a towel slung low on his waist, his curly hair wet.

'Nice bath?' I ask, looking over my shoulder.

'So good.' He rubs his thigh. 'Those bath salts are a miracle.'

'You still OK to do my calf?' I ask in a squeaky voice. *Be natural, Lottie. For god's sake.*

'Oh, yeah, of course,' he says, and I know he'd forgotten. 'Let me just get changed.'

He drops his towel and begins rummaging in his underwear drawer. I soak him in – god, he's hot. I want him, and not just because I should. Not just because we're married and we should be fucking. I *want* him, just as much as I did when we first met.

Theo pulls a pair of boxers on and yanks a clean white T-shirt over his head, then clambers onto the bed. 'Right, what seems to be the issue?'

I laugh at his faux-formal tone. 'My left calf, here,' I say, reaching round and rubbing at a random area below the back of my knee. 'It's twinging.'

'Lie down properly, get comfy,' he says, pushing my shoulders gently until I drop my face down onto the bed. God, that was hot. Was that hot? Is that what constitutes hot now?

I listen as he flicks the cap on the bottle of oil and squirts some into his palm. My skin is fizzing with anticipation; I want his slick hands all over me. He smells like his peppery shower gel, zingy and fresh.

He rubs his palms together, and then presses his warm hands against my leg.

Immediately, my body reacts. There's an instant ache, an urge.

He rubs slow circles across my skin, and I let out an involuntary moan. He pauses. 'That OK?'

'Yes,' I say breathlessly. 'It feels good.'

Theo's hands are below my knee, but still, it feels so suggestive. I feel like a Victorian woman, having her ankle touched with the tip of a finger. It's electrifying. I hope Theo feels the same way; I shaved my legs this morning and my skin is smooth and soft, the dress I've put on short and risqué. If he just moves his hands slightly higher . . .

'I can feel it in the back of my thigh now,' I say shamelessly, my voice muffled by the duvet.

'Here?' His hands slide up, past the back of my knee and to my thigh. He's about three hands away from my arse. I'd love for him to take it from here, to creep his hands upwards – something I'd have been certain of him doing just six months ago – but I can't take the risk that he'll act of his own accord.

'A bit higher,' I say.

'Tell me when.'

I let him slide his hand up my leg until his fingers are almost up the hem of my dress before I say, 'There.'

He continues with slow circles, applying gentle pressure with the tips of his fingers, and it's almost more than I can bear. I want him to dip his hand between my thighs, to discover for himself that I haven't got any underwear on. He shuffles about on the bed, lifting his hand off me for a moment, and when he puts it back down, his fingers graze my bum cheek through my dress. I gasp, and he pauses.

'Does it hurt?'

'No, no,' I say quickly. 'It's just so relieving. It feels so nice.'

'I know what might feel even nicer,' he says, his voice deepening. Excitement immediately flutters in my throat. My heart thumps with anticipation. This is it. He's going to lift my dress up, flip me over, climb on top of me, his hands finding my breasts, tugging his boxers down, pushing himself—

From nowhere, Theo begins karate-chopping my leg.

'Oh,' I say involuntarily, my voice box vibrating with the rhythm of his hands. 'That's . . .'

'Good, isn't it?' he says happily.

I feel my body sink into the bed, the excitement and anticipation draining out of me as quickly as they came. Is he really that oblivious? How can he be missing all of my hints, all of my attempts to bring us together? He's never needed much of an opening in the past; I'd only have to be bending over to pick something up off the floor, or taking my bra off at the end of the day for him to initiate something. How is he suddenly being so dense?

Then, as my body trembles with the force of a ferocious massage I don't need, a worse question comes to my mind. What if Theo knows exactly what I'm doing here, but is choosing to ignore it? What if he's all too aware that I'm attempting to initiate something, but is skirting around it on purpose?

The thought is horrifying; the idea that I'm being blatantly horny and thirsty, like some kind of randy horse – and that my own husband is trying to avoid me precisely *because* I'm attempting to have sex with him – is mortifying.

'That's enough,' I say suddenly, rolling onto my back and sitting up. Theo freezes, his oily hands hovering above the bed.

'Did I hurt you?' he asks, confused.

'No,' I reply as I get off the bed and stand up, pulling my dress over my head and rooting around, naked, for my pyjamas. I don't attempt to cover myself up, or to hold my body in a way that might be more attractive. What would be the point? Theo is either repulsed or indifferent to the idea of being physically intimate with me – how can I possibly make things worse?

And as I throw the ugliest, comfiest pyjama T-shirt over my head, the knowledge that I just lied to him thrums in my chest. Because he did hurt me. He *is* hurting me. And I'm running out of the self-esteem I need to keep taking it.

*

I have two sausage dogs, a boy and a girl. The girl is the opposite of a people pleaser: she knows her own mind, and she won't be convinced to do anything she doesn't want to do. The boy, on the other hand, is a dopey teddy bear who wants love and affection more than anything else in the world. He'll do anything for a cuddle, a stroke, or a snuggle on the sofa. But there is one occasion in which he won't do what he's told. If we're out walking and he spots a rabbit in the field, he will immediately start the chase. I'll call him back, and there'll be a moment where he'll pause, his eyes not quite meeting mine, like he's pretending not to see me. And then, inevitably, he'll carry on chasing the rabbit anyway.

These days, my husband is like our dog. He can hear me calling him; I think he's all too aware that I'm trying to bring us back together. But in the pause, he decides to pretend he hasn't seen me. He decides to plead ignorance, swerving my advances artfully, and carry on with his life as if our physical relationship doesn't exist.

I'm two weeks into my experiment with The Cliterati *now, and I have to admit that I'm losing hope. I can see that the activities my husband and I are doing together should work – for a normal couple, who are just in a bit of a rut, they'd be just the ticket to get things going again. But for us, they aren't. There's something more profound going on than a bit of a dry spell. Something a bit of Tantra and a massage can't solve. It's like my husband is actively avoiding me, like he's purposefully looking away when he sees that I'm trying to be physically close to him. I'm disappointed and frustrated and tired, and I don't know what to do next.*

I sit back in my office chair and read through my write-up. I'm exhausted after only having a few hours' sleep last night, and I know the whole thing reeks of pessimism. But what else can I say? I don't want to give a false report, to pretend to feel something I don't. There might be people listening to the podcast who are going through exactly what I am, and surely honest solidarity is more helpful than castles in the sky?

I remember that I told Isa and Tilly that Theo was in on the experiment, and wonder whether they'll guess from my write-up that he might not be as clued-up as I'd made out. Then I decide it doesn't make a difference either way; the result is the same.

Just before I hit send, I wonder whether referencing sausage dogs is playing with fire a little too much. With the descriptions I've given of Boodle's behaviour, it wouldn't take a cosmic leap for Theo to put two and two together. I change it to 'Irish terriers' and fire off the email, feeling quite clever.

That should throw anyone who might listen off my scent, while still being emotionally honest.

I pick up my phone and begin flicking through Instagram.

'Petra wants you,' Harry's voice murmurs from over my shoulder.

I start, turning around. 'What? Why?'

He shrugs. 'Something about the tote bag advert?'

My stomach drops. Shit. I was supposed to put the Facebook advert for our printed tote bag live two days ago – I completely forgot. I look up; Petra is in her office, staring at me.

'Bollocks,' I mutter.

'Everything OK?' Harry asks as I get to my feet. He slumps in his own chair and regards me over his mug.

'Yeah, fine,' I say. 'Just didn't sleep well.'

He looks like he wants to say more, but I'm already walking away, weaving through the desks towards Petra's office.

'No need to come in and sit down,' she says as I poke my head in and knock on the glass, as if she might have been startled by my sudden arrival outside the glass wall. 'Where's the Facebook ad?'

I decide honesty is the best policy, because really, who else can I blame but myself? Mark Zuckerberg? 'I completely forgot,' I say, keeping my voice low. 'I'm sorry. I'll do it right away.'

Petra sighs and takes her glasses off, rubbing the bridge of her nose with her fingers. 'Lottie, I asked you to lead this initiative because I thought you could handle it.'

'I can handle it.' *But this isn't my job,* I want to add. *I'm supposed to be engaging with the community, not doing online marketing.* I know what her answer will be, though.

Marketing *is* engagement. It's reaching people, bringing people in who might not have known about us before. It still doesn't mean I don't hate it.

'The bags have been in the shop downstairs for two days without any advertising. Do you know how much that might have cost us?'

What I want to reply is that the bags are ugly anyway – Emma Raynor's work is the kind of thoughtless non-art that rich people buy to make themselves look cultured. Instead, I inspect my nails shamefully, slightly shocked by my own bitterness. 'I'm really sorry.'

'I need your head in this, Lottie,' Petra says. 'OK? Don't let this happen again.'

I slink back to my desk, chastised, and Harry grimaces at me. 'Not good?'

'Forgot to put the Facebook ad up,' I say, sinking heavily into my chair and letting my head drop back.

'Yikes,' he winces. 'That's not like you.' He pauses. 'You know, I wanted to ask about the flyers for the tea set. Have you . . .'

'Shit.' I sit up. I haven't even started them. 'I'm so sorry. I'll have them with you by the end of the day.'

'No problem,' he says, though I know I'm holding him up. 'Whenever you have time.'

I puff out a breath and lean forward, unlocking my computer and loading up Meta's Ad Centre. The ad is already created, I just had to push one button. I click 'publish' and the stupid thing goes live.

'Lottie,' Harry says, watching me. 'Are you sure everything's—'

My phone begins buzzing in my pocket, cutting Harry off, and I slide it out. It's Isa. 'One sec,' I say to Harry, 'I've got to get this.'

I hurry into the kitchen, which is mercifully empty, and close the door behind me.

'Hello?'

'Hi, Lottie, it's Isa.'

'Yes, hi – is everything OK?'

She sighs heavily. I get a sense of foreboding. 'Look, I've just read your latest write-up.'

'Yes?'

'I'm sorry, Lottie, but it's too negative. We're going for a light-hearted vibe here, trying to make people feel better, not worse.'

God. How many things can I fuck up in one day? I stare at the coffee machine, feeling despondent. But wait, no – it's not my job to sugarcoat things for *The Cliterati*'s listeners. I'm being paid to report honestly about my experience. Isn't the whole point of this thing for me to fix my sex life?

No, I realize with a rush of clarity. The point is to attract listeners and make the podcast money. Of course that's the point; what world do I live in?

And with that realization fresh in my mind, why am I *still* struggling to defend myself?

'But . . .' I manage, '*I* don't feel better.'

Isa sighs again, and I notice that the sound is more frustrated than sympathetic. 'I'm sorry about that.' She doesn't sound it. 'Is there anything positive you can say? Is the experiment having any impact at all?'

I think for a moment. It's true that I'm more in tune with myself, more aware of my needs. My self-defending resolve disappears. I need to give Isa something; they've taken a chance on me, and they're trying really hard to help me. 'I feel . . . I suppose I feel more attracted to Theo. More interested in having sex with him.'

'That's great!' She brightens. 'Let's rework it, including that.' I can hear her typing something. 'Increased libido,' she murmurs. 'That's really good . . .'

'Isa,' I say, clearing my throat. 'I think . . . I'm not sure any of it is working, though. Theo doesn't want me. Maybe this is all a waste of time.'

She tuts. 'No, no. Everything's fine. The teaser trailer had an incredible reception, and we've already recorded the first two episodes. Just stick it out. Something will work eventually.'

I nod, even though she can't see me. I need it to be true. I feel like crying.

'Lottie,' she says after a beat, her voice softening just slightly. 'It's going to be fine. OK?'

'Thanks, Isa. I really—'

'Great to chat, Lottie. Can you get that revised write-up to me by the end of today? Thanks! Ciao ciao.'

Her voice cuts off in my ear.

I let my hand drop, so that my phone is dangling by my thigh. I need to pull myself together – I'm only halfway through the experiment, and there's still hope. We're going to get nowhere if one of us doesn't hold out for an improvement; if one of us doesn't at least try.

While I hate to admit it, I know that a big part of my second-guessing this whole thing is the money. I suddenly have a big boost in my income, and I feel guilty about hiding it from Theo. I want to buy him that holiday we keep talking about, because maybe that's really all we need: some time alone together in a brand-new place, away from our usual environment. But how can I give him a gift like that without explaining where the money has come from?

My phone begins buzzing in my hand again, and I look at the screen. Unknown number. I swipe to answer, frowning.

'Hello?'

'Lottie, it's Tilly.' Tilly's unique voice rasps down the phone line, and I freeze. Am I about to get my third telling-off of the day?

'Hey!' I say, attempting to inject some brightness into my voice. 'How are you?'

'Good, good. Listen, I've just spoken to Isa.'

'I'm so sorry about my latest write-up,' I blurt, the words tumbling out of my mouth. 'I'm just having a bad day, and I didn't think—'

'I'm going to stop you there,' she says bluntly. I clamp my mouth shut. 'You have nothing to apologize for. If the tasks I'm setting you aren't working, they aren't working. I wish Isa had brought this to my attention sooner, but there you go . . .' She trails off, and I sense some unsaid bitching in the silence. After a breath, she continues, 'I'm so sorry this is proving trickier than we first thought, Lottie. But I promise you, I'm with you in this, OK? We're going to keep trying. I think we need to change tactic.'

The kindness in her voice, the solid warmth of her certainty that she can help, brings the tears I'd been holding back to my eyes. 'Oh?' I manage.

'I'd like your next task to be an emotional one – physical contact off the table.'

I swallow and pull myself together. 'Right. It's just, I'm really keen that we get the physical side of our relationship back on track as soon as possible . . .'

'I think it's deeper than that, Lottie. I get the feeling there are a lot of things being left unsaid in your house, and until you bring those things to the surface, this problem isn't going to resolve itself.'

I'm nodding again. She's right. There's something bubbling underneath all this, and we need to dig it up. 'I'm down for that,' I say, hope once again flaring. 'Just tell me what I need to do.'

Chapter Thirteen

'I really feel like maybe you should have discussed this with him.'

Caro is sitting back in a wide armchair, an iced matcha clutched between her manicured hands. She takes a long draw from her straw.

'I didn't know how to bring it up,' I counter. 'Just the idea of talking about it is like . . .' I trail off, pushing my own straw back and forth in my iced caramel latte. We've been gifted a rare balmy day in March, and while it's not warm enough to sit outside, it is warm enough for iced beverages indoors at a heated café. 'Besides, we're going to discuss things now, aren't we?'

'He thinks you're taking him out for dinner, Lottie.'

'I am.'

'After you've tricked him into a therapist's office.'

She's right, of course. But the very idea of discussing things with a therapist is bad enough, never mind talking things through one-on-one beforehand. If I'd asked Theo to come to a therapist with me, it would have opened up a big discussion I'm not sure I'm prepared to have alone. I just don't know how to talk about this whole thing with him; it's been under wraps for so long, this big, unspoken elephant in the room, and it feels like too much for the four walls of our house to cope with. We've never had deep, heart-rending conversations before; we've never needed to. I wouldn't even know where to start. A professional, at least, will be able to referee us through the whole thing. Plus, Tilly says she sees the most success with her clients who engage in couple's therapy, and she's suggested that maybe, the thing I struggle the most with is actively bringing up the problem in the first place. If we're going to enlist professional help, I want that help to involve the actual act of broaching our dismal sex life.

'I'm bricking it,' I confess.

'Well . . .' Caro gives me an I'm-not-surprised look. 'I hope it works.'

'So do I,' I sigh. I flit my gaze again to the window, looking for Theo's figure approaching the café. My stomach is in knots. 'How's your week been?' I ask, trying to distract myself.

'I did a photoshoot for a couple who've adopted a baby puffin,' she says, chewing on a piece of ice she's fished out of her cup. 'On some big country estate. They invited me for dinner after and I ended up drinking a whole bottle of dessert wine and sleeping with the chef.'

'Christ.' I find myself thinking about Peter, and wonder what, exactly, the chef had that he didn't. But I keep my mouth shut.

'Mmm. I think they might have been mis-sold. Looked more like a blackbird than a puffin to me.'

'And the chef?' I can't help myself.

'Not bad, actually. Nice calloused hands from all the oven burns. Don't call me a convert, but I do think that yoni steam might actually have worked.'

I grimace, but before I can probe further, a figure appears on the other side of the window, and I look up, nerves shooting through me – it's Theo. Caro turns around, following my gaze, and he waves through the glass at her.

'Got to go,' I say, slurping the remnants of my drink and standing up. 'Wish me luck.'

'Good luck,' she says, raising her eyebrows. I pick up my bag and move towards the door, but she calls me back.

'Lottie.'

I turn around.

'Just . . . be honest, won't you? I know you don't find it the easiest to be direct, but it's not you, all this secrecy.'

I want to remind her that it was her who talked me out of telling Theo in the first place – but then I'd have to admit that her advice was exactly what I wanted to hear. I didn't need a whole lot of convincing to keep it all under wraps. 'Of course I will. That's the whole point of it,' I say after a beat, and I know I sound defensive.

She holds her hands up. 'OK. Sorry. Go. Go fix your marriage.'

I roll my eyes at her before stepping out of the door and plastering a grin on my face as I prepare myself to tell my husband that instead of an early pad thai, we're off to talk through our deepest issues with our brand-new therapist.

*

'So,' Theo says, linking his fingers through mine. 'What's brought this on?'

We're walking along the pavement in the direction of the therapist's office, unbeknownst to Theo. Him holding my hand buoys my mood; do we even need this? Am I completely overreacting? Maybe we should turn around, walk to Thai Khun, order our favourites, let the night's events fall where they may. Like old times. I lean into him, unlinking our hands and providing an opening for him to put his arm around my shoulder, but he rubs my back like I'm an elderly aunt and then steps slightly away, so that we're walking side by side again, unconnected.

No, we definitely need this.

Before I can answer his question, he squints ahead of us. 'We're going the wrong way. Thai Khun is back down there.'

He goes to turn around, but I take his hand again. Jesus Christ, here we go. 'Hang on,' I say. 'We're doing something else first.'

He stops and gives me a confused smile, anticipation dancing in his eyes. 'Oh?'

It dawns on me that he probably thinks we're going somewhere fun – a new little bar I've found, or to do a class at the arts centre. Just like when we did the tantric yoga, Theo believes we're on the same page. It's horrifying to me that lying and deceiving him are becoming easier than telling the truth, and I know that I personally need this therapist just as much as we do as a couple. I take a breath as we stand on the street, hovering outside the Post Office. Unease whooshes through me. 'Shall we . . .' I pull him to the side to make room for people coming and going with packages and envelopes.

'Is everything OK?' He must notice the expression on my face, because the curious anticipation gives way to a concerned frown.

I clutch his hand tightly. 'I've organized something for us. I think we need it, and I hope you'll feel the same, but I just . . . I didn't want to tell you until just now, because I thought we could talk about the whole thing *while* we're there, and then . . . yeah.'

He laughs uneasily. 'Lotts, you're not making any sense.'

I shake my head. *Just come out with it, Lottie.*

'I've booked us in for some couple's counselling,' I say in a rush. 'Just to talk through some things.'

Theo physically steps back. I hold his hand as he tries to pull it away. 'What things?'

'We can talk about it with the therapist. Please, Theo?'

He shakes his head. 'I . . . What? What . . . why don't you just talk to me? Do we not even get one conversation before we're in marriage counselling?'

Guilt hammers away in my chest. The things I've said for the podcast, the parts of our lives I've exposed. And I haven't even given him the courtesy of a conversation, of telling him there's a problem.

'Do you think everything's fine?' I ask hopefully. Maybe he does – maybe I'm being mad. Maybe if I just say, *Theo, why don't we have sex any more?* He'll smack his head and say, *Bloody hell, you're right. That completely passed me by. My bad. Let's go home and get freaky right now.*

But he doesn't say that. He looks away, his eyes finding

something in the distance at the end of the street. 'No,' he says after a moment.

My heart crumples. 'How long have you felt like that?'

He doesn't answer for a while. A minute passes, and then he turns his gaze back to me. 'Let's talk about it with the therapist, shall we?' He turns away from me and begins walking in the direction we were headed. 'You'd better lead the way.'

*

Gretchen Frodsham is hot.

From her picture online, she looked nice: blonde, a pretty blouse, a classic therapist. In person, she's an absolute bombshell: cool blue eyes; platinum hair cascading over one shoulder; high, full cheekbones; and a soft-grey silk blouse. It's low-cut enough to show just the very top of her cleavage, tasteful but suggestive, and her delicate hands lightly play absent-mindedly with her collar as she speaks.

The first thought I have is, *I bet Theo wouldn't struggle to shag her*. The second thought I have is, *Jesus, thank god I have a therapist*.

'You booked this appointment, Lottie,' Gretchen says, her voice like tinkling glass. 'Would you like to tell Theo and me why you've decided to come here today?'

Theo turns to me. We're sitting on armchairs next to one another, Gretchen poised elegantly on an identical one across from us, her shiny legs crossed. There's a vase of freshly cut flowers on a low table between us – expensive-looking. Some kind of upmarket subscription, I'd bet. I knew the podcast was paying, so I booked the bougiest therapist within a ten-mile radius.

I consider Gretchen's question. Would 'No, thank you' be an appropriate reply?

No – *come on, Lottie. Say what you need to say.*

'I'd like to know what Theo thinks the problem is.' Complete bailout.

Theo sits back and folds his arms, looking emotionlessly at Gretchen. 'I actually had no idea we were coming here until five minutes ago, so frankly, I'd prefer to hear from Lottie. Evidently there's something going on that I'm not aware of.'

'You just said that you didn't think everything was fine,' I reply. 'Just now, outside.'

He still won't look at me. He talks to me through Gretchen, like we're two parents gearing up for a divorce, speaking via our children. 'I hope Lottie will forgive me for considering there might be a problem when I'm having surprise marriage counselling sprung on me. I thought we were going out for tom yum soup.' He runs his hand through his curly hair: his trademark tell of frustration. He's *really* annoyed with me.

'I want to know what your problem is,' I push.

He jerks his head towards me. 'What's *your* problem?'

'I don't have one!'

Theo laughs; a short, incredulous sound. He looks back at Gretchen as if to say, *Are you hearing what I'm hearing?* He's so rarely like this – short and snappy and tight-jawed – that it makes anxiety well in my belly.

'Lottie,' Gretchen leans forward, resting her notebook on her lap. 'I think Theo might be saying something important here. You organized this appointment because you believe there's a problem that needs resolving. If Theo also thinks there's a problem, we can come to that later, but for now I think we should begin with the reason this appointment was scheduled. Do you think you can tell us?'

Why can't I say it? I've dragged us here; what was I expecting?

Really, though, I know exactly what I want – I want Theo to tell me why he won't have sex with me. I wasn't lying when I said I didn't have a problem. I *don't* have a problem. I love my husband and I want to be physically intimate with him. The issue evidently lies with Theo. Doesn't it?

Gretchen and Theo are staring at me expectantly.

'I worry that we've become distant,' I manage.

Theo nods, and I feel a mix of fear and relief – he agrees, but why?

'Distant how?' Gretchen asks.

'In bed,' I say quickly before I can backtrack. And then, to soften it, 'You've started reading books about planes instead of . . . spending time with me.'

Theo blinks. 'Lotts, you're scrolling through your phone before you've even got under the duvet most nights. What do you want me to do?'

I falter. That's not right, is it? But even as I'm wondering, I know it is. Didn't I confess exactly this to *The Cliterati*, when I sent my confession in? That most nights I couldn't be bothered? That it was easier to scroll on my phone than to initiate something?

Gretchen is regarding me inquisitively, like I'm a new species whose behaviour is quite interesting.

'I've been trying not to, recently,' I say weakly.

'Have you?' Theo shakes his head at me. 'You've been . . . different.'

'I've been trying,' I reply with a bit more force in my voice. 'I cooked a nice dinner for us.'

'And we had a lovely evening.'

'When I came to bed you were reading.'

This seems to make him pause. 'You're right,' he says after a moment. 'But you got into bed and immediately went on your phone again.'

I want to scream. I did, but that was after I'd tried everything I could think of to make him touch me. 'I tried to talk to you about a holiday.'

'And we did talk about it. We can't afford it, Lotts.'

'Does that mean we can't dream about it?' I ask, feeling lame even asking. 'Can't we even have ideas about things?'

'Of course we can.'

'Evidently not.'

'OK,' Gretchen interrupts. 'What I'm hearing is this, and correct me if I'm wrong. Lottie, you'd like more open and honest conversation with Theo, and the removal of some of those distracting life barriers that have come between you – phones, work, stress, and tiredness. Theo, it sounds like you want the same thing?'

No, shit, I haven't been clear enough. I've skirted around the topic too much and have been taken literally. I don't want to talk, I want to get nasty. How the hell do I bring that up now?

Theo sighs before I can interject. 'I do. But it's more than just a bit of life getting in the way,' he says, and my heart plummets. What is he about to say? Is he going to confess something awful – he's been cheating on me, he's leaving, he's been offered a job in Guatemala and can't say no? 'Things are just . . . off, recently. You're not yourself, Lottie. It's since that hen do, it's like . . . I don't know.' He looks unsure, hurt, and I feel a swooping rush of guilt. 'It feels like something's going on.'

'Nothing's going on,' I say quickly, forcefully. I grab his hands. 'Theo, nothing's going on. I just want us to go back to normal.'

He looks at me, his eyes searching mine as if they're looking for proof that I'm telling the truth. Jesus Christ, does he think I've cheated on him? At Jade's hen? All of this plotting behind his back, and me thinking he's completely oblivious. Of course he isn't oblivious. Of course he thinks I'm hiding something, and of course his mind has gone to the most obvious answer. I'm horrified.

'I swear to god,' I say, pulling his hands towards me. 'There's nothing. I'm just . . . I'm overthinking things. I want us to go back to how we used to be, and I'm trying too hard. It's making me weird.' I attempt a smile, and he returns it reluctantly.

'I'm sensing some real avoidance here,' Gretchen says softly. 'And that's not uncommon. Good communication doesn't come naturally to every couple. It's something we learn as we go, if we're willing to.'

I bite back my instinctive response: we *are* good communicators. We have talked about everything – from our decision not to have children to our deepest fears and beliefs. There isn't anything about me that Theo doesn't know, or anything about him that I don't know.

Or at least the latter part of that is true.

Although maybe that isn't, either.

Because maybe the truth is that we're good communicators as long as we're on the same page. As long as we're not communicating about something uncomfortable, that might get one of our backs up. We're good communicators as long as it's easy. The moment things get sore between us, there's no communication at all.

'I'd like to see you again next week,' Gretchen says, uncrossing and then recrossing her perfect legs. 'If that sounds good to you?'

Theo answers before I can even open my mouth. 'I'd like that very much,' he says.

*

If anyone could manage to go to counselling and emerge even more confused than ever, it would be me.

This week, my task was to attend couple's therapy with my husband, to try and get to the bottom of the issues that have led to our defunct sex life. The therapist diagnosed us with a chronic case of communication issues, which I resisted at first. We communicate brilliantly! We know everything about each other! But the fact of the matter is that, even in front of a therapist, even with so much on the line, I still couldn't admit to my husband what the problem was. I couldn't get the words 'Why won't you have sex with me?' out of my mouth. It felt too needy, too desperate, too humiliating. I managed to accidentally convince the therapist that we were just lacking one-on-one time instead.

Because while, yes, we might know everything about each other, we're very adept at swerving around anything in our way. We're like a river, furiously united until a rock is thrown into our path, at which point we split into two, lose sight of each other, and then come back together as if nothing ever happened. Until recently, I assumed that was good. I assumed it was healthy. Now, I realize it's probably a chronic case of avoidance.

So yeah, our therapist probably isn't far off base. It seems we suck at communicating in general.

One thing my husband did bring up is that I spend too much time on my phone. I feel like we're all guilty of that these days, and I didn't even realize I was doing it. It's embarrassing, having someone point out a habit of yours that you were unaware of. Embarrassing to think that they've been inwardly huffing about your behaviour without saying anything.

But it's also given me hope. Because now there's something I can do, something I have control over. I'll throw my phone into the nearest lake if it means reigniting the spark.

Watch this space.

Chapter Fourteen

63 Cross Street, 7 p.m. Wear something slutty x

Caro's text is as ominous as it is vague, yet here I am, walking down Cross Street at 6.57 p.m. wearing the too-short dress that failed to woo Theo the night of our romantic dinner and a pair of not-too-high heels. While I firmly believe women can wear any outfit at any age, I am in my mid-thirties and my days of being able to squat to pick things up in high heels while keeping my arse fully covered are behind me.

I can hear music coming from a few buildings ahead of me, and a glance at the door numbers beside me suggest it's my destination. I am not in the mood to be out – I've never felt less like partying – but the alternative is sitting at home with the dogs while Theo spends yet another evening at the gym with Dev. We had a brief chat last night after we got back from the therapist's office (needless to say we didn't go for the Thai meal) and ended up placating each other rather than actually getting anywhere.

He was unnervingly enthusiastic about the therapy, insisting we return; I managed to keep my phone away for the duration of the chat (twelve minutes) and promised to pay more attention to our marriage. But when we went upstairs, Theo went for a half-hour-long bathroom trip, and I got so bored that I watched a few TikToks until he came back. When I heard the bathroom door unlock, I threw my phone on the side and pretended I was asleep.

And that was that. We have successfully skirted around the whole issue, as we are evidently so skilled at doing.

As I approach, I spot Caro standing in the doorway of the building the music is coming out of, a half-finished cigarette between her plum-coloured lips. She looks incredible in a black leather skirt, fishnet tights and knee-high boots. Her camera hangs around her neck, resting on her ample cleavage. She is, as always, breathtaking.

'Wit woo,' she says when she sees me, looking me up and down.

'What the hell is going on?' I ask. And then, 'You look insane.'

She takes a mock bow and tosses her cigarette to the floor before grinding it under the heel of her boot. 'This, my friend, is an appendix.'

'You should put that in the bin,' I say.

'God, Lottie, no. We are not beginning the night self-righteously.' She kicks the cigarette end into a storm drain. 'Take that rod out of your arse and loosen up.'

I flick her my middle finger. 'What is this?' I ask again, peering beyond her to a dark stairwell leading downwards towards the music.

'It's Bring Your Friend to Work Day. Come on.'

She turns around and begins walking easily down the stairs, like she's wearing trainers rather than seven-inch platform boots. I hurry after her.

'What do you mean, an appendix?' I ask, raising my voice as the music gets louder.

'To your experiment,' she calls back over her shoulder. 'A little bonus exercise!'

Oh, god. 'Caro,' I say, tottering dangerously down the last few steps to try and catch up with her. 'I'm actually trying to get *away* from the experiment—'

The double doors Caro has just pushed her way through swing back in my face, and I huff irately as I push them back open. 'Caro, for fuck's—'

I stop in my tracks. Oh, sweet Christ. What fresh hell is this?

I've found myself at the back of a vast theatre, tiered rows of mostly empty seats stepping down towards a stage. The lighting is a dim red, and there's pulsing music pounding from speakers I can't see.

And there, on the stage . . .

I widen my eyes, feeling like I've walked in on something I shouldn't be seeing. On a chair sits a naked man, his hands tied in front of him, and standing behind him, a riding crop in her hand, is a woman wearing some extremely nice underwear.

'Close your mouth, you'll catch flies.' Caro has appeared beside me, and she's grinning.

'OK, I know Tilly's made me do some mad things,' I reply, not taking my eyes off the stage, 'but there is *no* way I'm getting Theo in this room.'

'Of course not! This is inspiration, Lottie.'

'For . . .'

She takes my arm and yanks me towards the bar behind us. 'Two Slippery Nipples, please,' she says to the barman before turning back to me. 'Be honest with me.'

I lean against the bar, doing my utmost to pretend that I am totally unfazed by all this, that my inner prude isn't screaming and covering her eyes. 'Always.'

'You and Theo strike me as a very vanilla couple.'

'I'm not sure there's a question there.'

'Well, are you?'

'Two Slippery Nipples.' The barman places two shot glasses on the bar. Caro picks hers up and nods to me, and I roll my eyes before throwing mine back.

'So?' Caro says, not even wincing.

I cough. 'Define vanilla.'

'Oh, god. If you even have to ask . . . Do you ever get out of the missionary position?'

'Yes! Well, at the moment, we don't even get *into* the missionary position . . .'

'Well, yeah. What about kinky stuff? A bit of light bondage? Role play?'

The thought makes me cringe. 'No.'

'Would you *like* to?'

'I've never thought about it.'

'Liar.'

I turn away from her, fixing my gaze on the stage. The man is now on his hands and knees, the woman pushing her crotch against his face.

'Jesus,' I say.

'Oh, shit.' Caro picks up her camera and takes a few shots, before letting it drop. 'I promised her I'd get some good ones of the cunnilingus.'

'What *is* this?'

'FemDom night,' she replies easily. 'Extremely private, members only.'

'We just walked right in.'

'Gav's on a fag break,' she shrugs. 'He won't mind me bringing you, though. As long as you have a go.' She clocks the expression on my face and bursts out laughing. '*Kidding.*'

I slap her arm. 'So this is what you're into?' I ask. 'Domination?'

Caro cocks her head, her eyes on the stage. 'Not really,' she says thoughtfully. 'Though I can see the appeal.'

'What makes you think I'd like it?'

She shrugs. 'Nothing. I have no idea if this is your bag. But everyone's got something.'

I drag my gaze away from the front and turn back to the bartender, who is wiping the counter languidly like he's doing the Monday shift at Wetherspoons, not pouring Slippery Nipples while a woman sits on a man's face twenty metres away. 'Can I have a glass of white wine, please? Any will do.'

'I'll go red,' Caro says. 'Fits the theme.'

When we've got our drinks, I scan the shadowy stalls below for an empty seat. 'Shall we sit down?'

Caro grimaces. 'I wouldn't.'

I frown, squinting again into the gloom. It's so dark in here, I can't see anything. 'What are they doing down there?'

She looks down at her camera screen, and for a moment, I don't think she's heard me. I open my mouth to repeat the question, but she thrusts the camera in my face. 'Here are some I took earlier.'

'Ah,' I say as she flicks through flash-lit pictures of couples in the seats below us engaged in activities I can barely even fathom. In almost all cases, the man is sitting or kneeling, the woman looming over him dressed in some kind of themed, slutty outfit: a nurse's uniform, army garb – in one instance, a full wolf costume. I say a silent prayer of thanks for the music, which I'm sure is covering up noises I don't want to hear. 'Yeah, no, I'm OK standing.'

Caro keeps flicking through the pictures, but I grab her wrist. 'Wait. Go back one.'

She flicks back, and I pull the camera closer to me. In the picture, a man is bending over a chair, and a woman is standing behind him, a paddle in her hand. She's wearing a half cat mask, and as the picture is being taken, she's turning towards the camera and pulling it down onto her face. My heart thumps uncomfortably. 'Jesus Christ,' I whisper.

'What?'

'That's Jade.'

Caro grabs the camera and peers at it. 'No fucking way. I thought I recognized her!' She looks at me, grinning in delight. 'Well *this* explains her penchant for dominating you.'

'She does not dominate me!' I retort instinctively.

'Wait . . . isn't Jade getting married in like . . . a month?'

'Two,' I correct, feeling sick.

'Hey, don't look so horrified. It's healthy. She and her fiancé have a very interesting marriage ahead of them.'

I look at the photo one last time, and then shake my head. 'That's not her fiancé.'

Caro winces. 'Oh, shit.'

I take a steadying sip of my wine. 'Maybe it's not her. It's a bit blurry; she was pulling her mask down.'

'Well, I've got some more pictures to take. Why don't we go and have a look?'

'No, Caro—'

But it's too late; she's already stalking off towards the side staircase. I clop after her, my wine sloshing in my glass. 'Caro!' I hiss, but she either doesn't hear me or chooses to pretend she hasn't.

I follow her down the staircase. At this level, I can hear some grunting, and I keep my eyes trained forward.

Caro stops every so often, asking questions and taking photos; I pause alongside her, inspecting the dimly lit posters on the wall. An Oasis tribute band is apparently playing here next Saturday. I am certain that whoever cleans this place is not paid well enough. We set off again, and then, about halfway down, Caro stops. 'There,' she says, pointing down the row.

I squint – the woman in the cat mask is about halfway along the row, a flickering light illuminating the exposed part of her face, and it looks like she's dripping something onto the naked back of her partner. I tell myself it's honey, maybe some extra virgin olive oil. Now *there's* a kink I could get behind.

'Come on,' Caro says, but I grab her arm.

'I can't!' I hiss loudly over the music. 'What if it's Jade and she sees me?'

Caro, to her credit, gives this some thought. 'OK, stay here. I'll go and ask if I can take some photographs, then we can go back up to the bar and check.'

'I'm going back up *now*,' I say firmly.

'Suit yourself. I'll meet you up there.'

I climb back up the stairs quicker than I thought I was capable of. I tug my short dress down at the back instinctively as I climb, before remembering where I am and accepting that really, my plain black knickers are probably the least interesting thing in this entire room.

Upstairs, I lean against the bar and take a gulp of my wine.

'First time?' The bartender is drying glasses now. His eyes look tired. Haunted, perhaps?

'Yeah. I mean, I'm not visiting. I'm not like . . . I didn't know I was coming here. My friend dragged me along.'

'Caro? Yeah, not much fazes her.'

'Doesn't it faze you?' I ask him. 'Must be weird, doing your regular job while all this is going on.'

He shrugs. 'I do the adult baby nights here, too. You get desensitized after a while.'

I ponder this, and find myself feeling quite sad about it. I can't imagine seeing so much debauchery that nothing does it for me any more.

Oh, god – what if that's what's wrong with Theo? What if he's watched so much porn, real sex doesn't do it for him any more? That's a thing, isn't it?

'You not into all this, then?' The bartender asks, gesturing vaguely towards the stage.

'No,' I say, making up my mind. The idea of tying Theo up and spanking him with our never-used table-tennis bats makes me feel decidedly un-horny. But I do wonder whether there's something to the point Caro is evidently trying to make. I've been trying to put the spark back into my marriage, to get us back to where we used to be, but what if where we used to be just doesn't cut it any more? What if those honeymoon hormones only carried us so far?

What if I need to spice things up in a more extreme way? Forget the tame lingerie and the candles – do I need to next-day-delivery a strap-on?

'Phew.' Caro arrives and throws herself against the bar. 'Sweaty down there.'

'Another?' the bartender asks.

'Go on then, Mick. Cheers.'

'Well?' I ask once he's turned away to prepare her wine.

'She let me take a few more pictures of her with her mask on. Sometimes, people say no to pictures, or they ask for their faces to be blurred. But if someone's got a mask, they're usually fine with it. I think some of them get a kick out of it.' She taps at her camera and then passes it to me. 'Have a look.'

'I feel weird,' I say, not looking. 'It feels like an invasion of privacy.'

'She knows the photos are going on the website, and it's not like she's naked.'

'No, but she thinks nobody knows who she is.'

'Maybe it *isn't* her. What if you don't look, and you walk out of here thinking you've caught your old school friend pegging some bloke who isn't her fiancé, and it's not even her?'

She has a point. If I'm going to feel uncomfortable around Jade for the rest of time, at least let me confirm I have reason to. I take the camera from her and look more closely.

I was right – the woman is pouring something onto the man's back. It's candle wax, and he's covered in it. Her blonde hair, up in a ponytail behind the mask, could be Jade's.

'The balayage is familiar,' I say. 'But then everyone has that balayage, don't they?'

'Same body type,' Caro observes.

'I can't say I've ever seen her in a corseted one-piece with a custom tail on it before,' I say, 'so I couldn't—' I stop.

'What?'

Shit. I fiddle with the camera buttons and zoom in to the woman's left shoulder blade. There's no doubt – it's Jade.

'Is that a tattoo?' Caro asks, peering at the screen.

'It's her dead dog's initials,' I confirm. 'She got it when we were in sixth form.'

'Her dead dog had *initials*?'

'Shit, Caro,' I say, pushing the camera back into her hands. 'What the hell do I do now?'

Chapter Fifteen

'It's champagne, isn't it? You can all see that, right? It's champagne.'

In a chorus of enthusiastically bobbing heads, the girls around the table nod their agreement. We're at Jade's pre-Big Day logistics meeting, and the bride-to-be is holding up a swatch of her wedding-dress fabric and waving it over a half-empty breakfast margarita.

It's definitely pink.

'What do you think, Lottie?'

Shit. Jade is looking right at me. I didn't want to come today, but I couldn't bring myself to cancel last-minute. I've had two margaritas already and it isn't even 1 p.m. – do I tell her, or do I not?

I already know I won't.

'Champagne,' I manage, nodding definitively. 'It's a beautiful champagne shade.'

'*Thank* you,' she says, sitting back in her chair. I note that her mother is absent today, and I wonder whether she really won't be invited to the actual wedding, after all. The whole thing is evidently getting on top of Jade, and we are all feeling the ripple effects, like the blast zone after a nuclear meltdown. There's something in the air, like at any moment she could burst into tears or start screaming. She's already done both twice, and we've only been here an hour.

I watch her as she turns to Holly-the-feet-pics-girl next to her and begins showing her something on her phone. If I look closely, will I see the lines where the elastic from Jade's cat mask dug in behind her ears?

I've wondered over the last few days whether Jade's fiancé, Matt, knows about her extramarital activities. Jade has an incredibly healthy sex life; we've all heard the stories. She and Matt are at it non-stop, their libidos aligning perfectly, and I know she's the envy of most of the girls in this room. Maybe they're adventurous; or maybe it's the freedom they give each other that keeps the spark alive. But I can't shake the feeling that Jade was doing something secretive that evening; the mask, and the extremely exclusive club . . . my instinct tells me Matt doesn't know anything about it, and that makes me feel all sorts of conflicted.

And if I'm right, it raises another anxiety for me to add to the list. If Matt doesn't know what Jade gets up to, *why* is she going elsewhere for her kicks? Does he not satisfy her urges, or share her kink?

What if Theo has a kink? What if the reason he's not interested in me is because our well-practised routine – usually under the duvet, and invariably once I've gulped down my contraceptive pill and put my nighttime pimple patches on – isn't cutting the mustard? What if he's going elsewhere, whiling away his evenings in sweaty basement dungeons getting candle wax dripped onto his newly toned back?

'Another margarita?' Holly's best best best friend, who strangely couldn't get a seat next to Holly and so has been shoved next to me, asks, her chin propped on her hand. She looks bored and irritated and moderately drunk.

'Keep 'em coming,' I say. She signals for the waiter and orders our drinks, then turns back to me.

'So. How are . . . things?'

'Good, good,' I reply. Neither of us know the first thing about each other, and anything we do know is buried under the eight shots of sambuca we each consumed at Jade's hen party. 'You?'

'Fine,' she says tersely, her eyes on Holly.

'Have you two had a falling out?' I ask nosily. The margaritas really are going to my head.

'No,' she snaps, and then quickly changes the subject, asking, 'Have you chosen your dress?'

Jade has given us a link to a website that sells bridesmaid dresses in a variety of colours and styles. She's chosen a pastel lilac for her bridal party, which makes the other bridesmaids' skin look like porcelain and makes me look like I've got jaundice. 'I'm going to go for the spaghetti straps, I think.'

Holly's friend pouts. 'I was thinking of going for that one.'

'We can both wear the same dress, can't we?'

She shakes her head. 'Jade wants us all different. Never mind. I wanted the strapless but Holly has chosen that one.'

She looks so pitiful, I actually feel sorry for her. 'You know what? I'll go for the capped sleeves. You have the spaghetti straps.'

For the first time, she looks at me. 'Really?'

'Of course.'

She visibly brightens, and as the waiter puts our fresh drinks in front of us, she shifts on her seat so she's facing me properly. God, why can't I remember her name? Why am I so awful at remembering names?

'Have you heard about the honeymoon?' she asks conspiratorially, taking a sip of her margarita.

'They're going to India, aren't they?'

She leans in, bringing with her a waft of salt and lime. 'She told Holly they might cancel it.'

'What? Why?'

She holds her palms up and raises her eyebrows. 'That's all I know.'

'Melissa!' Holly calls from the other end of the table, and the girl jerks away, flushing. 'What's the name of that place with the flaming sushi?'

Melissa immediately pulls out her phone and I watch as she taps into a favourites tab called 'Eats' and searches for the restaurant. On the other side of the table, Jade stands up and makes her way over to our side, doing her hostess rounds.

My heart rate increases as she makes a beeline for me. Immediately, all I can see is her blonde hair tied back behind a cat mask, holding a paddle aloft over the exposed arse of a man who is not her betrothed.

'Lottie,' she says, wrapping her arm around me. 'Have you picked a dress yet?'

'Mm-hmm, yep,' I say, swallowing. Can I smell candle wax? 'Capped sleeves.'

She pulls back. 'Aw, I think Jessica's chosen that one.'

'Oh. What's left?'

'The high-neck.' She beams, even though we all know the high-neck is the ugliest.

Great. I want to query why she even bothered asking me, considering I've already been assigned the last choice, but I smile instead. I'm still not entirely sure why I'm even a part of this bridal party, so I don't have a huge amount of skin in the game. Might as well just roll with it. I push down Caro's voice in the back of my mind – *she walks all over you*. 'Perfect.'

She claps her hands. 'Amazing! We're all sorted, then. Oh, that's such a relief.' She reaches for the drink she brought with her and winces, rubbing her bicep.

'Cramp?' I ask.

'No, just a bit sore, I . . .' She shakes her head, as if catching herself. 'Matt and I got a bit carried away the other night, if you know what I mean.'

The urge to ask some prying questions is sudden and strong, brought on by margaritas and the constant loop of thoughts about Jade I've had in the back of my mind since the kink dungeon the other night. Jade isn't my best friend in the world, but I care about her, and if she's not happy in her relationship, she shouldn't be getting married. But this is her pre-Big Day drinks, and I don't know the truth. I know what I've assumed, and I could be completely wrong. Is it any of my business?

'Oh, god.' One of the other girls slams her glass down. 'Do *not* make us all jealous again, Jade.'

Jade smiles and widens her eyes, feigning innocence. 'I have no idea what you're talking about.'

'Honestly, ten years and you're still all over each other,' Holly sighs, having joined us in our cluster at the end of the table. A jolt runs through me. Me and Theo have been together for less time; where did things go wrong for us? If Matt doesn't know what Jade's doing – and Jade is the envy of every woman here – what does that say about Theo and me? We were the golden couple, the one everyone thought was perfect. Jade is cheating on Matt, and if he has no idea, what have I potentially been missing? Holly carries on, 'I was listening to *The Cliterati* the other day; you know they're launching a whole series about sexless marriages now?'

My heart begins hammering for a different reason.

'You were asking us about that anonymous listener who wrote in at the dress fitting,' Holly says, her eyes boring into me. 'Weren't you?'

'You shouldn't marry someone you don't want to fuck every day,' Jade says definitively, saving me from responding. I can feel my cheeks pulsing with heat. 'It should be the baseline.'

'Ugh, I'm not sure I could cope with every *day*.' Melissa grimaces.

'Well that's how marriages implode,' Jade says self-righteously, as if she hasn't been married for a grand total of zero days. 'If you don't keep each other satisfied at home, one of you is going to go looking elsewhere.'

'Well there's no worry of that happening to you,' I find myself saying – anything to keep us straying further from *The Cliterati*.

There's a pause; so tiny, you'd miss it unless you were looking for it. And then Jade smiles. 'No. Definitely not.'

*

Theo and I are watching an old episode of *Benidorm*, at opposite ends of the sofa with the dogs curled up between us.

I say we're watching *Benidorm*; in reality, I'm watching Theo, who is watching his phone. Every few minutes, it lights up on the arm of the sofa and he grabs it, tapping quickly at the keyboard. We're halfway through the episode and he's replied to four messages already. I can feel a weird sort of emotion growing inside me – something primal and born of weeks of frustration.

'Ha!' I laugh loudly at something on the screen, though I have no idea what was just said. Theo jumps, flicking his eyes to me and then to the TV. He grins and laughs.

Is he hiding something?

I pick up my own phone. I've been trying to leave it in the kitchen, to actually be present in my relationship since our chat with the therapist, but now Theo appears to be breaking his own rules. I'm shocked and not just a little bit ashamed of how angry I feel. Theo is an incredible person; my best friend. I don't want to start resenting him. I need to work harder, move quicker. I'm not doing enough. I load up my latest email from Isa. It came through this morning, and I've been putting off responding, guilt gnawing at me. But now, as I reread it, I feel a swell of motivation rise in my throat.

Hi Lottie,

Tilly is just getting the last bits of your next task finished up, so should have details with you by tomorrow at the latest. In the meantime, I wanted to come to you with something pretty huge and see what you thought . . .

The first two episodes of the podcast are now edited, and we've played them to some pretty big people in the business, who have given us their feedback. Needless to say, they're blown away. They're predicting really big things from the series — they seem pretty hopeful at least one episode will be a multi-week chart topper! They've had a good look at Tilly's Instagram engagement since the announcement (and subsequent teaser posts) and listeners are really excited, so they anticipate this getting big on release.

Here's where things get interesting for you — it was suggested during a recent meeting that you and Tilly joint-pitch a book idea. Tilly has some good friends in publishing, and from putting some preliminary feelers out we can see there's quite a bit of interest. Obviously the conclusion of the podcast isn't written yet (though we very much hope it's a brand-new, sex-positive life for you and your husband, as that would really get our ratings up), but publishing is notoriously slow and if we want the book to come out before the podcast series is ancient history, we need to get the wheels in motion now. This would be a joint venture with you and Tilly, with you providing the anecdotal structure and Tilly providing the technical background and research, and I'm told an advance could be rather significant (split between the two of you — although of course weighted more favourably towards Tilly, seeing as she's bringing the technical expertise), as well as subsequent royalties.

So . . . what do you think? Exciting, right?!

> *Let me know ASAP,*
> *Isa*
> *PS We think this would work best if we 'unveil' you at the book cover reveal. People are already speculating about who you are, and this kind of big unmasking would be a great marketing tool. A promise like this would really drive up the advance, too. Every publisher wants to be the one that reveals the identity of a mystery person the internet is going crazy over!*

And then I swipe through to the other email, the one that came through from Tilly an hour or so after Isa's.

> *Hey Lottie,*
>
> *I know Isa's been in touch re: the potential book deal, and I know you're probably freaking out a bit. She's come in all guns blazing from the financial side (there's a reason I hired her – she's very good) but I wanted to send a quick note to reassure you that I'm thinking a bit bigger. The impact a story like yours could have on people who are struggling with the same issue you have can't be underestimated. I know from the work I do with my clients that many women feel very lonely in their relationship issues (I'm sure this is something you relate to) and that just hearing that they aren't the only one going through it is often the most helpful thing.*
>
> *There's an opportunity here for you to be the face of something big – to be the woman who steps out and says, 'No one's talking about this, let's change that.' It's scary, yes, but it's also profoundly brave and impactful.*
>
> *But if you don't want to do it, that's fine, too. The agency Isa works for actually owns the podcast (it's a very complicated and boring story) but I've always wanted* The Cliterati *to be run*

with authenticity and community in mind, not pound signs and whatever's trending. This is your decision, and it has to feel right to you. If it doesn't, I'm more than used to taking the heat from her, so I'll handle it.

If you need a chat, just let me know. I'm on the end of the phone whenever you need.

Tilly xx

Just reading both emails again makes my heart thump with nerves and horror. Imagining a world in which my face, my name and identity, are revealed to thousands of people as the woman behind the infamous sexless marriage makes me want to crawl into a hole and never come out.

But.

There's also a frisson of excitement running through me – there's the money, of course, but there's also the chance to be involved in something exciting. Something big. Something that could, if I do it well, make an actual difference to people's lives. That's all I've ever tried to do at the arts centre, and while I know I made an impact to a few individuals back before Petra took over, it wasn't much. My entire life has been small by my own design, and I'm struck by a sudden, insane urge to be reckless for once.

I look up at Theo, who is tapping at his phone again, a small smile playing on his face. There's that feeling again, bubbling under the surface, something potent and intense. It's the feeling of noticing that someone's drowning, and there's a life raft right next to you. The feeling of seeing a car crash about to happen, and stepping in to stop it. It's a feeling of power, of having the ability to save something precious placed in my hands.

Our relationship is worth fighting for, and I'm tired of feeling like the rejected party, sitting on the sidelines and waiting for things to happen for me.

The credits for *Benidorm* roll, and Theo doesn't notice.

I tap 'reply' on Isa's email, copying in Tilly.

Hi Isa and Tilly,
 I'd love to meet and chat about this. When are you free?
 All best,
 Lottie

*

'Tilly! Over here, Tilly!'

I gasp as something is thrown over my head, blinding me, and a hand grabs my arm, yanking me to the side. I stumble as I'm pulled across pavement and then grass, the noise of people shouting Tilly's name fading into the distance. And then everything goes quiet, and I'm released.

I scrabble at my face, yanking something soft off my head. It's an orange scarf – the one Isa was wearing thirty seconds ago. I blink in the darkness; we're in some kind of boarded-up pavilion in the park, and it stinks of wee. Isa stands in front of me, swearing, and when I turn around, Tilly is at the pavilion's opening, peering outside.

'I think they've gone,' she says, turning back to us.

'What the fuck, Tilly,' Isa seethes. 'Meeting at the park? What if they got a picture?'

'They didn't,' Tilly says, but she looks unsure. 'We were too far away.'

I only got to the park five minutes ago and already I'm wishing I'd stayed at home. I waited for Tilly and Isa to arrive at our pre-agreed meeting spot on the bench near the entrance gate, and had just said hello when someone with a camera started chasing us.

'No one was bothered when we met in the hotel bar,' I say confusedly. 'Why now?'

'People want to know who you are. TikTok sleuths are going mad over it. If Lottie's identity gets leaked,' Isa points to me, 'we're halving that advance. Do you understand that?'

'I'm more concerned about how *Lottie* might feel. I'm so sorry,' Tilly turns to me. 'Isa's right, meeting here was a really stupid idea.'

Isa sniffs. 'It stinks in here.'

I give Tilly what I hope is a reassuring smile, but my heart is hammering. 'I thought I'd been kidnapped for a moment.'

'Ha,' Isa says, yanking her scarf from me and wrapping it back around her neck. 'We can't discuss this here,' she adds, moving her shiny black shoe away from a broken needle on the floor. 'Honestly, Tilly, what were you thinking?'

'I thought we could walk and talk,' she says to me apologetically. 'This is my hometown, they're used to seeing me. I didn't think anyone would bat an eyelid.'

Isa taps at her phone, ignoring her. 'Right, here's what we're going to do. I'm going to leave with Tilly and get into a taxi, and I'm going to have it circle the park until I'm sure we're not being followed. Lottie, when I call you, come out and get in the car with us.'

'Right,' I say. 'So . . . sorry, you want me to stay in here by myself?'

'I don't see another way, I'm afraid. We can hardly walk out of here together.'

'God, Isa,' Tilly hisses. 'Lottie, *you* go and get in the taxi. Have it circle the park a couple of times; we'll wait here and join you in five minutes.'

'Right, so—'

'Silver Prius,' Isa instructs, taking my arm and pulling me towards the door as she rattles off the numberplate. 'Go, go, go!'

Then suddenly, I'm running across the park. I'm not sure *why* I'm running, but I've started, and I can't seem to stop. The grass is soggy under my boots, and a couple of times I skid, righting myself at the last moment. When I get to the gates, breathless, there's an Uber matching the description Isa gave me idling by the kerb. I open the door. 'For Isa?' I ask.

'Yup,' the driver says, and I slide in the back seat. I lean back against the headrest a moment, panting.

'Sorry, love,' the driver says. 'It's got both the pick-up and drop-off locations listed as . . . here. Where are you going?'

I feel like a bank robber in a cheap 90s movie. What the hell am I doing? 'Can you circle the park a couple of times, please?' I ask embarrassedly. 'Sorry. It's . . .'

'Oh, no need for explanations,' he says, setting off. 'I've done this before. Dodgy ex, is it?'

My head is too scrambled for me to formulate a proper response. 'Something like that.'

Evidently sensing my reluctance to engage in conversation, he does two laps of the park in silence. I look out of the window, feeling now like a member of the royal family on a tour of some dilapidated Victorian park.

It's right then that I have one of those moments, like I've

zoomed out and am watching myself from above. How did I *get* here? I was a happily married woman with a steady job, a comfortable routine, and a good idea of where I was going in life. Now, I'm in the back of a taxi evading paparazzi on behalf of a famous podcast host with whom I'm meeting to discuss a potential millionaire-making book deal while my wonderful husband, who has done absolutely nothing wrong aside from stop 'jumping me', sits at home none the wiser. What the hell am I doing?

I hiccup a laugh, and the driver turns around. 'You all right, love? Not going to be sick, are you?'

I shake my head. We round the final corner of the park a second time and the gates come into view. Isa and Tilly are waiting on the kerb, and I can already see that a woman with her pram has stopped just behind them and has pulled out her phone to snap a picture.

'If we could just pick these two up, please,' I ask. 'They'll tell you where we're going.'

He pulls up, and Tilly and Isa walk to opposite sides of the car and slide in the back, forcing me to squish myself in the middle. 'Right,' Tilly says, pulling out a compact mirror and inspecting her purple-lined eyes. 'Could you take us to 24 Peter Street, please?'

The driver puts the car in gear, glancing at us in the rear-view. 'You three all right?'

'Peachy, thanks,' Isa says curtly, and he raises his eyebrows and looks back to the road.

We set off, and I wonder what exactly we'll find at 24 Peter Street. This morning, I took the train half an hour out of my tiny hometown to this park in the place where Tilly grew up.

I've never been here before, but it doesn't look like the kind of place where there are hidden gems bougie enough for the likes of Tilly Carter.

'Do you come home often?' I ask for something to say. My thighs are squished together, Isa and Tilly pressing into me from either side with every turn.

'Most weekends,' Tilly says. 'I like the familiarity. London is so hectic.'

I'm surprised by this; Tilly strikes me as the kind of woman who's out every evening with her gorgeous husband, being fabulous at the best new places nobody else has managed to get into yet. But as we drive down the dull March streets, tired-looking Victorian semis whizzing past us, I wonder if I've read her wrong.

'Tilly is a contradiction,' Isa says flatly, as if she's read my mind.

Tilly smiles. 'I suppose I am a bit. I'm neither a homebird nor a party animal. I'm a bit of both. Right, here we are.'

The driver pulls up outside a terraced house like any other, with a neat front garden and little window boxes full of purple spring blooms.

We get out of the car and Tilly pushes the gate open with a squeak. We follow her up the front path, Tilly ahead, me in the middle, Isa following with her head bowed over her phone, typing furiously. I get the feeling she's been here before.

'Mum, I'm back!' Tilly calls as she unlocks the door and swings it open. 'Come in,' she says, stepping back to let me pass into the hallway.

Immediately, I feel my jaw drop. The house is like a bazaar, a treasure trove of trinkets and antiques displayed with organized chaos that feels homely and inviting and captivating all at once. The walls of the hallway are lined with beautiful clocks in tens of different styles, their pendulums ticking out of sync with one another; on a credenza to my left, there's a collection of thimbles, paperweights and origami cranes in bright colours. The walls are sage green with tiny daisies printed across the paper, and the worn rug on the floor is covered in leaping rabbits. I want to stop and look at everything more closely, but before I can, Tilly leads us through into the sitting room.

'Hello, love.' A woman in her late sixties is sitting on an ancient orange corduroy sofa, knitting needles in her hands and a long, multicoloured blanket pooling by her feet. 'Who've we got here, then?'

'This is Lottie,' Tilly says, and I wave and say hello.

'Ah, Lottie!' The woman smiles. 'I'm Esther. I've heard a lot about you. Have you had yourself a good rogering yet, my love?'

'Mum!' Tilly grabs my elbow and steers me back towards the hallway where Isa is waiting. 'You can see where I get it from,' she says, and I laugh. 'We'll be in the kitchen!' she calls back over her shoulder. 'If you want a cup of tea, say so now because I'm only boiling the kettle once!'

Tilly's mother doesn't reply, so we traipse into the kitchen, where a round table adorned in a patchwork tablecloth sits under a wide window overlooking the back garden. 'Take a seat,' Tilly says. 'I'll get some sustenance sorted.'

I can't believe I'm in Tilly Carter's family home. It's exactly what I imagined, but also the total opposite. Tilly is eccentric and kind and earthy, just like this house, but she's also a celebrity: made for city-centre apartments and expensive designer kitchens, not homemade doilies and a kettle shaped like a frog. Isa's right – she is a contradiction.

After a moment, Tilly puts a mug of tea in front of each of us, as well as a plate of thick white toast, lavished with melting butter. Isa glances up and then returns to her phone.

Tilly sits down, takes a sip of her tea, and closes her eyes for a moment. 'Right,' she says when she opens them again. 'Isa, do you want to fill Lottie in?'

Isa finishes typing, then finally puts her phone down. 'Right.' She props her elbows on the table. 'So, first of all, Lottie, we are very happy that you want to work with us on this book pitch.'

I try to interject, but I've just taken a mouthful of hot buttery toast, and I don't manage to swallow in time before she soldiers on.

'And we're obviously extremely excited for the unveiling, which we'll be pitching to publishers as a marketing strategy in the first instance. Tilly's got a contact at HarperCollins who is desperate to be shown the idea first, so we'll give her twenty-four hours to respond before sending it wider. Then, ideally, a bidding war. Now, in terms of the cut, obviously your contribution will be less significant, so we'd be looking at an eighty–twenty split for Tilly and yourself respectively. How does all that sound?'

I swallow. I'd been so sure the other evening, so desperate to reconnect with Theo by any means necessary (aside from, you know, having an adult conversation about it), but that fuck-it moment hasn't stuck around. I'm now panicking.

'What's the whole . . . idea?' I manage to ask. All this talk of money and pitching and marketing, and I have no idea what the book's actually about.

'It's a sort of companion to the series. It'll be your notes and reflections on the experiment alongside Tilly's expertise to back it up or offer explanations for things you might have felt throughout.'

I suddenly feel extremely uncomfortable. My skin prickles under my winter layers, my face heating up. I've allowed myself to be led into many situations in my life without asking enough questions – I wouldn't be sitting here now if I hadn't – and I need this to not be another one.

'It seems like I'd be putting quite a bit on the line,' I say unsurely. 'It's a lot of exposure. And everyone knowing who I am . . .'

'Fine, seventy–thirty. You've twisted my arm!' Isa laughs, glancing at Tilly. But Tilly isn't smiling; she's watching me over her tea, her face unreadable. 'That's fine, isn't it, Tilly?' Isa asks, but it doesn't sound like a question.

'Lottie has something to say,' Tilly says, sitting back, her gaze still fixed on me.

'What? No, I . . .' I trail off. Tilly doesn't break eye contact, just watches me, like a police officer waiting for a suspect to crack. I swallow. 'I just . . . I'm not sure the experiment's going the way I hoped.' I feel guilty immediately. Here I am, sat in Tilly's kitchen, having accepted not only her hospitality but her money and her help, too, and I've let her down. 'I mean, it's great. A fantastic idea. But I think it's me, I think maybe there's something broken in our relationship, and it's not the experiment's fault, it's ours. Maybe we're just not suitable candidates or . . . I don't know.'

Isa goes to interject, but Tilly holds her ringed hand up. 'She's not finished.'

I blink, taking a breath. 'I'm just not sure what I could write about. I feel like you want this happy ending, a sort of perfect narrative or a plan or something that other people can copy, something that might help people. Or at least I think that's what you want. And I'd love to help people. I'd love to be the bright, shiny redemption story and bring hope to other couples in similar situations. But I don't think that's how this is going to go. I don't think we're going to get back to how we were, no matter how much Tantra and lingerie and yoni steaming we throw at it. I just . . . I feel hopeless, and I can't lie to people. I can't pretend all of this is fixable when I don't know if it is.' To my horror, I feel a fat tear roll down my hot cheek. I swipe at it with the back of my hand. 'Theo doesn't . . .' I realize with a jolt that I'm about to confess my other secret: that Theo doesn't know about any of this. I haven't made it explicit in my write-ups, so they'd need to read between the lines to uncover the truth. I'm lying to everybody, but if I come clean now, what will they think of me? 'Never mind,' I sniffle lamely.

Tilly doesn't speak for a moment. She just keeps watching me, her gaze steady. Then she leans forward and puts her hands on the table.

'Fifty–fifty if I can fix your marriage,' she says. 'And if I can't, the deal's off.'

Isa starts, her eyebrows shooting up. 'Tilly, no, we—'

'They're my terms,' she says, snapping her eyes to Isa in warning. She looks back to me. 'All or nothing. What do you say?'

Chapter Sixteen

I don't know if it's the stress, the frustration, or the new world I'm suddenly immersed in, but it's like my husband has morphed into an entirely different person. Maybe it's just my perspective; maybe it's me that's changed, and he's exactly the same. But there's something distant and untouchable about him, and him not wanting me makes me feel simultaneously rejected and like I'm on the chase. I feel like I'm twenty-one again and the guy I fancy is giving me the cold shoulder. He's taken on this out-of-reach quality that makes me feel small, but also makes him seem more desirable, like a prize I want to win.

'Hey.'

I quickly minimize the email I'm composing and look up from the computer. Theo is leaning against the doorframe, wearing loose linen trousers and a shirt with the top three buttons undone. His feet are bare. Boodle stands up from where he's been curled around my feet and sniffs at Theo's toes.

'You OK?' I ask.

'What you doing?'

He doesn't say it like an accusation, but it feels like one. I've been replying to Isa's email about my latest challenge, the one Tilly is certain will fix things, and providing them with an update about how I'm feeling for the podcast. It seems impossible that he can't see the guilt on my face.

'Nothing,' I reply.

He steps into the room. 'We're seeing the therapist again tomorrow, remember.'

I nod. 'Yeah.'

'Anything you want to discuss?' He sits on the edge of the desk, his large hand pressed against its surface. His wedding band glints under the light of the computer, and I'm hit with that strange feeling I get every so often – this man chose to marry me.

'Don't think so,' I say lightly. 'You?'

He doesn't reply for a moment. Instead, he looks into my eyes, like he's trying to see what I'm thinking. I force myself to hold his gaze. 'You'll always be honest with me, right?' he asks softly. He's trying to hide it, but I can hear the undercurrent of vulnerability in his voice; the hope. I feel like I might explode with guilt.

I have to reply quickly – any hesitation will send alarm bells ringing – but I can't lie. 'If you think I'm seeing someone else, I promise you I'm not.'

I've already decided how I'm going to handle all this. If and when the experiment finally works, I'll come clean to Theo and tell him about the book idea. He'll be angry, I'm sure, but when he hears about the money, I'm almost certain he'll tell me to go for it. If the experiment doesn't work, he'll be none the wiser. Both eventualities make me sick with anxiety – either I have to admit everything, or I have to face the very real possibility that my marriage might not survive. Or both.

He sighs. 'I know. God, I don't know why I feel so . . .' He looks lost for a second. 'Is paranoid too strong a word?'

Any thoughts I might have harboured that Theo was doing something surreptitious behind my back vanish – he's not that good a liar. God, I hate myself. 'No. You're right, I have been different. It's not you. You're not going mad.' I can't gaslight him; I can't tell him what he's feeling isn't completely valid. But I can't tell him what I'm feeling either, not now – I'm in too deep.

'Anything I can do to help?' he asks, and I know he's being delicate on purpose. He doesn't want to ask the question directly in case he gets an answer he doesn't like.

'A hug?' I say, surprising myself. But truly, it's all I want right now: a hug from my best friend. A reduction in intimacy has been a reduction in all forms of contact, and it's easy to forget the less taboo, everyday ones.

He doesn't hesitate. He slides off the desk and gets to his knees in front of my chair, wrapping his arms around me and pulling me forward, so that my chin is resting on his shoulder. I squeeze him, breathing in the familiar, comforting scent of him, his warm breath in my hair. I've missed this so much, the warm closeness of him, our bodies pressed together. It's really not just the sex, I realize – it's all the physical touch I've been starved of, and this hug feels like the sweetest luxury, like sinking into a warm bath.

And then he kisses my neck.

This time, *I* don't hesitate. Instinctively, I lift my head, giving him freer access. He trails kisses up to my jaw, then across until his lips land on mine. It's not a tentative peck – the kisses we've been exchanging for the last few months. He parts my lips with his tongue and then we're properly kissing, our breath mingling, and my hands are in his hair.

His hands travel slowly down my back, making me shiver. He slips a finger under the hem of my top and runs his fingertip along my bare skin before pulling the fabric up and over my head. I help him, yanking at it until it falls to a heap on the floor.

I shimmy out of my bra and undo the last few buttons on Theo's shirt with fumbling fingers, my mouth hungrily finding his again every time we break apart. He takes my hands and tugs me up into a standing position, then pulls me to the window, where he drops the blind down. I undo his trousers and let them drop to the floor, then turn around and drop my own, pushing myself back so that I'm pressed against his bare chest, no clothes between us.

It's been so long, I'm rabid with it; I'd be embarrassed if I could actually think straight. Theo runs his hands down my arms, then lets them land on my hips. I bend forward, grabbing on to the windowsill, thinking for a moment how this is like that very first Valentine's Day we had – pressed against the window of the museum.

As I close my eyes to the feeling of Theo's warm hands

grabbing my ass, I'm hit by a surge of happiness. This is perfect. It's exactly how it should be, and I feel a sudden lifting in my chest, like a dead weight that's been pulling me down has been whisked away. It's all over. This period of drought, of questioning and distance: it was just a blip. A normal low period in an otherwise healthy marriage. There's nothing wrong with us; we're a happy, connected, sexually active married couple in our thirties. Nothing to see here.

And now I can pitch the book, knowing the story had a happy ending. I can tell Theo that *this* is the reason I did it: this, right here, this moment of pure connection between us. This is what it was all for. And surely he can feel it, too? Surely he'll understand. All I wanted was to get back to us. And with the money we can travel, see the world, fuck on all seven continents. And if he doesn't want me to do it, I won't. I'll delete Isa's number, never speak to Tilly again.

As long as we're with each other – *really* with each other – what else matters?

These thoughts have been happily zapping through my head as I've waited, poised, for Theo to push himself inside me. The delicious anticipation of it is almost better than the moment itself. I feel a smile spread across my face, satisfied in the knowledge that we're about to reconvene, that in just a second, we'll be having the kind of experience Moonbeam the tantric yoga lady would call 'transcendent'.

Any moment now.

I shimmy my hips back and forth, impatient. 'Are you torturing me on purpose?' I complain, laughing. He's always loved teasing me, really winding me up until I'm desperate for him. From the day I met him, he was different to the sexual encounters I'd had before, who'd count a bit of boob-grabbing as foreplay and just stick it in. Theo always wanted *me* to want it before he could enjoy himself. We always felt like equals in that regard. It wasn't perfect, of course; we had to teach each other about our preferences, to gently guide each other on occasions when things weren't that great for one of us. But that's the point: we kept each other as the priority.

OK, he's really dragging this out now. I turn to look over my shoulder, expecting him to be grinning at me, happy with himself for getting me all frustrated. 'Theo, please—'

He's not looking at me. He's looking down, and there's a frown on his face.

'What?' I ask. 'What is it?'

He snaps his eyes up. His cheeks are pink. 'Nothing. It's nothing, I just . . . it's . . .'

'What?! Theo, you're freaking me out.' Is there any quicker way to extinguish the flame than to have someone gawking at your vagina with a preoccupied expression on their face? 'What?' I ask again.

'It won't work!' he blurts. 'It's not . . . for fuck's sake.'

He turns away from me, whipping his trousers up off the floor. I stand up quickly, covering myself, and watch as he hops about, pulling his boxers up as fast as he can. He moves towards the door.

'Theo, it's OK.'

He whirls around, his mouth open. He clamps it shut. 'Let's not talk about this now,' he says after a moment, and then walks out of the room.

I lean back against the wall and let myself slide down, until

I'm sat on the carpet with my arms wrapped around my bare knees. I listen as Theo heavily shuts the door to the bathroom and the shower roars on.

And for the first time since all of this began, I allow myself to properly cry.

This isn't the first time this has happened; when we were in our twenties and having big nights out every weekend, we'd sometimes have some alcohol-induced difficulties getting things going. But it was never a problem. It's never felt like this huge, heavy thing that Theo needs to be ashamed of. He has never run away like this before. Why? Why are things suddenly so abnormal between us?

What if it isn't shame? The thought hits me from nowhere, and I wish I could put it back. What if it's guilt? What if the reason he can't get it up is because he's already used it elsewhere? But he sounded so honest before, so vulnerable. Was it a double bluff? A classic case of the guilty party projecting onto their partner?

Or am I doing exactly the same thing?

I rest my forehead on my knees and press my damp eyes against my cool skin.

Maybe the worst really is going to happen. We'll never fix this. There'll be no solution, no book, no advance; a disappointing end to the podcast. And Theo and I will be cast into the sea of our own crap; there'll be nobody to guide me any more, no structure to help me navigate this mess. We'll be adrift, alone, avoiding each other as we slowly trundle towards the inevitable end of our marriage.

*

'Free bookmark! Come and see our tote bags!' I wheel my arms enthusiastically in the direction of the arts centre, but inside I want to die. 'Choose your print!'

Across the cobbled pedestrian street, Harry is engaged in conversation with a middle-aged couple in anoraks. He's dressed like a giant egg, and much to my dismay, so am I. Somehow, Petra has enough in the budget to make us look ridiculous in public, but not to buy a packet of digestives for Chatty Tuesdays. We're promoting a new two-day exhibition we've got coming up, for an artist called Aisha Garratt, who paints pictures of household objects that sell for tens of thousands. *The Egg* is her most famous piece, so we've had these papier-mâché monstrosities made so that we can attract more attention and, in the meantime, try to flog more of the bloody tote bags.

I edge closer to Harry, gingerly readjusting the widest part of the egg around my hips. I have to be careful; one knock and there'll be a hole in the side of my costume. Harry stopped the anorak-clad couple ten minutes ago and thus far has not managed to get them through the doors of the arts centre. As I get closer, I catch a few words of their conversation – I believe they're talking about the best hotels in Mallorca.

'Hello!' I say loudly to a woman as she walks past, trying to get Harry's attention and remind him to stay on task lest Petra make us do another day of this tomorrow. 'Would you like to come and look at our latest exhibition? I'll give you a free bookmark.'

That last part came out a bit desperate, but whatever. The woman shakes her head, pointing to the AirPods in her ears, and hurries past. Harry remains locked in an irrelevant conversation. I huff, glancing up at the first floor of the centre. Sure enough, Petra is looking out of her window and down at the street, her beady eyes following me and Harry. She gives a little wave and I pretend I haven't seen her.

I decide I've had enough and trot across the street. 'Harry,' I say, grabbing his arm and smiling apologetically at the middle-aged couple. 'I need to discuss something with you, please.'

'Oh, we'll let you go,' the woman says with a look of thinly disguised relief on her face. As usual, I'm not the only one who's desperate for Harry to stop talking. They hurry off, and Harry turns to me.

'What's up?'

'I'm *bored*,' I say, moving my arms enthusiastically, giving the impression that I'm attracting pedestrians to talk to me. In reality, I need Harry to talk to me because I physically cannot be left alone with my own thoughts right now.

'I meant to ask you, actually,' he says, waving at a little boy in a pushchair. 'Jas has been on at me to invite you and Theo round for dinner forever. If I don't get something in the diary soon he is going to kill me in my sleep.'

I laugh; I can't imagine Jas – soft-spoken, impossibly sweet, the calm foil to Harry's mania – so much as sharing a cross word with Harry. 'Jas is an angel.'

'He is, but he's an angel with an agenda. He's got some chicken thing he wants to try out, and you're to be the guinea pigs.'

I hold up a fan of bookmarks to a passing group of women, plastering a smile on my face, while continuing my conversation with Harry. 'Theo's quite busy at the moment,' I say. 'But I'd love to pop round.'

It's true, Theo is busy. He's busy avoiding me. Since last night, we haven't said two words to each other. I fell asleep on the little sofa in the study, and when I woke up, he'd put a blanket over me and left for work. He hasn't messaged once, and usually we'd have exchanged three or four by lunchtime. We're due to meet for couple's therapy this evening, but I don't want to go. It all feels hopeless, and I don't know what Gretchen can do for us at this point. Can she make Theo tell me why he won't have sex with me? Because while I know I haven't asked the question outright, I've made it pretty obvious that I'd like to know. And if he hasn't put the effort in himself – the effort I'm making, however misguided, the attempts to bring us back together – it means something. And it means even more that he hasn't discussed it with me off his own back.

And then there's the question that underpins the rest, the one that's wrapped itself around my heart and keeps me awake at night: what if I don't want to hear what he's got to say?

'You're welcome whenever you like,' Harry is saying to me, thrusting leaflets at people as they pass. A man stops momentarily and Harry pounces, ensnaring him in conversation before he can get away. My phone buzzes in my pocket and I pull it out, keeping my back to the arts centre. Before Petra, having our phones out wasn't a problem. We're professional adults, and we were trusted to manage our own time – and did so, successfully. But Petra has a thing about 'slacking', something she defines entirely as using phones and chatting.

It's an email from Isa. This morning, I'd retrieved my draft reply from where I'd minimised it last night and deleted the whole thing, rewriting it to fit the new circumstances. I asked for a pause, to have some space from the experiment. I can't see how I can engage Theo in our next task when he won't even talk to me. From reading just the first line of her reply, I already know I'm shouting into a void.

Hi Lottie,

I'm afraid there's absolutely no wiggle room here. Episode One is out in less than a week, and we need them coming weekly after that. Editing takes a while. We're down to the wire. Thanks in advance for soldiering on even though things are difficult, as your contract dictates.

Looking forward to seeing your next entry soon.
All best,
Isa

My stomach plummets. Shit. I read my contract properly, and I knew there was a clause about upholding my end of the bargain, but I thought there'd be some space. I thought, stupidly, that I'd be allowed some room to have an emotional response to all this and some leeway in how quickly I acted on Isa's instructions. If I don't do as my contract says, I have to return all the money I've been paid so far. And it's a lot.

Something bops me on the head, and I look up from my phone, blinking. Caro is standing in front of me, her dark shiny bob pulled back at the sides, wearing a pair of black dungarees and a fleece. She's holding an empty folder.

'What the hell are you wearing?' she asks.

I immediately feel better. 'What are you doing here?'

'I've just delivered some prints to a guy at the chippy; I'm on my way home. Was going to text to see if you wanted to come down from your prisoner's tower for a coffee. Didn't know you were back working the streets.'

I glance up at the window. Petra is peering out again. I thrust a bookmark into Caro's hand. 'Come and see our new tote bags,' I say, opening my arm and leading her through the doors of the gallery. Once we're inside, I steer her into the back storage room and yank the giant egg over my head. 'It's lunch time,' I say, stretching my arms wide and then flattening my hair back down. 'Fancy a sandwich?'

'Music to my ears.'

I tell Harry what I'm doing, interrupting him mid-flow as he talks to a young girl about the pros and cons of Pinterest, and then walk off up the street with Caro, purposefully not looking up to tell Petra where I'm going. Immediately, good-girl guilt gnaws at me, but I'm feeling wound up and rebellious, once again sensing myself nudge against a breaking point.

'You're tense,' Caro says as we join the back of the queue at the sandwich shop. 'What's going on?'

I fill her in, telling her all about our failed sex attempt last night, our scheduled therapy this evening, the book deal, and the next task in the experiment. By the time I'm done, we're walking out of the sandwich shop clutching roasted vegetable and houmous rolls in paper bags. Caro leads us over to a bench in the square, a few streets away from the arts centre, and takes a big bite of her sandwich before replying.

'So let me get this straight,' she says, wiping houmous off her plum-coloured lips. 'If Tilly can fix your sex life, you get a shit tonne of money. If she can't, you're screwed *and* the whole thing gets pulled.'

'Yes.'

'And the experiment doesn't seem to be working, as evidenced by Theo's inability to get it up last night.'

'Exactly.'

'But Tilly thinks the next step is going to be what cinches it.'

'I'm not so confident.'

'*And,*' she continues, 'you've got couple's therapy this evening, but you don't want to go.'

'What's the point?' I ask.

Caro regards me for a moment, plucking a strip of pepper from her sandwich and dropping it into her mouth. 'What do you want?'

'I want my marriage to go back to how it was before.'

'No, from me. What do you need to hear right now?'

I give this some thought as I chew. Evidently, the way I've been doing things hasn't worked. I don't know if Caro has the answers, but she certainly has a different perspective. We often ask each other for advice, and the answers are sometimes given with considerations about our individual personalities, but I've never considered actually doing what *Caro* would do, despite her regularly telling me to make some huge, mad move that's totally out of character. Doing what Lottie would do obviously isn't getting me very far, so why don't I try being someone else for a change?

'I want to know what you'd do. If you were in this situation.'

Caro beams. 'God, I've been waiting almost twenty-five years to hear those words.' Without hesitation, she continues, 'I'd sack off the therapy. I'd throw everything I've got at getting my husband into bed with me. Have you thought about the club the other night, about spicing things up a bit? Trying something new?'

'I can't even get him to touch me, Caro. How am I getting him to whip the handcuffs out?'

She pops the last bite of her sandwich in her mouth and rubs her hands together. 'You know what you need to do, Lottie? You need to take the reins. Stop waiting for Theo to realize what you're doing and make it happen all by himself. Listen to Tilly and do as she says.' This isn't the first time someone has used these words with me, and they ring uncomfortably true. *Take the reins*. 'Get your phone out.'

'What? Why?'

She raises her eyebrows expectantly, and I oblige, sighing.

'Text your darling husband and tell him you won't be going to therapy tonight. Tell him that if he wants to see you, he's going to have to meet you at The Golden Oak Hotel, and that he'll find you waiting for him at the bar. Book a room, change your environment, and follow Tilly's instructions to the letter.'

'I can't just book a room on a random Tuesday—'

'Lottie, you're being paid an absolute fortune. Book the fucking *suite*, for Christ's sake.'

She's right, of course. I'm being my typical conservative, worrisome self. It's time to try a different tactic. 'Fine,' I say, pulling up my chat with Theo. Every time I think I've hit a wall, it turns out I've got one more tiny droplet left in the tank. 'Fuck it. What's the worst that could happen?'

Chapter Seventeen

I am not exaggerating when I say I have never felt like a bigger bellend in all of my life.

I am sitting on a high stool at The Golden Oak Hotel's wraparound bar – the same bar I met Tilly and Isa in for the first time. It feels like a different place in the evenings; the space is cosy and dimly lit, populated with people wearing smart dresses and open-necked shirts, and, most glaringly, instead of wearing my denim pinafore dress and white pumps, I'm dressed like some kind of Temu Tomb Raider.

I went straight to Caro's house after work and she did my full makeover by herself, explicitly vetoing any input from me. In her words, 'Every decision you've made this far has been utterly wank, Lotts, so let's just give it a rest, eh?'

As part of tonight's task, Tilly had asked me who Theo's celebrity crush was. I confessed to her, and then later to Caro, that he's always had a thing for Lara Croft. That was stupid of me, as I am to Angelina Jolie as Lambrini is to champagne, but here we are. Caro took the brief and ran, scraping my hair up into a sky-high ponytail and then weaving through some extensions to create a plait that lands somewhere near my arse. I'm wearing a skin-tight black vest top and high-waisted pleather trousers with heeled boots. My makeup is heavy on the eyes, light on the lipstick. I look like a completely different person.

Actually, sat here in this hotel bar, I look like a very specific kind of different person – and it's not Lara Croft.

'Hi,' a man says, sliding into the seat next to me. 'Can I get you another drink?'

'I'm not a sex worker,' I say quickly. I learned after the last guy came over twenty minutes ago that it's best to state this outright before a conversation gets underway. Where the hell is Theo?

The man looks affronted, the warm flirtatiousness leaving his eyes as he leans back. 'I didn't think you were.'

'Oh,' I say, feeling bad. 'Sorry. I'll have an Anna Banana then, please.'

'You're all right, actually,' he replies sulkily, getting up quickly and moving away.

Ugh. Part of me wanted Theo to see me here, looking like a different person, having a drink with a different man. Maybe that would have got some passion going. I chastise myself – I have never been a game-player. This whole situation is bringing out a side to me I'm not sure I like very much. Deflated, I order myself a second drink and check my phone. Nothing from Theo since he replied to my message at lunchtime. I read it through again as I nibble at my thumbnail.

> Me: *I'm not coming to therapy. Meet me at The Golden Oak Hotel bar at 7 p.m.*

> Theo: *Fine.*

It wasn't quite the intrigued, thrilled response I'd hoped for, but given the circumstances, it's probably better than I deserve. I'd accepted that he'd want me to do some explaining once he got here, but it's now twenty past seven and there's no sign of him.

The bartender places an Anna Banana on the bar in front of me and looks at me sadly. Good god, this is bleak. I'm sat here alone, dressed to the nines like some kind of greased-up dominatrix, loudly proclaiming to anyone who enters my radius that I am categorically not a sex worker. How exactly did I get here?

'Just waiting for my husband,' I say, picking up my drink with my left hand and wiggling my wedding ring at him.

He nods, flashing me an appeasing smile – the kind one might give to an elderly man who claims he's waiting for his long-dead wife to return from the shops. He moves off.

I slump lower in my chair. *Come on, Theo. Where are you?*

I pull out my phone to message him, but a shadow falls over me.

'Lottie?'

I look up. He's standing there wearing a loose shirt and green trousers, his hair still damp from the shower. His eyes scan me up and down, that confused line appearing between his eyebrows, and all of my resolve drains out of me in an instant. Genuinely, what the fuck am I doing?

No. No, Lottie, do not back down. You've come this far. *Take the reins.*

'Oh, it's not Lottie, actually,' I say, and I'm pleased to note that there's only a slight tremor in my voice. 'It's Lara.' I stick out my hand.

Theo's gaze flicks down to my outstretched palm, as if he's never been offered a handshake before. After a moment, he takes it. 'OK . . .'

'What's your name?' I ask. God, this is awful. In any other circumstances, I'd be laughing. *We'd* be laughing. But there's still that awful tension between us after last night, after weeks of disconnect. We're taking things too seriously, but not in the way we should be. It feels . . . cold.

Theo pulls out the stool next to me and sits down. He orders a beer and turns to me.

'Lottie, I think we really needed that appointment with Gretchen. We—'

'It's Lara.'

He closes his eyes briefly and takes a breath. 'OK, Lara. What the hell is happening?'

'You tell me,' I say. 'I've only just met you.'

'What have you done to your hair?'

'My hair is always like this.'

The bartender plonks Theo's pint on the bar and gives him a quick look. It says, *Good luck to you, pal.* Theo takes a sip and rubs his index fingers against his temples. After a moment, he turns to me.

'Fine. I'm Jack. I'd really like to discuss the reasons why a couple who is clearly struggling might be avoiding their therapy appointments.'

I swallow. 'Oh, let's not talk about such serious things,' I say. Why am I suddenly in *Bridgerton*? I cough. 'Tonight's for having *fun*.'

'Are you drunk?'

'On the promise of this evening.'

His mouth finally quirks up into a half smile. 'You're mad.'

'Get to know me and you might find out.' I'm surprised to find that I'm actually beginning to enjoy myself. I don't have to be Lottie right now, with all her anxieties and secrets and weaknesses. I can be Lara, and I can refuse to answer any questions that don't pertain to me. I will only give answers to queries about raids, tombs and tight tops. I've never seen the film, though, so anything going into more specific detail will have to be avoided.

'All right,' he says finally, leaning back on his stool. 'I'll play. Tell me about yourself.'

I take a sip of my drink and give him what I believe is a coquettish look. 'I'm Lara. I'm thirty-five and I'm single. I've been looking for a man who meets a very specific set of criteria.'

Tilly told me I had to define exactly what I was looking for. She said this evening wasn't about me objectifying myself to turn Theo on, but about me stepping into another role and asking for what I want. When I told her I didn't *know* what I wanted, she said I'd figure it out. I guess this is me figuring it out.

'What's that, then?' he asks, quirking an eyebrow.

I don't give myself too much time to think. I filter out all my usual Lottie-isms – the umming and ahhing, the 'if that's OK's and 'maybe's – and speak directly. 'I need a man who wants to take me upstairs right now and make me feel good.'

Theo widens his eyes. 'Wow. If only you had a room.'

'I *do* have a room, Jack,' I say, pulling the keycard for the top-floor suite from my pocket and placing it on the bar between us.

Theo pales. 'Lottie . . . we can't afford—'

'It's *Lara*,' I say firmly, frustration creeping into my voice now, 'and it was a gift.' It's a lie, but it's a small one in comparison to the rest.

'A gift from who?'

'I'm afraid that's none of your business,' I reply. 'But don't worry. If you're not interested, I can take my criteria elsewhere.'

I scan the bar, wondering whether I might have gone too far. But that's role play, isn't it? I'm not actually going to go and ask one of the many men in here who think I'm a sex worker to take me upstairs and have their way with me.

'So?' I say once I've done an exaggerated amount of peering at the various men in the room. I recross my legs and rest my elbow on the bar, fluttering my eyelashes. 'Should I—'

I stop. Theo isn't looking at me. He's staring at his phone. I bite my lip so hard it hurts. 'Theo— *Jack*, I'm sorry, have you found something more interesting? I can go . . .'

He still doesn't look up. I feel that new, not-yet-familiar surge inside me. I try to swallow it down, but I've been sitting here for half an hour, waiting for my husband, who I've been trying to seduce for weeks without success; who is making me feel like the smallest, most undesirable person in the world; who is slowly drifting away from me and seemingly doing nothing to stop himself; who is my best friend and my constant and who has lived so much of my adult life with me; with whom I share a house and two dogs and a history spanning over seven years; and who, right now, even as I struggle to breathe in my horrible pleather trousers with my head pounding from the pull of my hair and while I *absolutely embarrass* myself in an attempt to have sex with him, is ignoring me and staring at his phone. After he told *me* I spent too much time on mine.

'I'm sick of this,' I find myself saying.

Theo's head snaps up.

I scrape my bar stool back and swipe the hotel keycard off the bar. 'Finish your drink alone. I'm done.'

I go to stalk past him, but as I do, he reaches out and grabs my arm. I shake him off. 'No, Theo, leave me alone.'

I catch his eye as I pull away, expecting him to look apologetic, or hurt. But he looks angry. His brow is furrowed, his mouth turned down. Instead of asking me to stay, pushing me to talk to him, he thrusts his phone in my face.

All of the blood rushes from my head. My ears start ringing.

On his screen is a message from a fellow teacher, Greg, whose name I recognize vaguely from past functions we've attended together. It's a screenshot of a news article, followed by a question.

Tilly Carter spotted enjoying a morning in the park with assistant and mystery woman.

And there, clear as day, standing in the park right next to Tilly and Isa, is me.

My eyes travel to Greg's question, and I know in that precise moment that my world is about to implode.

> Mate, isn't this your wife?

*

Fuck. Fuck, fuck, fuck, fuck.

I'm lying on the super-king-sized bed in The Golden Oak Hotel's premier suite, a towel on my head and my ever-buzzing phone in my hand. I scroll the gossip news sites, looking at the two or three pictures someone managed to snap of me before Isa flung her scarf on my head and marched me into the druggy pavilion. Some sites have photos of me being herded, covered, across the grass, further adding fuel to the fire of rumours that is already raging about my identity.

As I read, notifications flood through at the top of my screen. The bridesmaids' group chat has been a flurry of activity, and as I scroll, I see a new one from Holly-the-feet-pics-girl come through.

> Lottie, you dark horse! THIS is why you were asking us all those questions!

As far as I can tell, nobody has publicly identified me yet, but people I haven't spoken to in years keep messaging me with links to the post along with lines of *??????* and I know it's only a matter of time before one of my less loyal acquaintances shops me. *The Sun*'s headline is the most damning:

Sex Podcast's Sexless Woman Unveiled? Who is Tilly Carter's Anonymous Guest?

While I know he didn't understand what he was reading – Theo wouldn't know who Tilly Carter was if someone held a gun to his head – he knew I'd been up to something. He knew, I could tell, that he had turned over the rock that covered all of my deceit. The niggles of doubt he's been harbouring for months, the suspicions he brought up with hot-Gretchen-the-therapist, the subtle differences in my behaviour. His friend Greg's message provided a thread for him to tug, and I couldn't do anything to stop it.

So I didn't. Theo asked me one simple question – 'What the hell is going on, Lottie?' – and I couldn't answer. I hadn't prepared myself, hadn't written a palatable explanation in my head yet. I thought that, when the truth finally came out, it'd be me controlling the narrative. I couldn't think straight, and so the only thing I managed to say, the thing that now I'm convinced has made things a hundred times worse, was, 'I can't do this. Don't follow me.'

Then I walked past him, across the lobby, my legs wobbly, and pressed the button for the lift. I stood and waited, five seconds, ten, then stepped inside when the doors opened. When I looked out as they slid closed again, he wasn't even looking at me. He was tapping at his phone, his mouth open.

And now, I imagine he's sitting at home, pulling on that thread until the whole tapestry pools at his feet, laid out for him to finally see and understand.

My phone begins ringing in my hand. Caro. I decline the call and silence my phone before putting it face-down on the bedside table. I've fucked it. I've well and truly fucked it, and there is nothing I can do.

I clamber off the huge bed and pad through to the bathroom, where I splash my face with ice-cold water. Actually, there is not *nothing* I can do. There are so many things I *should* be doing right now. I should be answering the phone to Caro, seeking her advice. I should be sending Theo flurries of texts, begging him to talk to me. I should be at home, trying to sort out my marriage, not wearing a complimentary dressing gown as I unwrap a tiny bar of goat's milk soap.

Should, should, should. It's how I've lived my entire life – I should get a fulfilling job, buy a nice house, marry a nice man. I should turn up on time, not upset anybody, avoid confrontation. I should push my own needs and desires down to make room for what I ought to do: be a good employee, not rock the boat, avoid discussing sex with my husband. I should not be too much.

And this is categorically too much. Avoiding everybody and hiding out in the premier suite of the local hotel – paid for using money earned secretly while allowing a nationally acclaimed podcast to do a deep dive into my sex life without my husband's knowledge – is truly off-the-scale too much. Is this what they mean when they talk about people having breakdowns? When people finally snap? They do say it's always the ones you least expect, don't they? And I am the most unlikely of candidates.

I make my way back into the bedroom and open the minibar I drank one and a half Anna Bananas downstairs, and the warm fuzz they gave me is rapidly dwindling. The contents of the minibar are included in the price of the room, so I unload it all onto the desk under the TV, snap open a can of tonic and a miniature of gin, and then mix myself a generous G&T using one of the teaspoons by the kettle. I swipe up a packet of M&M's and plonk myself on the armchair by the big window, propping my slippered feet up on the low table in front of me.

Outside, the town is twinkly and quiet, making my stay in this room seem even more obscene. I've lived within a three-mile radius of this exact spot for my entire life; if I was going to give myself a surprise night away, I could have picked anywhere else. The thought makes me uneasy all of a sudden.

I sip my drink as I crunch my M&M's, my eyes staring unseeingly out of the window. Right now, this is fine. Right now, I'm in a bubble, and real-life consequences haven't come knocking. They're just outside, though, raising their fist against the door. The way I'm behaving is like some huge metaphor for the way I live my life. Run away and hide; bury my head in the sand. And isn't this exactly why? Look what happens when I raise my head above the parapet.

The last people I'm interested in speaking to are Isa and Tilly. The cat's out of the bag now; there's no damage control to be done. Getting involved with them was my first and biggest mistake; each decision to continue working with them was just another to add to the list. And for what? Money? My relationship with Theo is worse than ever, and I'm currently being embarrassed in front of everybody I know. I have to go to work tomorrow, and if just one person has seen my face in the news, it'll be everywhere. Petra listens to *The Cliterati*; there's no way she won't have heard.

The thought is horrifying, an embodiment of my own personal worst nightmare. It's going to be days and weeks of this, a lifetime of never forgetting what I've done. Once it's out there, it's out there, and it's never going to go away.

So no, I decide as I reach the last dregs of my drink, I'm not going to speak to a single soul. For tonight, one last time, I'm going to continue doing what I do best. I'm going to turn off my phone, squeeze my eyes closed, and pretend the real world doesn't exist.

*

The next morning, mildly hungover, I traipse into the hotel lobby like I'm being led to the gallows. It's one minute to ten, the last possible moment for me to check out. Just twelve minutes ago, I was in bed sending a text to Harry, asking him to explain to Petra that I'd eaten a dodgy biryani and would be in a couple of hours late. My lies are as transparent as the bags under my eyes, but frankly, I've got enough on my plate.

When I finally drag myself to reception, I'm dismayed to see the bartender from last night sitting behind the desk.

'Good *morning*,' he says cheerfully, and I can't blame him for the glee on his face. If I worked here, a situation like this would be the highlight of my day. 'Did you enjoy your stay with us, Mrs Croft?'

I curse myself for using a fake name; it's even more mortifying in the starkness of the morning. And is it me, or does he emphasize the 'Mrs'? I vividly remember him watching me as I disappeared in the lift last night. I wonder if he had a heart-to-heart with Theo in my absence. 'I slept great,' I say, avoiding his eye and sliding my keycard across the desk.

'I'm so glad.' He taps at his computer and hits enter, then

smiles at me while the printer groans in the background. 'You've had a haircut, I see?'

I pretend to fish for something in my bag. 'Sorry?'

He reaches behind him and whips a piece of paper from the printer. 'Next time, please do feel free to ask for a second keycard, free of charge, if your husband's joining you.'

OK. He's really taking the piss now. 'I'm sure my husband will ask you himself if he needs one,' I reply sweetly. I don't know where this sass is coming from. It's like I've spent the last month trying to hold up a dam against a torrent of water. Now that it's burst, I feel unsettlingly relaxed, like I'm metaphorically lying down and letting it all wash over me. After all, how could things possibly get any worse?

The bartender-cum-receptionist at least has the decency to flush a little bit. 'Here's your final bill,' he says curtly.

I tap my card against the reader and then shove it back in my purse. 'Thanks so much for a lovely stay,' I say. 'Though your Anna Bananas were a little sickly. I prefer the way your colleague makes them.'

I turn on my heel and clip across the lobby, my squeaky shoes only slightly ruining the effect, and push my way out onto the street without a backwards glance.

Before I've even got down the front steps, I run smack bang into Caro.

'Umph,' she says, holding her hands up and grabbing me by the shoulders. 'Jesus, Lottie!'

'Sorry,' I say, yanking one of my bags back up onto my shoulder. 'What are you doing here?'

'Looking for you, obviously. Everyone's worried sick. What the hell is going on?'

I shake my head. 'I just can't talk to anyone right now.'

'Uh-uh,' she says, shaking her head too. 'Sorry, nope, that shit won't fly with me. We both need coffee and I need answers. Come.'

She grabs one of my bags with one hand and takes my wrist with the other, then proceeds to drag me down the steps and along the high street. I stumble as I go, wincing against the bright daylight, but relievedly allowing us to fall into our usual roles and letting her lead. Now, in the bustle of the outside world, my bluster is quickly deserting me. We reach the door of a little independent café that opened a couple of months ago and she pulls me inside and deposits me at a table by the window.

'Stay,' she says, and then turns and strides to the counter.

I stare out of the window for a moment, my mind blank, and then check my watch. I should have been in work an hour and a half ago. I'm sure they'll all be ostensibly sympathetic about my food poisoning once I finally arrive – I haven't had a day off sick in three years – but while I'm still absent, I know links will be being shared and whispered conversations had in the kitchen. I sink down lower into my seat.

A moment later, Caro dumps an iced caramel latte in front of me, the coffee sloshing over the sides, and sits down in the seat opposite. I open my mouth but she holds up a finger, takes a sip of her own Americano, closes her eyes, and then puts her mug down.

'OK, go,' she says.

'One of Theo's friends sent him an article while we were at the bar,' I say monotonously, the reality of my situation suddenly hitting me like a punch to the stomach. 'It was a picture of me with—'

'Tilly Carter and her agent in a park,' Caro finishes. 'Everyone's seen it.'

'Shit.' I bury my head in my hands. I haven't checked the news since I silenced my phone last night. 'Shit, shit, shit. Does everyone know I'm the podcast girl?'

Caro winces, and I have my answer. She leans forward. 'It's just suspected, though. I'm sure you could just say you bumped into them, said hi because you're a fan—'

I shake my head. 'No. No more lying, Caro. How can I reconcile with Theo and have it all based on *another* lie? He'd never trust me again.'

'Fair enough,' she concedes. 'So . . . what are you going to do?'

I stare out of the window again, lifting my latte unconsciously to my lips. The caffeine is slicing through my hungover, couldn't-care-less fug even further, and I'm feeling increasingly like I want to emigrate. 'I'm going to go to work,' I say, keeping my eyes on the street outside, 'and then I don't know.'

'You have to talk to Theo.'

'What do I say?' I ask, finally dragging my gaze towards her. 'How can I explain any of this?'

'How were you going to explain it when the book got announced?'

'Part of me didn't think it would. And if it had, things would have been different. Me and Theo would have been different. If we'd just managed to have sex, everything would have been better. None of this would have happened.'

Caro looks at me like I'm stupid. 'Lottie, you know that's not true.'

'The money would have made it better. He'd have understood.'

She shakes her head. 'You know your husband. He's taught Year Six at the same school since he graduated. He doesn't give a shit about money. And neither did you until recently.'

Her words sting. 'I didn't hear you saying any of this until it blew up in my face.'

If I thought she was going to back down, I was wrong. 'You're missing the point. You've lost sight of what's actually important, Lotts, and it isn't the sex or the money.'

'You told me not to tell Theo! You told me to keep my mouth shut.'

'Before you ran away and started co-hosting a podcast and negotiating a book deal!'

'I didn't see you stepping in and telling me not to.'

'I'm sorry, I forgot you were a two-year-old who can't make autonomous decisions without guardian oversight.'

I slam my half-empty glass down. 'Why are you so *angry* with me?'

'Because you're being pathetic! You're making these big, ballsy decisions but you can't even own them. If you're going to do it, Lottie, *do it*. Don't half-arse it and hurt people in the process.'

I get to my feet. Caro watches me, her face unreadable. 'You can't act like my life is all some big exciting piece of gossip until it gets serious,' I hiss.

'And you can't act like you're the only one with problems,' she spits back, and immediately, I see regret flash across her face.

'Oh,' I say, and my raised voice has the people on the

next table turning in their seats. 'I'd love to hear about your problems if you'd ever discuss them with me! Talk about burying your head in the fucking sand, Caro. I'm a novice compared to you.'

She stares at me, hurt etched across her face. I feel a stab of self-loathing. How has it come to this?

'So, what?' she asks as I gather my bags, my hands shaking. 'You're just going to go and pull a shift at the office like nothing's happened? When are you going to stop hiding, Lottie?'

I don't have an answer to her question. I don't know anything, except that I can't hear any more of this right now.

And so, for the second time in twelve hours, I turn my back on someone I love and walk out of the door.

Chapter Eighteen

As I walk into the office, an exaggerated hush falls over the room. Last night, I'd convinced myself that I could handle this, that I didn't give a shit what people thought any more. But now, without a stiff G&T inside me and still reeling from my argument with Caro, I am predictably mortified. I walk across the carpeted office, trying to make myself as small and invisible as possible, and I see someone in Accounting minimize *The Sun* as I pass.

Noting that Harry's chair is empty, I make a beeline straight for the kitchen, dumping my overnight bags under my own desk as I go. I find him in there wrestling with the coffee machine once again. When he turns and sees me, he straightens. 'Bloody hell, Lottie.'

I slump against the counter. 'Don't.'

He stares at me for a moment. 'That was one dodgy biryani.'

'I hate myself,' I say truthfully, burying my face in my hands and peering at him through my fingers. In a really small voice, I ask, 'Not everybody knows, right?'

Harry turns away and begins using a paper towel to wipe at an invisible stain on the countertop.

'Oh, god,' I groan.

'What the *hell*, though,' he says, turning back to me, evidently unable to help himself. 'You've been working with *Tilly Carter*? Jesus, Lottie! That's like . . . wow. What was she like? Are you actually doing the series? Someone in the *Daily Mail Online* comments said something about a book—'

'Harry, my life is over.'

'OK, sorry, yes. Let's talk about that bit. God, honestly, you're the last person I'd have expected to . . . no, yes, sorry, right. Let's rationalize.' He pauses for a minute, then looks at me seriously. 'This has nothing to do with your job, so it's nobody's business whatsoever. If you don't want to talk about it with anybody, you don't have to.'

'It's so *embarrassing*.' I feel like I might cry again. 'The whole office knows I'm in a sexless marriage, and that I got so desperate I started working with a podcast to help me sort it out. That's *mortifying*, Harry, whether it affects my work or not.'

Harry nods sympathetically. 'I know.'

'Thanks!'

'Well it kind of *is*,' he says, wincing. 'But hey! It does explain why you've been so weird recently. And why you kept asking about Petra's sex life.' He catches the look on my face and holds his hands up. 'Mate, it's not the end of the world. It's actually iconic, if you think about it.'

I stare at him, deadpan.

'It *will* be iconic. You just need to give it time, Lottie. People move on. Everybody will be talking about something else within the month.'

'And by then I'll be divorced and fighting for custody of the dogs.'

Harry blanches. 'Divorced? Are things that bad? Surely Tilly can help, she's a sex counsellor—'

'It's not that. I lied to him. He's found out about all of this at exactly the same time everyone else has.'

Realization dawns on Harry's face. 'Oh, shit.'

'Yeah.'

'What's he said? Is he . . . angry?'

'I haven't spoken to him.'

'What, at all?'

I shake my head. Suddenly, it all feels unbearably overwhelming and hopeless. I'm struck by the urge to walk out of the office door and to the train station, to buy a ticket to somewhere I've never been before. The urge, once again, to run away and hide.

'Let me make you a coffee,' Harry says quietly, flicking on the kettle. 'It'll have to be instant; the machine's still buggered.'

The kitchen door squeaks open and Londa, one of the other community engagement officers, pokes her head round the door. 'Oh, Lottie, there you are.' Her cheeks are flushed pink, and I almost laugh at how much she's failing at pretending she's been looking all over for me. Everybody out there knows exactly where I am – they watched me make my way to the kitchen like I was in some sort of carnival procession.

'Sorry, yes, I'm coming,' I say, moving towards her. I'm already two hours late, and now that I've arrived, I'm fannying about in the kitchen – A for effort in both the personal and professional columns today.

'No, it's not that.' She grimaces apologetically. 'Petra wants to see you.'

I throw a glance at Harry and he widens his eyes, shaking his head. I remember his words just a few moments ago – *This has nothing to do with your job . . . If you don't want to talk about it with anybody, you don't have to.*

I follow Londa out into the office, where people are now doing a really shitty job of pretending they're *not* watching my every move. As I walk past the interns' desk (not notorious for being a hive of any kind of productive activity at the best of times), I can see that one of them is watching a TikTok of a woman overlaid on top of the now-infamous picture of me, Tilly and Isa in the park.

'. . . and all the news sources have now confirmed that they've identified this woman as Charlotte Carmichael – you can see her LinkedIn profile via the link in my bio . . .'

One of the others elbows him sharply and he jumps, glancing up and spotting me and then scrabbling to lock his phone and silence the video. But it's far too late.

This has nothing to do with your job.

If everybody has found my LinkedIn, they've found where I work. I've watched these kinds of armchair detective investigations play out before: someone always contacts the company. Asks if they know what their employee has been up to.

But I'm a born-again virgin with a marriage problem, not a murderer. Surely there's a difference.

My heart thuds uncomfortably against my ribs as I knock on Petra's glass door. She looks up from behind her desk and beckons me inside with the flick of a finger, and then rises to her feet.

As I step in and close the door behind me, she does something I've never seen her do before. She walks over to the glass wall of her office and begins pulling the blinds down.

Oh, fuck. This is *not* good.

On the other side of the glass, the whole office gawps until the last blind swishes down over the door and blocks them from view.

'Sit down, Lottie,' Petra says.

Mutely, I let myself fall into the chair opposite her desk. I feel wretched, completely exposed and humiliated. I am such a stupid, stupid idiot.

'Petra,' I manage. 'I'm so sorry, I . . .'

'If you think you're here to discuss your recent appearance in the tabloids, you're mistaken,' she says coolly. 'Your personal business is your own.'

Relief floods through me, interlaced with a thick dose of shame. She knows – of *course* she knows – and she pities me. I can see it in her eyes. But I won't be forced to talk about it, or to defend myself. I haven't even figured out what my defence *is*. Surely, I need to explain myself to my own husband before I self-flagellate in front of anybody else?

That said, the blinds are down. The blinds are never down. Something tells me I'm not here for a promotion.

Petra sighs and steeples her fingers together. It's the first time she's talked to me without simultaneously typing. Unease twists in my belly. 'Lottie,' she says. 'I put you on the shop project because you have an impeccable record and you seemed keen to do it. Your ideas can be a little sentimental at times, but you're a hard worker.'

I feel a flare of irritation. Sentimental? When I started working here, we only stayed afloat because of people from the community getting involved and donating. Petra wouldn't be sitting where she is now if it weren't for the very people she now seems intent on pretending don't exist. I was brought on to bring good, local art to more people, not to bring people with money to not-so-good, pretentious art.

'I know you've had issues in your personal life,' she says stiffly, not meeting my eye, 'but it's not an excuse to drop the ball quite so fantastically.'

I blink. I try to tell myself I have no idea what she's talking about. In my mind's eye, though, I can see my to-do list, long and neglected. I can see Harry asking me repeatedly whether I've done things I haven't. I can see flagged emails I never followed up on. 'Is this about the Meta advert?' I manage.

Petra sighs again. She turns to her computer, clicks her mouse a few times, and then leans back, reading from her screen. 'I've had an email this morning from one of our London clients. He was expecting a promotional package from us, and he hasn't received it. I checked the post logs, and unless you didn't record it, it was never sent. Twelve of the shops you were supposed to distribute flyers to haven't seen hide nor hair of them. I emailed you last week about the dinner event at the end of the month, and you haven't replied to me, and from asking around, you haven't even booked the venue. The other day, when you were meant to be doing street outreach, you took a two-hour lunch. When you're here, you're either on your phone, googling something non-work-related, or in the kitchen, chatting.' She looks at me. 'Shall I go on?'

'No, thank you,' I whisper. Good god, she's made a list – a list of all my failures. And she's absolutely right. I haven't been doing my job. I haven't been present whatsoever. And while it'd be easy to blame it on my lack of passion for the new direction the centre has taken, I know that's only a small part of it. The truth is that my head isn't in it. This podcast has taken over my entire life.

'Finally,' she says, and her face makes my stomach swoop, 'there's Anita Hassan.'

Shit. Shit, shit, shit. Anita Hassan is a sought-after artist we were trying to book for an exhibition in just over six weeks' time. I was supposed to reach out and get her booked in weeks ago. There'll now be a gaping hole in the schedule, an empty gallery for a week, and it's unlikely we'll find anyone up to Petra's standards to fill it at such short notice. 'I'm so sorry,' I breathe, shame consuming me. I half rise from my chair. 'I'll go now, call her directly. I'll—'

'I've already called. She's fully booked.'

I sit down in my seat again heavily. My head drops. I don't know what to say.

'This isn't like you, Lottie.'

'I'm so sorry,' I say again, feeling tears building in my eyes once more. 'I'm just . . . it's been . . . it's been hard.'

'I gave you a warning a couple of weeks ago,' she says plainly, 'and nothing has improved. If anything, things have got worse.'

'I'll get straight on it,' I say, taking a breath and sitting up in my seat. 'I'll fix everything else, I have it all written down—'

She shakes her head. 'Lottie, your mistakes have cost the centre a lot of money. Our numbers are terrible. I can't trust you to lead this any more.'

I sit back. How can a few lapses in attention from me – albeit big ones – have caused so much financial damage? I know I messed up, but surely I can't be the sole reason things are failing. I'm mortified, but at the same time, underneath, there's a frisson of relief. Maybe now, I can go back to doing less fancy work – work I'm more passionate about.

Petra is still talking. 'I won't be announcing this until later, so please do keep it to yourself for your colleagues' sakes, but we are having to consider redundancies.'

My heart drops into my stomach. *Redundancies?* 'Because of me?' I whisper dumbly.

'It's a multitude of things,' she says, wafting her hand as if I wouldn't understand. 'I just need you to be aware.'

The subtext is very, very clear. You're off the project, and you're first on the chopping block.

'Petra,' I say leaning forward, 'this job is everything to me. It's been everything to me for the last ten years. I'll do anything to keep it.'

For a moment, she looks like she might capitulate. There's a softness in her expression I haven't seen before. But then she swallows, sits back, and turns to her computer. 'If you could work with Harry on the next exhibition for now, please. Take his lead.'

When I don't move, she flits her eyes towards me.

'You can go,' she says, and I'm dismissed.

*

I walk up our front path with the strangest feeling. Memories come flooding back to me: the day we bought this place, running to the door, wrestling with each other to be the first person to put the key in the lock. The second spring we lived here, when we finally got around to planting the borders with bushes that are now triple the size. We'd worn old university T-shirts and kitchen gloves and dug into the cool earth under the warm sun, flinging bits of soil at each other and then, when things escalated, an entire baby bush, its roots spraying mud across the path. The day a Jehovah's Witness slipped on the ice on his way up to the front door, and we had to bring him inside to stop him from freezing to death before his church arrived to pick him up. We ended up agreeing to attend a summer service in the end. He was very persuasive.

I let myself in with my key and wait for the sound of claws on wood as the dogs come running. But the hallway stays silent as I close the door behind me.

'Betty! Boodle!' I call.

Nothing.

I kick off my shoes, the sick feeling in my tummy getting stronger, and walk into the kitchen. It looks exactly the same, except the dogs' beds and bowls are missing and there's a bright yellow sticky note on the breakfast bar. I read it with what's left of my thumbnail in my mouth.

L,

Gone to stay at Dev's for the half-term week. Taken the dogs, cancelled the walker. Please don't contact me. I'll come to you when I'm ready.

T

I sink into a crouched position, the note crumpled in my hands. Oh my god, he's moved out. He's actually left me. I reread his words. They're so cold. He's unbelievably angry with me. Will he ever forgive me?

Without thinking, I stand up, walk back out into the hallway, put my shoes on, and leave through the front door. I start walking quickly, my mind humming, my feet thumping against the pavement. For the tiniest instant, I let the worst thought in: I'm going to lose my job and my husband. Then I brush it away. I'm going to fix this; I'll fix all of it.

As I walk, I check my phone, finally flicking it off airplane mode for the first time since last night. I have hundreds of notifications: messages and missed calls from family and friends, from people I haven't seen since secondary school. Emails from addresses I don't recognize – presumably journalists – asking whether I'll do an interview.

But nothing from Theo.

As I'm swiping through, deleting everything, my phone begins ringing in my hand. Isa. I pick it up on impulse.

'Lottie? Jesus Christ, thank god. Where the hell have you been?'

'I had to turn my phone off,' I say. 'It's been . . . what the fuck.'

'Listen, don't panic,' she says quickly, her voice crackling with excitement, 'this is actually *really* good. Interest in tomorrow's launch episode has gone through the fucking roof. We've had three more publishers reach out, which is obviously going to drive the advance up to the nth degree. One's suggested giving you a makeover, throwing in some decoys in the months leading up to publication. Having Tilly photographed with other random women, you know. Get people really speculating before we reveal that it was you all along. There's no—'

'Isa,' I interrupt.

'Yes?'

'My husband has left me.'

She's silent for a minute. 'Oh, shit.'

'I can't carry on with any of it,' I say, my voice flat. 'It's ruined everything.'

I hear her take a sharp breath. 'No, no, Lottie, that's not true. You still have one more task to go; this one could fix everything. You can't give up on it now when you're so close to the finish line. You have to keep trying—'

'Trying what, exactly?' I find myself asking coldly. 'I don't actually currently have a partner with whom to even *attempt* to have sex, Isa.'

'Lottie,' she says, her voice firm, and I can almost hear her switching gears, 'your contract states . . .'

She rattles off a host of legal terms, but I'm not listening. I'm thinking about what Caro said to me earlier: *You're being pathetic! You're making these big, ballsy decisions but you can't even own them. If you're going to do it, Lottie, do it. Don't half-arse it and hurt people in the process.*

And she's right. Of course she's right. She's my best friend; she knows me better than anybody, and I know from watching her self-sabotage over the years how frustrating it is to see someone hurt themselves and be powerless to stop it. She did tell me not to tell Theo, but then she encouraged me to be open and honest with him. She told me the lying wasn't me. But I carried on anyway, seeing my opportunity to make a difference from the shadows, anonymously, risk-free.

Don't half-arse it and hurt people in the process.
Isa is still talking.

'I don't care about my contract,' I interrupt. 'You can have all the money back. Bye, Isa.'

I click off and shove my phone back in my bag.

I'm outside Dev's house.

Before I can think too much, I stride up the path and rap on the door. It's silent for a moment, and I can hear my heart pounding in my ears. And then a shadow appears behind the glass and the door swings open.

It's Dev, and his eyes widen when he sees me. 'Lottie.'

'Is Theo in?' I ask. My breathing is shallow; I've never done anything like this before. I'm not a confrontational person. But I need Theo to come back to me. 'Please, Dev, I need to speak to him.'

He shakes his head. 'He's out.'

I look beyond him to the hallway; I can see Theo's running trainers, but that doesn't mean much. 'Where is he? Where are the dogs?'

Dev sighs, blowing air into his cheeks. 'The dogs are fine. Theo doesn't want to speak to you at the moment,' he says gently.

'I know.' I run my hands through my hair, tugging at my roots. 'But I need to talk to him. I need to explain.'

'What happened, Lottie?'

I shake my head. 'I thought I was doing the right thing.'

'Did you?' The way Dev is looking at me, like I'm delusional and a liar all at once, makes me want to die. 'Or did you just never expect him to find out?'

My eyes fill with tears. I've known Dev as long as I've

known Theo; he's a kind, true friend. To have him seeing me in this negative light is painful and humiliating beyond measure. 'It got out of hand,' I say eventually, blinking and looking up at the sky, trying my best to push down the swell of sadness. 'I didn't expect it to go this far. I only ever wanted to do what was right for us.'

He shakes his head. 'You know I love you both. But I've got to have Theo's back on this one. You understand that, right?'

I nod. 'I just want to see him,' I say quietly.

Dev doesn't reply for a moment, instead looking at me, his eyes searching mine. 'Just give him time, Lottie,' he says eventually, standing back and pushing the door closed. Just before it shuts, he gives me one last sad smile. 'Look after yourself, OK?'

And then he's gone, and I'm left standing on the doorstep, wondering where my husband is and how I'm ever going to get him to come home.

Chapter Nineteen

Now, some of you may remember an anonymous confession we received a few weeks ago from a woman whose marriage had taken a rather un-sexy turn. A seven-year itch, if you will. She was feeling frustrated, hopeless, and – as those who tuned in will recall – possibly a bit drunk. That episode was, unexpectedly, our most successful to date. We were blown away by the responses, and we had so many of you asking us to talk more about this, that we just thought – why not take it one step further? Why not do a full series on the subject? And, to really spice things up, why not bring our anonymous confessor along for the ride?

And so finally, here we are. Guys, I am so excited to be bringing this first episode of Long-Term Lust to you. There's been so much speculation about what direction we're going to take this in, and today, the suspense is over.

Here's how things are going to work. Every week, our anonymous confessor – who we'll be calling The Horny Wife – will be undertaking a task, prescribed by me, to try and get her sex life back on track. She'll be reporting back and letting us know how it went, and we'll unpack that right here with a host of professionals at the top of their field, so that you know whether to try it yourself at home. So if you're struggling to get things going in the bedroom, you're in the right place. We've got a weekly deep dive into why it's happening, who or what might be at fault, and what you might be able to try to help fix it.

Now, before we get into our first task – and a little spoiler alert here, it involves Tantra – let's remind ourselves of our Horny Wife's initial confession . . .

I stab pause on my Spotify app and lock my phone. I am lying in our bed alone, the morning sun peeking through the curtains, feeling like absolute shit. The first episode of the podcast has officially just dropped, and I can't listen. I don't want to hear Tilly and her expert guests discussing my drunken Instagram message, analysing my ramblings about my shitty sex life and questions about why my husband won't jump me – especially now I know that everybody I know knows it was me. I don't want to hear my own crappy little report from our tantric yoga session, and imagine Theo listening to the same thing, feeling hurt and betrayed and like something that was just ours has been publicly broadcast for the world to pick apart.

How did I let this happen?

It's Saturday, and I've zombied my way through the last two days of work, tagging along with Harry and letting his chatter distract me from my own mess. I promised to do better at work, and I've been up late the last two evenings, trying to play catch-up on all the responsibilities I've neglected. But no matter how hard I try, I always end up checking my phone every five minutes like a lovesick teenager, completely unable to focus. Theo hasn't replied to any of my messages, the latest of which reads simply, PLEASE TALK TO ME. I haven't spoken to Caro since our falling-out at the café, and I miss her. I miss the dogs so much it hurts. I miss the life I had before I messed it all up.

Isa has called me at least five times a day, but I let her calls go to voicemail each time. My inbox is filled with emails from her – the last came through yesterday evening and it says, *Lottie, you are in breach of your contract. Please don't make me escalate this unnecessarily* – but I ignore every one.

My phone begins buzzing in my hand again, and my heart trills in anticipation of it being Theo. But it isn't, it's just an unknown number, so I toss my phone onto my bedside table and clamber out of bed. Downstairs, I pull a caramel iced latte out of the fridge and stare into our tiny back garden. What lengths have I gone to to get laid?

I find myself thinking about Jade, and about all the women who wrote in to the podcast saying they related to my story. What lengths are we *all* going to? I plonk myself on the sofa and scroll through Instagram, double-tapping the posts from my favourite influencers. One – a beautiful blonde woman who makes her own jam – is cuddled up with her husband on the sofa, her head nestled on his shoulder. I feel a pang of longing for Theo that is so strong I swipe off the app.

I load up TikTok instead, flicking through video after video, only breaking out of my trance when there's a sharp rap on the front door. I look up, startled; the sun is high in the sky and my iced coffee is warm on the coffee table.

Could it be Theo? Or Caro? I scramble to my feet and pad quickly down the hallway before swinging the door open.

Tilly Carter is standing on my doorstep.

'Lottie,' she says, putting her hand against the door as if she's worried I might close it in her face.

For a moment, I don't speak. I become distinctly aware of the fact that I am standing here in one of Theo's old T-shirts and a pair of his boxers, which have a saggy, empty bulge at the front. Tilly, on the other hand, is wearing a huge lime green smock dress and a mustard yellow headscarf, her copper fringe poking out of the front. 'How do you know where I live?' I manage eventually.

'It's in your contract,' she says. 'Not technically legal of me, but hey-ho. Can I come in?'

'I'm not dressed.'

'You're not naked, and that'll do for me.' She steps past me and into the hallway, where she kicks her Doc Martens Chelsea boots off. 'Lead the way,' she says, turning to me.

Helplessly, I lead her into the kitchen and swipe a pair of Theo's jogging bottoms from the washing basket on the floor before pulling them on ungracefully. 'Coffee?' I ask.

'That'd be great.' She's already sat herself on the sofa, her legs crossed beneath her. 'Lovely house.'

'Thanks.' I flick the kettle on and take a deep breath before turning around. 'Tilly, I can't carry on with the podcast. Theo's left me. It's ruined everything. It's not your fault, and I'm sorry, but—'

She holds a ringed hand up. 'No. I'm sorry. None of this was supposed to put you in any kind of trouble. Isa is . . . she's a fucking fantastic agent, but she's ruthless.'

'She won't stop calling me.'

'I'll speak to her. You can talk directly to me from now on.'

I shake my head. 'I'm not carrying on with it. I'll send the money back. I'm so sorry. I just . . . I can't.'

She leans forward, her elbows on her knees. 'Listen. We've already recorded the first five episodes; we're just missing the last one. It's not due out for five more weeks, Lottie. We can fix things before then.'

I turn my back to her, pouring hot water into a mug and stirring through some coffee granules. The people-pleaser in me is screaming at me to say yes. I've committed to this, and I have to see it through. I can't let Tilly down. But I don't see how I can. Carrying on will just be yet more proof to Theo that I'm choosing this over him, over our relationship and our privacy.

I ask Tilly how she takes her coffee and deposit it on the table in front of her before taking a seat in the armchair by the TV.

'I'm not doing it,' I say firmly. 'I've alienated my husband and my best friend over this thing; I can't do any more damage.' Amidst all the self-loathing, I feel a flutter of pride. Good for me.

She raises her mug to her lips and takes a sip before setting it down and interlacing her fingers in her lap. 'So what's your plan, then?'

I frown. 'My plan?'

She smiles. 'Have you forgotten that I'm a relationship expert, Lottie?'

'No, I know. But like I told Isa, I don't have a husband to have sex *with* right now. So all of it's pointless.'

'Podcast or no podcast, I promised you I'd help you get your sex life back on track. What comes before *that* is getting your relationship back to a healthy place. Wouldn't you agree?'

I hesitate, feeling like there's a trap coming. Then, cautiously, I nod.

'And so, I'll ask you again: what's your plan?'

I look up at the ceiling, my hands outstretched on the arms of the chair. 'Keep trying to get him to talk to me? He's back in work on Monday, so he'll have to come home for more clothes before then.'

Tilly cocks her head. 'I mean . . . it's a bit passive, isn't it?'

I blink. Well, yes, it is, but what else am I supposed to do? Camp out on Dev's doorstep with a megaphone? Turn up at Theo's PSHE class and declare my remorse in front of a group of ten-year-olds? 'I'm not sure there's much more I *can* do.'

Tilly takes another slurp of her coffee and then gets to her feet, brushing the stiff fabric of her dress down. 'Think about it, Lottie. Despite what Isa might have conveyed, I'm not only in this for the money. I made a deal with you, and I don't intend to back out of it easily.'

She rustles towards the door, and I spring to my feet and hurry after her. 'Tilly, I'm not just having a bad day,' I say desperately. 'I'm serious when I say I can't carry on with this. I know I'm a huge pain, and this has ruined everything, but—'

She turns around as we reach the front door, stopping me mid-sentence. 'I only want you to do two things, Lottie. Firstly, don't interact with Isa any more – come directly to me. And secondly, think about it. I'll leave you alone until you've decided.'

I have decided, I want to say. But before I can get the words out, she's swept through the front door and pulled it firmly closed behind her.

*

On Sunday evening, I hear the sound I've been waiting for for almost a week.

The sound of Theo's key in the lock.

I'm sitting in the bedroom, wearing my nicest casual outfit: a rust-coloured linen top and wide-legged cream trousers. My hair is freshly washed and up in a shiny ponytail, and I've painted my finger- and toenails an off-white, with no smudges, despite the fact that my hands were trembling when I applied it. I've cleaned the house from top to bottom and have filled all the dried-up diffusers with a refill liquid I found in B&M called 'fresh linen meadows'.

At the sound of the front door opening, I stand up, my heart thudding. He's back. I walk to the top of the stairs and look down, watching him as he unlaces his shoes and stacks them neatly next to mine. The dogs rush around by his feet, sniffing the floor, their tails wagging, and I feel like I might cry.

'Hi,' I whisper. Betty and Boodle spot me and scamper up the stairs on their short legs. They circle my ankles and whimper, and I squat down and pull them close to me, letting them lick my cheeks. Theo doesn't move. He stands in the hallway, looking up at me. He looks tired; dark circles have formed under his warm brown eyes, and his hair is a mess. He's wearing one of his least favourite T-shirts – a clear sign that he's run out of clothes. I notice he doesn't have a bag with him.

'Are you OK?' I ask, straightening up.

'I'm just here for some clothes,' he says, his voice colder than I've ever heard it. I feel my heart splinter. It's what I expected, but a small part of me hoped he might be coming back. I hoped he'd had his space and was ready to talk.

He walks up the stairs without meeting my eye and walks past me into the bedroom, being careful not to even brush against me as he goes. I hover in the doorway as he opens the wardrobe and starts pulling shirts off their hangers.

'Can we please have a conversation?' I ask quietly.

He doesn't answer. He pulls a holdall from the bottom of the wardrobe and starts stuffing his clothes inside, unplugging his charger from the bedside table, fishing through the washing basket for underpants I haven't got round to washing.

'Theo, please—'

'I listened to your podcast,' he says, and his voice is scratchy. 'I'm sorry you find our relationship so weird and uncomfortable.'

My breath hitches in my throat. 'No, Theo, I—'

He picks up the holdall and marches past me to the bathroom. I follow him again. 'If I could just explain exactly what I *meant*—'

'I know *exactly* what you meant,' he bites back as he tosses deodorant and dental floss and shower gel into his almost-full bag. 'You made yourself very clear.'

'I did it for us!' I cry helplessly. 'I just wanted us to—'

He wheels around to face me. 'And I didn't deserve the courtesy of a conversation before the most intimate details of our lives went public, did I? I didn't deserve direct communication of some sort?' His eyes are wide and hurt, the thin layer of anger not disguising the very real pain I've caused.

'Of course you did,' I whisper. 'God, Theo, of *course* you did. I fucked up.'

'Yeah,' he says, and his eyes leave mine. He walks past me once more and goes back down the stairs. This time, I don't follow him, instead watching as the dogs hurry after him. I watch as he puts his shoes on.

'Let's talk now,' I beg, taking one step down. 'We can communicate now, start again. I handled this all wrong, and I want to make it better. If you'll just hear me out—'

'Stop calling me, Lottie, please,' he says, so quietly I almost miss it. 'I really don't have anything to say to you right now.'

I feel like I might collapse. 'When?' I ask desperately. 'When can we talk?'

He looks around him, his palms up, as though the answer might appear on the walls of the hallway. After a moment, he sighs and lets his hands drop. 'I don't know,' he says, turning away from me. 'I don't know.'

And then he opens the front door, and he and the dogs leave me standing at the top of the stairs, completely alone.

Then, suddenly, as the sound of the door slamming fades into the gaping silence of my empty house, I have a striking realization.

I have lost almost everything that is important to me. I have hurt the people around me and I have been a total, complete fanny about it all. I've been so scared of people being cross with me, of people leaving me, that I've gone about things in a sneaky, cowardly way – and what's the outcome? Everyone *is* cross with me and everyone *has* left me.

I caused this mess, and it's not going to resolve itself while I sit and mope at home. Nobody's coming to save me; nobody's rebuilding my bridges for me.

This is on me.

I sit down on the top step and pull out my phone. Then I scroll through until I find the recently saved contact information of the person who started this whole thing – the only person who's still willing to help me – and I put the phone to my ear as I wait for Tilly Carter to pick up.

*

> Me: *Caro, I'm so sorry. I've been selfish and ridiculous and I have no excuses. I love you and hope you're OK.*

> Caro: *I can't believe you stormed out on me.*

> Me: *I know. I've behaved in ways I'm not proud of. Can I make it up to you?*

Caro: *If it's another yoni steam, I could be persuaded.*

Me: *Maybe something better? Can you be free Monday to Wednesday? Tilly's offered me something, and I want you to come with me.*

Caro: *Not sure I can condone any more podcast stuff. It's sent you loopy.*

Me: *No podcast stuff. This is extracurricular hehe.*

Me: *Sorry, no jokes. I know you're still mad at me.*

Me: *Caro? It's a girls' thing. A retreat. I know you'll love it. Promise.*

Me: *Just trust me?*

Caro: *Fine. Just tell me where and when.*

*

'And then maybe there's something *more* we can do with *The Egg*. Could we put an egg hunt up the high street? Could we do some unhinged egg painting? We could dress like eggs again; we have the costumes in the storage room, don't we, Lottie? Although I'm not thrilled with how they turned out. *The Egg* is a pearly blue, but our costumes had a more pinkish tinge. Londa, could we match the colour? I'm sure there are some acrylic paints left over from that Painting Your Idol in Space class we did . . .'

Somehow, I've made it to Monday afternoon. I haven't slept for almost forty-eight hours, and I'm running solely on iced caramel lattes and sheer grit. Harry is leading our community engagement meeting, and we (though it's a very loose definition of 'we') are brainstorming ways to get people interested in our Aisha Garratt exhibition. Her drawing of *The Egg* sold last year for almost £50,000, and its owner is allowing it to be exhibited among her newer work to draw in the crowds.

'Couldn't we just get T-shirts?' Londa asks. She's the least creative of our group and, privately, I think the least arsed.

'We can do better than that!' Harry says, outraged. It's the kind of statement I'd have come out with just a few months ago, pushing Londa and the other less animated members of the team to think creatively, but right now, I'd let Harry dress me in that head-to-toe papier-mâché egg costume and parade me down the high street to crowds of people screaming 'Humpty Dumpty!' if it meant I didn't have to participate in this meeting. My eyes keep flitting to the clock, my stomach in knots.

'How's it going here?' Petra has appeared at the door to the meeting room. It's not highly unusual for her to pop in and see what we're up to (i.e. micromanage and stick her beak in), but the way her eyes keep flicking towards me, I know she's sizing me up. Seeing whether I'm trying harder. I try to think of something to say that makes me sound invested in my job, but fail.

'Just discussing the Aisha Garratt exhibition,' Harry trills. 'We were thinking of centring the final stage of the outreach campaign around *The Egg*, seeing as we already have the costumes and the street work went well. Maybe we could get stickers printed, car stickers, and—'

'Sounds great,' Petra interrupts. 'Lottie, as you're leaving early, could you send over those print mock-ups?'

'Yes,' I say, getting to my feet. I came in early this morning to get these done, and now I'm glad I did. 'Harry, can you fill me in when I'm back?'

He nods, and I follow Petra out of the room to my desk. She watches over my shoulder as I attach the files to an email and send them to her. A few weeks ago, I'd have been irritated at her need to watch me do such a simple task, but now I don't blame her. I haven't proven myself to be very trustworthy recently.

'Thanks.' She goes to move away once the email has disappeared from my outbox, but I stop her.

'Petra.' She turns back. 'Thanks for letting me take this time. I . . . I'm going to get things back on track here.'

She nods, but I can see the wariness in her eyes. She doesn't believe me. 'You'd better go,' she says, nodding to the clock on the far wall, and then turns and strides back to her office.

I gather my things, my nerves jangling. Then I head down the fire stairs and out into the alleyway down the side of the gallery. When I emerge onto the high street, I look around, scanning the people milling back and forth along the row of shops. My heart sinks. She's not here.

'Lottie.'

I whirl around, and my heart soars. She came.

'Caro,' I say, pulling her instinctively into a hug. She

stiffens, then hugs me back. When we release each other, there's an uncomfortable moment where neither of us speaks.

'Well?' she asks, folding her arms.

'Have you packed a bag?'

'And cleared my schedule, as instructed,' she bites back. '*And* brought the car, seeing as yours has been sequestered by your angry husband, so if you'd like to tell me exactly what the *plan* is—'

'OK, OK, yes, I know, you're still pissed off with me,' I interrupt, holding my palms up. 'And I'm sorry. I'm super, super sorry. But this is some world-class, exclusive retreat thing, and I promise you're going to like it. And if it makes you feel any better, I'm probably going to hate every second.'

A smile tugs at her lips. 'That does make me feel a bit better.'

'Come on, then,' I say. 'It's my turn to take you on an adventure.'

Chapter Twenty

'What the hell is this place?'

We've only been driving for half an hour, but it's felt like forever. Caro and I have always been perfectly at ease with each other, but she's pissed off, and she's making me work for it. She's answered all of my small-talk questions monosyllabically while yanking her butter-yellow Mini around the sharp corners out of the town centre and onto the country lanes, and although I'm rightfully in her bad books, I swear she's enjoying herself.

Now, Caro is staring through the windscreen at what is, to me, a familiar set of wrought-iron gates. This time, the sun has only just set and the rain isn't lashing down, but there's no mistaking where we are.

'Theo says it's an old Romanesque monastery,' I say as I pull the car door open. Just the thought of Theo and his fascination with architecture makes sadness well in my throat, so I duck my head and hurry over to the buzzer.

Moonbeam – our tantric yoga instructor – greets me through the speaker and the gate swings open. I turn to Caro as I slide back into the passenger seat, my composure firmly back in place. 'Ready?'

Caro looks at me as she puts the car in gear, and for the first time since we met up, there's an excited sparkle in her eyes. 'This place looks *fancy*.'

'Apparently the waiting list for a spot is like, a year long.'

She lets out a low whistle as we crawl up the drive and the house looms into view. As we pull into a space, she side-eyes me. 'Don't think everything's cool and dandy now. We have a lot to talk about.'

'Roger that,' I say, nodding once.

'But holy shit,' she says, craning her neck to peer through the windscreen at the towering estate. She grabs my arm excitedly. 'Lottie, this is incredible!'

My mood lifts; we're joking again, and I know Caro is going to love this. Like Theo, she's up for anything, and I hope more than anything that we'll just have fun – laugh, make memories, be silly.

We clamber out of the car, and Caro looks at me over the roof. '*You've* taken two days off work for this?'

I nod, moving to the boot and popping it open.

She doesn't move. 'You never take time off work.'

I yank our bags out, plonking Caro's huge case on the floor and swinging my rucksack onto my back. Her words make me uneasy; she's right, and now is the worst possible time to ask for favours from Petra, with my shoddy work and the potential redundancies hanging over me. But this is Caro; there's nothing more important than her and

Theo. I stand up straight. 'Well, I have,' I say eventually. 'Come on.'

We walk up to the front door, where just a few weeks ago, Theo and I arrived in the rain to do our couple's tantric yoga. Has it really only been that long? It feels like a lifetime ago. Back then, I thought we had issues because we didn't touch very often. Now we don't even talk.

When I called Tilly the other evening, I told her I'd had an idea. It came with a caveat, though: I needed a few days to think through the details, and I needed two places on Moonbeam's upcoming Women's Holistic Identity retreat. Tilly didn't even hesitate to agree. Once I'd had my first try at being assertive with a nationally famous podcast host, asking Petra for two days off was much less daunting.

'So you're writing about this trip?' Caro asks.

'No,' I reply honestly as the door closes behind us. 'This is just for us.'

Inside the stately home, it's a different scene again. The reception space is the same, with the curved desk and the shiny floor and yellow walls and tall ceilings, but now there are people wandering around: women of different ages, some in pairs, some alone, drifting out one doorway or walking more purposefully towards another. I remember with a jab the way Theo had been mesmerized by this space, his endless questions. At the time, I'd wanted him to shut up, but now I'd do anything to have him bore me to death with facts about architecture and Boeing 737s.

Moonbeam is behind the desk this time, her long white tunic making her look like some kind of receptionist from heaven, and she smiles when she sees me. 'Lottie,' she says. 'It's so lovely to see you again.'

I smile, knowing as I always do when I'm with Caro that I'll be able to take a backseat as soon as the greetings are over. But then I reprimand myself: no, I'm in charge today. It's my turn to take the reins and let Caro enjoy the ride. 'Hi, Moonbeam. Great to see you, too.'

'You two are booked in for our Women's Holistic Identity retreat, am I right?'

'That's right.'

Moonbeam peers at me worriedly. 'I heard the episode about the yoga. I'm sorry it wasn't as useful as it could have been.'

Oh, look. If it isn't yet another consequence of my own stupid actions coming back to bite me. Not only am I betraying Theo with my decidedly non-anonymous confessions, I've also shit-talked people I thought I'd never see again but who are now right in front of me. God forbid I ever find myself in a room with the yeast-infection-giving yoni-steamer therapist again.

'It wasn't your fault at all,' I say hurriedly. 'I had a great time. It's just my husband, the situation . . . it's complicated.'

Caro reaches out and squeezes my hand, and I feel another piece of our friendship slot back into place.

'Well that's why you're here!' Moonbeam says brightly. 'To focus on *yourselves*. Shall I show you to your room? Then you can get yourselves settled and have a look at the activity list. There's something for everyone, so you can pick and choose as you like.'

She leads us across the big foyer and to a door to the right, which opens up onto an even larger space with a huge wooden staircase ascending through its middle. We climb the stairs and navigate a warren of corridors lined with doors, most of which are closed but some of which are open, and I peer inside as we pass, noting cosy libraries and sitting rooms. 'Feel free to use any of the communal spaces whenever you like,' Moonbeam says, turning round and noticing me nosing. 'They're open twenty-four-seven. We only ask that you respect other people who might be in there; if people are sitting quietly, please try to do the same. Ah, here we are.'

We stop outside the final door at the end of the corridor. A plaque on the outside says 'Robin'. Moonbeam inserts an ancient-looking key and swings the door inwards.

I physically feel my jaw drop. The room is on the corner of the building and has two huge Georgian windows on each wall, letting in the last of the evening light. There are two single four-poster beds made up in the whitest cotton, with soft linen curtains draped around their sides. Each has its own bedside table, where warm lamps cast a soft light across the worn hardwood floors. On the far wall, beyond the second bed, is a set of wooden patio doors that lead out onto a small balcony. Under one of the windows is an old wooden leather-topped desk, the view beyond it showcasing the rising moon above pink-tinged rolling fields.

'Wow,' Caro says, striding inside. 'This is . . . wow.'

'I'll leave you ladies to it,' Moonbeam says. 'You'll find the activity list on the desk, and if you'd like to join us for dinner, it's in an hour downstairs. If you get lost, just ask someone and they'll point you in the right direction.'

She steps out of the room and the door clicks softly closed

behind her. Caro immediately spins round to face me. 'Fucking *hell*,' she says.

'It's really nice.'

'*Nice?* This is like . . . Jesus.' She throws her suitcase on the bed nearest the bathroom. 'When did you become the one with the cool contacts?'

I force a smile and walk over to the bed at the far end, by the balcony. Dumping my bag on the floor, I let myself fall onto the soft sheets. I groan with pleasure. 'My god, it's comfy.'

Caro sits down on the other bed. 'Holy shit.' She bounces back up again and walks around the room, picking things up and inspecting them before putting them down again and moving on. She swings open a small door in the corner. 'There's a bath!' she declares gleefully.

I feel a warm swell in my tummy – it's one of my favourite things in the world when Caro is happy like this, and now that she's bouncing around in front of me, it's glaringly obvious that she hasn't been for some time. When was the last time I saw her this excited? When she first got with Peter?

Surreptitiously, I check my phone. Still nothing from Theo. I tug at the curtains around my bed until they're half closed, cocooning me in a linen cave. I close my eyes. I'll just rest for a moment, get my energy back.

The bed jolts as Caro plonks herself down. I peer at her; she's holding a thick sheet of cream paper. 'OK, so tonight's the welcome dinner – six courses. Obviously we're doing that. Then there's a moon goddess ritual out in the garden. Oh my god, a midnight tea ceremony in the forest. They have a *forest*, Lottie. Then tomorrow morning—'

'Caro,' I say, propping myself up on my elbows. 'Can I just stay in this evening? Please? I'm so tired.'

She pouts. 'You have not brought me here so we can lock ourselves in the room. I cancelled a Furry shoot for this.'

I want to defend myself, but really, I had hoped that we might just hang out. Repair things between us, maybe watch a movie, do some yoga. But this is Caro; of course she's going to want to do all the things.

'You can go,' I say. 'I just need to rest I think.'

'I know you've booked this whole thing for me, but you'd benefit from some of this stuff, too,' she says, scanning the paper. 'You still need to fix your marriage, remember.'

'With a *tea* ceremony?'

She narrows her eyes, and I capitulate – I'm here for Caro, I've got to push my own heartbreak to the side. I sit up. 'I'll make you a deal. If you let me stay here and catch up on some sleep this evening, you get to decide everything we do for the rest of the stay.'

A wicked grin spreads over her face. 'Sounds *great*.'

I find myself smiling back, despite knowing that I'll pay dearly for my night in, and for a moment, our eyes meet and it feels like all is completely forgiven between us. But then she flicks her gaze away and stands up.

'Right,' she says, clearing her throat. 'Help me decide which of my outfits best conveys "Here to non-ironically connect with my womb". I want to make a good first impression.'

*

The house is deliciously silent, the kind of quiet people in London pay thousands to escape to for just a couple of nights.

I'm lying where Caro left me, watching the moon through the gauze of the curtains around my bed, my eyes heavy but my mind whirring. It's *too* quiet without Caro chattering, Theo snoring, the dogs to feed, the usual street sounds outside.

All I can think about is where Theo is at this precise moment. We've probably spent a total of ten nights apart since we started dating, and this past week has almost doubled that number. Is he thinking about me? Is he lying in bed, too, staring at the same moon, wondering how we're going to come back from this? Or is he out somewhere with Dev, losing himself, pretending our problems don't exist? Or, worst of all, is he going through the logistics of the worst ending to this story imaginable? Is he drafting emails to lawyers, making enquiries about getting the house valued, googling 'Who keeps dogs after divorce'?

I reach through the curtain and grab my phone from the bedside table. My chat with Theo is still resolutely silent. I only have two new messages, both from Caro, reading:

> Caro: *They have wine!!*

> Caro: *Omg, sat next to a woman who makes her own tampons – SOS!!!!*

I reply, then instinctively swipe into TikTok before closing the app again. Something tells me distracting myself isn't what I need right now. I open my Photos app. Yes, I decide, I need to torture myself instead.

I have to scroll back quite far to find a photo of me and Theo together. In the past year they've dwindled, our attention to recording memories of our relationship evidently fading around the time our sex life started to fall off a cliff. I stare at the last picture we took together until it blurs in front of my eyes: a selfie at the tapas restaurant in town, specifically taken so that we could capture the couple behind us, who were necking so aggressively the woman knocked a bowl of olives onto the floor.

We look . . . happy. Not quite as happy as we do a few photos back, but certainly happier than we have been for the past few months. I remember we ordered rosemary focaccia with olive oil and balsamic vinegar, and our favourite red wine. We talked about my latest issue with Petra, Theo's most troublesome students, whether we were going to get the dogs new harnesses before or after the winter. I was excited about some new ticket I'd found for him – two pairs, to something called AirCon in Bristol. It was usual, daily stuff. But we were interested in each other. I wanted to hear about his life and he wanted to hear about mine. We wanted to dissect the tiny mundane details that compiled to form our coexistence. Those things were important to us. We shared an interest in the familiar bubble that surrounded us. Our lives were so intertwined it was impossible to imagine ourselves as separate people, untouched by each other.

Yet here I am, lying in a single bed in the middle of the countryside, with no idea whether I still have a marriage or not. And there he is, out there somewhere, without me.

I lock my phone and hold it against my chest, closing my eyes and hoping that wherever he is, Theo can feel the silence I'm offering him, my heartbeat conveying everything I need to say across the distance between us.

Chapter Twenty-One

'OK, so I took pity on you this morning and let you sleep – you've missed breakfast, which was incredible, by the way – so you'd better have recuperated some energy for this morning's activity, because—'

Caro cuts off midway into the room when she sees me. I'm lying in my bed, my eyes pink-rimmed, the sheets pulled up to my chin. I've barely slept all night; I dozed off until Caro came in and filled me in on her evening downstairs, and I listened with envy as her words became heavy and her breathing deepened and she slipped into a peaceful sleep. I tossed and turned until the sunrise began filtering through the curtains, and then pretended to be asleep when I heard her getting ready for breakfast. Once she'd left, I gave in and started looking at photos of Theo again, going as far back as when we first met, when we first bought the house, when we brought the dogs home. I've been lying here crying ever since.

'Oh, Lotts,' Caro says now, hurrying over and plonking herself on the edge of my bed. She reaches out a hand to comfort me, but there's still everything that's messy between us, and she pulls back at the last minute. Her brow creases in concern. 'I'm sorry you're sad.'

'I'm fine,' I say, forcing myself to shuffle into a seated position. 'I'm sorry. I'll get ready now, I'm just . . .' I trail off as another fat tear rolls down my cheek. 'Shit.'

Caro stands up and plucks a tissue from the desk under the window, then sits back down and hands it to me. 'It's all going to be OK, you know,' she says quietly. 'Whatever happens.'

I nod, pushing the tissue against my eyes. I'm desperate to step up for Caro, to show her I'm actively participating in the mending of our friendship, but I feel so heavy and tired. 'Can I stay here?' I ask after a moment, when the tears don't stop. 'I think I just need—'

'No.' Caro says firmly. 'Doing this – hiding out, not showing up – is exactly what's got you into this mess in the first place.'

I sit back. Her words sting, but I know they're true. Still, I can't help pushing just once more. 'Honestly, Caro, I've barely slept for a week, I—'

'And you won't sleep now,' she says, standing up. 'What you need is to face the day. Come on.' She strides over to the windows and begins yanking the curtains open. I wince as the bright light hits my sore eyes. She wheels around and looks at me, and I can see a familiar mischievous brightness etched across her face. 'Besides, I seem to remember we made a deal last night.'

'I know . . .'

'I endured an entire dinner with a woman who weaves sanitary pads out of cotton she grows in her renewable greenhouse in the Highlands. I know *so* much about weaving, Lottie. I drank almost an entire bottle of wine by myself and I still remember every single thing. And you promised me that if I did that, you'd let me pick our activities for the rest of the stay.'

I pull the sheets around my shoulders. 'You said the dinner was nice.'

She waves a hand. 'One of the best meals I've ever had. But that's not the *point*. You've dragged me here, when I'm still actually quite cross with you, and you're not helping your case to win back my friendship by lying in bed like some kind of sick Victorian child.'

She sounds mean, but she isn't. This is Caro's version of love: *get up, brush yourself off, get on with it, and I'll hold your hand while you do so.* I offer her a weak, hopeful smile. 'But I'm making a compelling case otherwise?'

'No,' she says bluntly. 'Now hurry up. We've got a class to get to.'

I eye the activities list on my bedside table. 'Caro, I am not painting my own vulva.'

'You don't paint your *vulva*,' she says, looking at me like I'm insane, 'you paint a picture *of* your vulva.'

'And how exactly is that supposed to work?'

'Mirrors,' she says as though it's obvious.

'I'd rather die.'

She strides over to me and yanks my covers back. I cry out as the cool morning air hits my skin, and snatch to pull them back, but she tugs them away. She looks down at me defiantly. 'I am not painting my vulva alone.'

'Pick something else! Anything. Anything but the vulva painting. I promise I'll come.'

She narrows her eyes. 'Anything?'

Why do I already feel like I'm going to regret this? I nod.

She whips the piece of paper off the bedside table. 'Excellent,' she says once she's scanned through it again. 'We need to be downstairs in twelve minutes.'

*

Exactly thirteen minutes later, Caro leads us into an already-full room on the ground floor, apologizing for our tardiness. I balk as soon as we enter, grabbing her by the sleeve.

'Why do I see mirrors?' I hiss.

She glares at me. 'Lottie, come *on*.' She obviously sees the reluctance still plastered across my face, because she grabs my hand and tugs me forward, her voice softening. 'I promise you won't have to get your vulva out.'

There are two spaces left, right at the front, and each contains a yoga mat and a full-length mirror. Mercifully, I see no paint. A woman I haven't seen before stands in front of us with her own mirror and mat, smiling serenely, a stick of incense burning perilously close to her bare feet. She has a wiry thin frame and a bony face, and tangled brown-grey hair down to the backs of her thighs.

'That looks like a full house,' she says softly once Caro and I have sat down. 'So welcome, everybody, to today's tantric mirror work session. I'm Miranda.'

I turn to look at Caro, widening my eyes. More Tantra? Caro studiously ignores me, smiling pointedly at Miranda, and I turn my gaze to the front again. This is for Caro. If this is what she wants to do, this is what we'll do.

But I just *know* she's doing it to mess with me. She might be feeling sorry for me, but she's also still rightfully annoyed, and watching me squirm is exactly the kind of thing that will make her feel better.

'Now, this is a safe space, and everyone is free to work at a level that feels comfortable to them. That said, if you'd like to remove some or all of your clothing, please do so now.'

Good god. I can hear rustling behind me, the sound of multiple women shedding their outfits. Miranda pulls her top over her head, so that she's standing in just her low-rise linen trousers and bralette. Beside me, Caro does the same. I stay sitting, trying not to catch a glimpse of anyone else in the room (a near-impossible task with a giant mirror in front of me) as I sit, uptight, in my jeans and turtleneck. Somehow, *I* feel like the weirdo.

'Now, let's begin in a seated position,' Miranda says, positioning herself cross-legged in front of her own mirror. I catch a glimpse of nipple in the reflection in front of me and avert my gaze, only for it to land on a woman who's totally naked three rows back. This is a nightmare. 'Gaze into your own eyes. What are they saying to you?'

With relief, I focus on my own face. I look tired and pale, and as though I'm attending a seminar, not a spiritual retreat. My hair is pulled back into an unflattering bun and yesterday's mascara is smudged above my cheeks. I look into my own eyes. This is what Theo must have seen when we were here: my worried gaze staring back at him. I remember his deep brown eyes fixing on mine, then flicking away. In the mirror, I note that I look sad. I answer Miranda's question silently: *my eyes are telling me I am unhappy.*

'Today we are going to honour the divine within,' Miranda murmurs. 'We see ourselves through the eyes of truth, not shame. Keep going.'

Keep going with what? I want to ask, but Miranda has stood up and moved towards the door. I look over to Caro, who is staring at herself serenely. She evidently notices that I'm looking at her, because she flicks her gaze towards me and raises her eyebrows, angling her head towards the mirror. 'Look at yourself!' she mouths.

I stick my tongue out and reluctantly turn back to my mirror. Behind me, someone tuts, and I feel a flush of embarrassment. But then, hang on, why am *I* embarrassed? I'm not the one sat here with my tits out behaving like I'm on a third date with myself.

Suddenly, from nowhere, there's a spritzing noise and a damp mist sprays across my cheek. I gasp.

'Rose water,' Miranda says softly. She's appeared beside me carrying a spray bottle of pink liquid. She spritzes it around the room, moving from woman to woman. 'Clarifying.'

I wait until she's out of sight and then use my sleeve to dry my skin.

'Who do you see?' Miranda asks. Somewhere, someone is breathing extremely heavily. 'A woman who is afraid?'

'Yes,' someone whispers.

'Or a woman who has survived? Who has desired and hidden and pushed down?'

Someone begins weeping.

I look into my own eyes again. I see a woman who has betrayed.

'Let us hum,' I think I hear Miranda say. I turn to look at Caro. She's staring at herself, seemingly lost in whatever it is we're doing.

Miranda lets out a low, throaty, droning noise, and one by one, people join in until it sounds like there's a swarm of bees in the room. I press my lips together, panicking as laughter trembles in my chest. *Don't* laugh, Lottie. Do *not* laugh. I try to think of something sad. *My husband has left me.* The urge to laugh quickly subsides.

'Look at yourself!' Miranda cries, and the humming abruptly stops. 'You are beautiful, desirable, soft, and solid! You are Mother!'

Oh, Christ, no, the laughter is back. I'm shaking with it. Beside me, I think I see Caro twitch.

'Touch your skin. Stroke it. Your stretch marks are rivers, your breasts sacred homes. That belly you feel so ashamed of? It's the centre of your intuition, the very heart of your feminine instinct. Touch yourself with softness, with the gentleness that is your divine birthright.'

The only skin I have uncovered is that of my hands and my face. I clutch my hands together in my lap, digging my nails into my palms. I cough, releasing some of the giddy energy building at the back of my throat. I hear Caro do the same, and for a moment, I think it's going to push me over the edge.

'Now hold your hand to your belly and look at yourself. *See* yourself. And repeat after me. I see you.'

'I see you,' we chant. My voice wobbles, the giggles almost breaking free.

'You are enough.'

'You are enough,' we reply.

'I forgive you.'

My voice falters. I look into my own eyes, and for a brief flash, I see everything reflected there. Not just my own shitty behaviour, my lies and secrecy and betrayal, but my hurt, too. The pain of feeling unwanted, the fear of asking for what I want in return. I see myself through Theo's eyes, a human being who has tried and has gone about things the wrong way. A human being with the capacity to cause pain but also to endure it, and choose an unwise path as a result. The laughter dies in my throat and something else rises instead, pressure building behind my eyes.

But I can't do it. As women sob and whisper and murmur around me, forgiving themselves for their sins, I look deep into my own eyes and keep my lips tightly closed.

*

'OK, well *that* was ridiculous,' I say with a rush when Caro and I are finally outside. The session ended ten minutes ago, but I had to wait for Caro to get dressed and have a brief catch-up with the half-naked tampon lady she was sat next to at dinner last night, and we've only just broken free. We've come straight outside, where the sun is shining on the estate's manicured gardens.

Caro lights up a cigarette. 'You *loved* it,' she says.

'I did not. It was mad.'

She gives me an exasperated side-eye as we begin walking. 'Oh, don't be such a miserable sod. You must have got something out of it.'

I don't answer. I'm reminded that I had a very similar

conversation with Theo after our tantric yoga session. I needed him to feel something, and was devastated when he said he didn't. But now that it's me, I just don't seem to be able to relay what I experienced in there. Could it be that our communication was so broken down, he couldn't open up to me? That it was easier to laugh it off instead?

Really, all I got out of that session was the satisfaction of knowing that I did something for Caro. We've been there for each other whenever we've needed it over the years, but recently I've dropped the ball, and I've got a lot of making up to do. If staring at myself in a room of naked women is what it takes, so be it.

'What did *you* get out of it?' I ask Caro as we round the building and emerge onto a striped green lawn, bordered with tall, swaying tulips.

'I found some self-acceptance,' she says confidently, taking a drag of her cigarette.

I snort. 'You? Self-acceptance? You're the most self-assured person I know. Your life is great.'

Suddenly, she stops. I take another two steps forward and then turn around. 'What?'

She stares at me, her eyes flashing. 'This is exactly what I mean.'

'What?' I ask again, flummoxed.

'You're not the only one with problems, Lottie.'

I take a step back, shocked at the anger in her voice. 'I know.'

'Do you?'

I blink, totally caught off-guard. We've never argued before, not like this. 'What's going on, Caro?'

She shakes her head and turns away from me, looking out across the hills as she lifts her cigarette to her lips.

'Caro,' I say, stepping towards her. 'I've been shitty and preoccupied. I know that. But it's been a really crap time, and—'

'Forget it,' she says, tossing her cigarette onto the grass and moving past me.

I watch her stalk off towards the house, my mind reeling. What the hell was that?

But really, the answer is niggling at the back of my mind – it has been for a while. Something is up with Caro, and I haven't tried hard enough to find out what it is. Have I made the same mistake with my best friend as I did with Theo? Sensed them changing in front of my eyes and averted my gaze, not wanting to see anything that might upset the delicate balance of my carefully constructed life?

Because I've tried getting to the bottom of this – I asked her when we did our yoni steam, tried digging in when she was at mine – but I never probed too much. I let it drop at the first sign of resistance.

I didn't want her to tell me something I didn't want to hear.

*

Lunch consists of extremely healthy food prepared in an extremely delicious way. We have couscous with chickpeas and juicy red peppers; pasta with fresh tomatoes drenched in olive oil, a rich romesco sauce, and the crunchiest lentil crispbreads. Everything is laid out in the middle of the huge table in the dining room, which sits under high ceilings with exposed wooden beams. The patio doors beside us are open and the spring breeze is blowing in across the hills, making the gauzy curtains flutter.

But I'm not enjoying any of it, because the tension between Caro and me is so thick you could cut it with one of the vintage butter knives.

'I'm Sasha,' the woman next to me says mere seconds after I've put a piece of lemon-marinated tofu in my mouth. I chew and swallow too quickly and almost choke, so desperate am I to talk to someone else and break the weird funk that's hanging over this meal.

'Lottie,' I croak, holding out my hand. 'Nice to meet you.'

Sasha has the kind of white-blonde hair that's almost impossible to find on an adult, and the smoothest, milkiest skin. Her eyes are bright blue, and she's wearing a loose vest dress that dips low to reveal most of her left boob. Sasha is not the kind of woman who needs to wear a bra. She's the poster girl for a retreat like this – the type of person who would set up an Instagram account to document the renovation of a builder's van into a quirky mobile home.

'Girls' trip?' she asks, nodding at Caro, who has begun chatting to the woman beside her.

'Yeah.' I try to smile. 'What about you?'

'Oh, you know,' she says vaguely, 'just passing through.'

'Are you on your way somewhere?'

She smiles quizzically. 'No. I'm just . . . here.'

'Ah, OK.' I turn back to my meal. What do I say to that? I fork some tahini broccoli into my mouth. 'Have you done something like this before?' I come up with once I've swallowed.

She nods. 'A couple of times. I find it transformative.'

I sense Sasha and I aren't going to walk away from here as best friends.

'Hi!' Caro says beside me, nudging her way into the conversation. 'I'm Caro.'

'Sasha. Lottie was just telling me you're on a girls' trip.'

'Yep.' To the untrained eye, it seems like a simple, uncomplicated answer. But I can hear the subtext underneath.

Sasha looks at us thoughtfully. 'I did a retreat last year in Penzance. It was all about personal philosophy. Do you know your personal philosophy?'

The words are meaningless to me, but Caro answers immediately. 'Fuck it, could be dead tomorrow?'

Sasha breaks into a grin. 'I wouldn't word it exactly like that, but I'm the same.'

'How would you word it?'

Sasha's face is serious. 'The veil is thin, the clock is ticking, my soul is hungry.'

I blink, stifling a laugh. I can't wait to get back to the room and see Caro's impression of Sasha: her intense stare, her statue-still posture. If she's talking to me by then. I shovel a spoonful of couscous into my mouth.

But surprisingly, Caro is nodding beside me. 'It's more woo-woo than I'd go, but that's exactly it. What are we here for if not to make the most of each day?'

'Exactly! So many people just sit in these flat, empty lives, accepting that work-sleep-repeat is all there is. And why? Because they're scared. They're terrified of stepping out of the socially acceptable way of living and realizing that they've missed out on the whole world. It's a complete tragedy.'

Caro nods, leaning forward now. 'You're so right. I always feel like there's not a minute to waste. I can't bear the idea of looking back and seeing that I just sat there, not moving, not going after what I wanted.'

I put my fork down. I'm starting to feel a bit sick. Caro and Sasha keep talking, leaning towards each other over my plate, getting more and more animated. While I hope it isn't, everything they're saying feels like a personal attack. Because it's true: I have spent my entire life scared. I've lived small, and I've stayed quiet, and I've convinced myself I'm happy. I *was* happy. I'm not Caro, big and impulsive and reckless. But was it all a lie? Because my relationship wilted right before my eyes, and really, I've hated my job for years now. And what have I done about any of it? Ignored it, or tried to fix it from the shadows, hiding anonymously. I've never looked a problem in the eye in my life.

But does Caro really go after what she wants? Or does she just run away from anything remotely resembling commitment? They look the same from a distance, but up close, one is driven by bravery and the other by fear.

I blink and push my chair back, shocked at the bitterness of my own thoughts.

'Just nipping to the bathroom,' I say, rising to my feet. Sasha and Caro barely glance at me as I edge around my seat and walk across the dining room to the main doors. Once I'm outside, I skirt the bathroom and go straight to our room, where I sit on my bed and go through my text chain with Theo again. I haven't messaged since he asked me to leave him alone, but my previous string of desperate attempts to communicate sit at the bottom of our chat, unanswered.

> *Please, Theo. I miss you.*
>
> *Can we talk? I'll explain everything.*
>
> *I know that nothing I can say will make what I've done better – I fucked up. But can we start again?*

Promises of explanation and face-to-face conversations – hundreds of them, and he ignored every single one. And why wouldn't he? I've had months to offer him an explanation for my behaviour, to have a direct and honest conversation with him, but I didn't bother until the shit hit the fan.

I don't know how much time passes, but I scroll slowly back through my chat with Theo until the blue wall of my messages becomes interspersed with grey, and for a moment, I let myself imagine that a conversation we had two weeks ago about spaghetti bolognese is one we're having right now. Then the bedroom door clicks open and I look up to see Caro standing in the doorway.

'Lottie? I've been looking everywhere for you. You OK?'

'Yeah, fine,' I say, sliding my phone into my pocket. 'Just needed a minute.'

'I'm sorry,' she says, coming in and sitting opposite me. 'I didn't mean to exclude you from the conversation there.'

I shake my head. 'You didn't at all. I just felt a bit off.'

She looks at me for a moment, then turns her gaze out of the window. When she looks back at me, the hardness that's been in her eyes since our argument in the café has gone.

I feel a rush of love and gratitude for this woman sitting in front of me, my best friend, who has given up her time to be here with me. She's putting up with my mopey bullshit, despite this retreat being my gift to her, and despite the fact that I've neglected her and pushed her away for weeks now. This is what we do: we look after each other come rain or shine, and while it might not be the most stable time in my life, it's my turn to step the fuck up. I sit up straight. 'We need to have a proper chat, don't we?'

'We do.' She stands up. 'But not now. We've got our next class to get to. Come on.'

Chapter Twenty-Two

At the back of the estate, a place I haven't seen until now, there is a huge yurt on the lawn. It's like a giant wedding marquee, except it has no windows and is khaki brown. Caro and I step across the soft grass until we reach the entrance, where a warm, dry, incense-laden smell is drifting out into the spring air.

Inside, the yurt is exactly what you'd expect: thick woven flooring dotted with wooden posts rising up to a huge canvas exterior. The light is warm and reddish from the sun filtering through, and spores of dust and pollen float in the air. Around the space are strewn clusters of random items: cushions, foam rollers, drums, notebooks, empty bins. Several women are already gathered in the centre, where Moonbeam is holding court, yet more incense burning at her feet. Caro and I join the huddle.

'Welcome to our primal release workshop,' Moonbeam is saying. 'Some of you may have tried variations of this before;

perhaps you know it as sacred rage or anger-embodiment work. Our aim here is to put down what has been assigned to us as females – niceness, amenability, politeness, prettiness – and access our raw, unfiltered selves. We release the rage that has inhabited your womb, your bones; the womb and bones of your mother and grandmother. We are not here to play a role today, ladies. We are not here to make each other feel comfortable. We are here to express our raw power. How does that sound?'

An enthusiastic rumble ripples through the group. I fight the urge to nudge Caro, to make her laugh. She's watching Moonbeam seriously, her eyes keen with interest.

'Great. We'll begin in our stations. Go and pick an area with a few objects in it, anywhere you like, and once we're settled we'll get started.'

People scatter, and Caro and I find a spot near the wall of the yurt, where there's a rolled-up yoga mat, a saucepan, a huge pillow, and an IKEA storage bin.

'Now,' Moonbeam says once everyone is hovering near what looks like the unwanted lot at a charity shop, 'close your eyes.'

I shuffle a little closer to Caro and squeeze my eyes shut.

'Feel the anger. You might not know it's there, but it is. It's under your skin. Where has it come from, and where is it hiding? Who taught you that smiling was better than screaming?' Moonbeam waits a beat while we process this slightly baffling question. 'Now, I want you to give yourselves permission to make *noise*. You were not born to be quiet. In this space, anything goes. There is no one to disturb, no one to get offended or troubled by your primal energy. You can scream, grunt, roar, moan. Hit, punch, throw. Whatever comes, allow it.' And then, in a quieter voice, she says, 'But please do be aware of other people; we accept no liability for damage or injury to persons or personal objects.'

I flick my eyes open and look at Caro, grinning. But she's not looking at me. Her eyes are still tightly closed.

'And now . . . RAGE!' Moonbeam screams.

The room erupts. Women throw themselves at the ground, picking up pillows and pressing them against their faces, screaming into the fabric. Someone grabs a drum and begins smacking it while howling, her head tilted to the sky. Next to me, one lady rolls across the floor, growling like an injured bear.

I look at Caro, my mouth hanging open. 'What the—'

But Caro is holding the rolled-up yoga mat aloft, pounding the ground with it, her shiny black hair flying this way and that. 'Fuck you!' she screams. 'Grow up!'

In front of me, a woman is curled on the floor, clutching a saucepan that she beats with her fist. 'Where were you?' she moans.

'Lottie.' Moonbeam has appeared by my side. 'Would you like to join in?'

I realize I'm standing awkwardly, staring dumbfounded at the chaos around me. 'Erm. I don't think I'm angry about anything right now,' I say apologetically.

'Are you sure?' she asks, raising her voice over the commotion. 'A lot of our surface-level emotions are rooted in a deep anger, a deep sense of injustice. Can you dig a little deeper?'

I'm not sure I want to, but I don't want to upset Moonbeam, who is already being very kind considering how rude I was about her tantric yoga course. I rack my brains as someone launches themself against the side of the yurt, bouncing off the stiff fabric and landing in a heap on the floor. I feel sad, not angry. I feel bereft. I think back to my ignored messages to Theo, the crack I felt in my heart when he stood at the bottom of our staircase and said he didn't want to talk to me. I think about how angry Caro is – with me, but with something else, too. Something I haven't helped her work through, because I've been so wrapped up in my own self-created mess.

And then I realize, suddenly, that yes, I'm angry. I'm angry with *myself*. That anger is so fierce, so visceral, that I almost can't look at it. I took something beautiful, something perfect, and I shattered it all. I let myself get carried away with promises of quick fixes and anonymity and subterfuge, and instead of bringing us closer together, I hurt the person I care most about in the world. I reach down and pick up the IKEA bin, then hold it in front of my face. Moonbeam looks at me and nods, smiling, like she's seen the thoughts I've just had zapping by in the space of a few seconds. She steps back. 'Let it out, Lottie,' she says.

I shove my head in the bin and scream louder than I ever have before. The rage tears at my throat, making my eyes water. My scream is directed entirely at myself, at the way I've lost Theo, and almost lost Caro, too. I thought I had my whole life together, but really I was just scared.

And then, unbidden, Sasha and Caro's conversation over lunch comes back to me.

So many people just sit in these flat, empty lives, accepting that work-sleep-repeat is all there is. And why? Because they're scared.

I *am* scared. And if I ask myself why, I know it's because rocking the boat is something I've programmed myself to avoid. I need to make people like me; I need Theo to desire me; I need my boss to think I'm doing a good job. If not, they'll reject me, and I'll be all alone. But what do *I* want? Do I want to run soulless marketing campaigns for artists I don't believe in? Do I want to wait for my husband to come to me, to show me that he wants me, before I can feel good about myself?

So, yes, I'm scared. I'm scared that people won't like me, that my husband will leave me, that I'll lose my job and be humiliated, and that my nice, postcard life will topple down. But more than that, underneath the surface, I am simmering with rage. Because while I'm undoubtedly the villain in this story, I have also sacrificed myself and my wants and my integrity and my *identity* for other people. For their opinions and their ideas of who I should be. And it has got me precisely nowhere.

And it's only now occurring to me, as I let myself scream into a plastic box in a yurt in the middle of a field, that perhaps betraying Theo in this way was my attempt at actually *doing* something. There's a part of me, one I've tried to push down, that wanted this mess. The part of me that showed up the night of Jade's hen party and sent that anonymous confession is the same part of me that accepted Tilly's offer, wrote the posts, entertained the book-deal conversations. And it's an angry part of me – a part that's saying, *I don't have to sit back and accept. I can do big, insane things, too.*

It rumbles in my chest, the part of me I've pushed down my entire life finally rushing forward. My own needs, my own wants, my own decisions. I don't want to be palatable, not really. I want to be forceful. I want to look my life in the eye and shake it into submission.

I don't want to wait for someone else to give me permission.

I let my scream roar into a crescendo, and then throw the bin to the floor and turn to Caro, who is punching a pillow with all her might. She looks up at me, sweat sticking her hair to her forehead, and grins, before tipping her head back and howling. I lift my arms up in the air and roar at the ceiling of the yurt, and she runs forward and throws her arms around me, laughing into my ear.

'We can do anything!' she cries. 'We don't need to be scared!'

And it's only then, as I'm howling and sweating and laughing and gripping someone I love with all of my heart, that I finally start to wonder whether maybe, I might survive this. *We* might survive this. No matter what's happening with my marriage, my job, my life, no matter what's going on with Caro, we will make it through. As long as we have each other, we'll make it through.

*

There isn't time for me to dive deeper into this with Caro, because the moment our primal release workshop ends, we're swept up in a herd of people heading out of the yurt and towards the forest. The sun is dipping in the sky, and Sasha catches up with us as we're following a well-beaten path through the grass to the tree line.

'Hey,' I say as she appears by my side. Her cheeks are pink and her eyes are bright. 'Were you at the primal release workshop? Wasn't it amazing?'

'*Incredible*,' she says breathlessly. 'You were really taking something out on that pillow, Caro.'

'It was *so* good,' Caro says. I peer at her. She's never been a particular fan of woo-woo anything; she's fiercely independent and always absolutely fine, seemingly in no need of any external guidance from the universe, god, or anybody else. But she's really leaning into this – laughing about it, yes, but also throwing herself into the activities, getting lost in them like she's sinking into a hot bath with sore muscles. Now that I'm attuned to the fact that Caro's going through something, I'm like a detective on the hunt for clues. What part of her is she trying to soothe?

As we enter the cool darkness of the forest, Caro and Sasha chatting across me, the noise of the outside world falls to a hush. After a few minutes walking through the pine trees in the dusk, the path below us a carpet of soft pine needles, we emerge into a clearing. In front of us is the perfect cosy campfire scene: overturned logs are arranged in a wide circle around a stone centrepiece covered in flower petals and crystals, and in the middle, there's a crackling fire, a column of smoke snaking up into the sky. Each log has a folded blanket and a notebook on it, and the air is thick with the smell of burning wood and the sound of birds' evening song.

The group falls silent – this place feels sacred, deserving of respect. We each choose a log and sit in the fading light. I instinctively pull my blanket over me, running my fingers over the embossed cover of my notebook as I stare at the flames in front of me.

A few moments pass, and then a bell rings. From my left, a woman emerges from the trees. Was she hiding back there, waiting to make her entrance? The thought ruins the effect somewhat. She floats into the centre of the circle, colourful robes draping over her large chest, and begins slowly moving around the fire.

'Welcome to the forest, sisters. Welcome to your sacred home. My name is Starlight. We're here this evening to remember ourselves. To rediscover who we are underneath the layers of our lives.'

This is very peaceful. There's something nostalgic about it; I feel like I'm on a PGL trip. I pull my blanket up higher.

'I'd like to invite you first of all to share your goddess name for today with the group. It doesn't have to be perfect, just whatever comes to mind. We'll start with you.' She points to a woman across from me. Immediately, my palms begin to sweat. What fresh hell is this? A *goddess name*?

What do I say? Aphrodite? Aside from being wholly inaccurate, is that arrogant? I don't know any other goddesses.

I fling my blanket off me as the question makes its way quickly around the circle. I'm boiling all of a sudden. Some women answer confidently, having evidently done this kind of thing before: Sunshine Sparrow, Lunar Fox, Gaia. Others seem unsure, but think on the spot: Glenda the Brave, Lioness Lisa. This is horrifying.

Aside from shortening Charlotte to Lottie, the only nickname I've ever been given was by Caro, who, for a brief period in Year Eleven following a dinner-hall disaster, started calling me Spaghottie.

The question comes to me. Starlight smiles at me expectantly. In an instant, I make a decision. 'Spaghottie,' I find myself saying. Beside me, Caro snorts and claps her hand over her mouth.

'I'm sorry?' Starlight takes a step forward.

I swallow. 'Spaghottie,' I say, with more authority this time.

She nods. 'Right. Yes. That's . . . unique. Welcome, Spaghottie.'

We move on to Caro. She looks Starlight in the eye and says, quite seriously, 'Tony.'

'Tony,' Starlight repeats, and glances between us, as if she's not quite sure if we're teaming up to take the piss or not. I press my lips together, images of Tony's Pizzeria and those stodgy margheritas appearing in my mind. Starlight moves on unsurely, and I reach out and grab Caro's hand, my eyes still trained forward, and give it a squeeze.

She squeezes it back.

'Fantastic,' Starlight croons when she reaches the end of the circle. 'Now, if you'd like to open your notebooks, you'll find a piece of paper inside.'

Surely enough, tucked inside the front cover of my book is a folded list. On it are written eight different 'goddess archetypes'.

'Take a moment now to find the archetype that most aligns with who you are today. Your central energy this evening. Make notes, draw, access whichever parts of you you need to make your choice. When you've decided, make your way to the corresponding shrine and take an item to adorn yourself in your identity.'

I follow Starlight's gesture and look more closely at the trees around us. Every five or so, there's a collection of objects around or on the trunk – feathers, veils, wind chimes, swords – and nailed to the tree is a wooden plaque stating the corresponding archetype. At the base of one, there's a glistening crown, shining in the fading light.

The clearing falls quiet as everyone reads, the fire crackling in the background. I scan the list. The Mystic, The Creative, The Warrior. Instinctively, I identify with The Lover, who is described as submissive, demure, loyal, sensual. But I *want* to be one of the others. I want to describe myself as powerful, assertive, wild, creative, intense.

Someone stands up, and as soon as they do, others begin to follow. Several women are heading for the shrine called The Queen, where the crown sits. As the two women at the front near, they pick up the pace, evidently trying to beat each other to the title spot. One stumbles on a log and flies to the floor, and the other rushes forward and takes the crown, plonking it on her head before turning to help her competitor.

Next to me, Caro stands up. She makes her way over to The Warrior shrine and picks up a shining silver bracelet, slipping it onto her wrist. Sasha stations herself at The Creator with a paintbrush.

I'm one of the last people still sitting. I'd feel stupid, pretending to be something I'm not. I stand up and walk over to The Lover, the only shrine not yet populated by anybody. I awkwardly pick up a silk scarf and wrap it around my neck.

'Now,' Starlight says when we're all in position, 'walk the circle. Make eye contact with your fellow goddesses. Feel how it is to inhabit this energy, to be the divine woman you know is inside you.'

We set off in different directions, some of us going clockwise, some anti-clockwise. I feel like a complete idiot, the only Lover among us in my scarf. Even in an activity where we can choose to be anything, I chose to be quiet and submissive. Am I just unimaginative, or am I really that scared? I think back to the primal release workshop just half an hour ago. I felt such a sense of passion, of wanting to take my life by the reins and cajole it in the right direction. So why, here, am I unable to channel that same energy?

I pass Caro, who is holding her silver-bangled wrist aloft like some kind of monarch. She sticks her tongue out as she passes me and I hold my foot out to trip her, but she deftly swerves it, flipping me off as she goes. I can't stop myself grinning; if Caro is giving me the middle finger, it means she's forgiving me.

'Now introduce some movement,' Starlight says. 'Dance a little, move, *be* the energy.'

It's easy to separate the wheat from the chaff here, and I am definitely the chaff. One of the Queens begins a series of aggressive pelvic thrusts, jerking herself around the circle like some awful woodland Michael Jackson. Caro shimmies across the clearing, looking beautiful under the darkening sky. I wiggle my arms a bit.

We carry on like this for what feels like forever. I feel a desperate urge to be alone in a dark room. One of the women I saw rolling around in the yurt earlier is on her hands and knees, prowling through the leaves like some kind of badger. I awkwardly bob my head from side to side, and several times I catch Starlight looking at me pityingly.

'Lovely, ladies,' Starlight says eventually. 'I can feel the power crackling in the air. You are all incredible. Now it's time for our crowning ceremony. Gather around the fire, please.'

We huddle in, standing arm-to-arm around the flickering flames. Caro is across from me, and her eyes dance in the firelight. From the trees, shadowy figures emerge, and I wonder for a second whether we've all been lured here on false pretences and are about to be sacrificed to the goddess of insanity. But they're holding what look like stacks of leaves, and as they come closer, I see that they're crowns made of foliage and flowers. One is deposited on each of our heads, and then the shadowy figures disappear.

Say what you will, but this place is *impeccably* organized.

'And now we speak our truth,' Starlight says into the ensuing quiet. 'The forest is listening.' She holds her palm up. 'I'll begin. I will not dim my light for others' sensibilities.'

She nods to the woman to her left, and we begin yet another declaration circle. I don't know what I'm going to say. What kind of truth is expected of me? What is a *truth* anyway? Everyone always bleats on about speaking your truth, owning your truth, living your truth. What is a truth, and more to the point, what's mine? Some people want to express the identity they feel is theirs, but which they've never felt safe to share. Some people want to speak up about trauma they've experienced. Some people want to hold their hands up and say, *I'm depressed, but I've been putting on a brave face. This is my truth*. What's mine? Is it deeply embedded within me, some kind of unresolved quirk of my personality? A part of my history that needs expunging, an integral centre of my very being that has to come to light for me to fix things?

'Spaghottie?'

I realize that the circle of women is staring at me, waiting for my answer.

'I will grow up and own my bullshit,' I say plainly.

Chapter Twenty-Three

'Well *that*,' Caro says, taking a sip of her drink, 'was something.'

We're sitting on the balcony off our room, sharing a bottle of wine Caro managed to steal untouched from the table at dinner. The moon is a huge yellow orb in the sky, covering the rolling hills in front of us in an eerie, milky light.

'I have never felt more out of my comfort zone in my entire life,' I reply.

'Well, that is kind of the point.'

'Yeah, you're right.' I readjust myself so that I'm facing her. 'Caro . . .'

She looks at me and sighs. 'I'm sorry.'

I blink. '*You're* sorry?'

'I was really harsh with you. You're not a shit friend. The way you were there for me when I broke up with Xavier . . .' She trails off, narrowing her eyes at me. 'Don't say it.'

'Lips sealed,' I say, sliding my index finger across my mouth. But it *wasn't* a breakup. The deadbeat drug dealer Caro was dating (and even calling it 'dating' is playing fast and loose with the truth) was just there one day and gone the next. The two-week stint she had at my house to recover was painful to witness, but I was more than happy to be there for her.

'I was a mess,' she continues. 'And then I met Peter, and I wasn't a mess any more. And that's the problem, isn't it?'

'What is?' I ask, although I know what she's going to say. She's coming to the realization everyone around her had a long time ago: Caro is only happy when everything is new and exciting.

'I can't commit to anything.' She shrugs sadly, looking out across the fields. 'For the longest time I was *so* jealous of you and Theo. You fit so well together, you both seemed so happy. And I just kept asking myself, "What's wrong with me? Why can't I be that happy?" Because it's not like I've never had the chance, you know? It's just that every time I get the chance I throw it as hard as possible off the nearest cliff.'

I nod, not quite knowing what to say for a moment. 'But you were right to be angry with me,' I say. 'I was self-absorbed and like, *so* irresponsible. I don't know what happened to me. I don't know what's *happening* with me. But if it helps, at least now you know me and Theo weren't perfect, either.'

She scoffs. 'Of course that doesn't help, you wally. I *want* you to be happy.'

'And I want you to be happy, too.' I reach out and grab her hand over the tiny balcony table. 'What's brought all this on? What happened?'

She shakes her head. 'Nothing. Or . . . I don't know. I think

Peter sort of . . . did something to me. Like, it was the same story: we got too close, I ran away. But this time, running away didn't feel fun and exciting and freeing. It felt wrong. But I did it anyway, because I don't know how else to behave.'

'Oh, Caro.'

She swipes at her eyes and I stand up, pulling her head into my chest for a hug. 'Do you want Peter back?'

She sniffles. 'I want to date and party and stay young forever. I want to move to Edinburgh. I want Peter back.' She pulls back and dabs at her cheeks with the sleeves of her jumper. 'But I can't have all those things, can I?'

I sit back down. 'No,' I say after a moment. 'I guess sometimes you have to figure out which thing feels least painful to sacrifice.'

She nods, swallowing. 'You've never struggled to sacrifice.'

'No, but then I've never been able to do anything even remotely brave, either.'

'Except doing a casual podcast collab and getting yourself a book deal behind your husband's back.' She smiles.

'That wasn't brave,' I say firmly. 'That was so, so cowardly of me. If I was brave, I'd have sat Theo down and talked about our issues. I'd have told him the moment I sent that confession in. I'd have involved him in my talks with Tilly – and at the least told Tilly that he wasn't in on it. I had a million chances to be brave, and I threw every single one of *those* chances as hard as possible off the nearest cliff.' I smile back at her.

'God, we're fucked, aren't we?'

I laugh. 'No. Because we have each other.'

This time, Caro reaches over and grabs my hand and gives it a squeeze.

'And,' I say, feeling suddenly more sure than I have in a very, very long time, 'because I have a plan.'

*

I must be setting a new record for the least amount of sleep a human being can function on. Despite the comfy beds and half a bottle of wine, I tossed and turned all night, looming reality stealing any chance of rest. Despite my mind being made up, what lies ahead of me is still daunting. On the drive home this morning, I asked Caro whether she was glad we'd gone to the retreat. She said yes, but that she had a lot of thinking to do, and I told her to come to me when she was ready. I'm not about to let her struggle alone, but I know that whatever decision she makes next has to come from a place of self-reflection, and self-reflection takes time. God knows I've had some of my own to do.

I'm sat at work looking like a zombie (although smelling like a freshly plucked rose thanks to the complimentary toiletries in the retreat's shower) and very much toeing the line. I might not have slept more than a handful of hours over the last week or so, but the limited energy I do have is being poured into proving that I *can* do my job, and that really, I'm very bloody good at it. I've spent the last hour putting together a new flyer for a mixed exhibition we're holding in October; I'm ahead of schedule, but I want to prove to Petra, and my team, that I am hauling myself firmly back on track.

I blocked my Instagram notifications days ago, and haven't been tempted to check it, but now, as the desks around me fill up, I click through to the app absent-mindedly, intending to go through to one of our artist's pages to cross-check the email address in her bio for our promotional material.

But before I can even make it to the search bar, the number on the paper aeroplane in the corner smacks me in the face.

I have over a thousand DMs.

My heart leaps up into my throat. I click the little icon and scroll through, reading the previews of the first however many without opening them.

Hey Lottie! Just wanted to reach out to say how much the series . . .

YOU HAVE SAVED MY SANITY!! I had no idea anyone else was . . .

LOL I've tried tantric yoga before and you have to basically surr . . .

Please tell me you're writing a book . . . I would buy like ten cop . . .

Don't you think it's disrespectful to your relationship to be airing . . .

I swipe the app closed and put my phone face-down on my desk. From the twenty or so that I read, the positive responses far outweigh the negatives, but those negatives . . . they're like a gut punch, feeding into the fears I've had all along: I have done something bad. I have hurt my husband. I have exposed the most intimate details of our relationship. And if this is how the public is feeling, how is Theo himself processing all of this?

No. No more of this. It's time.

I stand up before I can think too much, and walk on slightly shaky legs across the office to Petra's door.

I rap once on the glass with my knuckles. 'Petra?'

She looks up from her computer briefly, then back to her screen. 'Lottie,' she says, her fingers not pausing once over the keys. 'You're back.'

'Yes,' I reply, stepping inside and closing the door behind me. 'Do you have a minute?'

She continues tapping. 'Of course. Sit down.'

I decide not to. Instead, I hover by her desk, trying to find the words. *Come on, Lottie.* I bring back the memories of the retreat, of screaming into an IKEA bin. I roll my shoulders back and lift my chin. I can do this. 'I have an idea I'd like to run by you.'

'Oh?'

Here goes nothing. 'Have you managed to secure an artist to fill Anita Hassan's slot?' When I left the other day, the gallery calendar still had a glaring hole where I'd failed to book the artist we needed in time. The date will be here in just over a month, and getting someone good secured at such short notice is a monumental task.

'No,' she says curtly, and I feel a familiar twinge of shame.

I push it down and soldier on. 'You mentioned that you were looking for high-profile guests to appear at live events at the gallery?'

'Yes.'

'I think I have one for you.'

Finally, Petra's fingers still. She looks up at me.

I take a deep breath. 'Tilly Carter from *The Cliterati* is very interested in running a live show of the podcast here.'

Immediately, anxiety surges in me. I've said it now, and I can't take it back. The idea came to me when I was talking to Caro on the balcony at the women's retreat. I meant it when I said she couldn't have everything – she couldn't date Peter *and* be a single party girl *and* move to Edinburgh. But it got me thinking: what if I can finish the podcast *and* get Theo back? What if I can get him to listen to me not through endless unanswered texts but through speaking to him publicly, using the podcast to reach him? I'd already told Tilly that I'd carry on with the podcast before I went away with Caro, but I'd warned her that I needed a couple of days to think about how I wanted to do things. When I called her this morning, she was thrilled with the idea of hosting the final episode at the gallery, but I warned her that I'd have to speak to my boss first. It was a safety net; I knew that if I changed my mind, I could just tell Tilly that Petra had said no, and the whole thing would be over before it had even begun. But now, Petra is looking at me exactly the way I knew she would: with extreme interest.

'That's a fantastic idea,' she says, immediately beginning typing again. 'We'll need a collaborating artist, of course. We'd be looking at next year, to get someone contracted and the space set up—'

'It'd need to be in Anita Hassan's slot,' I say.

She stops again and stares at me. 'In five weeks.'

'Yes. It'd be the final instalment in the Long-Term Lust series.'

The words hang between us. She knows I'm a part of that series. The whole world knows. 'I assume you would be . . .'

'Participating, yes,' I say.

She blinks, and I can see that she's computing in her head – this is my personal life, something we never discuss, and we're blurring the line here. 'And you would be OK with that?'

'Yes.'

She turns back to her computer and clicks a few times. 'Five weeks is extremely tight.'

'Yes,' I repeat. 'But you can trust me. I'll make it work.'

She puts one finger to her lips as she clicks around, presumably looking at her calendar. After an excruciating amount of time, during which I almost shout 'Never mind! Forget it!' three times, she sits back in her chair. 'If we do this, it's your project. I want your full ownership. Ask for whatever help you need, but don't disrupt the projects we're already working on.'

The subtext is clear: mess this up, and you're in even deeper shit. Prove to me that you can do this.

And despite my dislike of Petra's management style, her words trigger something in me. I love my job. I want to do well. I want to prove that I'm still Lottie the Community Engagement Officer, bringing people into the gallery simply to engage with art – no pretentiousness or deep pockets needed. For two years I've watched my power to reach my community become smaller and smaller, have watched the gallery and its clientele change before my eyes. Here's my chance to yank that power back, just for one night.

I look Petra in the eye. 'Absolutely,' I say.

Chapter Twenty-Four

'You've got everything? You're sure?' Caro is standing in the doorway, dressed in a floor-length red jumpsuit and giant gold hoop earrings.

'Yes. No, wait.' I run back over to the computer and stare at the document again.

'Lotts, you've changed that thing three times just this past hour. It's perfect. Let's go.'

On impulse, I delete the final line, type something else, then send it to print. 'OK, last time, promise.'

'Uber's here,' she says, glancing at her phone. 'You all ready?'

I take one last glance in the mirror. I'm wearing my slutty dress again, and my highest heels. My hair is soft around my face, and I've done simple makeup with a dramatic lip: a coral pink that Caro insisted would make my skin glow and which, I have to admit, does the trick.

I tuck the still-warm papers from the printer under my arm and blow air into my cheeks. Riffling through my bag, I count my purse, keys, phone, charger. I grab my jacket from the hook behind the study door. 'Ready,' I say.

Caro links her arm through mine as we totter down the stairs and to the front door. As we make it to the gate at the end of the path, where our Uber is idling, she squeezes me. 'You've got this.'

As it is with all journeys to somewhere you don't want to go, it flies by, and within what feels like thirty seconds we're pulling up outside the arts centre. My heart is in my throat. It's still two hours until the live recording, but already people are gathering, peering through the windows at the covered artwork due to be unveiled before the show. Above the entrance door, there's a huge sign advertising *The Cliterati x Arts Centre, 2nd May*. Beside the words, there's a photo of Tilly with a microphone, and next to her, a silhouette of an unknown woman, a question mark on her face. Me.

'Relax,' Caro says, spotting my expression. 'You've seen it a hundred times.'

It's true; I've been walking under that sign every morning on my way into work for the past two weeks, and every morning, I feel a heady mix of sickness and anticipation. Now, though, it's on a completely different level. Now, it's actually happening, and despite having woken up about ten times during the night in a panicked cold sweat, I haven't backed out. Yet.

Part of me told myself that if Theo came to talk to me, I'd hit the brakes on the whole thing. If he reached out or showed up at our front door, I'd shut everything down. We could have a normal, private conversation about our sex life and the distance between us and rebuild things behind closed doors, like a normal married couple.

But he didn't.

He hasn't called or texted or showed up. The announcement for the live podcast special went out almost as soon as Petra agreed to host it at the gallery, and I wonder if for him, it was the final nail in the coffin. So I've left him to it, in the hopes that respecting his boundaries will make him more open to listening to what I have to say.

Even if sometimes, in the middle of the night, I question whether respecting his boundaries might involve *not* airing my thoughts on our marriage to a live audience and tens of thousands of Spotify listeners. But Theo is romantic, and while we've drifted a lot over the last few months, I know him. He's a gesture guy, a big fan of PDA and expressing himself regardless of who's watching. I'm more of a wallflower, but I'm hedging my bets on him knowing me well enough to understand my motivations here. He knows I wouldn't do this for attention; I'm so far out of my comfort zone, I wouldn't do it unless it was absolutely necessary. It's all for him – all for us.

The Uber slows down outside the main entrance, but Caro directs the driver round the back, where there's a fire door and far less visibility. I feel like some kind of influencer, hiding from the paparazzi. It's so not me, I feel like I've accidentally stepped into a parallel universe.

When we stop down the back alley, I get out of the taxi on shaking legs and duck in through the fire door, letting out a breath I've been holding since we left the house. My relief is short-lived, though, because no sooner than Caro has joined me inside, Petra appears at the bottom of the stairs, looking like she's on her eighth coffee of the day.

'Lottie, hello, you're here,' she says, stopping a foot away from me. She's wearing a gorgeous androgynous suit – muted grey, shoulder pads, and flared trousers – and her short dark hair is slicked perfectly back from her face, exposing her high cheekbones and makeup-free skin. Despite looking like the next James Bond, though, she is giving off an air of extremely heightened emotion. Petra is not a fidgety person, but I can feel the air around her vibrating.

'Hi, Petra,' I say. I haven't had much to do with her over the last few weeks, our paths only crossing when I'm asking for approval for one thing or another. Two weeks ago, she let me and Harry spend an entire day out of the office flyering for the event – we went as far away from the gentrified areas of town as possible, walking for hours in the rain putting invites through letterboxes. She also agreed to let me give half the tickets away for free to low-earners in the community, who snapped them up as soon as the sale went live. While I know she didn't approve of my tactics, I also know she's aware that this event hinges on me, and I've used that fact to my advantage. Besides, the attention the gallery will receive from being associated with the podcast will more than make up for the reduced ticket profits.

'We've made a temporary green room in the storage room for you, Lottie,' Petra says now, her cheeks flushed. 'We'll need to look into getting something more permanent for the future. For real guests.'

I bite my tongue; Petra doesn't realize how insensitive she is sometimes. Caro, who had been peering into the gallery room behind Petra, steps towards me and drapes her arm over my shoulders. 'You must feel very fortunate to have Lottie working here. What an amazing opportunity for the centre.'

Petra nods, seemingly oblivious to the jibe. 'It's certainly put us on the map. Lottie, Tilly's waiting for you in the green room.'

'OK,' I manage, my voice wobbly.

I totter past her, Caro in tow, and into the gallery. Immediately, I stop. It's been transformed in here: the walls are covered in shrouded artwork, and all the standing easels have been removed to make space for velvet chairs set up like a wedding ceremony, with a walkway down the middle leading to the window, where two big armchairs sit on a low stage, facing one another. Each one has a microphone on a low table beside it, and I feel my stomach clench. I avert my eyes. At the far end of the room, there's a table lined with Prosecco glasses, ready to be filled during the post-show unveiling of the art.

Caro squeezes my arm. She walks over to the wall and goes to lift the corner of one of the shrouds, but I stop her. 'Harry spent about six hours ironing those shrouds yesterday. He'll kill you if he sees you touching them. Come on.'

We walk over to the door of the storage room, but before I open it, I stop.

'I wouldn't have done any of this without you,' I say to Caro.

'Not sure if that's a compliment or not.'

I laugh. 'Me neither.' My eyes find the stage again, and a rush of anxiety overwhelms me. 'Fuck, Caro. What am I doing?'

She takes my cheeks between her hands. 'You're speaking to your husband. That's it. Ignore everybody else, look at Tilly, and speak to Theo. He'll be listening.'

'What if he's not?' This thought has occurred to me hundreds of times over the last few weeks. What if Theo doesn't listen to the podcast? What if he's already decided there's nothing I can say?

But that's not the Theo I know. The Theo I know is considered, kind, open-minded. He'd let me have my say before he moved on from me for good. He'd see the romantic gesture behind what I'm doing, and he'd try to understand; I'm sure he would.

'If he's not listening live, there's no way someone won't send it to him,' Caro says. 'And there's no way he won't let his curiosity get the better of him. You would.'

'Not if I thought it was going to be yet another embarrassing critique of my sex life.'

'And when he hears it isn't . . .'

'OK,' I say, nodding. This is the millionth time we've had this conversation. 'I'll shut up.'

'To the green room?' she asks, making her voice posher for the last two words.

I laugh. 'It's really nice of Petra to have set this up when she's been so busy,' I say, pushing the door open with my shoulder, and as I do, I turn my head enough to see the door into the gallery, where Petra is standing, watching us. When she sees me looking, she turns quickly and walks away.

Inside, Tilly is sitting on a new white sofa, which has been pushed up against the wall of the storage room. There are new shelves lining the walls, meaning there's considerably more floor space than there used to be. There's no dressing table, but there's a standing full-length mirror in the corner. She stands up and walks over to us, enveloping us each in a hug.

I take a deep breath, nerves wriggling in my stomach. 'You look amazing.'

Tilly is wearing a huge pink sphere of a dress, with puffball sleeves and a round, excessive skirt that stops mid-thigh. Her milky white legs are almost entirely covered in red, thigh-high, platform cowboy boots, and her shoulder-length orange hair has been curled into an upward flick at the ends. She looks like a Barbie, and I instantly feel like a second-rate New Look basic bitch.

'So do you!' she croons. 'Look at those legs!'

'This is the seductress dress,' Caro confirms. 'Used to drive Theo crazy.'

'I can see why.'

'Not any more, apparently.' I laugh awkwardly.

Tilly puts her hands on her hips. 'Right, well, instantly we're going to be winding that negativity *right* down,' she says. She strides over to the back of the room and plucks a bottle of sambuca from her bag, along with a stack of plastic cups. She lays three out on the coffee table in front of the sofa and pours a big glug of clear liquid into each. 'Sit, and let's go over your letter.'

Caro and Tilly take the sofa, and I take the seat opposite them: an office chair that's been draped with a throw in an attempt to give it a homely vibe. Just the thought of reading my letter to Tilly and Caro is making my heart race; how am I going to do this in front of a hundred people, knowing that thousands more are listening?

'Where's Isa?' I ask, buying myself some time.

'At her office. We've had a bit of a . . . reshuffle,' Tilly says, and then sits up straight. 'To be honest, we were long overdue a conversation about our individual roles in all of this since the podcast started getting big. We thought it best if she just manages the financial side of things from now on.'

I nod, reading between the lines. Isa isn't the most diplomatic people person; Tilly can sort that part out herself. I find myself relieved she's not here with her manic texting and constant references to figures and stats.

I pick up my plastic cup, knock it against Caro's and Tilly's, and then throw it back. It tastes like nightclub toilets and hangovers, and I'm reminded of the last time I drank sambuca: Jade's hen party. The last time everything was normal, the night I put all of this into motion. I wince, but the sharpness cuts through the panic momentarily. I shuffle the pages of my letter in front of me, but before I can start reading, the door swings open behind me.

'Petra,' Tilly says, smiling. 'Join us for some Dutch courage? Lottie's about to do a run-through of her letter.'

I turn around. Petra is standing in the doorway, a bunch of sunflowers in her hand. She gives a small shake of her head and steps towards me. 'I just wanted to give these to Lottie. To say good luck.'

'Oh.' I take the flowers from her, the paper crinkling in the silence. This is so unlike Petra, so . . . *sentimental*, that I don't quite know what to say. She's the same cool, indifferent Petra, but there's an awkwardness to her, and I can see the discomfort in the set of her shoulders. 'Thank you so much, Petra. I—'

'I have things to sort out,' she says, and then turns on her heel and strides back out into the gallery, closing the door firmly behind her.

I stare for a moment at the big, bright sunflowers. The idea of Petra choosing these would almost be laughable if I didn't feel so touched.

Before either Tilly or Caro can say anything, the door whooshes open again. This time, it's Harry in the doorway, beaming in a chequered suit. 'There she is!' he cries, rushing forward and clapping me on the back. 'The big day has arrived. How are you feeling? I've had a thought – what if you did a big entrance to a theme song? Maybe we could get two of the guys upstairs to hold some big feathers, do a grand reveal. If you—'

'We've already got the intro sorted,' Tilly interrupts gently. 'Love the ideas, though. Kind of wish we'd thought of the feather thing. Shot?'

Harry nods enthusiastically and squeezes himself between Caro and Tilly, who pours four more shots as introductions are made.

'Right,' Tilly says once we've knocked our drinks back. 'Lottie. Hit us with it.'

I clear my throat, shuffle my papers, and when I can put it off no longer, I begin to read. As I go, I try to imagine everyone who might hear this. I try to see myself through the eyes of the audience – will they judge me for what I've done? When I confess that my husband didn't know about any of this – that I *lied* – will they hate me? But no matter how hard I try, the words I spent all night typing sound fake and empty, and all I can see is the hurt etched on Theo's face. The way he looked at me when he left our house, declaring he didn't want to speak to me. I stumble over my words, my tongue feeling thick in my mouth, and the whole thing is disjointed and clumsy, devoid of emotion. As I come to a close, I raise my eyes to look at the three mismatched people opposite me, and I can see that they feel the same way.

There's a beat of silence.

'That was great!' Harry breaks it first.

'Practice makes perfect,' Tilly says, but she looks worried.

'Lotts.' Caro leans forward until I meet her eyes. 'You can only do what you can do. It's going to be *fine*.'

'Oh, god,' I say, panic rising. 'Evidently not! I'm not cut out for this! It's not me! What am I doing?'

The door swings open once more. It's Petra again, holding a clipboard. 'People are coming in now,' she says tightly. 'Be ready in ten.'

'Fuck,' I say.

Tilly grins. 'Time to get this show on the road, folks.'

Chapter Twenty-Five

My heart is going to beat out of my chest. I'm standing in the 'green room', listening to Tilly greet the cheering crowds of people who have filled the gallery. She's incredible at what she does, jovial and hilarious and riding the energy of the room. I, on the other hand, am peering with terror through the crack in the door. Caro and Harry are sitting at the back; Petra is by the door with her clipboard. I can see Jade and a couple of the other bridesmaids sitting near the middle of the left section, and I feel a pang of gratefulness.

I haven't made a big effort with any of them, with everything that's going on, and I wanted to show I cared, as well as putting my hands very firmly in the air and admitting that yes, the Horny Wife on the podcast was me, and I know that you all think I'm insane, but how do you fancy coming to the guaranteed sell-out live show? I offered early-access tickets on the group chat – my first message since the flurry of question marks and links when my face appeared in the papers with Tilly – and the girls snapped them up. Holly-with-the-feet-pics replied, 'I wish you'd told us it was you from the start; I'd have told you *everything*.' And there went yet another point in the 'don't be a secretive weirdo' column.

As I scan the room, Tilly waves at the crowds and sits down, subtly calming the audience, introducing the show, welcoming everybody to the gallery.

'This has been an absolute rollercoaster for *The Cliterati*, and I'm not kidding when I say it's gone way further than any of us could have imagined – least of all our resident Horny Wife.' Someone whoops, and I think I might throw up. 'We never could have predicted just how *many* of you would relate to her story, and we certainly couldn't have foreseen where her journey would take her. We hoped this would be a redemption story, a renewing of a couple's connection, a refinding of their physical pleasure.' Tilly pauses for effect. 'Things didn't quite work out like that.'

I haven't heard any of this before; the script was written without my input, so that my response will be natural and authentic. I'm not sure Tilly appreciates that my natural and authentic response to this exact situation is sheer, throat-gripping panic.

'So I won't keep you on tenterhooks any longer,' Tilly says excitedly. 'There's been a lot of speculation about the identity of our anonymous confessor, and right here, in this room, you're about to discover exactly who she is. You're part of something exciting, and I wish our live listeners at home could feel the energy in here. It's fucking electric.'

A cheer goes around the room. I, for one, wish the storage room had a window I could climb out of.

'So, without further ado, it is my absolute goddamn *pleasure* to introduce the fantastic, the funny, the fierce . . . Lottie Carmichael!'

The room erupts. I don't move. What – and I have never felt anything so strongly – the *actual* fuck am I doing? What am I doing? I'm standing in my work's storage room, while one hundred people wait outside for me to appear. I'm about to record a live podcast about my sex life. My husband is neither talking to me nor living with me. I have royally, totally, absolutely taken myself on the weirdest, most fucked-up adventure of my entire life.

And I can't finish it off. I can't see it through to the end.

I can't do it.

Tilly is keeping the crowds cheering, but there's a slight frown on her face as she looks towards where I'm hiding behind the door. 'She's making us work for it!' she calls, half laughing.

Petra is peering towards the storage room, her lips drawn in a tight line. She starts to move across the back of the room towards me. I feel like I'm either going to pass out or be sick. Caro turns around in her seat and looks at me, somehow finding my eye peeking through the gap. She gives me a look. It's a look she's given me hundreds of times during our friendship: when I was nervous to ask the teacher for an extension on my homework; when I had my first date in sixth form and didn't want to leave the house; on my wedding day, when I stood behind the closed church doors and asked her if she thought I was doing the right thing. It's the look that says, 'You've come this far.' It says, 'Don't let fear win now, right as things are about to get good.' It says, 'Put your big-girl pants on and fucking do it, Lottie.'

And so, just as Petra arrives outside, her hand outstretched to turn the handle, just as the cheers are dying down and the crowd is starting to mutter between themselves, I swing the doors open and step out into the gallery.

The space explodes into noise again, and I stand, unmoving, in the storage-room doorway. Immediately, there's the flashing of iPhone cameras, people turning in their seats and contorting themselves to snap a photo.

'There she is!' Tilly cheers. 'Come up and join me, Horny Wife!'

Somehow, I manage to take a step forward, and then another. I wish I hadn't worn these heels. Blindly, I make my way up the aisle between the chairs and towards the stage. I'm reminded of my wedding day, of every eye being on me, but this time the gazes aren't loving and adoring – they're hungry. They're frantic.

I make it to the stage and Tilly stands up, reaching out a hand to help me climb the step in my shoes. She squeezes my fingers and I lower myself gratefully into my seat. I made it. I'm up here. I did it.

'Phew!' Tilly sits opposite me and makes a show of fanning her face. 'That was *insane*. Well, everyone, here she is. Our anonymous confessor, our Horny Wife, here in the flesh. Lottie, welcome! How are you feeling?'

I blink. There's a microphone below my chin, angled upwards from the table beside me. 'Shellshocked,' I find myself saying. My voice comes clear and loud through the speakers, making me jump.

There's a ripple of laughter around the audience. Tilly beams. 'Well, I'm not surprised. You've been on quite the journey. How have you found it?'

I cast my eyes around the room, then quickly look back to Tilly when I see too many expectant faces staring back at me. 'It's been . . .' I stop. I can't seem to string a sentence together. I force myself to take a breath and swallow. 'I'd say it wasn't what I expected,' I manage, 'but I didn't expect anything, so it's been one big learning process.'

'I bet. Well, you've all heard me jabber on enough over the last few weeks, so let's get our other listeners involved. I believe we've got Annie on the line, who's also struggling with her husband. You feel like the spark's died, is that right, Annie?'

A woman's voice comes from somewhere. 'Hi, Tilly! Hi, Lottie! Wow, this is so exciting. Erm, yes, so I'm in the same boat as Lottie, really. Everything's just become so routine, we've stopped doing it entirely. I'd love your advice, Lottie, as someone who's been there.'

She goes quiet, and Tilly looks at me, eyebrows raised. I realize everyone is waiting for me to answer. I knew the format of the show when we were organizing it; I've lived and breathed the schedule for the last five weeks. But now that it's in motion, the reality of what I'm doing hits home. What advice can I possibly give to a woman in my predicament? 'I don't know what to say, Annie,' I say eventually. 'I haven't figured it out yet myself.' I pause. I can't leave this woman hanging, thinking there's no hope. Surely I've taken something from this, some small morsel of wisdom I can pass on. And then I realize that of course I have, and that it's time for me to come clean.

'There's actually something most people in this room don't know, and that's that this whole time, I kept my involvement in this podcast secret from my husband.' A hush falls on the audience. I make eye contact with a woman on the front row who is staring at me with buggy eyes. 'I thought I'd write in to the podcast, get some advice, fix things. Maybe that's where you're at, too, Annie. I'm hoping this won't run away from you the way it did me, but . . .' I laugh, and the audience joins in. A rush of relief fills me – they don't hate me. 'What I *would* say is: talk about it. Don't scheme and plot. If you love each other, and you know you want to be together, just have a conversation. There's a place for sexy lingerie and out-of-the-box couple's activities, but I think those things are best done when you've both agreed to them in a joint effort to revive things. When you're on the same page.'

Annie thanks me briefly, and then we're on to the next caller. We carry on like this, with me giving advice I'm not sure I'm in any way qualified to provide, until Tilly takes us to audience questions. She points to a woman at the front, and one of the gallery workers hurries over with a microphone.

'Hi, Lottie! As I was listening to the show, I was wondering how you managed to stay sane throughout it all. It just felt like things went from bad to worse, and while it was really entertaining to listen to, I wondered how you were coping. What kept you going?'

My eyes instinctively flick to Caro. 'My best friend, Caro,' I say without hesitation. 'I've known her longer than I've known anyone, even my husband, and without her, I wouldn't have done any of this.' I correct myself, 'Not that she forced me to do anything.' I laugh, watching the mock-horror on her face. People turn to follow my gaze and she beams under the attention. 'But she's always encouraged me to go for things, and I never really have until now. She's so brave and beautiful and ballsy, and I guess she, and this podcast, have taught me that I can make big, scary decisions. And that even if they blow up in my face sometimes, I'll survive.'

There are a few 'aww's and murmurs of appreciation, and Caro gives a mock bow, but when she looks at me, I can see that she's touched.

'Always the girls,' Tilly cheers. 'And our next one . . . there, on the other side, at the back.'

The microphone-wielding woman hurries to the other side of the back of the room, to where a man has got to his feet.

My heart stops.

It's Theo.

He's standing there in his white shirt and green linen trousers, his curly hair tousled, his eyes locked on me. The microphone is brought to his face.

When he speaks, his voice is clear, emotionless, and direct. 'I'd like to know why Lottie felt she couldn't just talk to her husband. If he means as much to her as she says he does, why didn't she feel she could have a conversation with him?'

For a moment, I just look at him. It is so heart-wrenchingly good to see him, like a drug, like a lighthouse in a storm. But his face is unreadable, distant. Pain flares in my chest. His eyes are still locked on mine, and as I look back at him, I try to convey everything I feel: *I'm sorry. Please hear me. I love you.*

He looks away. His eyes find Tilly, who is sitting forward in her chair, evidently oblivious to the fact that it's Theo, my actual husband, in the room. 'You might need to repeat the question,' she says, putting her hand lightly on my arm. 'I'm not sure Lottie heard it.'

'Of course,' Theo says, still addressing Tilly. 'I wanted to know: if Lottie cares so much about her husband, why is she doing this to him?'

A shocked hush falls over the room. I feel like I've been publicly slapped, the question firing across the gallery like a whip. Instinctively, my eyes find Caro. She's staring, open-mouthed, at Theo. She looks back to me, her eyes wide, and puts her hands out, palms down, gesturing at me to calm. To relax. I clear my throat.

'My husband isn't actually speaking to me at the moment,' I say after a beat, my voice wobbly. 'But if he were, I'd hope he'd listen to me when I tell him I would never intentionally do anything to hurt him. This all blew up so quickly, and so much more hugely than I expected, and I made decisions I regret. But those decisions came from the same place that sits inside me today. Love drove me to seek help in the first place, and that same love has me sitting here now, still certain there's something worth saving. My husband is the most important thing in the world to me. I—I love him. So much.'

Theo opens his mouth to speak again, but Tilly jumps in. 'I'm afraid that's all the questions we've got time for! It's flown by, hasn't it?' I turn in my chair and throw her a look, wanting her to please, god, just let it run over. Let me hear what he has to say. But she gazes out at the audience and carries on. 'We do have one last treat for you before we wrap things up, though – the series finale, the last chapter, the full stop. Lottie's final entry into *The Cliterati*'s Long-Term Lust series. So, without further ado and for the final time, Lottie, take it away.'

I look up, intending to meet Theo's eye, to make sure he's listening before I start reading. I want to make it absolutely clear that this message is intended for his ears.

But he isn't there.

Somehow, during Tilly's segue into this final section, he has slipped away.

I swallow back the tears that threaten to come. I had him. I had him here, listening. And I missed my shot.

My eyes scan the room, just in case he's moved, but he really has gone. His chair sits empty. I finger the pieces of paper in my lap, swallowing down the emotion and frustration. People stare at me expectantly.

Tilly stands up and crouches next to me, covering my microphone with her hand. 'Imagine he's in the room, Lottie,' she whispers. 'Nobody else, just him. Just picture him, right here.'

He was here, I want to reply. *He was right here.*

I squeeze my eyes shut. In the quiet, it's easy to imagine that there's no one else in the room with me. I picture Theo, not as he was a moment ago, but as he was on our wedding day when the church doors swung open and I stepped forward and got my last glimpse of him as my boyfriend. My fiancé. He was standing by the altar, dressed in a navy blue suit, but I didn't notice the pocket square or the shiny shoes or the brand-new tie. He was beaming, and the only thing I could see, the only thing I can see now as I squeeze my eyes closed, quick as a flash, is the light that came from his face. The warmth of him, the big, fat, sunshine-y home that he was, and the way I wanted to run to him, throw the bouquet to the floor and fuck the whole thing off, just so we could be together, us two.

I open my eyes, fold my pieces of paper in half, and tuck them down the side of my seat. I sit forward and lean into the microphone.

'I hope I don't offend any of you when I say this, but right now, I'm not talking to you.' The room is deathly silent, a collective breath held. 'This podcast episode could get one listen, there could be one person in the audience tonight, and that would be enough for me. Because despite what people might think, and despite the sudden fame I've gained from this, there's only really one thing that matters to me, and that's my other best friend. My husband.' I shuffle in my seat, searching for the words. 'I didn't start all of this with the intention of setting anything in motion. I didn't send in that anonymous confession assuming it'd lead to a podcast series and a live show. I didn't go ahead with the experiment expecting it to turn me into some kind of relatable millennial marriage hero. I wanted to stay anonymous for a reason – because I was doing all of this for my marriage. I was frustrated, hurt, and lost, and I made a snap decision to share that hurt and frustration with someone I thought might be able to help. That was my sole focus, my only goal: fix the gorge that had formed between me and my husband. And if I was being offered free advice from a sex and relationship therapist to help me along the way, count me in.'

Tilly gives a little wave, and a laugh goes around the room. I forge on, looking at the empty chair where Theo was sitting just a few moments ago.

'So, Theo, let me talk to you. Let me tell you what I've learned. This experiment didn't fix our broken sex life. It didn't make us want each other like we did when we were in our twenties. In all the ways this experiment was supposed to work, it failed. We are further apart than ever; it has sent us spinning backwards, to a time before we even met. The time when our lives were separate bubbles and we didn't exist to each other.

'But in one way, this experiment has been enormously successful. It has taught me that a marriage, even one as strong as ours, takes effort. Even when you're best friends, there are days when you have to pull yourself up and prioritize, to remember that relationships need nurturing, and that just because a plant is thriving, doesn't mean it will continue to do so if you stop watering it. This experiment has taught me that the modern world is full of distractions. It's easier, now, to scroll instead of seeking real connection. It's easier to watch Netflix than have a chat over dinner. And when you don't make a conscious effort to retain those rituals, those sacred moments, the outside world will take over. None of us are immune to it, but it's a personal choice to disengage that we have to make.

'Most of all, Theo – and I mean no offence to Tilly here – this experiment has taught me that you and I don't need Tantra or new lingerie or role play in hotel bars. It's so much simpler than that. We need each other, in the most basic sense: I need to hear you, and you need to hear me. Because there are so many things neither of us are saying, and if we aren't here to hold each other's mess, why are we here at all?' I take a deep, shaky breath and grip the microphone. 'I don't know if you'll listen to this, and if you do, you might not want to hear me. What I'm saying might not change your mind. Because I know that what I did was reckless and stupid, and I know that

I betrayed your trust. But I'm hoping that you'll forgive me my first indiscretion, the first wild and badly thought-through act of my life. The first time I've put myself out there. Because it's still me; I'm still Lottie. And I love you so much.'

And with that, I sit back in my seat, and this destructive, transformative chapter of my life finally comes to a shuddering close.

Chapter Twenty-Six

Somehow, I manage to walk and wave, walk and wave, all the way off the stage and down the aisle between the chairs to the green room. As soon as the door shuts behind me, and the noise of the hundred or so people outside muffles, I fall into Caro's arms.

'He was here, Caro,' I say, the tears finally breaking loose. 'He was here, and he left, and I fucked it all up.'

'Shh,' she soothes, rubbing circles into my back. 'That's it, let it out. You're OK. You're fine.'

'Who was here?' Tilly asks from behind me, looking perplexed. 'What happened? You did so well!'

'Theo,' Caro explains for me. 'He was the one who asked the last question.'

Tilly's mouth drops open, and I can almost see her mind whirring. Having Theo in on the show would have been an explosive addition. 'Now you say it . . . god, of course. I wondered why he was being so brutal.' She stops and then widens her eyes in excitement. 'That means he heard your speech. It was beautiful, Lottie. I was worried when you started improvising, but . . . wow. People were stunned. There's no way he won't at least be willing to have a chat after that.'

'He didn't hear it,' I say, pulling myself away from Caro and swiping my arm across my face. 'He left after he asked the question.'

Tilly's forehead creases. 'Oh, love. I'm so sorry. You did so brilliantly. Just give him some more time?'

'She's right, Lotts,' Caro says. 'It was beautiful. And the fact he turned up means he hasn't completely shut off any idea of reconciling.'

I sink down onto the sofa. I feel suddenly completely wiped, all of the adrenaline and nerves that had been carrying me through draining away and leaving me exhausted.

'Wait here.' Caro slips out of the green room door and returns a minute later with three glasses of Prosecco balanced in her hands. 'I know this feels like a shit moment,' she says, handing them out, 'but I think it's really important that we take a minute to actually realize what you've just done. You sat up there and said what you needed to say. You put yourself on the line, even though it goes against everything your play-it-safe personality tells you to do, and you did the fucking thing.'

Tilly raises her glass. 'She's right, Lottie,' she says. 'To doing the fucking thing.'

I clink my glass mutely, but none of it is registering. What was it all for? What was any of this for if Theo is just going to continue hating me forever? I have so colossally fucked up, I can't even bring myself to absorb it.

'I'm really sorry to do this,' Tilly says, perching next to me on the sofa, 'but we have the art unveiling, so we need to be back out in two minutes.'

'If you're not up to it—' Caro starts.

'No,' I say, standing up. This is important – the culmination of five weeks of hard work, and bigger than me. There are people out there who want to engage with art, and an artist who deserves recognition. 'I'm fine. Let's go.'

The next thing I know, I'm back in the bustling gallery, clutching my warm glass of Prosecco, and people are taking photos of me and trying to talk to me and shouting, 'Lottie! Hi, Lottie!' and Caro is gripping my arm with the force of a velociraptor and asking people to 'excuse us, please, thank you, beep beep, excuse us', and then we're back at the stage and I notice that the chairs have been removed, and eventually, Caro releases me and steps down and I'm all alone.

'Hello, everyone!' Except I'm not alone, because suddenly Tilly is standing next to me, addressing the room. 'Welcome back! I hope we all had a nice pause and got ourselves something refreshing to drink. Now, for the final part of our evening, it's time to unveil the *insane* collection that accompanies this show. It's an unusual one, but it perfectly captures the essence of what this series has been about, and I can't wait for you to see it. I'm not exaggerating when I say that when I saw this collection for the first time, it literally took my breath away.'

I scan the audience. They're waiting expectantly, cheeks pink from the Prosecco, eyes bright. Through the nerves and the exhaustion and the fog of overwhelm, there's a little beat of pride. Half of the people in this room wouldn't usually set foot in here, and even if just one of them comes back for a class, or to look at our next exhibition, and finds something in it, I've done my job well.

And now the last moment has arrived, and Tilly is turning to me. Apprehension churns in my stomach; have I done the right thing? It's too late now.

'So I'll ask our Horny Wife, the lovely Lottie, to do the honours, if she's ready?'

I step down from the stage and walk over to the far side of the gallery window, where a thick red rope hangs from the ceiling. Harry spent hours setting this system up last night, and I catch his eye across the room as I wrap my hands around the cord. He holds his crossed fingers up to me and offers me a nervous grin.

I yank the rope, and the shrouds covering the artwork on the walls fall simultaneously to the floor.

A gasp goes around the room, a collective murmur getting louder as people look from picture to picture. My eyes find Caro, my heart in my throat.

She's looking at the artwork with a crease on her forehead, and I can see the cogs whirring. Then her eyebrows shoot up, and her gaze snaps to me.

'We're lucky enough to have our resident artist in the room with us this evening,' Tilly says into the microphone. 'Give us a wave, Caro!'

The audience turns as one to follow Tilly's eyeline to the back of the room, where Caro stands, looking shellshocked. She lets her jaw hang open, then closes it and offers a stunned wave.

'Caro is an incredibly talented photographer,' Tilly says, 'and she's got a knack for capturing the most intimate scenes. Her work spans the whole spectrum of relationship moments: from weddings and the adoption of pets, to anniversary boudoir shoots and the most underground sex clubs. Her work is *so* perfect for the message we've discovered here during this series: that marriage, relationships, are not linear or one-size-fits-all. They're a collection of softness and passion, public joy and the deepest privacy. I hope you'll think of the journey we've all been on over the last few weeks, and about your own intimate relationships, as you enjoy this collection.'

The audience disperses, filling up their glasses and spreading around the room to take in the artwork. There's a shot from Caro's shoot with the couple who adopted a puffin; one from the kink dungeon she dragged me to (Jade is, obviously, absent); a landscape of a woman lounging on a spread of the greenest grass, her pale skin bright against the backdrop. I step down from the stage on shaking legs and weave through the crowds, searching for Caro. And then, as if the stars have aligned, a group parts and there she is.

She's staring at me, her face unreadable. Nerves twist in my gut. Caro's portfolio is public – it's on her website – but she has always stopped just short of exhibiting it publicly, even when she's applied and been accepted. I now realize this is her fear of commitment playing out again. Something like this takes her from word-of-mouth photographer to known-person-in-the-industry. Is it what she wants?

I close the gap between us. 'I know what you're thinking,' I say before she can speak. 'But sometimes we need a push from people who love us to do things that are terrifying but right for us. I wanted to repay the favour.'

She blinks, her eyes moving beyond me to her work, which people are poring over as they have animated discussions, glasses of Prosecco waving in the air.

'You're so talented, Caro,' I say earnestly, desperate for her to see how incredible she is, how much she deserves the world to see that, too. 'You're amazing, and—'

She steps forward and pulls me into a hug. I squeeze her back, relief making tears well in my eyes. Her hair tickles my face. 'Holy fuck,' she says into my ear. When she pulls back, she runs her hands through her hair, a smile spreading across her face. 'You completely one-eightied me.'

She meets my eye and grins, and for a whooshing second, despite the fact that Theo isn't here and that this whole thing might have been a huge flop, I feel a sudden rush of OK-ness. Of stability. Of *even if Theo never speaks to me again, there's always Caro. Here before, here forever.*

*

As soon as the exhibition is in full swing, I dump my untouched glass of Prosecco and find Tilly, who is having an animated chat with two women by a photo of a man dressed in full bondage, his exposed mouth spread in a delighted grin.

'. . . really captured the essence of what it *is* to be a sexual being. To be a whole person tied to another whole person, not just a husband or a wife – oh, hi, Lottie! We were just talking about how wonderful this evening has been.'

'We've had the best time,' one of the women says, holding

out her hand, 'and it's *so* good to meet you. My husband and I tried the hotel-bar role play and it completely transformed our sex life. It's such a shame it didn't work out for you.'

'Yes, no,' I find myself saying, shaking her hand and my head at the same time. 'Sorry, it's so lovely to meet you, but I have to . . .' I turn to Tilly. 'I've got to go.'

She nods once, understanding passing between us. 'Of course. I'll call you?'

'Sure.'

I say goodbye and then hunt down Caro, who has a small crowd around her. She gives me another squeeze and asks if I'd like her to stay over.

'No, thanks,' I reply. I'm so wiped, I can barely see straight. I'm indescribably happy for Caro, and glad that the whole thing is over, but I feel empty and drained. I leave her to keep waxing lyrical about her photographs and fight through the crowds towards the green room. Every step I take, someone tries to block my path, but I keep my eyes focused straight ahead. 'Sorry,' I say, 'excuse me.'

Petra is by the door, and on impulse, I push down my desire to call an Uber for three more seconds and approach her.

'Petra,' I say, and she turns around. 'I just wanted to say thank you—'

'The evening has been a great success. You're leaving, I take it?' Her face is unreadable.

'Yes, but I wanted to—'

'Here's your coat.'

It's only now that I realize she's holding my jacket, as if she was waiting to see me out. 'Thank you,' I say dumbly, taking it from her. 'But Petra, I—'

'Get home safe,' she says, and then turns away, back to her conversation.

I stare at her back for a moment, and then, without the bandwidth to push any further, shrug my jacket on and weave my way to the fire door and out into the alleyway. The evening is cool and damp for May, and there are only a couple of people out here, smoking and vaping, big clouds filling the small street. None of them look over as I stand with my back to the door and take a big lungful of air.

Fuck the Uber, I decide. I'm tired – more tired than I might have ever been – but I need to walk. I need to clear my head, or I'll go to bed with everything rattling around up there, torturing me.

I walk down the alleyway until I emerge onto the high street, where the lights from the gallery are casting a yellow glow across the tarmac. I peer inside as I pass; no one can see me, and for a moment, I just take it in. This big, weird, unexpected thing that I did. Did I make the right decision? I remember Theo's face as he stood at the back of the room. He was looking at me like he barely even knew me.

I push onwards, leaving the arts centre behind me, my heels loud in the silent street. My outfit worked when I left the house, but now my bare legs are chilly, and there's a cold breeze tickling at the thin fabric of my jacket. I stuff my hands in my pockets as I walk.

My fingers brush against a piece of paper. I don't remember having anything in my pockets when I left the house. Absent-mindedly, I pull it out and read it as I step onto the main road out of the centre of town.

L,
 OK, let's talk.
 T x

My heart canters in my chest. Suddenly, I'm not tired any more. I slip off my heels, my bare feet slapping against the cold, wet pavement, and begin to run.

Chapter Twenty-Seven

I stand on the street outside our house, looking at the light spilling out onto the garden from the living room window. It's a sight I haven't seen in weeks, and it makes my heart clench with hope. Theo's in there, and he wants to talk. Before I have time to consider the different ways this could go, I open the gate, walk straight up the path and slip my key into the door.

The dogs are leaping up at me before I've even stepped over the threshold, whimpering, their feet scrabbling against the floor. For a moment, I squat down and let them cover me with wet kisses, squeezing my eyes shut, running my hands along their silky backs. And then I stand up, dump my heels on the floor, rub my wet feet on the mat, and walk into the kitchen.

Theo is standing at the counter, his back to me, the roar of the boiling kettle filling the room. I watch him for a second, relishing in the brief moment before he realizes I'm here – the brief moment before I know which way he's going to take this.

His broad back is slumped slightly, his palms pressed against the work surface. His curly hair is clean and shiny, and he doesn't move as the kettle clicks off, like he's somewhere else entirely.

I am hit suddenly by the clear and indisputable knowledge that this man is my home. He is a part of me, a limb, half of my heart. He is the love of my life, my best friend, my world. And all I want, more than I've ever wanted anything ever, is to take the three steps between us and wrap my arms around his waist.

I stay where I am. Theo comes to, picking up the kettle and pouring hot water into a mug in front of him. I wait until he's put the kettle back in its stand before making myself known.

'Hey.'

He turns around quickly, knocking his mug and splashing hot water onto his hand. 'Shit.'

I'm by his side before I can think, taking his big hand and pulling it under the cold tap, rubbing my thumb over the red skin. I catch myself and move away, leaving him standing over the sink, his hand under the water. 'Sorry,' I say.

He shakes his head and flicks off the tap, then nods to the sofa in the living room. 'Shall we sit down?'

I walk over to the sofa, curling my bare legs under me while he pulls my favourite mug from the cupboard. He plops a teabag in it, pours hot water, lets it steep. I watch him, a mix of reluctance and anxiety brewing inside me. I want to hear what he has to say. Or do I?

Eventually, he brings the two mugs over and puts them on the coffee table. Then he takes a seat in the armchair opposite me. I swallow the ominous disappointment that he hasn't chosen to sit next to me on the sofa.

Neither of us says anything. After a moment, I realize

he's waiting for me to speak. Of course he is – unlike me, he doesn't owe me quite such a huge explanation.

'Theo,' I say, sitting forward, 'you left the show before you heard everything I had to say.'

'I heard it,' he says without a beat. 'I was standing outside the fire door, listening.'

I nod, relief flooding through me. 'So . . . you understand?'

'No,' he replies, shaking his head. 'No, Lottie, I don't. I don't know why you couldn't talk to me. When did we become the couple who don't talk?'

It's a question I've asked myself a hundred times over the last few months, and one I still haven't had the answer to until now. 'We never really talked, Theo.'

He shakes his head at me, but I know he knows it, too. 'We did. We talked about everything – how we didn't want kids, what we wanted from our careers; we know everything about each other.'

'We've been lucky,' I correct. 'We gel so well together, there was never . . . we never needed to have big chats about our differences.'

'I didn't think we had any.'

'But we *do*,' I say, leaning forward. 'Not fundamental, deal-breaking, relationship-altering differences, but we're still two people. We can't be on the same page about everything – it's not realistic.'

He blows air into his cheeks. 'I know.' He runs a hand down his face, then turns to look out of the window, where the moon is peeking from behind a cloud. 'But we used to talk about everything,' he says.

'Everything that wasn't a sticking point between us. We

glossed over those, skirted around them until they fixed themselves.'

He nods. I know he knows what I'm talking about, but it's hard. It was hard for me, too – to accept that our perfect relationship had its flaws. 'It'll just take some practice,' I say, using the future tense hopefully.

'You didn't need practice to discuss our life with a stranger and thousands of hungry listeners.' He's hurt, and rightly so. One quick promise to do better isn't going to fix this. 'I don't understand how that was easier than sitting down with me.'

The pain is so apparent on his face, I want to cry. 'No, Theo, it's not that straightforward. It's not that I didn't want to talk to you.' I cast about for what it is exactly that I'm trying to say. 'It's that it was anonymous. I didn't have to sit and look anyone in the eye. And I think . . . I think part of me didn't want to hear what you had to say.'

He frowns. 'What do you mean?'

'I tried so many times to make you . . . want me,' I say, mortification sending blood rushing to my cheeks, 'but it didn't work. I thought you didn't like me, or you'd got bored of me, or . . . it felt like if I brought it up, you'd tell me something I didn't want to hear.'

He raises his eyebrows. 'Like what? I'm cheating on you? I don't find you attractive any more?'

The words slice through me – they're exactly what I've most feared hearing. 'Do you?' I ask quietly.

'Of course I do! There's no one else. You're beautiful, I love you, I love our life.'

'So why? Why did we stop talking? Why did we stop . . . wanting each other?'

He throws his hands up. 'Neither of us made an effort. I wasn't making excuses when I said you were always on your phone. Or we're watching something. Or I've got marking. Or we're too tired. It just happened; slowly, yes, but it happened.'

'But then I started making an effort! I tried! I couldn't have been more obvious. Don't tell me you didn't notice.'

'Of course I noticed.'

'So why didn't you reciprocate?' I'm raising my voice now, my emotions high. 'Why don't you want to have sex with me?'

'It's not as easy as that.'

'Of course it is! It's biology!' I'm riled up now, leaning forward in my seat, pleading with him. Each time, he was being wilfully ignorant. He could see me there, trying, and he didn't reciprocate. 'Why, Theo? Why didn't you reciprocate? Why—'

'Because it doesn't fucking work!' he shouts.

The silence that follows is loaded, ringing in the air. My mouth is dry. 'What doesn't?' I ask after a beat. 'Us?'

He shakes his head roughly, his cheeks coloured. 'Me,' he says, and it hits me with a slap that he's embarrassed. Whatever this is, it's hard for him to talk about. 'I can't . . . make it work,' he says gruffly, nodding to his legs. 'When things got quiet between us, I started overthinking it, got too in my head. When we tried, a few weeks ago, it happened again, and I just . . . I can't bear your disappointment.'

And just like that, everything becomes horrifyingly clear. I take my mind back to the last time we actually had sex – not the failed attempt in the study, but a good six months or so ago. It'd been a while, and we were both going through the motions, a pre-bedtime under-the-sheets affair. Then, from nowhere, Theo stopped. When I asked him what was wrong, he said he wasn't in the mood, but I'd felt him soften before he clambered off me. Now, I'm ashamed to remember not thinking much about it at all, actually feeling relieved that we could go to sleep after a busy day and not bother with the whole thing.

'I've never been disappointed with you,' I whisper.

He doesn't meet my eye. 'I've lost all perspective on it,' he says quietly. 'It's become this huge thing, this obstacle . . . I wanted to talk to Gretchen about it, but you didn't want to come to the session. And then it turned out it was an even bigger issue than I feared: you were doing a whole podcast on it.'

Shame and regret rush through me, but before I can reply, he continues, 'There's always been pressure on men to perform,' he says. 'And Jesus, women have had it so much worse. And now you're owning your sexuality, asking for what you want, and it's amazing. It's hard-earned and well-deserved, and it's a fucking good thing that these podcasts and books and resources exist, because everybody deserves to have good sex. But I think sometimes, people like Tilly forget that we're not robots. We can't always just switch it on and keep it on, even if a woman wants us to. Porn's unrealistic messaging affects us in a small way, too. And the pressure to be right for you, to perform . . . god, Lotts, it's not your fault. But I feel . . . inadequate.'

For a moment, all I can do is look at him as the reality of what he's saying slams into me. How egotistical I've been, how self-centred. I thought it was all about me; I thought he was being selfish and negligent by not giving me what I wanted when I wanted it. Isn't that exactly what women have been complaining about men doing for centuries? The playing field isn't equal, but I'm ashamed that I've neglected the human being in my husband, the person behind the 'man' label I've tarred him with.

'Theo,' I whisper, standing up. I take two steps across the rug and clamber onto his lap, discarding the awkwardness and distance and tension that's brewed between us for weeks. I hold his cheeks gently between my palms until his big brown eyes meet mine. 'I am so, so sorry.'

He swallows. Then he leans forward and presses his forehead against mine. 'It felt like you'd outgrown me,' he says.

I hold him tighter. 'No. *No*. Theo, I don't need you to be anything more than what you are. I don't want anything from you except *you*. How you've always been. I just need us to talk. I can't bear this distance between us. I miss you.'

'I miss you, too,' he whispers.

'We don't have to have sex ever again, as long as you'll talk to me. Laugh with me, be with me.'

He huffs a laugh. 'Ever again? Now you're just being ridiculous.'

I pull back and look at him – really look at him. 'I'm so sorry for everything I've done. I need you to know that every single decision I made – and admittedly, there were some poor ones – was for us. I thought, stupidly, that I was bringing us back together. I thought it'd all stay a secret and it'd all work out. I thought it would bring us closer again.'

He doesn't speak for a minute. Then he lifts his hand up and strokes the back of my neck. 'And hasn't it?' he asks.

And really, what else is there to say?

Chapter Twenty-Eight

'Does it feel weird, being on this side of things?' Theo glances at me from behind the steering wheel as we cruise along our road. Last time we were in the car together, it was dark and rainy and our relationship was in tatters, but now, he's smiling at me behind his sunglasses, light dappling through the trees either side of the street.

'It does a bit,' I say, crossing my bare legs under me in the passenger seat. 'But I'm actually quite enjoying being the one in the dark. As long as it's a nice surprise.' I poke him in the arm.

'Of course it is.'

I grab his hand and intertwine my fingers with his, suffused with pure, unadulterated happiness. We're both glowing, radiating positive vibes around the car, and we can't stop touching each other: an arm stroke here, a head on a shoulder there. It's a post-coital glow, except for one key qualifier – there's been no coitus. We've spent the last three nights wrapped around each other, cuddling and holding and making space. Weirdly, it's been infinitely more intimate than sex ever was.

Not that I don't miss sex, of course. In fact, I miss it more than ever. Sometimes, it's physically painful being so close and not taking that final step. But it'll come when it comes, and from the willpower I know we're both exerting at different moments, something tells me it's going to be explosive when it does.

'I still can't believe you're a celebrity,' Theo says as we enter town. I rack my brains, trying to guess where we could be going. 'Do you think you'll get recognized?'

'No!' I say, laughing. 'I mean, if you're taking me to the arts centre, Petra might know who I am . . .'

I finally answered the phone to Tilly yesterday, and she was delighted to hear that Theo and I were patching things up. She was even more delighted to tell me about the reception the live show had received. She's offered me something by way of thank you – something so huge I can barely process it – but I'm saving that conversation with Theo for later. No secrets; just good timing.

Theo pulls into a parking space and yanks the handbrake up. I look around, realization dawning. I haven't been here in years.

'You're joking,' I say, laughing.

'Lotts,' he says seriously, taking my hand. 'I never joke about line dancing.'

I'm still laughing as we get out of the car, and Theo links his arm through mine and pulls me to the entrance of the church hall we met at all those years ago at our first line-dancing class. He swings the door open to reveal a very similar scene to the one I encountered the first time I came here: a group of people, most of them elderly, milling about and waiting for the class to start.

The instructor smiles at us and takes our names, evidently not remembering us from seven years ago, and then chivvies us all into two lines. Then she hits play on her portable speaker, and the hall fills with happy country music. I look to my left; Theo is beaming at me, and I realize that the same stupid grin is plastered across my own face, too.

As the instructor leads us through the first steps, it all comes back to me. The step and cross, the hand on the belt, the swaying hips. And the other things, too: the stolen glances at Theo when I thought he wasn't looking, the way he'd somehow always get the space next to me, the way his fingers managed to graze me during the turns, even when there was plenty of space.

This is where it all began – our silliness, our love for each other – and now, with every uncoordinated step to the left and then right, I feel even more sure that this is exactly where we're supposed to be. Together again, just us two, working to our own rhythm, and finding a new pace, too.

*

'Holy shit, I haven't had that much fun in so long,' Theo says, plopping a piece of crispy calamari into his mouth. 'When that lady did a spontaneous "Yeehaw!". . .'

I laugh, remembering. We're sitting in our favourite tapas restaurant in town; the same one where we took that last happy selfie of us, with the couple kissing in the background.

We've ordered one of everything on the menu, and the food is piled between us: chorizo in tomato sauce, patatas bravas, creamy aïoli, crusty bread. The vibe is high, celebratory, but I can feel the prickles of anxiety nudging at my periphery. I don't want to ruin things with what I'm about to tell Theo. We've come so far over the past few days, it'd be easier to wait, make sure we're really solid before I come clean.

But no. I promised myself and, by definition, him: no more lies.

'Theo,' I say, wiping my hands on my napkin and leaning forward. 'When I spoke to Tilly yesterday, she had something else to tell me.'

Worry flits across his face, and I feel a pang of regret. That's his knee-jerk reaction now, because of me. A few months ago, he'd have been curious, interested. Now, he assumes it's something he's not going to like. He smooths his expression, putting down the piece of bread he's just picked up. 'Oh?'

'She wants me to work with her, full-time, on a new show they're making. It's about sex in your thirties. She wants me to interview women about how their sex lives are, and use the clips on-air for her to give advice and get expert opinions on.'

Theo doesn't reply for a moment. 'And she wants you because you're a success story?' he asks, but he's not being sarcastic. 'We haven't . . . we're still working on things, Lotts.'

'I know,' I say. 'That's why I've said no.'

He blinks. 'What?'

'I've turned her down. The money would have been insane, but there's already the book deal, and I want us to keep working on the physical side of our relationship together, without anyone else's input.'

He shakes his head. 'But it's an opportunity—'

'And I took that opportunity. Putting that side of our life up for public dissection isn't something I want to do again. This is us. Me and you. We'll figure it out our way, like we do with everything else.'

Theo nods, but I can see he's having mixed feelings. I know he'd rather I didn't do it, but he's struggling with me turning something down because of him. 'OK,' he says after a moment. 'But I meant it when I said it's all about communication. If you want to do something mad that involves our relationship, let's just talk it through first.'

He smiles, and I grin back. 'Well, funny you should say that . . .'

'Oh, god. Why am I terrified?'

I laugh. 'It's just an idea, and I've pitched it to Tilly with the caveat that I have to discuss it with you first.'

'Go on . . .'

'I want to do a series about long-term love. Something uplifting, speaking to people in long-term relationships, old and young, and digging into the good stuff that ties people together.'

He's quiet for a moment, and then a smile tugs at the corner of his lips. 'That sounds really good.'

'You think?' I ask, feeling a rush of relief. 'Really? I'd want to chat about us, but I'd run everything by you first, and it'd be softer stuff – how we walk the dogs together every Sunday, no excuses, or how you always bring me a croissant back from your Friday morning run. More . . . taking care of each other than railing each other.'

Theo bursts out laughing. 'Yeah, OK. I give you permission

to discuss my bakery offerings to you. And you can tell them how you always buy my favourite beer for the weekend, and how you batch-cook my favourite lasagne for when I've got marking night. The cutesy stuff is yours for the taking. Just leave the butt plugs out of it.'

'You've bought a butt plug?' I ask, widening my eyes. 'Things *are* about to get interesting.'

'Whatever floats your boat, Mrs Carmichael,' he says, dipping some bread in olive oil and offering it to me. 'Is that everything, or should I prepare myself for a prime-time TV show about love eggs next week?'

I laugh. 'Not *quite* everything,' I say, wiping my hands again and reaching into my bag. 'This is for you.'

Theo raises his eyebrows as he takes the envelope I'm offering him. He opens it carefully, pulls out the contents, and then looks up at me, blinking. 'You're kidding.'

'Twenty-one days over your summer holidays,' I say. 'A full road trip of the United States. And, if you look here on the itinerary . . .' I point to about halfway down. 'You'll see we're staying for two nights in Seattle.'

'Seattle . . .' he murmurs, and I can see the cogs whirring. His eyes widen when it finally clicks. 'The Museum of Flight,' he says.

'Where you'll find . . .'

'A guided tour of the interior of a Boeing 737.' He grins, half laughing, half mesmerized. He leans across the table, the corner of the itinerary dunking into the garlic aïoli, and kisses me hard on the lips. 'God, I fucking love you.'

'I fucking love you, too.'

Chapter Twenty-Nine

'God, look at that.' Caro is sitting across from me on the armchair, her legs tucked under her and her elbow propped on the armrest. She's pulling a slice of Tony's pizza from its box, the cheese stretching as far as her arm can lift it. 'A work of art,' she says, snapping the cheese with her fingers and taking a big bite.

'Come on, Caro, what's going on?' I ask, my patience now completely spent. She arrived at the same time as the pizza, and ever since she sat down, I've noticed something different about her. There's a restless energy coming off her, a sort of anxiousness I've never seen before. It's not that same heaviness she's been carrying around the last few months; this is new. But despite the three times I've asked now, she won't come clean.

'Nothing, nothing,' she says through a mouth full of tomatoey dough. But she won't meet my eye. 'First day back tomorrow?'

'Yep.' I took a week's annual leave after the live show, and with Theo's school having a week's break for half term, we spent lazy days with the dogs, planning our road trip, leaving the house only to go for long walks, buy muffins and coffee, or attend our line-dancing classes. 'Caro,' I say, forcing her to look at me. 'Out with it.'

She swallows and blows air into her cheeks. 'Fine!' She throws her pizza crust back into the box. 'So the exhibition is doing really well.'

'That's great . . .' I say, waiting for more. Caro's photos have been up at the gallery for a week, and her residency is coming to a close. 'But?'

'No but. It's doing much better than expected.'

'Caro! Tell me.'

'All right! They've given me a bit of an extension,' she says.

'OK . . . and this means . . . ?' I'm already running through the arts centre's calendar in my mind: we've got a new artist from Birmingham showing next week, and there's no way it'd be moved this last-minute.

'They're offering me a six-month residency,' she says in a rush, her cheeks flushing. 'A *proper* residency, Lotts.'

'Oh my god, Caro, that's incredible!' I'm thrilled for her, but I don't understand. 'But . . . at the gallery? I don't . . .'

'No, not here.'

'Where, then?'

She picks up the crust again and twiddles it between her fingers. Then, finally, she meets my gaze. 'Edinburgh,' she says.

I can physically feel the grin spreading across my face. 'Stop it.'

She beams. 'For real.'

'You're doing it? You're finally moving to Edinburgh?'

'Only for six months!' she says, and there's a mix of anxiousness and elation in her voice. 'And you'll have to come and visit me. I'll come back all the time, and—'

'Caro, of *course* I'll come and visit you, and of *course* you're not going to come back to your tiny, boring hometown all the time just to see me. You're going to be busy showing loads of important people your incredible photographs, you nutter.'

Her eyes are sparkling. 'And . . .'

'And what? Oh my god, how can there be more?'

'We might have to schedule your visits. I might have someone else coming to see me pretty frequently while I'm up there.'

I stare at her. 'Tell me you're about to say what I think you are.'

'It's early days!' she says, holding her hands up. 'Don't get excited! But yes, me and Peter are sort of . . . giving things a shot again.'

Before I know what I'm doing, I've launched myself off the sofa and thrown myself on top of her.

'Stop!' she squeals, laughing as she bats at me with her pizza crust.

I haul myself back to my seat and beam at her. 'These are big, scary things, and you're doing them,' I say, remembering her words to me at our primal release workshop.

She nods. 'I'll miss you, though.'

'I'll miss you, too,' I say. 'But hey, maybe *The Cliterati* will do a live show up in Edinburgh.'

'Well obviously we have to make *that* happen. When do you start?'

'In about a month,' I reply. Tilly has green-lighted my Long-Term Love project, so I'm just waiting for my contract to come through before the start date gets finalized. 'But seriously, Caro,' I say, leaning across the table and grabbing her hand, 'I am so fucking happy for you.'

'I'm really grateful, Lotts,' she says, squeezing my hand back. 'I would never have put myself forward like that.'

I snort. 'I know better than anyone how much a push from the right person can force you out of self-sabotaging stupidness. No offence. And now you're doing the damn thing. You're getting out of here and going back to Edinburgh.'

'Except this time I'm not running away,' she says with a wink.

We each grab a piece of pizza and tap the cheesy points together in a cheers. 'You know you can always talk to me,' I say firmly. 'Always.'

'I know. You too. Tell me before you tell a podcast next time, yeah?'

'Deal. And you call me before you do another midnight flight from Peter. I'll talk you out of it.'

'Yes, sir,' she says.

I pause, my pizza midair. 'No matter how far apart we are, nothing will ever change, you know?'

'Never.'

'And hey, maybe all that moonlight manifesting actually worked,' I muse, nibbling at the edge of my slice. 'Because here it is. Your big fucking dream, coming to life right before your eyes.'

She beams at me, my big-eyed, beautiful best friend, and I've never seen her look happier. 'Love you,' I say.

'Love you, too, Lotts,' she says. 'Now eat up, we need our energy. We've got big-girl shit to do.'

*

In the staff kitchen, Harry and I are watching a thin trickle of dark coffee pour out of the machine and into an awaiting mug.

'My god, Harry,' I say quietly. 'I think you've done it.'

He looks at me, and I swear there are tears in his eyes. 'I think you might be right.'

The machine beeps to a finish, and he picks the cup up tentatively, as if too fast a movement might cause the coffee inside to disappear. I watch as he lifts it to his lips and takes a small sip.

'Well?'

A slow grin spreads over his face. 'Fucking fantastic.'

I cheer, and he immediately sets about making me one, too. 'Frothy milk?' he asks as he stabs at the buttons on the front.

'Probably best not to push our luck?' I suggest.

'You're right.' He hits the button for a simple black coffee and turns to me. 'So? When are you going to do it?'

I nibble at my thumbnail. 'Soon.'

'Soon?' He tilts his head. 'Lottie.'

'I know,' I say. 'I *am* going. In a minute.'

'What are you waiting for?'

'She's finishing her Starbucks. She's always in a better mood after her Starbucks.'

The coffee machine beeps again, and Harry thrusts the mug into my hands. 'You're such a baffling creature.'

I laugh. 'Why?'

'You've done the most bonkers, out-there things over the last few months, yet *this* is freaking you out.'

'I sort of got sucked into those,' I clarify. 'This is . . . yeah.'

'This involves you proactively *choosing* something,' he says. 'I'd say you owe yourself that, don't you?'

I consider this for a moment. He's right, of course. Even the most passive individual can live an extraordinary life if they rumble along with a wild wind. If I want to put my new-found assertiveness to good use, I *have* to do this. And frankly, I *want* to. 'Old habits die hard,' I say, jumping off the counter. 'But they do die if you whack them enough times.'

'That's the spirit,' Harry says, grinning. 'Go get 'em.'

I lift my mug in salute and walk out of the kitchen before I can talk myself out of it yet again. Outside, I walk straight past my desk and across to Petra's glass door. I rap my knuckles against the pane three times.

'Come in,' she calls.

I open the door, walk inside, close it behind me, and sit in my usual chair in front of her desk.

Petra looks up from her computer, her eyebrows raised. 'Lottie, hello,' she says.

'Petra, I need to say something,' I begin, letting the words rattle out of me without too much thought. 'I think we're very different people, and I think we have different goals for the arts centre, and I think all of that is fine. But I think we've been working with crossed wires, and really, we both want the centre to be a success in our own way. I'm really sorry for losing sight of that goal for a while. I dropped the ball, and

I know you had to do a lot of work to sort out my mistakes. I'm sorry,' I say again.

Petra blinks at me. 'Right. OK. Well, thank you.'

I nod. For a moment, neither of us says anything.

After a beat, she clears her throat. 'I know I'm not the easiest person to work with,' she says, red blotches appearing on her neck. 'I am aware that I can be quite . . . cold. I think it makes me good at my job, but I can miss the more emotional details at times.'

I wasn't expecting this. 'Well, that's kind of how it works, isn't it? That's why we work in teams. We all bring different things to the table.'

She nods, picks up a pen, then puts it down again. 'Regardless, I apologize for neglecting my duty of care to you as your manager during a difficult personal circumstance.'

I'm not sure what to say here; I'm almost certain those are the exact words in the HR manual. But still, it looks like she means it. Before I can respond, she carries on.

'Speaking of useful skills, I'm glad you're here, actually. I told everyone else while you were away, but the gallery is doing much better since the live show. There shouldn't be any need for redundancies.'

I smile. 'That's great.'

'Actually, we have the space for some promotions. I wondered whether you'd be interested in becoming the Community Engagement Manager, overseeing the whole team. It'd be a big step up in responsibility, so obviously it would come with a nice hike in pay, and—'

'Me?' I interrupt.

She pauses. 'Yes.'

'My performance has been awful.'

'Well, yes,' she says, nodding. 'But the council is looking for more outreach to the wider community, and I know it's something you're very passionate about. Something you used to do very well before you were moved into more of a marketing role.'

I can't help myself. 'Before you moved me into more of a marketing role.'

A smile twitches at the corner of her mouth. 'Yes. I'm not sure all of my skills are directly transferable to this kind of business. I'm still learning.'

'I'm delighted to be asked,' I say truthfully, but inside I'm reeling. This is the last thing I expected, and I didn't come in here with a plan for this. Now, the next steps I'd mapped out seem less clear. What do I do?

'Your work with the live podcast special was exceptional,' she says. 'You're evidently very skilled at what you do.' She clicks at her computer. 'Shall we set a start date for a month's time? That'd give you time to transition and set up the new role.'

I hesitate, unsure how to word what I need to say next. 'I actually came in here to ask you something,' I say. 'I'm going to be working with *The Cliterati* again in a month or so, and . . .' I weigh up my options quickly and decide to shoot straight. Regardless of my recent success at work, the centre is still hurtling forward on corporate, pretentious tracks – and my organizing of the *Cliterati* event didn't help its image as a home-grown crafty hub at all. We're on the map, and while I did manage to get our community through the door, it's still not the place it once was. And with Petra at the helm, it's unlikely to ever be again. I take a breath. 'I was thinking of handing my notice in. You know I'm not in love with the direction the centre has taken, and I'm going to be too busy to do both. I love this place, but I think I've outgrown it. Or rather, it's outgrown me.'

Petra sits back in her chair. For a moment, she doesn't speak. She taps at her computer, and then faces me again. 'How long will you be working with the podcast?'

'About six weeks.'

She looks beyond me, to the office through the glass wall. 'What if I offer you an unpaid sabbatical, followed by full rein of community engagement? You can angle it however you want. Start Chatty Tuesdays again, run some more concessionary-rate classes. You'll come to the management meetings, have a say in how the place is run.'

I can barely believe what I'm hearing. 'Why?' I manage.

Petra sighs. 'Because you're right, Lottie. When I started here, this place had heart, and it doesn't feel like it does any more. I think you might *be* that heart. And while I can't offer it myself, I can make sure the right person brings it to the table.'

I search her face for signs that there's a catch here, some way in which she's trying to box me in even further. But all I see is the hopeful face of a woman who is trying, in her own messy, misguided way, to do the right thing.

And god, can I relate to that.

After a moment, I stand up and hold out my hand. 'I'd love to.'

Chapter Thirty

The marquee is lit up like a carnival, with fairy lights winding round every available object and snaking up to the ceiling to merge in one giant, starry spectacle. The space is dotted with white-linen-covered tables, with huge pillar candles dancing in the middle of each one, illuminating the detritus of a mass-catered mediocre wedding meal. I'm lucky enough to have a seat facing the head table, where Jade's mum – reinvited at the last minute after conceding that the dress was champagne, not pink – is merrily taking photos of the wedding party with her flip-cover-adorned iPhone. On the dance floor in front of me, Jade is doing some kind of lunging TikTok dance in her wedding dress while her new husband watches on, clapping enthusiastically.

I tug for the hundredth time at the high neck of my last-choice bridesmaid dress. 'God, I can't wait to take this thing off.'

Theo leans back in his chair beside me, his cheeks flushed from the free wine and his shirt collar open, exposing his chest hair. 'I can't *believe* you didn't do the worm at our wedding,' he says, watching Jade on the dance floor.

'A wasted opportunity,' I agree, leaning my head on his shoulder. 'You excited for tomorrow?'

He laughs. 'Dev texted earlier, asking whether he should pack his kaftan.'

I lift my head up and look at him. 'Dev has a *kaftan*?'

'He wears it every morning. It doesn't leave much to the imagination. I'm going to tell him they're banned; I saw more than enough of it when I was living with him.' He pauses. 'You're going to be all right getting to Edinburgh?'

'Of course,' I smile. Tomorrow, I'm getting the train to Edinburgh to see Caro for a couple of nights in her new place – an apartment she's rented right near the castle. While I'm there, I've used some of the podcast money to book Theo and Dev a lad's holiday. They'll be going twenty minutes up the road to Moonbeam's 'Divine Masculine' retreat: a two-day affair that mirrors the retreat Caro and I did, but for men. It seemed only fair that Theo get to stay in his new favourite building after everything I put us through. I'm giddy at the thought of the stories he'll come back with.

One of the first things we did after that first week off together was book in for a full batch of couple's therapy. We were doing well, working through things on our own, but as I've learned over the last few months, a little help from the outside can be very useful – as long as you're both on the same page.

'Sorry.' A guy across the table – the boyfriend of Holly, the feet-pics girl, I believe – leans forward. 'I've been resisting all night, but I'm six pints deep and I can't hold back any more. You're that podcast girl, aren't you?'

I freeze, glancing at Theo. It's the first time I've been recognized with him, and I have no idea how he's going to take it. While we've been doing our sessions with Gretchen religiously, working on our communication, and are more solid than ever, this is a sore spot, and it might be too soon.

''Tis us,' Theo says cheerily. 'The sexless couple.'

I laugh relievedly. The guy stands up and throws himself into the spare chair next to Theo. 'You've helped so many people,' he says to me, and I feel that same flutter of happiness I get every time someone tells me that what I did had some kind of positive impact. He looks between me and Theo. 'You've got to help *me*, man.'

Theo raises his eyebrows. 'Help you?'

'We never have sex any more,' he says, jerking his head towards Holly, who is barefoot on the dance floor, taking photos of her toes under the colourful lights.

'Ah,' Theo says, picking up his glass. 'I hear that's quite common.'

'I don't even like feet,' he says desperately. 'It's all she wants to talk about, but I don't like them.'

'I'm just going to check how Jade's doing,' I say, rising to my feet. I nudge Theo as I go, and he widens his eyes at me, blatantly imploring me not to leave. I flash him a wink and hurry over to the dance floor. I'll save him soon, but I need to talk to Jade before the night goes on any further, and I've just seen her sit down to rest her feet.

'Hey,' I say when I reach the top table. Jade looks up from where she's taking her shoes off. She looked stunning this morning, but she is even more so now with her skin slightly dewy and her hair tousled from the dancing.

'Hey, gorgeous,' she says. 'You having a good time?'

'Amazing time. It's been such a beautiful day, Jade.'

She smiles. 'I meant to ask you earlier; could you get up early tomorrow and collect up all the photographs? They're scattered all around the hotel lobby, and I want everyone to see them on their way up to bed, but I don't want the cleaners to chuck them in the morning. I've asked my mum to do it but she's three sheets to the wind and she'll probably forget.'

Instinctively, I begin rearranging my schedule. This is our first evening away together in years, and we were looking forward to a small lie-in before we have to head off for him to make it to the retreat on time. I wonder whether I can stay up later, wait until everyone's in bed and then grab the photos, or set an alarm for six and then head back to bed once I've collected them. But my feet are tired and the neck of my ugly dress is scratching against my skin, and I really want to enjoy a lazy morning with Theo. The room wasn't cheap, and it's so rare that we get to sleep in, with the dogs usually waking us up at dawn. I've been here since early this morning helping with the prep, and Jade's mum only turned up when the makeup artists arrived, along with most of the other bridesmaids. Over Jade's shoulder, I spot her maid of honour chatting to her mum, laughing about something.

'I'm sorry,' I say to Jade after a beat. 'I'm not going to be able to do that. Maybe you could ask one of the others to help your mum, then she won't forget?'

Jade blinks at me. 'Oh,' she says. 'Erm, yes, OK, no problem. I'll ask someone else.'

I smile. 'Congratulations again; it's been such a gorgeous celebration.'

'It has,' she says, her eyes softening as they land on Matt. 'God, I'm lucky, aren't I?'

'Very,' I agree. Together, we watch as people whirl across the dance floor, whooping and laughing. The tasteful band was replaced with an old-school cheesy DJ about an hour ago, and people are jiving to 'Karma Chameleon' and 'Sweet Caroline' like there's no tomorrow. I turn to Jade. 'It's—'

'I know you saw me,' she says. She's still fiddling with her shoe straps, and for a moment, I think I've misheard her.

'What?'

'At the FemDom event. I know you saw me, Lottie. With Caro. I put two and two together when I listened to the podcast.'

I don't know what to say. 'Jade, I—'

'My relationship isn't perfect,' she says quietly, her eyes once again finding Matt, who is talking animatedly to the best man by the bar. 'But we love each other, we're honest with each other, and we make each other very happy.'

I stew over my words for a moment, and then decide to just directly ask the question that's been irritating me ever since that night at the club. 'But you have such a brilliant sex life,' I say. 'Why?'

She swallows, her gaze dipping. 'The stories I tell . . .' she says. 'They don't always involve Matt.'

I stare at her, shocked. While I knew the situation in the sex dungeon was a possible act of infidelity, I imagined it was a one-off, or that at the very least there was no intimate touching involved. But the stories Jade tells are obscene, explicit. 'What? Does Matt . . .'

'Yes, he knows,' she says calmly. 'That's the way our relationship works.'

'Is this why you've cancelled the honeymoon?' I ask, remembering Melissa's whispered gossip at the bottomless brunch.

She frowns. 'Cancelled? No, we just swapped from India to Bali. Got a better deal.'

'Oh.' The pieces slot into place, but I still can't wrap my head around the way her marriage is going to work. The way they're essentially married friends, who sleep with other people.

'But how do you—'

'I have a lot of friends,' she says, looking at me. 'But maybe you've noticed that I'm not very . . . close with any of you guys. Matt's my best friend. My whole world. I can't imagine spending my life with anybody else.'

Well, that explains a lot. The numerous bridesmaids, the distant friends Jade has collected over the years; none of us really ever getting that close to her. I want to ask more, but I stop myself. It's really none of my business. And the way Jade and Matt are looking at each other now, across the room, I know with certainty that they love each other. If I've learned anything from the last few months, it's that relationships are complex, nuanced things, and that nobody on the outside really understands. Whether you're married and monogamous, serially dating, or in an open relationship, it's baffling to anyone who isn't living it. And we're all just trying to make it work in our own way.

Besides, I know how it feels to have unexpected people peering into your sex life, and it's not something I'd wish on another person – even if both Jade and I did something to invite the scrutiny.

'As long as you're happy,' I say eventually.

Jade smiles at me. In her eyes, I can see the emotions I felt on my wedding day: overwhelm, exhilaration, love, the simultaneous panic that it's almost over and a longing for bed.

'You look so beautiful,' I say, planting a kiss on her cheek and leaving her to what's left of her big evening. I walk across the marquee to the champagne table, where I pick up two fresh flutes before turning to look across the room. Theo is still trapped in conversation with Holly's boyfriend, and when the other man bends to retie his shoe, Theo makes a throat-cutting gesture at me.

I stride across the space until I'm standing in front of them. 'Theo,' I say, putting my hand on his shoulder. 'Our car alarm's going off and I can't figure out how to get it to shut up.'

Theo leaps to his feet. 'Sorry, mate, back in a sec.'

The man gapes at us as we walk away from the table, and Theo snakes his arm around my waist. 'A minute too long,' he murmurs into my ear, 'but thanks for the rescue.'

I pass him one of the champagne flutes and steer us towards the marquee's exit. 'Come on.'

'Where are we going?' he asks as we step out onto the dewy grass, the music quietening behind us. When I don't reply, he stops. 'Wait, is the alarm actually going off?'

I turn to face him. We're standing alone on the lawn, the big hotel we're staying in tonight towering above us. The moon is bright and yellow, and I feel warm and merry from the late-spring heat and the wine. I trace a line down Theo's chest, undoing another of his shirt buttons as I go.

'Ah,' he says, the marquee fairy lights dancing in his eyes. 'I *see*.'

I reach up and pull him down to me, and our lips meet hungrily, Theo's breath hot against my own. I pull away and he grabs my hand to keep me there, but I take a step back towards the marquee, taking a sip of my champagne. 'We should probably get back to the party, though,' I say coyly.

In one quick movement, Theo has swept me up into his arms, our champagne flutes tumbling onto the grass. I shriek, laughing, as he carries me across the field towards the hotel's grand entrance, his strong arms wrapping around me just like they did on our wedding day three years ago.

'Come on, Mrs Carmichael,' he growls as we near the front door. 'Let's get you out of that dress.'

Acknowledgements

Ah, the gushy bit! First of all, thank you for dedicating your precious reading time to Lottie's story – I hope you feel it was a worthwhile journey, and that your Google history is now awash with yoni-steamer searches and overpriced primal rage retreat booking requests. Writing this book took quite a bit of research into a world I wasn't very well-versed in, and my targeted ads are now a thing to behold (underground kink dungeons, anyone?).

A big thank you to my agent, Rebeka, who is a wonderful guiding light and a brilliant champion of her authors. I couldn't wish for a better agent! To the whole team at Darley Anderson, thank you for your consistent hard work and support; I'm honoured to have you guys on my team.

I am immensely grateful to my editor, Billy, whose editorial insights were invaluable and whose vision for this book was so well-aligned with my own. Thank you, Billy, for making the weaving together of this story so seamless and joyful! Working with Avon has been such a dream come true, and I'm hugely thankful to the whole team for their hard work. Thank you Debbie Chapman for your proofreading, and a special shout-out also has to go to Rachel, whose copy-editing skills had me reassessing the power of the human brain. Your attention to detail is incredible, Rachel – thank you for lending your eagle eyes to my words. (My spelling of 'canapés' as 'canopies' will forever humble me.)

I have to thank my number one writing buddy (with whom, incidentally, I never write) and overall amazing friend, Holly, whose emotional support and gin cocktails are the cornerstone of my sanity during the writing process. A massive squishy thanks also to Zara, whose love and friendship have seen me through the best and the worst times. There's really very little in life that a good bitch and some reminiscing can't solve. Alex, Lauren, Amie, Charlotte, Adam, Daniela, Millie – thanks for always buying my books and being such lovely friends.

(I'm at the point in the writing of this where I'm brainstorming new yet natural ways to say thank you without actually writing the words 'thank you', and I'm failing. So we will continue.)

Thank you to my family, immediate and extended, for their enthusiasm and support of my slightly unconventional career path. Big love to the Hargreaves lot especially; you guys are my cheerleaders and I appreciate it more than you know. To my in-laws, Silvana and Franco, thank you for being such a warm and supportive second family – I couldn't have married into a better one. Nora, my OG hairy child and big crazy horse, you are an angel. Thanks for being your weird, bonkers self.

Finally, thank you to Stef and my hairy daughter, Salsiccia. You two make up my tiny nuclear family (not unlike Lottie, Theo, Betty and Boodle), and I thank the universe every day that I have you both by my side. It's a rare gift to find someone who will witness you hunched over a laptop, snapping that you can't talk right now because this sentence makes no *sense*, and who will respond by bringing you a cup of tea and offering to do the hoovering. It's a less rare gift to find a small creature to bite your ankles while you're racing to a deadline, but I appreciate it all the same. I love you both to the moon and back.

Wondering what to read next?

Don't miss the hilarious and uplifting book-club novel that will give you a Richard Curtis experience, perfect for fans of David Nicholls, Amanda Prowse and Jojo Moyes.

What if you could relive any day again? Would you remind your husband to take out the bins? Or would you be brave? Go back to a moment that could change everything?

Check out the funny, insightful love-letter to female friendship, perfect for fans of Dolly Alderton and *The Bold Type*!

Thirteen years. Three women. One annual sleepover.

From the #1 bestselling author of *The Cruise*, embark on an unforgettable journey and sail through Norway's winter wonderland to see the spectacular Northern Lights.

Pack your bags for the adventure of a lifetime.